FOR MONEY
OR LOVE

Visit us at www.boldstrokesbooks.com

Praise for *Like Jazz*

"This book is a top of the line winner that grabbed me, held me, and more than entertained me from start to finish!...I totally recommend this book; it is capable of being enjoyed on many levels, from different angles, and in its totality. Please do not miss this thoroughly satisfying book!"—*Rainbow Book Reviews*

"An excellent debut and an excellent book: well-developed, engaging characters, good plot, great setting."—Rainbow Awards 2014

By the Author

Like Jazz

For Money or Love

FOR MONEY OR LOVE

by

Heather Blackmore

2016

FOR MONEY OR LOVE

ISBN 13: 978-1-62639-756-9

This Trade Paperback Original Is Published By
Bold Strokes Books, Inc.
P.O. Box 249
Valley Falls, NY 12185

First Edition: September 2016

CREDITS
Editor: Shelley Thrasher
Production Design: Stacia Seaman
Cover Design by Sheri (graphicartist2020@hotmail.com)

Acknowledgments

I'm grateful to Radclyffe and all the staff and associates at Bold Strokes Books who work tirelessly on behalf of their authors.

To my perspicacious editor, Shelley Thrasher, without whom I'd be tempted to say clichéd things like you're the cat's meow whom no one holds a candle to: thank you for your sound guidance.

Shelly Lampe: your love, encouragement, mad copy-editing skills (who knew?), and laughter not only see me through, but make me look forward to all that's next for us.

Beta readers Kathy Chetkovich, Chris Paynter, and Chuck Eyler provided incredibly valuable feedback. The book is better for your efforts. Thanks especially to Kathy for always starting with the positives before delving right into what needs fixing, and to Chris for your shrewd suggestions and unwavering support ever since *Like Jazz*.

Marketing goddess Jennifer Zeszut greatly improved my attempts at folding in real-world marketing strategies; any mistakes and improbabilities are solely mine.

Fellow authors Kris Bryant and Cindy Rizzo—finding you guys has been a wonderful bonus along this writing journey.

To my readers: thank you for choosing to spend time with Jess and TJ. I truly appreciate when you take a moment to let me know something resonated with or amused you. You make all the difference.

For my mom

Because I miss you and your laugh,
because I love the idea that
a lesbian romance novel is dedicated to you,
but most of all
because you loved me.

CHAPTER ONE

Jessica, I want you to help get our intern acclimated to the firm."
The Diet Coke Jess was sipping shot up through her nose, drops of it landing on her silk Chanel blouse. She should have opted for the sparkling water.

As the burning sensation ebbed, she stared at her father in disbelief, silently ticking off the reasons she must have misheard. One, this was so not her thing. She was the head of marketing, not a babysitter. Two, her father rarely asked her to perform any actual work and never held her responsible for anything. Why her, why now? Three, intern? Derrick Spaulding was worth billions—with a B. His investment advisory firm was small but highly respected, with billions of assets under management. Interns should occupy as much space in his head as sunlight.

It wasn't possible she'd heard him correctly.

"You expect me to believe you're interested in an intern's first day?"

"I'm interested in her project. As you should be. She'll be doing a case study on the firm, and if it goes the way Philip intends, it will be taught at some of this country's best universities."

Philip Ridge and her father had been college roommates. He was the dean of Griffin University's business school, where the two had met as undergraduates.

"Have Gary handle it," Jess said. Gary Treanor was the firm's chief operating officer, her father's right-hand man and stepson. Unlike Jess, he was a fixture at the office.

"I don't want her to focus on the side of the business Gary handles. I want you to show her other aspects."

"Such as?"

"How you and Brooke manage to bring in so many new clients."

Of course. Brooke. This was Derrick-speak for her sister's ability to sell anything to anyone, but he was being kind enough to include her. Brooke could sell sand to Saudis and portable heaters to Algerians.

"If she's doing a case study on the business, shouldn't she spend her time with the investment managers?"

"I want her to focus on sales and marketing, without which we'd have a sliver of the assets under management that we have."

It was as close to a compliment as Jess had ever received from him in a business context, and she took to it like gum to a shoe. "I'll help in any way I can. What do we know about her?"

"According to Philip, she was the impetus behind the program." The Derrick Spaulding MBA program was a sixteen-month accelerated curriculum that included a two-year nonprofit-sector service requirement post-graduation. It was Ridge who ensured that if Derrick made a sufficiently large contribution to their alma mater, he'd work his magic to get the program named for Derrick. Jess was well associated with it because Derrick's donations were one of the things she adored most about him and one of the reasons she worked so hard, albeit surreptitiously, on Magnate's behalf. The higher Magnate's profits, the more Derrick gave to various causes. Prospective investors interested in learning the character of the firm's founder found an extensive bio on the corporate website, much of which related to Derrick's philanthropic interests.

Jess closed her eyes and placed two fingers against each temple as if channeling an otherworldly entity. "Okay. I'm getting brainy, dull, and single-minded. Am I close?"

Derrick offered his winning smile. "Once you're through with her? Not a chance." He winked.

Another compliment. Apparently this internship was a bigger deal than she anticipated. "You haven't met her?"

Her father shook his head.

"Do we know if she has more than the social grace of a hyena?"

"Except for her chronic halitosis and unseemly body hair, I imagine she'll be fine."

Jess loved it when her father bantered. At home—at least when her stepmother was out and she dropped by—he proved a great foil, engaging her with humor and interest. Work was another story, where he scarcely acted as though they were related. She could probably unicycle in front of him wearing a gold-lamé bodysuit that shot sparklers out of her bustier, and he wouldn't notice. She treasured these unguarded moments, wishing desperately they could share more of them. But she'd take what she could get.

"Bring a little Listerine and some tweezers?" she asked.

"And a brush for the dandruff."

"I'll put it in my purse."

"My little Girl Scout. Always prepared."

Jess kissed her father on the cheek. "For you? Anything."

❖

TJ evaluated her outfit. The black pantsuit was the same she'd worn to her mother's funeral four years ago. She had two suits and three blouses, all of which fit more loosely than they once had. Although her internship was paid, she wouldn't receive her first paycheck for two weeks. That meant rotating through her meager choices until she could go shopping at the thrift store. At a posh firm like Magnate Investment Securities LLC, her clothing would stick out like an unruly cowlick.

The shoes were presentable yet uncomfortable. There was no way she could make the walk from the bus stop to the firm's corporate office in the unforgiving synthetic materials. TJ didn't own a briefcase; she'd have to make do with her backpack—yet another thing that would scream of the differences between her world and theirs.

She took a deep breath. Focus on the positive. The opportunity. She had every right to this internship and would do whatever it took to succeed.

At her sister's door, TJ knocked as she entered. "Wake up, Kare." The lump in the bed didn't stir. "Kara! Up. Now."

From under her pillow, Kara peeked at her clock. "Go 'way."

"You need to be up before I leave or you'll never get to school. Come on. Up."

"I have another hour."

"Not for the next three months you don't. I have to catch an earlier bus, which means you have to get up too. Take a shower, eat your cereal, and study."

"Ugh." Kara covered her head with her pillow.

TJ walked over and snatched it out of her hands. "Kare. You promised."

"Okay. Okay." After sitting up, Kara rubbed her eyes. "I'm up."

She crawled out of bed and gave TJ the once-over. "You look nice. Funeral attire is perfect for a corporate job. Good choice."

"I'm not sure when I'll be home, so eat when you're hungry. There's leftover pasta and garlic bread. And a little salad left in the blue Tupperware."

"Are you kidding? If you're not home, I'm starting with the M&Ms." Kara padded into the bathroom. "Good luck today."

❖

After offering a beverage and exchanging pleasantries, Gary Treanor asked TJ, "What do you want to get out of this internship?"

"An understanding of how the firm's achieved such extraordinary success in a field rife with competition. I'd like to write a case study that shows the primary factor the firm has leveraged to allow it to consistently excel."

"You've given it some thought."

"Yes, sir."

"I'm not sure it's in our best interest to let the secret sauce out."

TJ expected the COO's question and launched into her prepared spiel. "It could be another tool you use to gain clientele. Something's obviously working, and reporting on that methodology, especially in the form of an objective study published by a prestigious university, might benefit you. But the firm doesn't have to commit to anything. I'm already operating under a nondisclosure agreement. It's up to the firm to decide if it wants to confine it to my professors and me or publish it."

"Tell you what. Let's start you in marketing. We spend millions annually to find new clients and educate them about the benefits of moving their assets to us. I'll have you work with Jess, our head of marketing. Meanwhile, I'll consider your case study."

TJ's optimism was waning, but she didn't let that fact show. This wasn't a marketing internship. She was here to learn how to operate a successful business and understand how it differentiated itself. "That sounds great."

"Follow me. If she's here, I'll introduce you."

Gary started to lead her down the hall but stopped. "Her lights are off."

TJ heard someone mumble, "So to speak," from behind a cubicle wall.

"Let's set you up close by," Gary said.

After signing payroll forms and being issued a laptop, TJ began filling the time scouring the Internet for articles on Magnate and its charismatic owner. The hustle and bustle surrounding her was as easy to tune out as the conversations she ignored when she waited tables.

Two hours later, she decided the laptop was an expensive paperweight for what she was getting from it. Thin and sleek, it would provide more value as a warming pad for a resourceful feline. Without access to the firm's trading software and client account records, and someone to train her to utilize them, TJ might as well be reading her leadership book. She was ignored and left without any tasks. If this was supposed to be a case study in mindfulness and living in the moment, she'd missed the memo.

TJ was a doer. These people were supposed to train her, not pay her to fog a mirror. She briefly considered contacting Professor Ridge, but she was supposed to be acquiring leadership skills. The order of the day was action, not kvetching.

She decided to focus on what she knew so she could ask educated questions when the time came. It was hard to argue with facts. Magnate had a stellar record of beating the market. Bull and bear markets provided the overall trends, which the firm necessarily followed, but it tended to best the category indexes by ten or more points. In its seventeen-year history, through which it saw two major market collapses, Magnate had posted negative returns in only three years.

Derrick Spaulding was Wall Street's golden boy. He'd worked his way up the ranks of the NYSE before branching out on his own and taking clients with him. That entrepreneurial spirit had served him well and brought an influx of interested clients. He defied conventionality by opening an office on the West Coast and maintaining only a small one in Manhattan. There were, of course, detractors on the Street, claiming the consistently high returns were impossible and thus fabricated. Nevertheless, his reputation remained untarnished. During interviews he reminded naysayers that an independent accounting firm audited his firm annually. He had nothing to hide.

A sudden change in noise caught TJ's attention. Phone conversations muted as a cheery voice crescendoed. TJ turned toward its direction. A late-twenty-something blonde was making her way through the office, waving to some and chatting briefly with others.

TJ couldn't describe fashion to save her life. An image of Monty

Python's Keeper of the Bridge of Death popped into her head. She would undoubtedly face a question requiring her to know what the hell a décolletage was and be cast into the gorge of eternal peril when she erred. She had learned all she knew about it from scanning magazines lining the checkout stands at the grocery store. But if TJ had to describe this woman in one word, it would be fashionable.

Her blond hair curled at the ends and stopped at the top button of her jacket. She wore a long-sleeve, black suit jacket that buttoned just below her cleavage, which her red lace blouse seemed to make stand out all the more. Her matching black pencil skirt and black high heels limited the woman's stride to require nearly two steps for every normal one.

That was all it took for TJ to amend her earlier thought. Not fashionable. Airheaded. Watching the woman's ridiculous half-step attention-seeking performance, TJ briefly wondered whether she'd stumbled onto the set of a reality show where the gorgeous woman chooses her male quarry and leaves with him to fulfill some sort of everyman fantasy involving a hot tub and plenty of naked women.

Jess removed one of two wine bottles from a rectangular box. The label was blank except for the words RED WINE. "Gather 'round, gentlemen. Come see the latest promo." She handed out the bottle to be passed around. "Anyone can do generic and mediocre. But what do you get when you pair your demand for quality with your desire for personalized attention?" She lifted the second bottle. The label was elegant. "Spaulding" was embossed in gold calligraphy above the vintage, and the distinguished Golden Oak picture hugged the lower half of the bottle. "You get uncompromising."

The men clapped and whistled.

What Jess didn't say was how each of the prospects from the firm's own Pebble Beach Classic would be getting a box, the second bottle personalized for him or her. The accompanying invitation included a unique toll-free number that would allow the answering account rep to identify the caller for a custom experience.

"Golden Oak doesn't partner with anyone," someone said.

"Really? Hmm. Maybe it's a mistake." Jess winked. She didn't delve into the details of her lengthy pursuit of the brand. The winemaker had refused to allow any co-branding until she convinced them of the good PR they could achieve at little cost. They embraced her idea to allow each Classic attendee to purchase up to six of the personalized bottles (names of individuals were acceptable but company names were not), which were twice as expensive as retail. Golden Oak pledged the net proceeds to the firm's university fund. Even if the customer didn't pursue a relationship with the firm, the only path to getting the special bottles was to call and provide the unique code on the invitation. The prospect would feel good about his or her exclusive purchase, the firm, the winemaker, and the charitable contribution. Down the road, some would become Magnate customers.

Jess never revealed the effort behind her marketing coups. Her reputation was that of a spoiled princess who got by on good looks and Daddy's money, and she excelled at maintaining it. She occasionally paraded a new promotional item around the office to keep the team convinced that some marketing transpired, but she kept her hard work to herself. When she wanted to stand out, she did so on physical appearance, not brainpower. Female Spauldings simply did not compete for thought leadership.

The men in her office seemed to believe new clients arrived at Magnate's door due solely to the superior market returns it earned. Reality suggested otherwise. It took brand awareness—the figurative pounding into people's consciousness the positive results to be achieved by changing investment firms. That awareness required significant amounts of capital to maintain and expand. Thankfully, due to the overconfidence of her colleagues and the façade she cultivated, it was easy for Jess to let the staff continue their beliefs.

TJ heard the group provide several more accolades before breaking apart to return to work. The blonde headed past TJ toward the corner office. That the woman was walking like Morticia Addams reminded TJ of her own funereal attire, and she again felt her socioeconomic status like a tattoo on her forehead. TJ brushed the thought aside; she'd earned this chance.

Stopping at the door, TJ knocked on the frame and peered in just as the blonde set down her purse. "Excuse me." Blue eyes met hers.

"Yes?"

"Are you Jess?"

"I am."

"I'm TJ, the new intern. Gary said I'm to work with you."

Jess crossed the office and extended her hand. "Nice to meet you. Welcome to Magnate. Please come in." She gestured to one of the guest chairs as she took a seat behind a gorgeous wooden desk with stunning marquetry. Likely handcrafted in Europe, it probably cost more than TJ would make this decade.

"What a beautiful piece of furniture," TJ said, mindful not to run her finger across its edge like she wanted.

Jess took a moment to appraise it, as if she'd never seen it before. "I suppose it is. A little something I picked up years ago in Italy, but to be honest, I haven't really noticed it in forever. I can already tell you'll be good for me." She smiled warmly. "Now let's get straight to the hard questions. Is TJ your given name or a nickname?"

Amused by the softball she was thrown, TJ replied, "Nickname. My real name's very feminine. It's awful."

Jess laughed. "Do tell."

It was TJ's turn to smile. "Not on your life."

"Ah, the gauntlet is thrown already. Mark my words: I'll get it out of you. Tell me a little about yourself. I'm familiar with your MBA program. You must be smart."

TJ sank into the soft leather chair and ignored the comment. She didn't want to start off their get-to-know-you by tooting her own horn. "You're the head of marketing?"

"Or the tail. I'm the only one *in* marketing, so you can decide which end I am."

"The high end."

Jess sat back. "Then I'm doing something right, since our asset minimum for clients is ten million."

"It must be tricky talking about managing assets."

"How so?"

"Don't be offended at the comparison, but when I'm waiting tables, I'm constantly getting inappropriate responses to my questions. Diners often purposely misconstrue an innocuous 'Is there anything else I can bring you?' or 'Can I interest you in dessert?' as sexual. If your typical client is an older white male, I imagine you get a lot of innuendo regarding managing assets. Yours." If TJ waitressed in anything as suggestive as what Jess wore, which wasn't particularly revealing, she'd be pawed incessantly.

"How do you handle that?"

"Politely. They have no right to call me babe or honey, yet they think they do, and I don't want to negatively impact my friend's restaurant by calling them out on their improper behavior."

"And you want your tips," Jess suggested.

"Not at the expense of doing what's right. If it wouldn't adversely affect my employer, I'd have no trouble telling them theirs is no way to treat a woman."

"I hate to disappoint you on your first day, so I'll be sure not to tell you that we don't typically discourage our more politically incorrect clients. They like an audience."

TJ smirked. "Thanks for not telling me."

"But speaking of waiting tables, may I take you to lunch? One of the benefits of getting in late is I can head to lunch as soon as I get here and forgo the need to do anything at all constructive."

TJ wasn't sure of the proper protocol here. She expected to work through lunch and had brought hers. Yet Ridge had counseled her to be open to everything they threw at her and ask for more. She heeded his advice. "That sounds great. Thank you."

"Let's go."

TJ followed as Jess baby-stepped through the office. TJ kept her eyes on the back of Jess's head instead of the tight-fitting fabric that surrounded her backside. The woman obviously worked out. And although the outfit seemed designed to garner notice, TJ wasn't about to be caught checking out her new boss.

As they exited the building, Jess walked toward a sleek black sedan from which a stocky, forty-something man in a suit emerged and opened the rear door. Once Jess sat and swung her legs inside, the driver opened the opposite door for TJ, and she sat with none of the grace of her companion.

TJ scanned her surroundings. The plush leather interior and dark-tinted windows made her feel she was with some sort of celebrity. In front of each seat was a monitor for video entertainment, and the wood-trimmed console between them offered individual climate controls and a smartphone charger. "I've never been in a car like this."

"The amenities become more impressive every year. I could do without the heated door panels and armrests, but I confess to taking advantage of the hot-stone massage feature on occasion," Jess said.

"Hot-stone massage?"

"You've never had one?"

TJ shook her head.

"It's kind of like someone's gently poking you with warm snooker balls. Want to try?" Jess reached for the remote control, but TJ stopped her hand.

"I'll take your word for it."

"We'll eat at Donatello's, if that works for you. Michael Warren Davidson is executive chef."

"Sounds like a serial killer or assassin," TJ said while tracing her fingers along the interior's curves.

Jess cocked her head.

"The middle-name thing. John Wayne Gacy, John Wilkes Booth, Lee Harvey Oswald, Michael Warren Davidson."

"I'm sure he'd be honored to be in such esteemed company," Jess said wryly. "I take it you haven't heard of him?"

"No, but I've a feeling you and I don't run in the same circles." TJ pulled on a small handle in the console and stared as a metal arm slowly rose, revealing a laptop table. "They've thought of everything."

"This model comes with an option for owners of small dogs. They swap this console for a car seat with a safety strap and removable cover for easy cleaning. The airbag goes there." Jess pointed to the area between the monitors.

"You're pulling my leg, right?" TJ folded the tray back into its compartment.

"You must be sensing the shiatsu option designed to help you stretch while you ride."

TJ felt beneath her seat before narrowing her eyes. "Okay, you got me. Fido's SOL and there's no shiatsu. Does this mean there's no hot-stone massage?"

"Now that's most definitely real." Jess pressed the remote control. "Close your eyes and enjoy."

Moments passed in silence, the road noise so muted that TJ occasionally peeked out her window to see if they were still moving. "Mmm. Sold. This feels wonderful. How about we go for a drive and skip lunch?"

"And miss our chance at being poisoned by the infamous Michael Warren Davidson?"

"We could get takeout and eat in here. Die happy."

"Where do you live, TJ?"

TJ stiffened, the question effectively cooling the heated seat. She didn't want to lose their surprisingly easy banter. "Maddiston. On South Cedar, near the old theater." South Cedar was in an industrial area of Maddiston, the city that abutted affluent Montgomery Hills. Most people didn't realize there was any housing there.

"The abandoned drive-in?"

"That's the one."

"Yikes."

TJ sat straighter. "We all have to live somewhere."

"Sorry. I just meant that area lacks…well…is it safe?"

"The neighbors watch out for each other. It's home. And it's close to the bus station."

"That's a good thing?"

TJ eyed her companion. "Why wouldn't it be?"

"The transients and drug dealers, to start."

TJ shot out her hand to turn off the massage. She was about to cross a line but could stop it as well as an open palm against a moving train. "People need to get to work or school. We don't all have a car service at our disposal."

"I didn't mean to offend you. As to this," Jess waved a palm to the interior, "I don't drink and drive, so when I'm entertaining like I am tonight, I use the service. It also makes it easy to ensure others in my party get home safely."

"Admirable."

"Yes. I can tell from your tone."

TJ's voice was still too controlled. "More people should use other means of transportation if the alternative is driving drunk."

"Unless that alternative is a limousine." Jess's irritated tone mirrored TJ's.

TJ regretted her comment. She'd responded to judgment with judgment. Regardless of anyone's means, she strongly believed no one should drive while intoxicated. TJ's years of watching her mother kill herself with alcohol informed her decision to minimally partake of it; she needn't condemn folks like Jess who took a different, yet responsible route.

"Whether you walk, take a taxi, ride with a friend, or use a limo, anything's far preferable to killing or injuring someone, and if I made it seem otherwise, I apologize. Frankly, as guardian of a teenager, I appreciate your foresight in ensuring there's one less drunk on the road tonight."

The remaining minutes passed in silence, with TJ lost in her own thoughts. As the Mercedes slowed to a stop, TJ became aware of her surroundings. A valet approached and opened her door. TJ stepped out onto a busy thoroughfare cordoned off by two orange plastic cones. She hoped the valets on this side of the street received hazardous-duty pay.

Once they were inside, an impeccably dressed host immediately acknowledged them but held up a finger while he finished his telephone conversation. Several couples occupied waiting-area benches, though TJ suspected the majority of the lunch queue was enjoying adult beverages in the adjacent bar until called. After the host hung up, his eyes alighted on Jess and he smiled.

"What a pleasant surprise, Ms. Spaulding. Please come with me." He pulled two thick rectangular menus from a slot and led them through the opulent dining room. White linens covered the tables, walls and ceilings were adorned in red-and-brown-patterned velour, and wooden dining chairs held crimson cushioning. Warm hues emanated from candles within glass globes on each table, adorned with elegant formal place settings. TJ forced a smile in response to the host pushing her chair forward as she sat.

"I recommend either the risotto or the swordfish, but I've never had anything here I didn't enjoy," Jess said as she perused the menu. "The beet salad or Castelvetrano olives make an excellent first course. I find four courses too much if we want dessert."

TJ's stomach dropped when she saw the prices for the three-, four-, and five-course options. The three-course option cost more than her monthly bus pass, and that was before tax or tip. She wasn't expected to pay for the meal, but she wouldn't be able to enjoy spending more for one meal than she spent on groceries for two weeks. Worse, when she'd heard how the host greeted Jess, she realized her dining companion was none other than the daughter of Derrick Spaulding. One of the online profiles she'd read on him mentioned his family. How was she supposed to relax in the company of the founder's daughter?

Finally, Jessica Spaulding seemed completely immune to the excess surrounding them. Her head, which never swiveled from the host's lead during the walk to the table, was now bent as she studied the menu. She acted as if she had no notion of how special this type of dining experience would be for the vast majority of the population. It seemed Jess looked forward to eating here as much as TJ did to eating at McDonald's, which was to say she didn't.

TJ found herself in a quandary. She couldn't feign illness because she needed to return to the office. She couldn't back out of lunch because she'd already agreed to it, no matter that she hadn't known her companion's lineage or the destination. Honesty was the only way forward.

"Ms. Spaulding."

Jess raised her head. "Please. It's Jess or Jessica."

"I can't eat here."

It took a moment for Jess to reply. "I should have asked whether you had any food sensitivities. But they can accommodate almost anything. Vegetarian, vegan, gluten-free—"

"I'm not comfortable having you pay for a meal like this when I can't return the favor. I'd offer to go Dutch, but honestly, I can't spend this kind of money on one meal."

Jess set her menu down. "I'd never ask anyone to lunch and expect reciprocation. Also, I'm not paying for it. It's admirable of you to be concerned with the cost, but this is a business expense. Magnate's picking up the tab, no strings attached."

TJ shook her head. "I'm not comfortable with it."

Jess's narrowed eyes gave away her exasperation. "Is this because of my comment about the limo?"

"No. It's because I can't accept something for nothing."

"It's *lunch*. A normal part of everyday business. Someone new starts, you take them to lunch. End of story."

"I'm sorry."

"Fine. It's a progressive town. Pretend we're on a date."

"I don't date."

"Can't imagine why," Jess said under her breath. She was flabbergasted. When did having lunch become such a big deal? Why was she suddenly having so much difficulty with this intern? She didn't need the drama. Abruptly, she grabbed her purse and strode over to the host, not bothering to see if TJ would follow. If TJ wanted to get out of here so badly, she would. "Victor, please forgive my horrid manners for leaving so soon." Jess cut him off before he could get a word in, surmising from his wide eyes that he believed the staff had screwed up. "As always, I appreciate your exemplary service and promise I'll be back soon."

Her driver was waiting in a no-parking zone out front and immediately pulled the car forward. Jess was so furious she nearly threw open the door but kept her manners and allowed him to open it. Moments later, TJ slid in next to her.

"Back to the office, please." Jess had done her duty, having tried to play nice with the intern. Now, she'd toss the keys to Gary. He was in the office daily, which was where TJ would be spending her internship. Jess had no need to be involved. He oversaw the financial-modeling and market-research aspects of the business, which were the areas TJ would want to focus on.

She stewed over their conversation. With prospects and clients, Jess routinely steered clear of controversial topics and ignored irritating comments made by those she wooed because most of them liked to listen to themselves talk. She had no desire to change their ways of thinking; she aimed solely to get them to move their money stashes to the firm. It was amazing, the power of her acquiescence to whatever they said. They never put two and two together to realize she let them win any present argument so that they'd feel more impressed by her. It defied logic. But this intern wasn't a prospect, and Jess had no reason to play her usual smile-and-nod bobblehead.

Still, Jess felt an uncharacteristic wave of guilt. She should have kept her dating rebuttal to herself. TJ hadn't done anything wrong or said anything disdainful—well, except for the comment about the limo, for which she'd apologized. She had merely voiced her unease.

And admittedly, the teenager comment intrigued Jess. TJ hardly seemed older than a teenager herself. Jess couldn't imagine living in TJ's neighborhood or pushing her own needs aside for someone else. Motherhood was not in her five-year plan.

The silence in the car was so thick Jess grew irritated with the incredible German engineering that effectively negated the road noise. She pivoted to face TJ. "My sarcasm was completely uncalled for, and I'm sorry. I've never had a lunch outing turn south so quickly. I'll make sure Gary takes care of everything you need for your internship." She shifted her body so she again faced the window, but realized she wasn't finished and turned to TJ once more.

"Also, though I said it derisively, frankly I can't imagine why you don't date. You're obviously smart or you wouldn't be in the program, and look at you. Your cheekbones are perfection, you have a celestial nose my stepmother's friends pay plastic surgeons to emulate, and your gray eyes are hypnotic. You could have any man you wanted. Assuming he let you pay," Jess couldn't help adding.

"I don't have time, and even if I did, I wouldn't be interested."

"In dating?"

"In men."

Jess was incredulous. "Did you just come out to me?"

"I did."

"How is that possible?"

"That I'm gay?"

"That it was easier for you to come out to me than have lunch with me."

"Having lunch with you wasn't the problem. Having lunch *there* was the problem."

"Because of the cost."

"Yes."

"You ax prospective dates based on income?"

"It wasn't a date."

"That wasn't the question."

"I told you, I don't date."

The reasons were becoming all too clear. TJ was attractive and likely hit on routinely, but she had a damnable pride that probably put off potential suitors faster than claiming an STD. "When someone asks you out, do you hand them a job application to weed out anyone above a certain income level?"

"Come to think of it, that must be why the number of billionaires knocking on my door has trickled lately."

"You do realize you're interning at an organization that caters to people for whom a lunch like that is the equivalent of eating at Subway?"

"Good to know I wasn't wrong."

"About?"

"The fact that you didn't appreciate a single facet of the experience."

"You mean the food I didn't get to order? You're right."

"The service, the uniforms, the muted conversations, the fabrics, the art, the heft of the wine list, the window treatments, the menu choices, the view!"

TJ was right. Jess hadn't noticed any of those things. She'd been trying to welcome the newcomer and instead was being criticized for not being awed by a site as familiar as her hand. Jess kept her remarks as cool as steel. "If you can't accept wealth, you're interning at the wrong establishment. We market to people and organizations with hundreds of millions, and yes, billions of dollars. If you can't stand to be in a room with them, I suggest you rethink the next few months."

The sedan slowed to a stop outside the firm's offices.

Jess remained seated. "I won't be back today. You're free to leave for the day or have Gary give you something to do."

❖

With a free afternoon, TJ stopped by the blood bank, which often gave movie passes to thank donors. Today was no exception, and she gratefully accepted.

Once home, she went to Kara's doorway, pleased it was uncharacteristically open. Kara, sporting the look she'd adopted in middle school of black skinny jeans, T-shirt, and a men's cardigan, lay on the bed playing her Nintendo. The handful of games she owned was long stale from overuse, but TJ had come to believe that to Kara they were like dog-eared books. The stories were familiar, the characters old friends. Maybe it didn't matter that they couldn't afford new games every week.

Negotiations took place over homework and movie selection, and they dissected the movie's strengths and failings during their meal.

TJ didn't require too much family time except for dinner, and typically Kara would immediately head to her room afterward. Tonight she lingered, rimming her water glass with her finger.

"How'd it go today?" Kara asked.

TJ spoke over her shoulder as she scrubbed the plates. "Fine, I suppose."

"Must've been pretty bad for you to leave early."

"The person I've been assigned to isn't exactly…I'm not sure I can learn from her."

"So, like, Mr. Ferris?" Kara's freshman-year foreign-language teacher had been as helpful to the students learning Spanish as whistling to communicate with birds. Kara had complained, suggesting she'd learn more from Spanish language audiobooks than attending his class. TJ had agreed, and instead of suffering in his class each day, Kara went to the school library and followed the lessons. She was now in Spanish AP.

"I don't know if she's that bad, but we definitely don't see eye to eye."

"About what?"

TJ didn't want to talk to Kara about her exchange with Jess. But it was rare these days for Kara to be so unguarded, and TJ didn't want their time together to end. When their mom had died—which to TJ was far too passive a way to describe it—TJ had been forced into a guardianship for which she was ill prepared. Kara blamed herself for the loss while TJ blamed their mother. As Kara grew older, she retreated into her games, growing more sullen and standoffish.

Cars were the only thing these days that pulled Kara out of her doldrums, a subject that often put the two of them at odds. Their relationship had morphed into a bifurcated not-parent, not-sibling thing TJ couldn't describe. Now, their closeness was sporadic. She didn't know how much of Kara's moodiness was due to normal teenage angst or to feeling worthless.

For several months after their mother's passing, Kara, twelve at the time, had often cried that she wasn't good enough—wasn't enough, period—to keep her mother interested in this life. Since then, Kara never talked about their mother. And neither did TJ.

TJ set down the glass she was cleaning and dried her hands. Two chocolate muffins had been warming in the oven, which she tossed into two bowls. She dropped a dollop of ice cream onto each one and sat next to her sister, who immediately began to eat.

"I haven't been able to stop thinking about something she said." TJ interpreted Kara's full-mouthed mumbled question as only a sibling could. "Scary I understood that." TJ sucked on a small bite of the mint chocolate chip. "She asked if I weed out prospective dates based on income."

"You talked with your boss about dating? On the first day?"

"Not talked about it, exactly. It came up."

"Did she hit on you?"

"No! God, she's straight as a pole."

"Paulina Zeilinski just transferred from Warsaw, and she's anything but."

TJ pushed her sister's shoulder. "Smart aleck. Fine. Straight as an arrow. Broom. Line."

"How do you know she's straight?"

"She wore a sign."

Kara returned the shoulder push. "Do you?"

"Do I wear a sign?"

"Weed out prospective dates based on income?"

"I don't know. It's not like women come up to me and say, 'Hi, I made two million last year and here's a copy of my 1040. Want to have dinner?'"

"Probably not a great pick-up line."

"For a lot of women, it would be."

"Gross."

"I know. But part of me thinks she's right. What if I judge people based on how they live? More specifically, their earnings? How does that make me any different from people who judge me based on the sex of the person I prefer in my bed?"

Kara grinned and waggled her eyebrows. "Sex and bed. You never talk sex and bed." She scooped another spoonful of ice cream and muffin into her mouth.

"Never mind."

"She rich?"

"As Croesus."

"Who?"

"Iranian Bill Gates, sixth century BC." Unless a history lesson related to automobiles, Kara lost interest, so TJ often modernized and packaged historical facts into sound bites to keep their conversations on track.

"She hot?"

"What does that have to do...were you not here for the part about the arrows and lines?"

"What if...what if a beautiful, bright heiress worth bazillions asked you to dinner?"

"How could I enjoy the meal? How could I ever pay her back? I'd sit there and think of all the ways I'd fall short and how I couldn't remotely give her anything she's used to."

"Why would you need to pay her back? Dude. Pretty—"

"Don't call me dude."

"Don't interrupt. Pretty, smart heiress is—"

TJ scoffed. "You can scrap smart."

"Goes without saying if someone asks you out. But dimwitted heiress is asking you on a date, not pulling out her little black bookie book to track who owes who."

"Who owes whom. And I can't accept something for nothing."

"I'm speaking colloquially, Grammar Police. She wouldn't be asking you to. She'd be asking you to respond with, like, part of you, not part of your checkbook. She's surrounded by people who could do that, but she asked you. What if you're the antidote to her having to deal with all the Class As trying to get into her pants because they paid for some fancy dinner?"

Class As were assholes. TJ didn't allow Kara to swear. When either wanted to call someone a nasty name, they were Class As.

"I don't know that I could prevent them from trying."

"If she knew you were by her side, she wouldn't care that they did."

"Fake heiress in said fake situation sounds intriguing, but don't you have some homework to finish?"

"So she's hot."

"Homework."

CHAPTER TWO

W hy can't she learn about sales? You'd make a far better teacher," Jess said.

"She's gay?" Brooke asked, completely sidestepping the question.

Jess pushed the eggs on her plate around with her fork, feeling every bit the petulant child. After telling her sister about the disastrous outing with the intern, the only thing on Brooke's mind was business. Brooke wasn't inquiring out of personal interest. "You're not going to help me, are you?" Jess asked.

"Interesting."

Jess watched the wheels turn in her sister's mind. Brooke was hatching some scheme. "You could make her get your coffee every morning," Jess said.

"I don't need another assistant on my heels like a Chihuahua. Is she pretty?"

"What does that matter?"

"I want to know if she's attractive. Describe her."

"I don't know. Ask Gary."

"Come on. Are we talking Grace Kelly or Winston Churchill?"

Despite herself, Jess snorted. Brooke could always make her laugh. "Definitely not Churchill. But not Grace Kelly's kind of pretty. Not as feminine. More like...I don't know. Attractive for sure. Good-looking."

"Pantsuit, no makeup?"

Jess nodded. "With eyelashes that could fan Cleopatra, who needs it? Dark-brown hair in a shortish, wavy bob I'd call contemporary messy. Trim. Tall."

"Invite her to the party."

"Why?"

"She sounds just like Muriel's type."

If laid flat, Muriel Manchester's dollars could blanket the globe twice over, covering the Earth's landscape with green and white pictures of elderly white men with bad hair. Magnate had been trying to land Muriel's business for ages.

"We're not playing matchmaker," Jess said.

"No. We're trying to show Muriel we embrace diversity."

Jessica laughed. "Since when?"

"Since always."

"We don't employ a single person of color, almost no women, no gay people, and no one with a disability."

"That doesn't mean we're averse to doing so. In theory. And we have our first lesbian. Might tip the scale with Muriel."

"Even if TJ accepted, how exactly do you propose we inform Muriel of our incredibly diverse practices? Hire Neil Patrick Harris for the evening's entertainment and throw a rainbow LED necklace around TJ that flashes 'I feel pretty'?" Though the thought was ludicrous, the mental image of subjecting her father's typical guests to such a display amused her. It would definitely spice up the evening.

"First of all, she's an intern. You don't invite her. You insist she attend. Second, it's not about getting her together with Muriel. It's about us being accepting and welcoming, conveniently in Muriel's presence. Make sure she brings a date."

"You want a lesbian couple parading around one of Daddy's parties." Jess had been at the receiving end of too many of her stepmother's public smiles that said "What a pleasant surprise" concurrent with the disparate murmured audio that said, "What in God's name is this?" Lilith would call security at the sight.

"There needn't be any parading. We're not talking drag queens. We're talking you and me laughing and getting along swimmingly with our lesbian guests. Bonus if Muriel happens to notice."

❖

TJ walked along the side path beyond the courtyard, carrying a Tupperware container and a cup of water. The firm's offices disappeared from view as the walkway wound through the sheltering trees to a minipark.

Dropping onto a bench seat, she closed her eyes and inhaled the garden scents of lavender and jasmine. Alone in this small sanctuary, she simply enjoyed the moment. The peacefulness of this spot reminded her of home. Daily she traveled unforgiving streets only to cross the threshold to her apartment and joyfully leave the world's ugliness at the door. Here in this setting, the yards separating her from the firm's office felt like miles, and she reveled in the divide.

Day two of one of the most sought-after internships imaginable, and she had yet to learn anything. Three months wasn't long to gain a comprehensive understanding of a business and write a lengthy case study about an aspect of it that warranted examination. TJ had hoped to document the strategy and execution that made Magnate's success exceptional, but being stuck in marketing without a marketing expert made the task seem impossible.

Another deep breath helped temper the frustration. Lunch break meant taking time out, and damn it, she would focus on this moment outside, not what was waiting for her inside. Breathe in. Breathe out. In. Out. How did she get here?

TJ cleared the plates from table twenty-three and wondered whether someone had switched them for natural stone tiles. After two hours on her feet without a break, they felt that heavy. The Saturday-night shift meant more tips, but the work was exhausting.

She approached the middle-aged couple at table nineteen and faltered mid-sentence as she recognized her former teacher. "Nice to see you, again, Professor." It was the fourth time in two months she'd waited on him. "One might get the impression you had something on your mind other than the bouncing beef tenderloin."

Professor Ridge introduced his fellow diner. "Deadline's Friday, TJ."

TJ addressed Diane, his companion. "Would you care for a glass of wine or cocktail this evening? Perhaps a citrus martini?"

Diane bent down for her purse and pulled a card from a cardholder. "If you'd like help with any part of the application, please call me. I'm a graduate counselor and can provide feedback on your essay, personal statement, and statement of purpose. Whatever you need. And yes to the martini."

TJ placed the card in her vest pocket and eyed Ridge. "More of the soft sell, Professor?" She had to give him points for tenacity.

"This program was made for you, TJ. I'd say don't disappoint me, but don't disappoint yourself. This is a great opportunity, and you know it."

Ridge had been one of the few attendees at her mother's funeral. He was the only teacher—the only person—she'd told of her difficulties caring for a parent with end-stage alcoholism, playing guardian to a tween, and working full-time while taking night classes. Four years ago, when the strain of her family's fragile finances had finally forced her to abandon her educational aspirations and take a second job, she visited him during office hours to apologize for dropping his course. She'd broken down in his office under the crushing weight of her obligations.

Ridge had found a way to help. One of his friends owned Zelda's, the restaurant where she now worked. On the strength of Ridge's recommendation, the friend hired her. The increased tips at this more upscale restaurant allowed TJ to scale back to one job and re-enroll in school.

Ridge was intent on her applying to a new accelerated program that would allow her to earn an MBA in Nonprofit Management. It targeted the best and brightest underserved students, those with limited finances. The program only provided loan/scholarship awards that carried a service obligation. The loans were forgiven when graduates hired by qualifying nonprofits met the two-year service commitment. Otherwise, the loan became due with interest.

Businesses that had integrated philanthropy models similar to those of Salesforce and Google wanted to be seen as community-focused and socially aware. They supported the program by providing paid internships. Interns would gain real-world business experience and prepare a case study as to the primary element (e.g. supply-chain management, customer service, product innovation) that set the company apart. The university would select the best report to polish and publish in its prestigious *Business Review* as best of breed, an honor for any business.

Ridge had told TJ he'd had her in mind from the outset of the program's design. TJ was adamant about her lack of interest in grants or scholarships designed for financially struggling students. Yet she didn't want to incur massive student loans. Even if she were willing to go into debt, no funding sources covered both student and family expenses. As her family's breadwinner, she had no options.

Until Ridge. His creation brought industry and nonprofits together, aligned their goals, and promised positive outcomes for student, firm, and foundation alike. For students like TJ, who wanted to run her own charity one day, Ridge's program was perfect.

TJ started at the sound of footsteps, and when she looked up, her eyes met Jessica Spaulding's. Tension crept into her shoulders. Yesterday's exchange had stayed with her more than she wanted to admit. Three months was a long time to work in close proximity with someone with whom you didn't see eye to eye.

What was it about the woman that was so bothersome, like a stiff clothing tag on a shirt collar that wouldn't lay flat against the skin?

Jessica stopped several feet away with a wary gaze TJ assumed she mirrored. She tried not to white-knuckle the plastic container. Was Jess here to dismiss her? Maybe that shouldn't surprise her. Mouthing off to the big boss's daughter was probably as smart as hiking Everest in flip-flops. At least she was being granted privacy rather than being humiliated in front of other staffers. The kid gloves were an unexpected touch.

Jess stepped forward and offered her hand. "Hi. I wanted to introduce myself. I'm Jessica Spaulding. You're the new intern, I presume?"

TJ's momentary confusion gave way to relief. Jess wasn't here to terminate her. Setting aside her lunch, TJ stood and shook hands. "Yes. TJ Blake. Nice to meet you."

Jess sat across from TJ. "I'm in marketing."

"I believe I'll be working for you."

"No one works for me. If anything, we'll be working together."

"Sounds good," TJ said.

"I'd love to take you to lunch tomorrow, but some rather unscrupulous hackers have targeted us, forcing us to temporarily close our corporate credit-card accounts. I'm afraid it's every woman for herself until we can clear that up. That means I can drive us, but you'd have to pony up for your meal. Not very welcoming, I know."

"Sounds serious." TJ appreciated the artifice. Apparently Jess had taken her words to heart about not wanting an expensive meal.

"It is. I'd offer to cook, but that would be even more disastrous. National-guard level. We can always postpone if you'd rather."

"No, no, no. I'm happy to pay for my meal."

"Any suggestions as to where we should eat?" Jess asked.

"How about Waverley Beach Park?"

"There aren't any cheap restaurants there. There's only Le Papillon and Manresa's. Fine dining."

"Let's go to Al's Sandwich Shop and split a deli sandwich and their world-famous coleslaw. They provide napkins, utensils, paper bags, and cups for water. We'll take everything to the park and sit on a bench overlooking the ocean."

"No dessert? Dessert is essential," Jess said.

"They'll toss in two Andes mints for free."

"Excellent. Ande and I go way back. How much will this lunch set us back?"

"Seven dollars. Three-fifty each. Million-dollar view."

"Perfect. We'll take my car," Jess said.

"Is it safe?"

"Doubtful. I'll be driving."

"Does it have airbags?"

"Only for canines."

❖

Once TJ finished her lunch, she dropped by Jess's office for an assignment.

Jess grabbed her keys and purse. "Let's go to the Players' Open. It's one of the top tennis tournaments in the world, and it's local. We're sponsoring it, and we've got a suite. I'll drop you off here afterward." Jess passed TJ and headed for the exit.

"What will I be doing?" TJ asked, sliding into the passenger seat.

"Getting a sense of how we gain and keep customers. It's not all about investment returns, believe it or not."

"It's admittedly a stretch to imagine having enough money to invest, but if I did, returns are the only thing I'd care about."

"All our investors have multiple channels through which to invest. Our job is to differentiate ourselves. If we can get our clients to value our services—including investment returns—on a different level than they value others', we give ourselves the breathing room to occasionally drop out of the top quartile without repercussion because of comprehensive value perceived." Jess gave TJ a quick smile before shifting her eyes back to the road. "Not that we've ever dropped out of it."

During the drive, Jess shared some of the methods Magnate used to try to stand out from other investment advisory firms while TJ listened. Everything Jess said made sense and sounded far more astute than anything TJ had come to expect from her.

Once they arrived and turned the car over to the valet, Jess led TJ through the stadium grounds and up to the VIP boxes. The suite they entered was spacious. Several young servers stood shoulder to shoulder, ready to do the bidding of a client. A set of rectangular tables housed nonalcoholic beverages and snacks, and each small round table set up for more intimate conversation had a small menu atop it for custom orders, including alcohol.

TJ passed through the sliding-glass door between the suite and the spectator seats reserved for suite guests. She was so close to the tennis players she could see the sweat beading on their foreheads between points without having to glance at the television monitors overhead. Jess joined her for the next two games, and as the players switched sides, she indicated for TJ to follow her into the suite. There, she introduced TJ to one of the two investment advisors manning the event, who brought Jess up to speed as to which clients and prospects had thus far attended.

TJ's attention turned to a seated ruddy-faced man in his fifties speaking with another man while holding a young server around the waist. Each time the server made a move to depart, the man tugged her back and laughed with his male companion. The young woman was trying to peel the man's hand from her waist as politely as she could, clearly uncomfortable.

TJ watched the man pull the server onto his knee like she was a child and he was Santa Claus. But these were no reindeer games. He was intoxicated, and the more the young woman tried to disentangle herself, the more he laughed. A quick scan of the room for any sign of someone to come to the woman's rescue bore no fruit until she was finally able to make eye contact with Jess. TJ flicked her head in the direction of the drunk. Jess followed TJ's gaze, watched the scene for several seconds, and met TJ's eyes. She shrugged. TJ looked at her pointedly and tilted her head in a manner that suggested Jess take action. Jess shot back a warning and shook her head.

TJ crossed the room seconds later. "Get your hands off her," she said as she stood over the man.

"I beg your pardon?" he replied as his laughter died.

"She's not your chattel."

His red face reddened further. "How dare you—"

"Mr. Torrington," Jess interjected. She scooped his free hand in both of hers, shook it, and offered him a wide smile. "How lovely to see you. I'm so glad you could make it." She nodded to the other man. "Mr. Adams. Thank you for coming." She then turned to the server and lost all geniality. "I'm still waiting for the drink I ordered ages ago. I'd appreciate it if you'd resume your duties instead of chatting up our guests." The startled woman looked like she was about to cry. Jess barked at TJ. "This isn't what we pay for. Please handle it."

TJ had no idea what just happened but didn't need to be told twice to get the woman away from the Torrington creep. Her anger, already at the boiling point when she confronted Torrington, was shooting into the stratosphere with what she witnessed from Jess. How could Jess take the situation out on the unfortunate and powerless young woman?

She steered the server out of the suite. "Are you all right?"

The woman kept her gaze to the floor and nodded.

"Where's your manager?"

"This way," the woman said with a nod of her head toward the hallway.

As they started forward, Jess burst through the suite entrance and rushed toward the server.

Before Jess could say anything, TJ put her arm between them. "Haven't you done enough?"

Jess glared, pushed TJ's hand away, and returned her attention to the woman. "I'm so sorry for that man's behavior. I'd like to talk to your manager and get you sent home."

The woman's chin trembled. "But I didn't do anything wrong."

"No, you didn't, which is exactly what I intend to tell your manager. Can you get him or her for me?"

"So you can get me fired?"

"I don't intend to get you fired. I thought you might be more comfortable heading home than going back in there."

"You didn't order any drinks from me, and I wasn't chatting up that man."

"I know. I didn't want the situation to escalate." Jess shot TJ a glance. "He's drunk, and if confronted, he's either going to deny any wrongdoing or insinuate that you brought it on yourself. I had to trump up a reason to send you out. Now where can we find your manager?"

"I can't leave this soon into my shift. I need the money."

"How much would you make if you stayed?"

The woman shrugged. "Thirteen dollars an hour plus tips. I'm still on for three more hours."

Jess reached into her purse, thumbed through her wallet, and extracted five one-hundred-dollar bills. "Here. Will this cover it?"

Wide-eyed at the sum, the woman nodded and tucked the money in her pocket. "I'll go get him." The server rushed down the hallway.

"Hush money?" TJ asked venomously.

"What? No. She shouldn't have to remain on shift after that."

"No, but you'll pretend to blame *her* so that man can stay without rebuke and continue to act like an ass with anyone else of his choosing?"

Jess crossed her arms. "I said what I said in there in order to do the least damage possible for all involved."

"No. You said it so you could avoid having me tell him to his face that his behavior is unacceptable."

"He's a client."

"I've no doubt," TJ spat.

"I see. You told me yesterday you accept certain objectionable behavior because you don't want to negatively affect your friend's restaurant. But I can't do the same."

TJ snorted. "It's not the same thing at all. Your friend Torrington was physically assaulting the poor girl. That goes well beyond sexist comments."

"Assault's a bit hyperbolic, isn't it? They're in a public place. Torrington doesn't get violent or touch in places he shouldn't."

TJ couldn't believe what she was hearing. "He does this *repeatedly?*"

Jess sighed. She dug through her purse and drew out her office keys and valet ticket. "You're here to learn what makes businesses succeed. The time will come when you'll have to decide whether to show a prestigious client the door due to bad behavior or find a way to live with it. If you prefer to leave, take my car back to the office. I'll finish up here and either have one of the guys drive me or take a cab."

TJ stared at the objects in her palm. They hadn't been here long, she hadn't gotten much of a sense of any of the marketing aspects of the event, she was once again aware of a rift between Jess and her, and Jess was right. She was here to learn, and she'd have to handle sticky situations with donors.

Jess closed TJ's hand over the keys. "I'll see you tomorrow." With that, Jess disappeared into the suite.

TJ tried to get her head into a more conciliatory space before following. She found Jess laughing with Torrington and Adams, sitting close to Torrington as if they were old friends. Occasionally Jess would swat at Torrington's arm in a flirtatious manner, which sent TJ's blood pressure skyward.

When the manager arrived, TJ handled it herself, relaying to him what had happened, apologizing for their client, and informing him that his server handled the situation admirably. She didn't add that the client hadn't even had so much as his wrist slapped. Well, that wasn't exactly true. He was getting his wrist slapped playfully by a beautiful blonde who seemed to have regressed into some caricature of herself, the way she'd been when she arrived at the office yesterday.

TJ spent much of the next hour mingling but found she desired to remain in earshot of Jess. Jess mostly giggled, smiled, nodded, and gaily swatted. She asked questions the men would answer jovially and, as if they thought they were charming and brilliant enough to carry the conversation, didn't bother asking Jess's input on anything. Jess acted as if there was nowhere else she'd rather be. This persona was a stark contrast to the woman with whom TJ had shared the car ride over. A game-show line popped into her head: Will the real Jessica Spaulding please stand up?

After Torrington departed, TJ and Jess returned to the car. Jess turned on the radio after taking TJ's hint she wasn't in the mood for conversation. Halfway through the forty-minute drive, Jess lowered the music and broke the silence between them. "I feel as though I kicked your puppy."

TJ laughed, despite herself. "That was random."

"You wanted a different outcome."

The insightful remark surprised TJ. "Yes."

"You wanted to punch his lights out."

TJ laughed mirthlessly. "Yes."

"And mine."

"Briefly."

"At least you're honest. Still angry enough not to talk to me?"

"I'm not angry."

"You're disappointed," Jess said.

"I'm not naive. I've been in the service industry long enough to know how these things shake out."

"Then what's bothering you?"

What *was* bothering her? That Torrington consistently got away with his unseemly pawing of a young woman was par for the course. She hadn't expected anything to the contrary. It *had* bothered her that Jess had been initially so flippant about it, shrugging when TJ brought it to her attention. Although TJ silently acknowledged that the server wasn't being assaulted, it didn't mean the sexual harassment should have been tolerated. As the most senior company representative in attendance, Jess should have stepped in immediately. Still, Jess had inserted herself directly into the line of fire afterward, allowing herself to be the target of Torrington's advances until he retired for the day. Moreover, Jess had quickly defused the potentially volatile situation TJ was stirring up, summarily extracting the server from her plight without harming Magnate's relationship with its client. As disgusting as Torrington's behavior was, it wasn't Jess's fault that his race, gender, and money allowed him to get away with it.

What was bothering her was her confusion about the woman seated next to her. Jess had as many riches as Fort Knox, part of the nation's uber wealthy that got away with exactly the kind of unforgivable behavior Torrington displayed. Yet she was approachable and unconceited. She was also a beautiful woman. Had she the smarts to go with it, Jess would be quite an attractive package. Certainly she'd shown flares of intelligence, but they were enmeshed among great swaths of doltishness. It was like being around Mister Ed: when you were alone with him, he was precocious; when others were around, he was simply a horse. TJ didn't appreciate feeling so disoriented around her and lashed out unfairly.

"We're not friends, Jess. You don't have to ask me what's wrong."

Jess nodded slowly. After a minute, she turned up the volume of the stereo.

TJ inwardly kicked herself for her childish reply. Jess was being thoughtful, and TJ was pushing her away because she couldn't neatly fit Jess into her rich-girl stereotype. She switched off the music. Before she could apologize, Jess cut her off.

"My father's having a little soiree in a couple weeks. Saturday the ninth. You're invited." Jess's tone was as warm as frostbite, belying the overture. TJ supposed she deserved it.

"Work-related?"

"Always."

"A party full of Torringtons. Lovely."

"If you intend to run a nonprofit one day, you'd better get used to schmoozing. Even if you have a development director, you'll be expected to press the flesh."

"I don't expect Magnate's clientele to be the kind of folks I'll be dealing with in the future."

"Don't be naive. One day you'll be soliciting donations. That means you'll need to get comfortable talking to people with money. Lots of it."

"Employees need time off with their families. I don't plan to be the type of employer who requires night and weekend..." TJ stopped short. The set to Jess's mouth suggested no latitude. TJ inhaled and then exhaled deeply, trying to keep calm. "You're requiring my attendance?"

"I'm inviting you to a party and giving you plenty of notice," Jess said evenly.

But Jess held no cards. "Magnate needs me to be successful in my internship so I'll be hired. Otherwise your idyllic inaugural graduate-program statistics will go up in flames. I'll pass."

Jess regarded her for as long as she could before endangering them on the road. "Percentages, not individuals, matter. You may think you, specifically, do, but you don't. You won't be able to secure any kind of recommendation from us. Yes, it would be ideal if you succeed here, but the MBA program will do so regardless."

TJ studied Jess, who'd gone from solicitous to Queen's Guard frigid in seconds. She owned to causing the change. "What I said before, about us not being friends, was uncalled for. I'm sorry. You confuse me, which makes me uncomfortable. When you asked what was bothering me, that's the answer. Please accept my apology."

Seconds ticked by with only the music playing in glorious surround sound. Standard road noise was apparently something the wealthy could opt out of on their vehicles. TJ wondered what the option cost.

Belatedly, Jess replied. "Apology accepted. Thank you for being honest. What exactly confuses you? I'm not particularly complicated."

TJ snorted. "First of all, you're a woman. All women are complicated. It's in the handbook."

"There's a handbook?"

"Lost in the Great Flood, unfortunately. Never made it onto the ark."

Jess tsked. "Could've come in handy."

"You're telling me."

"Okay, I'm complicated. But confusing?"

"You're different when we're alone." Gone was TJ's lighthearted tone.

"In what way?"

TJ wanted to say, "Smarter and more genuine," but that would be akin to telling Jess she was otherwise stupid and shallow. She wasn't at all sure-footed in this conversation. "More yourself." It was a shot in the dark. TJ knew the real Jessica Spaulding as well as someone in a grocery checkout stand knows the true lives of the celebrities splashed across the entertainment magazines.

Jess frowned. "My life's a dichotomy. At least usually. I'm either by myself or in a work setting surrounded by others. I'm not used to being shadowed." Jess drummed her fingers on the steering wheel for several seconds. Then she flicked her eyes to TJ and offered a smile. "You're throwing me off my game."

It was a cliché, but TJ sensed truth in the statement. Was Jess used to playing a cunning game when she wasn't alone? Did she purposely affect simplemindedness when in company? If so, why? "How long have you been playing it?"

"Turn of phrase."

TJ let it go for now. "Can we get back to this soiree matter?"

"Sure, though your apology doesn't buy you a get-out-of-jail-free card."

"I don't really do dresses," TJ admitted.

"It's black tie. That includes tuxedos. Rent one and expense it."

"You want me to wear a tuxedo to this shindig?" TJ couldn't have heard correctly. "You realize that could be construed as my being gay?"

"What does being gay have to do with wearing a tux? I have a tux. In fact, I have two. Gucci and Burberry."

"Will you be wearing one?"

"No. But there's no reason you shouldn't."

TJ mulled this over. Something didn't quite fit, like a woman trying to shimmy into her wedding dress on her twenty-fifth wedding anniversary. "Okay, what gives? I imagine my wearing a tux to this affair would go over like Ford's pardon of Nixon."

Jess sighed. "Muriel Manchester. Heard of her?"

"No."

"One of twenty-three female CEOs in the Fortune 500 and one of only three out executives among them. She's worth several billion, and we've been pursuing her for years since she travels in my parents' social circle. She insists the firm's an all-boys network and refuses to give us the time of day until we embrace diversity in the workplace. We want to show her we're not like that, or if we were, we've changed."

TJ gaped. "Have you *looked* around the office?"

Jess bit her lower lip. "I know."

"One lesbian staffer isn't going to change her mind."

"Probably not."

"Then what's the point?"

"One point five percent annually of billions in assets under management."

TJ tapped her fingers against the armrest. "I'd have to bring a date in order to make it perfectly obvious."

"Yes."

"I don't have anyone to ask."

"I don't imagine you'll have any trouble," Jess said.

TJ was oddly pleased by the notion that Jess thought so. While it was true TJ wasn't usually turned down, she rarely did the asking. There weren't enough hours in the day for dating. "Even if that were true, it's not dinner and a movie. Getting gussied up for a party with a group of strangers isn't first-date material."

"Ask a friend. No one would ever know she's not a real date."

TJ wondered how much to divulge. During the years of her mother's decline, after she'd moved back to help care for Kara, she'd lost touch with most of her friends. Long hours working and studying left little room for downtime, which she willingly allotted to her sister. Though she missed her friends, there was no contest when it came to being there for Kara versus having a social life.

"The idea is to prove to this Muriel Manchester, if she happens to notice, that the Spaulding clan is perfectly comfortable hanging out with homosexuals?" TJ asked.

"Yes."

"Are you?"

Jess was taken aback. "Of course I am. How can you even ask me that?"

"Not you. Your family. As a family-run business, your family sets the corporate culture."

It was a question Jess struggled with, especially as gay rights remained at the forefront of federal and state news, from marriage to marriage licenses to bathroom utilization to faith-based discrimination. If Derrick and Lilith knew any gay people besides Muriel, they didn't mention it. On more than one social occasion, Jess had overheard derisive comments made by her stepmother's friends on the subject of gay marriage. Her stepmother never corrected them. Gary never said anything bad about anyone except for their attire. Brooke said mean things about everyone. Jess had never heard her father bad-mouth gays, but Muriel had a point: Magnate was hardly a model of anti-discrimination practices in the workplace.

Jess blew out a breath. "I don't know." Whatever reaction TJ was set to give, Jess wanted to be honest with her.

After some deliberation, TJ asked, "Are you bringing a date?"

"I am." Jess infused the comment with as much excitement as she could muster. She wondered if it was convincing.

"Someone special?"

"Yes." It was a lie. Chad Astor was a known quantity. They dated occasionally, Chad always wanting more than Jess was willing to give. But as something of a player, he didn't pressure her because he could readily find women who were charmed by his good looks and moonstruck over his fortune. The fact that he was an Astor shot him straight to the top of Lilith's list of suitors for Jess. Too bad his brain was two sizes too small for his opinions. He wasn't an awful person and could be fun at times. Best of all, as far as Jess was concerned, he was low maintenance. They mutually used each other to attend various social engagements when the other was available.

"Okay."

Jess heard the disbelief in TJ's answer, turning it into two syllables and lilting the "y" upward.

"You don't even notice when you do it, do you?" TJ asked.

"Do what?"

"Slide into your public persona."

"I don't know what you mean."

"The way you said, 'I am' and 'Yes.' It's as if you're trying to believe what you're telling yourself."

"You don't know me well enough to make that kind of statement."

"Fair enough. How would it go over with your family if you brought a woman to the party?"

"Everyone including Muriel knows I date men. She'd see through it immediately. It would be so obviously platonic, what would it accomplish?"

"Sorry. What I mean is, for the sake of argument, pretend you actually wanted to date a woman. How would it go over with your family?"

Jess deliberated. "I don't know. My parents' friends are fairly conservative, and my stepmother's all about what people think. She'd freak out about what it would mean to her reputation, and my father would probably defer to her in terms of how to handle it. I think they'd be disappointed."

And there it was. It wasn't until she'd said it aloud that Jess hit on the truth. Her parents *were* homophobic—at least Lilith was. And Jess didn't have the backbone to stand up to it. She felt her face flush with shame. Would TJ notice? Thankfully the interior of the car was fairly dark.

"That's not an uncommon parental response, unfortunately. But at the risk of downplaying umpteen million dollars, the more important question isn't what Muriel thinks of Magnate, but whether my date and I will be sending a truthful message. If there's no will on your family's part for substantive change regarding diversity in the workplace, it's... artificial."

Now Jess felt like a pimp as well as a spineless drudge. She pulled into Magnate's parking lot. "I'm sorry I mentioned it. It was selfish and unfair of me to ask. Rest assured you're under no obligation to attend."

CHAPTER THREE

G ary knocked, entered Jess's office without waiting for a reply, and closed the door. It was his standard practice, and Jess appreciated it as much as breaking a nail.

"She needs new clothes," he said.

There were only two other women in the firm, one of whom, the receptionist, had been with them for several years. The other was Brooke. Therefore "she" could only be TJ. Still, Jess feigned ignorance for the sole joy of rattling Gary. "Who does?"

"Your intern."

"She's not *my* intern."

"Have you seen what she's wearing?"

"A suit. Perfectly suitable attire."

"Perfectly suitable satire. Don't tell me your internal fashion police haven't pulled out their riot gear."

"Around here, individuality gets expressed with an amount of fabric that would make a bikini blush: a quarter inch of shirt collar, half an inch of cuff, several inches of necktie. My fashion police head for the nearest doughnut shop as soon as I walk in here."

"No one's going to take her seriously if she doesn't dress the part."

"I don't see what it has to do with me."

"Who knows fashion better than you?"

"Gary, what do you want from me? I'm not her personal shopper. And even if I were, it's none of our business."

"Intern or not, each of us is a representative of the firm. How we dress communicates volumes about who we are and who we represent. Make it your business." Message delivered, Gary left.

For the eight hundredth time, Jess was treated not as head of marketing, but as head of vanity. Usually she'd be pleased at her success in maintaining the artifice. But every so often, it chafed. She responded the way she'd learned to in order to stay sane: she left early and went to her loft.

After catching up on industry news and drafting a blog post, Jess took a break and contemplated her dilemma. Ignoring Gary wasn't an option. He was COO, handpicked by her father to run the day-to-day operations of Magnate. He was no more insightful than a Magic Eight Ball, but he had fantastic fashion sense. If he deemed someone's wardrobe unsuitable, it needed to change.

More importantly, Jess needed to shift TJ's focus away from her. How better than by focusing on TJ's appearance? Their conversation en route from the Open had unsettled her, with TJ hinting Jess was putting up a front. She didn't need TJ to take that train of thought any further. Perhaps Gary's timing was perfect. By calling TJ out on her wardrobe, Jess could convince her of her superficiality and stop the inquiries into her world.

Spirits raised, instead of continuing to do the work no one expected of her, she returned to the office to do exactly what was expected of her.

❖

Settled back in her comfortable office chair, Jess lost her gumption to attack TJ's clothing issue. God damn Gary. Though the clothing discussion was inevitable, she'd derive no pleasure from it. Years of observing the hurt inflicted on less popular students by her wealthy friends regarding attire made her stay out of the fray. She always enjoyed wearing the latest fashions by the world's most famous brands, but the clothes spoke for themselves. She never felt the need to point out differences that were so obvious between her classmates. Bringing someone else down in order to lift herself up was never her MO. She'd been on the receiving end of that painful experience at fourteen and didn't intend to return the favor. She'd rather find another way to keep TJ at bay than by criticizing her.

Inwardly cringing at her mandate, she asked TJ to join her in her office.

She opted for the direct approach since TJ would see through anything else. "We need to discuss your outfit."

TJ quickly glanced down at what she was wearing before crossing her arm and legs in a defensive posture.

"I'm afraid that's not going to cut it," Jess said.

"I'm dressed according to the firm's business-formal dress code. I'm in a suit. Like everyone else here."

"You wore the same one Monday."

TJ's eyes gleamed with fire.

"You've also lost weight since you bought that. You practically need suspenders—which I don't recommend with those slacks—and your heels are too short for the length."

TJ blinked several times and clenched her jaw. She took a deep breath. "I'd like to get back to the *project* you've assigned, unless there's something else?"

Jess knew TJ was displeased by the work she'd given her for the day: applying personalized stickers to the backs of stacks of books they were mailing to financial advisors in their network. It was a task she normally outsourced, reserving a small box for the office to maintain the illusion she didn't engage in anything more worthwhile.

"You'll be meeting clients, representing the firm, representing Derrick Spaulding. Like it or not, *that*," Jess motioned to TJ's outfit, "does not."

Okay, this wasn't going well. Or maybe—now that Jess's goal was to shift TJ's scrutiny away from her—it was. The animosity pouring from TJ was so thick, Jess could spread it on toast.

Jess withdrew her wallet and keys from her purse. "Take my car. If you go to Saks Fifth Avenue at the Lakeside mall, charge whatever you buy to my account." She pulled out her American Express card. "If you want to go somewhere else, use this." She held out the card to TJ.

TJ stared at her. "That's your answer to everything, isn't it?"

"If you prefer to pay, I rescind my offer."

"I can't afford one button on a suit at Saks."

"Then why not let the firm pay?"

"I'm not a charity case."

Upon reflection, Jess should have expected some resistance from the woman who wasn't comfortable eating lunch at a posh establishment. "I didn't mean to imply you were. If you want to pay, I'm sure I can arrange a signing bonus or an increase in your stipend or salary or however it is we're paying—I haven't even finished my sentence and you're shaking your head."

"The university set the stipend. All of us get the same."

"I'm sure each employer has the discretion to—"

"I don't want special treatment. And it's no different than you paying."

Jess nodded. TJ had a point. "An advance then."

"Unbelievable." TJ strode to the door. "I'm sure plenty of stores carry brands you could afford. You don't have to wear Armani." But it can't be whatever that is, Jess thought.

"What I can and can't afford is none of your business." TJ exited, continuing past her desk and out the building, likely taking some time to calm down.

Damn the woman's pride. How was she going to get TJ into some Spaulding-approved clothing? And damn Gary for bringing it up in the first place. Her father would have handled it so much better. He was buttery smooth; he could make TJ believe a new wardrobe was as much a part of every intern's onboarding process as a laptop. At least now TJ couldn't possibly harbor any doubts about how superficial Jess was. That was a win.

Monday morning, Jess breezed past TJ's desk just after eleven. She'd been productive this morning, continuing to make headway on a special speaker event for select clients and prospects that'd made it big in technology. Many entrepreneurs turned around and invested in new startups, but lots more of their money was at play, and Jess aimed to convince these leaders to invest some of their windfall with the firm. One such entrepreneur had been with Magnate for years and was happy to oblige her request to speak at the event. A similar one she'd put together for leaders in the biotech industry had been incredibly successful, and she had high hopes for this one.

Time to dumb things down. She selected a bottle of nail polish from her stash. The resentment at playing into the hackneyed blonde stereotype usually faded when she arrived at the office. It was her mental downtime, and typically she was able to check her emotions at the door.

As soon as she passed TJ's workstation, however, she realized it wasn't possible today.

Earlier, thoughts of TJ had woven themselves in and out of Jess's consciousness until she'd become completely wrapped up in her work. She was concerned the intern might walk off the job after being told her outfits could use improvement. She'd long been conflicted about being judged by what was on her body versus in her head. Years of being pushed to focus on style and manners instead of studies had turned her into the duality she'd become: a numskull wrapped in a put-together package and an astute businesswoman recognizable to no one. Her identities were no less divergent than Clark Kent and Superman.

Telling TJ that her attire was lacking was no different than Jess's stepmother telling her to keep up with the latest fashion trends. It discounted the woman's mental acuity.

Yet the firm's clientele undeniably expected its personnel to dress and act in a certain way. As a marketer, Jess spent countless hours working to create and cultivate a specific perception in her clients' minds concerning the caliber of the firm's services. Despite the bruise to TJ's ego, how she dressed *did* matter. All the wishing in the world wouldn't change the fact that people did judge a book by its cover.

A sharp knock on her door frame pulled her from her musings.

TJ stormed into Jess's office, protocol be damned. "Excuse me, Ms. Spaulding."

Jess kept her attention on applying her nail polish. "You know to call me Jess, TJ." She dipped her wrist to display her fingernails. "What do you think? The shade's called 'mini bikini.'"

TJ bent over the guest chair and held its armrests. "I'm learning nothing."

"No?"

TJ started pacing. "I've been here a week. I'm supposed to be learning how Magnate's managed to beat the market in good times and bad. I have no access to any client records or financial modeling data. How am I supposed to create a case study if I'm not allowed to study anything? All I do is put stickers on books and print address labels. A monkey could do it."

Jess brushed some polish onto her pinkie nail. "I do it."

"This is the best you can do?"

"In terms of a retort?"

"In terms of work! You're the freaking head of marketing and you're sending out mailers? Christ. You should be working the gift-wrap counter at Neiman Marcus."

Jess blew on the wet nail. "Interesting way to talk to your supervisor."

"Supervisor? *Supervisor?* With blunt safety scissors and a jar of paste you'd be a glorified kindergartner. Anyone with half a brain would know your time would be far better spent paying a vendor to do it faster and at a fraction of the cost. But do you care about that? No. You care about what I'm wearing. I mean, it's like you're purposely parading around here like a Barbie doll because that's exactly what's expected of you. Must be nice to be the founder's daughter and have everything handed to you on a silver—"

That was when TJ saw it, the tiniest hint of truth that passed over Jess's expression, bringing her tirade abruptly to a halt. Suddenly she knew without a doubt that it wasn't always nice to be Derrick Spaulding's daughter. She wondered, too, if she'd hit on something else—the smallest shade of defiance that played across Jess's face as quickly as a sixty-fourth note in music.

TJ shoved her hands into her pockets and focused on the floor. "I…I'm sorry. I have no right. I spoke out of turn. This isn't working for either of us. You don't deserve to have anyone speak to you that way, and I don't deserve to be relegated to menial tasks. I came here to learn. I'll leave the laptop on the desk." As she turned to exit, she stopped at the sound of Jess's voice.

"Take this before you go." Jess opened a desk drawer, removed an envelope, and held it out toward TJ.

"What is it?"

"Letter of recommendation."

"But I haven't done anything to merit one."

"That's not what this says."

TJ folded her arms and shook her head. "You don't even see anything wrong with it," she said rhetorically. She stared at the thin rectangular paper, the contents of which offered a jump-start to her fledgling career. Only an idiot wouldn't accept it. "Thank you. But I haven't earned it." She left without further hesitation.

CHAPTER FOUR

K nock knock," Jess said as she tapped on the door frame to her father's study.

Derrick Spaulding raised his eyes from his monitor and smiled. "Sweetheart, come in." He walked around his desk and embraced her.

"You wanted to see me?" Jess asked.

Jess's father rarely requested her presence in his home office, as their business paths seldom crossed, and he didn't like to insinuate such affairs into family time. He gave her free rein of the marketing spend without holding her accountable for its successes or failures. She wished he did. To her, it was a testament to his lack of regard for her contributions to the firm. Brooke and Gary—who wasn't even a Spaulding—mattered; Jess didn't.

Aside from wishing he showed more interest in her work, the only complaint Jess had about her father was he worked too much, which included frequent visits to the New York office and meetings with prospects throughout the country. When he wasn't traveling and Lilith was off attending this or that social function, Jess would stop by the main house to have dinner with him. The one-on-one time was precious, and she wished they shared more of it. It was ironic that once she'd moved into the guesthouse, she saw less of him than she did when she lived miles away. But tonight Derrick hadn't asked to share a meal, and instead of being excited by the prospect of talking about work for a change, Jess found herself wondering if she was in trouble.

"I thought I'd check in and see how things are going with the intern." He returned to his chair, closed the laptop, and gave her his undivided attention. Derrick was one of those people who had the gift of making you feel like you were the most important person in the world. He was a good listener and asked questions. Unlike many tycoons, he didn't feel the need to talk about himself. His actions spoke for themselves; he didn't need a blow horn.

Damn Gary. Jess appreciated that her stepbrother didn't prevaricate, but the flip side was he was Swiss cheese with information whenever Derrick wanted to know something. Derrick had made his wife happy by bestowing upon her son a lofty title, but in practice it left Derrick with complete control over the firm.

"Not great, actually. She insisted on access to the client asset records, and when Gary put the kibosh on that, she wanted detailed marketing information instead."

"Which you didn't provide?"

Jess barely avoided wincing at his disapproving tone. "No, sir."

"Sweetheart, have a seat."

This wasn't off to a great start.

"I thought you were behind this program."

"You know I am, Daddy."

She was well aware of how he'd swooped in with a multi-million-dollar donation to his alma mater for the purpose of creating a graduate program for disadvantaged, smart, and ambitious students like he once was.

Jess thought highly of the program, though she had mixed feelings about the fact that it carried her father's name. It was akin to tithing in church—if you gave in order to be seen doing it, the gift was cheapened. Anonymous giving was about doing something good without regard to getting credit for it. But just because the Spaulding name was on something didn't mean it wasn't important.

The MBA program was a perfect case in point. When Jess assessed it objectively, Derrick Spaulding's name was associated with class and fortitude. Businesses partnered with the university because of the Spaulding brand. In turn, the program's students received unparalleled access to some of the best companies in the world. Moreover, with its focus on creating the next generation of nonprofit leaders, the program was providing a valuable service.

"Why did she quit?" Derrick asked conversationally.

Ugh, Gary. "She didn't find the position challenging." It was confusing, being asked to provide occupational stimulation when no one thought she did any actual work. Was Derrick aware she did more than she let on?

"Did you challenge her?"

"Not to her satisfaction, apparently."

"So she has backbone and determination?"

"Yes."

"And you let her go."

That it wasn't a question hit hard. She nodded. What could she say? TJ's grit and tenacity had meant nothing since they were giving her a recommendation at the outset of her tenure without requiring any proof of her capabilities, solely for the purpose of improving the program's hiring statistics.

"She sounds like the kind of student this program was designed for. I'd like to see her succeed here."

Tail firmly tucked between her legs, Jess assented. "I'll see to it, Daddy."

"I'm sure you will, honey."

Jess stood to leave.

"Be honest. It was the body hair that put you over the edge," Derrick said.

Jess turned back around, relief flooding her senses. Her father's humor was inching out from under the covers, and she was thrilled to see it. "I don't know. She's tough to take for a lot of reasons. I'd have sent her to my stylist, but how do you groom Sasquatch?"

Derrick mulled this over. "Garden shears?"

"Good idea, though it'll probably require something with more power. Hedge trimmer?"

"I'll send the gardener."

"Send two. It's a big job." Jess waved and headed for the door.

"Jessica?"

Once again Jess turned.

"You up for dinner tomorrow? We'll have the run of the place." This was Derrick-speak for Lilith being gone.

"I'd love to."

TJ was tiring of the silent treatment she'd been subjected to as soon as Kara found out she was working a shift at Zelda's. The slamming of the cupboards, the leaving of the milk carton on the counter, the attempt to take the cereal bowl back to her bedroom had made it reach its boiling point. Before Kara was through her bedroom doorway, TJ called out in warning, "You know better than to eat in your room."

Kara wasn't usually one for slamming doors, but TJ braced for the sound, not knowing what had gotten Kara so keyed up. Thankfully Kara returned to the kitchen wearing her earbuds and sat at the table. TJ wondered why, if Kara was so intent on tuning her out, she was impairing her own ability to enjoy the music with the noise she was making smacking the metal spoon against the side of the porcelain bowl. And was it really important to dunk every single cornflake into the milk? What was wrong with a little crunch?

TJ finished buttoning the black vest required of all Zelda's waitstaff and sat across from Kara, who scrolled through the music on her phone with one hand and fought renegade non-drowning cereal flakes with the other. When some milk went astray and spotted Kara's chin, TJ stopped her from using the back of her hand to wipe it and handed her a napkin. This act enabled brief eye contact, such as it was, during which TJ signaled for her to remove her earphones. Kara used the napkin before pausing her music. TJ repeated the signal, and Kara pulled the listening devices from her ears with an expression that said it was the largest inconvenience of her life to date.

"Wanna tell me what's up?" TJ asked.

Kara shrugged and took a bite of cereal.

"Any particular reason you left the milk out?"

"Might have seconds," Kara mumbled.

"Don't talk with your mouth full."

"Then don't talk to me when I'm eating."

TJ preferred to say, "I'll talk to you when I want to talk to you, and you'll use your manners like you've been taught." Instead she said, "I've got to leave soon. Would you set that aside for a minute so we can chat?"

Kara continued chewing a bite that, based on her facial expression following TJ's suggestion of a conversation, might as well have been a triad of sauerkraut, olives, and raw eggs. After swallowing, she folded her hands in her lap and kept her gaze on TJ.

"You're mad at me," TJ said.

Kara shrugged again.

If only TJ had a dime for every shrug! Kara's shrugs had become such a part of her, TJ wondered if they were part of some sort of physiological event associated with being a teen, the way menstruation began at puberty. If only she could invent some sort of maxi-pad protection for it. "You've seemed peeved ever since I quit my internship."

"Whatever."

On second thought, maybe the shrugs weren't so bad in comparison to the lip. "I spoke to Ridge. He's trying to get me into another company. The Zelda's thing is just for some extra cash in the meantime."

"It's your life."

"I'm not any happier with how things went at Magnate than you are. It wasn't a good fit."

"Are we done?"

"As soon as you tell me what's on your mind."

"I'm a hostage?"

"Hostage, no. Hostile, yes. But if you really don't want to talk, I won't force you."

Kara pulled her bowl close, donned her earbuds, and scrolled through her tunes.

TJ grabbed her jacket and keys. She stood behind Kara and pressed her hand over Kara's, pausing the music. She gave her shoulders a quick squeeze and kissed her temple. "Love you. I'll be back around midnight. Be good."

As TJ took the stairs, she recalled her relationship with her parents. Her father Jack had been her best playmate, always ready with an open ear and warm smile. And when she was growing up, her mother Evelyn was as good a mother as anyone could hope for. It was only in her alcoholic years that TJ's heart had hardened toward her, eroding what had been a strong bond and transforming it into a lingering bitterness. Yet when she was Kara's age, both were better parents to TJ than she could ever be to Kara. TJ's failings were the impetus behind her desire to either create a nonprofit that helped bereaved children and their caregivers or support an existing one. TJ could certainly have used the help. Kara rarely seemed to want to be in the same room with her these days, let alone share her thoughts and feelings. Did Kara have that kind of relationship with their mother before Evelyn became hell-bent on killing herself?

With the eleven-year age difference between them, TJ didn't have much insight into the kind of relationship Kara and Evelyn had had. If Evelyn were alive, would she have as much trouble communicating with Kara as TJ did?

For the thousandth time, TJ wondered whether their mother's death was the positive thing she'd once hoped it would be. It had been excruciating enough watching Evelyn slowly deteriorate into a person TJ barely recognized. But watching what her deliberate march toward suicide did to the light that once shone so brightly in Kara's eyes had been unbearable. Evelyn's metamorphosis from a spirited and joyful radiance into the somber shell of the woman she'd become after Jack's disappearance had been nearly as painful to TJ as having lost her father. But at least she'd been an adult when Evelyn began her descent into alcoholic oblivion. How much harder had it been on Kara, who was only eight when Jack never returned home and Evelyn abandoned them emotionally?

On the familiar bus ride to Zelda's, TJ hardly noticed the journey. The ever-present anger with her mother had flared, simmering beneath the surface. Whenever TJ and Kara failed to communicate, which seemed to be occurring more and more frequently, TJ's ire toward Evelyn spiked. TJ could never be the mother Kara so desperately needed, and TJ could never forgive herself for having wanted Evelyn's slide toward acute respiratory failure from alcohol to come sooner.

Angry tears slid down her cheeks as surely as Evelyn's journey into the abyss. What kind of daughter wished for her mother to die?

CHAPTER FIVE

Having had every intention of dropping by TJ's on her own, Jess quickly changed plans after driving through the neighborhood. Perhaps it was the warm evening that brought out the residents. The steps leading up to the front door of TJ's building were flanked by men of various ages and races decked out in what appeared to be the local uniform: white T-shirt and jeans. Shorts and tank tops would have been the better option in this heat, but Jess wasn't there to offer fashion advice. Every head followed her sports car as if it were a satchel of gold coins, and her foot never touched the brake. She was jumping to conclusions about their designs on her automobile, but she proceeded to make a hasty exit.

When she called the limo service, she requested Tim, whose neck was as thick as a hedge and whose body was the size of a refrigerator. At the curb in front of TJ's building, she instructed Tim to stay put and keep the engine idling.

Ignoring the whistles and various versions of "hey baby" tossed her way, and praying the dog responsible for the deep barking was leashed, she ascended the steps of Bleak House. Not that she'd ever read the Dickens novel, but the title popped into her head as she pushed open the building's broken front door. The stale, heavy air assaulted her senses first, as strong as a physical being pressing its weight against her chest. Surely she'd misread TJ's address? No, this was South Cedar all right, close to the long-deserted drive-in, exactly as TJ had mentioned her first day. Much of the stucco along the walls had cracked and peeled, stairs were warped and missing chunks, and minimal light came from bare bulbs. No one should live in this squalor. She ran up five flights of stairs to TJ's apartment and knocked on the door. Although she was sweating in the stairwell's stifling heat, she wished she'd worn a wrap so she could erect a barrier, however spurious, between herself and this place.

After her third set of loud raps, Jess had started back down the steps when a gravelly voice stopped her descent. "Who ya lookin' for?" Jess turned to see an elderly Caucasian woman wearing a stained housedress and ratty grayish slippers that might once have been pink. Hard to tell.

"TJ Blake."

"Ain't here. Try Zelda's."

"Is that a neighbor?"

"No, honey. Restaurant on Twenty-third. She waits tables there."

"Oh, right. Of course. Thank you."

"Tell the boys downstairs yer lookin' for TJ, and they'll leave ya alone. Tell 'em Stella says."

"I will. Thanks, Stella."

"Take care now." The woman shuffled behind her door and closed it.

When Jess opened the front door and bolted toward the awaiting limousine, several men blocked her path.

"What's your hurry, baby?" one asked. An uncollared rottweiler shifted at his side, staring intently at her.

Jess tried not to show how much she was shaking. Drops of sweat beaded on her forehead and above her upper lip.

Tree-trunk Tim opened his door and walked around the vehicle toward Jess. Men previously seated along the steps stood. She raised a hand to bring Tim to a halt. "Just got my wires crossed, gentlemen. I thought I was supposed to meet my friend TJ here, but Stella said she's waiting for me at Zelda's. May I tell her who's looking out for her? I'm sure she'd appreciate you've got her back."

"We always lookin' out for TJ. Tell her Uncle Pauly says to bring back some buffalo wings for Bruiser."

Apparently having heard his name, the rottweiler commenced his barking.

"I'll do that. Bye, all." Tim took a couple steps toward her to open her door, but Jess shook her head and pointed to the driver's seat. They entered simultaneously, and the car was moving before Jess could buckle up. Still shaking, she fumbled with the seat belt several times before clicking in.

Unaccustomed to such situations, Jess blinked back tears.

Moments passed before she could recall what had led her to this side of town. TJ. Why did her father insist she set aside her pride in order to reconcile with the obdurate woman? What kind of graduate program touted students who would act so disrespectfully? Why was she risking her life to speak to a woman who'd told her off?

She took steadying breaths before she smiled at her exaggeration. Okay, she hadn't exactly been threatened, let alone stood at death's door.

As they wound through the streets of Maddiston, Jess began to notice things—rather, their absence. Rarely did she focus on her surroundings, but she was suddenly as sensitive to them as if they emanated light and her eyes had been dilated. No trees. No grass. No parks. No playgrounds. Broken windows peppered the walls of the buildings they passed. Barbed wire topped the gates that surrounded many of the abandoned lots. Why would TJ and her sister live here? Why would anyone live here if they had the opportunity to leave?

Damn TJ. Jess had given her a golden parachute of sorts, and TJ hadn't taken it. With the firm's recommendation, TJ would have had multiple job offers. Within a few months, she could have packed up her belongings and found a safe apartment in a middle-class neighborhood. Even if TJ wasn't concerned for herself, didn't she care about her sister's welfare?

Jess's anxiety turned to dismay. What right did TJ have to hold her sister back from a better life? Was TJ's integrity really more important than her sister's safety? Didn't TJ's moral code account for anyone except herself?

She instructed Tim to take her to Zelda's.

❖

The restaurant was more upscale than Jess anticipated; she guessed the entrees cost in the twenty-dollar range. Groups stood outside and the waiting area was packed. She approached the maître d' and informed him she was a friend of TJ's. She told him she had an important matter to discuss and asked him to take her to TJ's section. He said he was about to seat a couple in her area, and when he asked them to follow him, Jess followed as well.

TJ visibly tensed when she caught sight of her but continued forward.

Jess grabbed TJ's upper arm as she tried to pass. "Do you have a minute? I'd like to speak with you."

TJ shrugged off Jess's hand. "Look around. What do you think?" She went to take the order of a group of four.

Jess approached the couple she'd just followed. "Excuse me." The couple looked up from their menus with curiosity. "I was wondering if I could use this table for a few minutes?" Jess extracted a hundred-dollar bill from her purse and laid it in front of them. "I need to talk to your waitress, and I'm afraid I've come at a bad time. I won't delay your dinner for long, I promise. Please explain to the maître d' so you can have this table when I'm finished. Is that okay?"

The young man pocketed the money, and the couple slid out of the booth. Jess sat, crossed her legs, and surveyed her waitress. TJ moved with purpose and grace. She brushed past staff and customers alike as if in a choreographed sequence, dodging shoulders, serving beverages, balancing plates.

After setting down a round of pink beverages two tables over, TJ finally approached. "Might I interest you in a drink or an appetizer this evening?"

"I wouldn't have pegged you as someone to give up so easily."

"May I suggest the garlic lemongrass curry fries or the wasabi crab cakes?"

"You're going to encounter a lot of adversity when you finally run your own organization. Are you planning to walk away from every difficult project you can't figure out within a week?"

"The lemon-drop and lychee martinis are also quite popular."

"I'm not some kid pulling your pigtails at recess, damn it. Stop ignoring me and stop acting like a child." Jess couldn't miss the movement of TJ's jaw as she repeatedly clenched her teeth. She'd finally gotten through.

TJ bent over the table, held its edges in a white-knuckled grip, and practically growled her response inches from Jess's face. "Difficult projects don't frighten me, *Ms.* Spaulding. I welcome being judged on my merits. You people might not give a rat's ass about the graduate program that bears the name of your firm's founder, but I do. I owe it to Professor Ridge and every single student who believes that graduates of the Derrick Spaulding MBA program have earned their rightful place alongside their wealthier Ivy League counterparts *not* to accept a recommendation for work I haven't done. When I receive my scroll at the university's commencement ceremony, I'll have earned it, or I won't be participating. Good evening."

Jess was proud of herself for not flinching. Although unsurprised by the vehemence of TJ's reply, she was nevertheless unsettled by it. TJ's voice had been a low rumble that nearly shook the table. Anger swirled like funnel clouds in TJ's charcoal eyes. Jess couldn't remember the last time she'd been in the presence of someone so passionate about an issue. Any issue. It was exhilarating, and she was more resolved than ever not to be so easily dismissed.

Keeping her eyes on TJ, Jess sat patiently. TJ wouldn't be able to ignore her for long without catching the notice of the manager, so she simply waited until TJ returned.

When TJ stood before Jess once again, she seemed to try a different tack. "You're a busy and important woman, and I appreciate your taking the time to stop by. If there's nothing else I can get for you—"

"Come back to the firm, TJ. I promise to work with you this time around. At the end of every week, we'll review your performance together. No prefilled recommendations. No monkey work. You'll either earn your keep, or you'll be back waiting tables in no time."

As Jess stared into those oyster-shell eyes that were coursing with animosity, TJ's penetrating gaze suddenly shifted, and she reached for her vibrating smartphone. She tucked her head down and covered her other ear with a palm.

Jess only caught the words, "Thank you, Doctor. I'll be right there," before a suddenly ashen TJ bolted away and bounded to the rear of the restaurant. Jess quickly slid out of the booth and pursued her.

TJ got a quick pardon from a woman Jess assumed was the proprietress, who, in a motherly move, shooed her out the door. TJ left through the back and Jess followed, ignoring warnings she was in an employee-only area. It took Jess little time to digest the fact that TJ seemed dazed and unsure of where to go. She stepped forward and grabbed TJ's hand.

"Come with me. We'll be there in no time," Jess said.

At the front of the restaurant, the Mercedes sat idling in the yellow zone. Jess opened its rear door and gently pushed TJ inside. Within seconds they were en route.

"Hospital?" Jess asked.

TJ nodded.

"Which one?" When TJ failed to respond, Jess grasped TJ's forearm. "TJ. Which hospital? Fairview or Mercy?"

"Mercy."

Jess felt the car accelerate. They were in good hands. Tim would have them there in minutes.

TJ sank into the seat and covered her face.

"Is it your sister?" Jess asked. At TJ's nod, Jess pressed for information. "Will she be okay?" Another nod. Thank God. Jess didn't know what to do. Although she was helping by providing necessary transportation, she was insinuating herself in a situation where she didn't belong. She reached across the console and gave TJ's hand a brief squeeze.

Once they arrived and TJ received instructions as to Kara's location, she took the elevator to the third floor and stopped at room 314. Jess followed her through the corridors yet remained in the hallway as TJ opened the door.

TJ was no stranger to hospital rooms, having spent countless days as a reluctant tagalong to her mother's personal hell. Evelyn Blake had been bent on killing herself by drowning in nothing short of eighty proof. TJ knew the sounds, smells, even the tastes. When her mother would refuse a meal, TJ wouldn't let it go to waste. Bland didn't mean inedible, though at times that was debatable.

But this was only the second time TJ had been in a hospital because of her sister. Twice too many. Kara was a smart, scrappy kid with a penchant for "borrowing" cars. Once she returned them, the displeased owner occasionally caught her. The owner didn't want to be charged with assault, and Kara didn't want to be charged with joyriding or worse. Neither fingered the other. One such incident had put her in the hospital. Make that two.

TJ swallowed a lump in her throat at the sight of her sister. Kara's face was red and swollen, her right arm covered her left side as if protecting it, her left leg was wrapped and raised, and her hair was matted down on one side as if an ice pack had rested there. She appeared much smaller in this setting, as if the bed was king-size and she was a kitten.

TJ pulled the visitor chair forward and sat, gently taking her sister's hand. "Hey, kiddo. I'm here." As her tears fell, TJ wiped at them. She felt powerless and would trade places in an instant if she could.

"TJ?"

Dr. Rebecca Stanfield stood in the doorway. TJ rose and extended her hand. "Dr. Stanfield. Good to see you again. How is she?"

"Please. It's Rebecca. Good to see you too, although obviously I wish it were under different circumstances."

As Rebecca filled TJ in on the extent of the girl's injuries, TJ returned to Kara's side. While jarring to see, Kara's facial injuries were superficial. Her ribs were mildly bruised, causing pain when she coughed. A kick had resulted in a mid-shaft fibular fracture, but Kara had been lucky. The fracture wasn't displaced, obviating the need for surgery. She'd be placed in a short-leg cast or immobilizer boot for several weeks and would need to undergo physical therapy for several weeks thereafter. As for her head, while this was her second mild traumatic brain injury, Dr. Stanfield didn't believe a CT scan necessary. However, she wouldn't rule it out while Kara's headache persisted.

Dr. Stanfield had treated Kara during her first trip to the ER, so she'd quickly homed in on the similarity to the previous assault. Yet Kara refused to answer whether she could identify her attacker.

"When I asked if she'd taken his car, she was mum. TJ, she can't keep doing this."

TJ nodded. "How long has she been asleep?"

"Not long."

"What can I do?"

"Get some sleep. I'll let her know you were here. We'll observe her overnight, and if all goes according to plan, she can be discharged tomorrow."

"Can't I stay?"

"You can, but she'll need rest, and so will you. Why don't you come back in the morning?"

"Okay. I'll just be a few more minutes."

"Would you like me to let your friend know?"

The question confused TJ. The doctor continued. "The blond woman waiting in the hall?"

Jess. TJ had completely forgotten about her. "No. I'll talk to her."

As they left the room, Jess was immediately at her side. "How is she?" Before TJ could answer, a voice called out from behind the half-circle nurses' station.

"Ms. Blake?"

"Yes?"

"Would you please stop by registration with Kara's insurance information? They don't have it."

TJ felt the blood drain from her face. What was today? The third. She'd quit her internship a week ago. As an employee, she'd been eligible to participate in the firm's benefit plans beginning on her hire date. Although the internship lasted only a few months, Magnate gave all full-time employees the option to enroll in its benefit packages, which were of the platinum variety. Magnate paid one hundred percent of employee health-insurance premiums and ninety percent of their dependents'. Believing her internship to be a sure thing, she'd canceled their previous coverage. In her anger over the mindless work she'd been assigned, she'd completely forgotten. At the moment, neither she nor her sister had medical insurance.

TJ's knees weakened almost to the point of collapse. Strong hands pushed her shoulders to the wall, keeping her upright. "Are you okay?"

Confused, TJ found herself staring into Jess's blue eyes. She nodded. "I…" She dropped her face into her hands.

Jess pushed open Kara's room, shoving TJ inside. TJ kept shaking her head, hidden in her hands. "What is it?" Jess whispered. "You're white as a ghost."

TJ quietly replied, "Doesn't matter. I…I'll figure it out."

"Can I help?"

TJ tried to smile. "Thank you, no. You've already done so much." Her voice cracked as she peered past Jess to her sister. "Thanks for bringing me here."

"Please. Tell me what's wrong." Jess nodded in Kara's direction. "Besides the obvious."

The compassion and concern in Jess's eyes briefly unnerved TJ, but she quickly dismissed it as she admitted to her failing. "I let our health insurance lapse. I don't know if I can reinstate it or if we're eligible for COBRA or what."

"You have health insurance through the firm."

"No. I quit, remember?"

Jess stared at TJ at length. TJ could practically see the gears turning. "You tried to. I don't remember accepting your resignation." Her tone was challenging, as if she dared TJ to disagree.

TJ blinked. Jess was handing her a lifeline. Could she accept the offer? TJ's medical premiums would be inconsequential to the firm's bottom line, whereas she could be repaying the cost of Kara's hospital stay and subsequent treatment for years to come. Just like with Evelyn.

No! TJ's father's words came roaring into her ears like an approaching freight train. Don't take something for nothing. She briefly squeezed Jess's hand. "Thank you, but I'm no longer an employee. I'll see if I can get back on the student health plan." Hopefully COBRA was an option. Then at least it would only cost thousands of dollars each month instead of tens of thousands in a lump sum.

"Listen to me. You're every bit as much of an employee as I am. No one's processed your termination. Come back to the office next week." Jess tilted her head to indicate Kara. "As soon as things are okay and settled and you can make it in. Like I said, no more busy work."

TJ hesitated. It was the simplest choice, but the easiest things weren't always the right ones.

Jess pressed her case. "You earned this internship, TJ. It's the hallmark of the MBA program and the best way to assure you of a job once it's over. I'm sure another company will be happy to take you, but we both know Magnate's in the top echelon of those participating."

"It's my mistake to own. I made the call to leave."

"And you can make the call to stay. But I'll understand if you don't think you can cut it." Jess's eyes danced with taunting.

Rarely one to back down from a dare, TJ stood taller and crossed her arms. "I was paid through the end of the month. That means I owe you two days of work without pay. I left a message for Gary but haven't heard back. Can you make sure my salary is reduced this next pay period?"

"I'll have Gary see to it."

"And you'll make sure I learn something?"

"I can't speak to your abilities. All I can do is teach you what I know and make sure my colleagues follow suit. It's up to you whether you digest any of it."

"Unless none of you can teach."

Jess visibly brightened. "Shall we find out?"

TJ nodded. Jess had been surprisingly thoughtful. She briefly wondered why she found that surprising—after all, she hardly knew the woman. But a glance past Jess brought her back to the reason they were here: Kara. With an apologetic smile, she brushed past Jess and sat beside her sister.

Shock jolted Jess once she finally focused on the bed. In it, a sliver of a person looked as though a bull had stampeded her. Her facial discoloration sharply contrasted against the paleness of her skin and the white of the sheets. What kind of calamity had befallen her?

Car accident? Fall? No, the injuries seemed almost like they were purposefully inflicted. Had she been beaten?

Jess felt intrusive. She didn't belong here. She wanted to offer TJ a ride home but didn't want her to feel rushed. Should she wait in the hall or leave? Jess gave TJ a small wave before heading to the door, but TJ beckoned her toward the bed.

Once Jess was by her side, TJ spoke softly to her sister. "Hey, kiddo. I want you to meet someone. This is Jessica Spaulding, my big, mean boss. Think *Devil Wears Prada*." She winked at Jess. "Jess, this is my…" TJ's voice caught and her eyelashes quivered with unshed tears. She swallowed hard. "This is my little sister, Kara, who's going to be just fine. Aren't you, kiddo?" TJ bent over the small figure and kissed her forehead. "I love you, sweetie. I'll be back bright and early, okay?" She caressed Kara's cheek. "Okay."

TJ darted in front of Jess, walked briskly down the hall, and disappeared into the restroom. Jess recognized the signs of a woman working to pull herself together.

Jess waited outside the bathroom. When TJ emerged, Jess extended her palm. "This is my insurance card. It has our carrier and group number. You'll need it for Kara's registration." She took TJ's elbow and steered her to the elevator. "There's cell-phone service in the lobby. While you're registering, I'll call the 800 number so we can get your subscriber ID." They entered the elevator and took the short ride down. "When I hand you the phone, give them your social, and they can look you up." Jess maneuvered them past technicians, patients, vistors, and wheelchairs as she held her phone to her ear and parked TJ in the registration queue. Once on hold, she said, "I'm taking you home, so don't even think about arguing." After answering and asking several questions, she handed the phone to TJ.

Registration completed, they exited through the lobby doors and found the Mercedes idling in the passenger loading zone. Tim had the doors open in five seconds flat, and they were on their way.

TJ leaned against the headrest and closed her eyes. They rode in silence. Jess kept her eyes on her, contemplating whether to break the quiet. She wanted to know Kara's prognosis as well as what had happened to her, though it wasn't any of her business. She was aware of it only because she'd happened to be with TJ when she received the call.

TJ opened her eyes. "Thank you."

Jess nodded.

They maintained eye contact as if both had something else to say. TJ did. "What little I thought I knew about you turned out to be completely wrong. You were everything I needed tonight. I don't usually lean on people, but I leaned on you, and you didn't let me down. I won't forget this anytime soon."

As the car approached the dilapidated apartment complex, TJ rolled down her window and called out to the men who were converging on them. To Jess, she said, "They'll leave us alone once they know it's me." Sure enough, upon recognizing her, the men returned TJ's greetings and returned to their cars and conversations. "It's hard to explain."

The Mercedes stopped and, with her hand on the handle, TJ hesitated. The moment was awkward. She wanted to give Jess a hug for being so strong and sure tonight. But they'd be working together, and that seemed an inappropriate gesture between colleagues. "Thanks again," she said, exiting the vehicle.

As she started up the steps, Jess called her name. Jess was out of the limo and walking toward her. She threw her arms around TJ. Startled at first, TJ returned the embrace. It was what she'd wanted. She let herself enjoy the warmth of the woman's body. Neither of them spoke, but that didn't stop their audience from doing so. Some of the men started making sexual comments and offering Jess their services if she needed comfort. Others were egging TJ on to escalate things to another level. Jess gave TJ's hands a squeeze and disappeared into the car.

TJ ascended the grime-ridden stairs. She'd long since stopped noticing the tenement's neglected common areas. They were a means to an end. Home was on the other side of her apartment door. It had been at her urging that they'd moved into this building. Her mother had opposed the idea but relented since TJ was paying all the bills. There was only one reason they were here: the school district.

TJ had done her homework before moving her family to this run-down building in an industrial area. In its heyday, this unincorporated district had been primarily a manufacturing area, but with most of the businesses long ago exporting those jobs to China, it had dwindled to a handful of remaining commercial properties. Only a cement manufacturer, a vodka distillery, and a truck-rental facility remained. The other older buildings were boarded up and fenced with barbed wire.

On the other side of the tracks, literally, was the wealthy city of Montgomery Hills. In its flat section were the businesses and restaurants. As you ascended the hills beyond, you entered the world of the privileged.

And, unquestionably, the privileged had great school districts.

During her online research, TJ had accidentally stumbled across the address of the apartment building. It was located on the only street outside the Montgomery Hills city borders included in its school system.

Although other school-age children lived in the building, none of them went to Montgomery Hills. The high-school-age kids were put to work by their parents or, more frequently, parent, and the younger kids were either kept home or dropped off at Vista, a poor district that, due to its interdistrict public-school-choice program, accepted students from neighboring areas.

Education had become important to their father, whose lack of a high school degree had vexed him throughout his short life. He had worked odd jobs, mostly as a bartender, with some side gigs in carpentry and construction thrown in. TJ had received a good education due to his hard work. After he died and it became obvious Evelyn wouldn't be carrying on his efforts to ensure Kara was equally educated, TJ had stepped in, researched the best schools, and moved them here.

She thought of her father and smiled as she unlocked the door. She'd upgraded its hardware as he'd shown her, and it felt solid and smooth in her hand. He'd taken her on some of his carpentry jobs and taught her the basics. He'd introduced her to the salvage store that sold high-quality used and recycled goods such as lighting and plumbing fixtures, hardware, windows, cabinets, and furniture. It was still one of her favorite shopping destinations.

It didn't matter that the landlord didn't pay for any of the upgrades she'd done to the place. It felt like home. During the first year at the apartment, she'd removed the bars from the windows; installed vinyl flooring in the kitchen; replaced the stained toilet, bathroom and kitchen sinks; retiled the shower and kitchen counter; re-carpeted the two bedrooms and living room; and repainted. Aside from the portable air conditioner that worked wonders on hot days, she was able to use inexpensive recycled items that, for the most part, appeared new. The only thing she made the landlord pay for was a refrigerator, since the old one leaked.

The worst feature of the apartment was the lack of natural light, as the windows were small and scarce, and she couldn't do anything about that. To tackle the problem, she'd selected light-colored paints and purchased used lamps for each room. She installed pleated blinds on the windows and added several mirrors throughout the apartment to encourage what little natural light they did have.

The best feature—perhaps its only innately good one—was the sound. The walls and floors were surprisingly thick, and the old aluminum-frame windows were dual-pane. Soft music from the stereo could drown out noisy neighbors and traffic.

As she closed the door behind her, she studied her surroundings and sighed. All her hard work had paid off. This would never be her first choice for a place to live, but she'd made it a warm and welcoming one. Standing on this versus the other side of the door was like being the deputy instead of the inmate. She admired the accent walls Kara had helped her paint. Her father would be proud of them.

Or would he? Kara wasn't here tonight. She was miles away, in pain and alone. TJ frowned. Was that her fault? By insisting they heed her father's wishes to give Kara a good education, had she pushed her into making poor decisions? She grabbed a glass of water and slumped onto the couch.

Ever since they'd moved here, Kara had become a little sister to many of the residents, a number of whom were younger males TJ suspected didn't shy away from illegal activities. They'd taken her under their wings and into their "garages"—which were the abandoned streets surrounding them—and taught her how to fix cars.

Since Kara wasn't interested in sports or other after-school programs, and TJ didn't have the means to enroll her in music or art courses, Kara spent her afternoons hanging out with the guys, working on cars. She was a quick study, with small hands that could reach things in tight spaces, and she didn't mind dirt or grease. Though her neighbors didn't pay her for the work she performed, they made up for it by teaching her everything they knew about vehicles.

Including how to steal them. *Borrow*, TJ reminded herself. The distinction Kara tried to place on it the first time she got caught (smugly explaining why joyriding was a different legal construct than theft) had so infuriated TJ that they didn't speak for two days.

TJ walked to the window and gazed below. As usual, the street in front of their apartment building was lined with cars, as was the feeder street perpendicular to it. Although she wasn't naive enough to believe they legitimately owned all the vehicles they gave Kara to work on, she also didn't believe it was fair to put the onus on Kara to somehow check. TJ couldn't be with Kara most afternoons, and these guys, for all their faults, looked after Kara as one of their own. Why didn't Kara drive these cars? They were at her disposal, and she was surrounded by a group of men who didn't care if she took them for a spin. Why swipe autos from other neighborhoods? Was it to see if she was capable of hot-wiring them? Was it to see if she could get away with it? Did she want to get caught?

TJ couldn't wrap her head around it. Such a smart kid to be doing such dumb things.

Dumb things Kara would never be involved in had TJ not moved them here. If they continued living here, Kara could remain at Montgomery Hills High. But would she stay out of jail through graduation? And would she survive until then?

TJ got ready for bed, her thoughts turning to Jessica Spaulding. What had that been all about? She'd been not only helpful, but thoughtful and surprisingly competent. Was she simply good in a crisis, or had the lobotomy elves returned what they'd borrowed? Although Jess was pretty, she was all-out attractive when she sounded smart and capable, which was exactly how she'd been this evening.

Maybe she was sharper than she let on because, in the firm, she was forced to play a role she was unprepared for or uninterested in. Neither prospect thrilled TJ because Jess would be a poor teacher in either case. The good news was that she'd mentioned she'd involve her colleagues as well. If Jess was true to her word, the internship would prove invaluable.

TJ slipped under the covers and closed her eyes. She missed Kara: her grunting reply when asked if she wanted a snack, the sounds in the bathroom as she showered and brushed her teeth, the way she mumbled "'Night" before turning in, the gunfire from her video games. Who would have thought she'd ever miss the thunder of virtual weaponry?

She thought of the kicks and punches Kara had suffered at the hands of someone who'd turned his limbs into real weapons. She wished she could comfort her sister the same way she'd been comforted by Jess, whose hug had been as welcome as a late winter. Even if Jess's promises turned out to be empty, nothing about her tonight had been.

Heart full, with thanks for Jess and in anticipation of seeing her sister tomorrow, she drifted off to sleep.

CHAPTER SIX

S till okay?" TJ asked as she opened the apartment door.
　　　"Yeah." Kara was sweating and irritable from the ride over and from having taken five flights of stairs using one leg, one crutch, and in places where the banister was broken, her sister. The cab driver knew how to brake and accelerate, but to him the concepts of coasting and maintaining speed were as advanced as quantum physics. Aware of her sister's propensity for motion sickness and her already throbbing head, TJ had asked him to drive more evenly. Her request was lost in translation.

　　　Kara maneuvered into the apartment on her crutches. "I'm going to bed."

　　　"Good idea," TJ said. "Your sheets are clean and I've laid out fresh PJs. How's the leg?"

　　　"Peachy. Let's do some leg presses."

　　　"Itching? Swelling?"

　　　"It itches."

　　　"Pain?"

　　　"Yes. She's about five-ten and her name's TJ."

　　　"You must be feeling better." TJ followed Kara into her bedroom. Kara sat with her leg out and scooted back on the bed. TJ angled the crutches against the wall within Kara's reach and propped a pillow under her cast to elevate it.

　　　"Not really."

　　　TJ crouched next to the bed. "No? Do I need to call Dr. Stanfield?" Though the doctor had proclaimed a CT scan unnecessary, TJ remained anxious. Kara's headache had improved somewhat but lingered.

　　　Kara shook her head slightly. It obviously hurt to do so.

　　　"What can I get for you?"

"Morphine."

"You can take two more acetaminophen in…" She glanced at her watch. "Two hours. I'll wake you. Anything else?"

"Mouth's dry."

"I'll bring you some water. Be right back."

TJ's phone vibrated as soon as she entered the kitchen. The display showed the same unrecognized number that had called three times earlier. This time she answered. "Hello?"

"TJ?"

"Yes. Who's this?"

"It's Jess. Jessica Spaulding."

"Oh, hey. Hi."

"I won't keep you. I just wanted to see how your sister's doing. Is she out of the hospital?"

"She is, yes, thank you. We just got home. She needs more rest so she's going to bed."

"That's great to hear. I'll let you get back to it. And if you need to take time off next week to handle anything, just give me a call or let Gary know. It's no problem."

"Thank you. I will. And thanks for calling. It's very sweet of you."

"Don't forget to take care of yourself too. Okay, see you Monday, unless we hear from you."

"Bye."

TJ returned to find Kara's eyes closed. She set the water on the nightstand and headed back out.

Kara's voice stopped her. "Who was that?"

"Woman I work for."

"At Zelda's?"

"No. Magnate."

"Thought you quit."

"We'll talk about it when you're feeling better. Want help with your PJs?"

"Not moving. Statue impression."

"I'll get you up in a few hours."

"'Kay."

TJ flipped off the light. As she was closing the door, she heard, "The hot one?"

Living with a teenager could be such a one-way street. When you asked questions, you were met with mumbles or glares. When the teen asked, she expected an answer.

TJ decided an honest reply would be the quickest way to end the conversation and get Kara to sleep. "Yes."

"What'd she want?"

"To check on you."

"Nice of her."

"Yes. Now get some rest."

"'Kay."

Jess had given her word, and now she regretted it. She'd promised to teach TJ, but what information could she appease her with without revealing too much about herself?

Jess replayed some of their interactions. TJ had turned down a golden parachute in the form of a recommendation letter because she felt she hadn't deserved it, and she wanted to ensure any action taken toward winning Muriel Manchester's business wasn't simply window dressing but part of a real commitment to change. These issues along with her reluctance to accept things like medical benefits, clothing, and lunch pointed to a level of virtue Jess didn't share.

It didn't make sense to her for TJ not to accept the recommendation and use it to land a decent-paying job that could get Kara and her out of Maddiston. She'd have to earn her stripes there, so what did it matter if she used all the tools at her disposal to help her get started? It wasn't as if the letter contained false information—TJ had performed her tasks satisfactorily, albeit over an abbreviated period.

Jess didn't understand or share TJ's sense of right versus wrong. If TJ learned that Jess was essentially wearing a mask at work every day and, worse, learned the reason behind it, she would quit again. No way would she continue to be coached by a woman who took the easy way out at the first sign of confrontation, a woman who prized her possessions above all else.

Assigning more busywork wasn't an option, so how should she proceed? She didn't want to hand over any of her real marketing files to TJ. She primarily did her work and research at her loft, saving her time in the office for contrived displays. Her colleagues believed the firm's reputation was all that was needed to bring new clients calling. Since most of the firm's staff had finance backgrounds, they gave little thought to how word was spread. To them, marketing was as useful as Swahili.

In truth, Jess had built a finely honed marketing machine. Knowing that high-net-worth (HNW) individuals as well as government and nonprofit asset managers engaged professional advisors to manage their complex affairs, Jess focused on events these advisors attended and insisted that Brooke and Derrick go. Face-to-face meetings at key industry events performed well for the firm; the subtle sale thrived.

To target HNW individuals themselves, rather than pay exorbitant fees to be the lead sponsor at a conference or event, Jess spent a fraction of the amount by securing the attendee contact information and sending personalized gifts to attendees in advance, such as what she did with Golden Oak wines. Brooke and Derrick then had brand awareness and rapport to build from.

Although recommendations gained through advisor networking were the best entry point for Magnate, Jess knew decision makers wouldn't switch firms without doing significant research. She made sure the firm's website was packed with market insights and viewpoints; she paid market experts to create timely and relevant Q&A-style education for investors; she retained a search-engine optimization agency to make sure Magnate showed well to treasury managers researching investment firms online and was easily found via the major search engines.

She knew what she was doing, and the firm enjoyed high conversion rates across all fronts.

Jess worked hard to achieve these results and took pride in the firm's success. Based on some intel from her professional network, Jess estimated the firm brought in twice as many new clients per year as other similarly sized investment advisors. The trick was trying to educate TJ without revealing all she did.

Since they'd already covered how Kara was doing—it was the first question out of Jess's mouth—she couldn't stall any longer.

Jess arrived at a decision. She wouldn't provide TJ with anything more than what she, herself, started with. She'd give TJ the ingredients; it would be up to TJ to create the entrée. If she was as capable as she was purported to be, she'd discover Jess's secret. But Jess wouldn't make it easy. And by then she might come up with a plausible alternative explanation to account for the firm's marketing prowess, one that would allow her to keep her success private.

Jess popped a removable drive into her laptop. As she moved electronic files, she said, "These are the lists we purchased last year. They're the attendees of each event we co-sponsored or received through networking. We know who they are and how we found them, which is all here. Every introduction has an origin. While we don't determine exactly which combination of our marketing touches led to closing them, we can at least assess the lead sources based on what revenue they ultimately drove and calculate a proper ROI for each activity in our tool kit."

After removing the pinkie-size drive, Jess handed it to TJ. "I'd like you to ignore our actions and results. Start with the lists. Research how you think it best to reach these people based on the associated event. Try to discern who they are and what incents them to alter their status quo. Your goal is to come up with two different initiatives designed to yield the most new clients. For the first, tell me how you'd proceed if you had five hundred thousand dollars to work with. For the second, you have two million. Any questions?"

As TJ reached for the drive, she asked, "Do I get to assume you or someone like you is available as an expert resource, or am I expected to proceed as if I'm the sole marketer?"

Initially Jess flushed at the compliment. No one had ever pegged her as an expert at anything. But she was uncomfortable. TJ hadn't even opened the lists, and she was already deferring to her. Jess didn't want to be seen as an expert. She spent many hours pretending the opposite. "You can allocate your budget as you see fit. If you want to pay for advice or work with an agency, assume it will come out of your budget."

TJ stood. "What's my deadline?"

Jess sat back and smiled. Setting expectations for deliverables was one of the most important tasks of any client-service business, and she was pleased TJ understood. "End of day Friday. But if you have questions along the way, stop by anytime."

❖

Jess dialed Renee, her personal shopper, and inquired whether she was available to meet at the local thrift store. Renee would be able to see her there in thirty minutes. Jess didn't like the thrift shop because the inventory tended to be too tightly pressed together, but it was in her affluent neighborhood and she knew a number of its volunteers.

After Jess gave Renee her best guess of TJ's measurements, she and Renee spent nearly ninety minutes working their way through the lightly used clothing until they'd found a good number of items likely to suit TJ. She instructed the store's volunteer to have the chosen clothes couriered to TJ's address and to include an invoice for twenty percent of the total price, half payable in thirty days, the other half in sixty days. The firm paid the difference and TJ would be none the wiser. In the unlikely event TJ ever entered the shop and wondered about the absurdly low prices she'd managed to get, Jess had the volunteer write on the invoice, "Thanks for being a part of our successful blowout sale! No refunds or exchanges."

Although Jess didn't own a single piece of clothing previously owned by someone else, she appreciated that, like her, so many of her neighbors recognized when they'd outgrown or tired of items in their wardrobes and that others less fortunate could benefit from their downsized closets. In some cases, Jess wondered whether the pieces had ever been worn.

Renee did a fantastic job, as always. The suits were easy to break into separates, the blouses current, and the shoes timeless. Jess was impressed at how quickly Renee was able to cull together different outfits from a random collection to which she'd had no previous exposure. Hopefully TJ wouldn't be so offended by the package that she'd refuse delivery. There was one way to find out.

❖

TJ finally wrestled the box into her apartment. It had taken some persuading to get the gang to allow the courier to carry the large box to her floor. At times she appreciated their protectiveness. At other times she felt as stifled by it as the heat in the stairwell.

As she lifted each carefully folded item from its thin paper wrapping, she found herself conflicted. Her instinct was to wield a black Sharpie and write "Return to Sender" on all sides of the container. But the clothes were all her size, meticulously cared for, and, as much as she hated to admit, stylish.

The brands were some she'd actually heard of. TJ couldn't understand how the clothes had arrived in such fine condition at what must be a fraction of their original cost. Kara, not one for fashion sense beyond skinny jeans and sweaters, pestered TJ to try on all the outfits. She was dismayed by Kara's approval of all the combinations she tested.

Swallowing her pride wasn't one of TJ's most reliable attributes. She'd had adequate time to reflect upon her clothing conversation with

Jess and wasn't pleased with her response. The firm, whether she liked it or not, could dictate its employees' attire—not the brands per se, but an expectation that each employee look their Sunday best. Admittedly, she wasn't happy with the choices in her closet, so while she hadn't appreciated how the message was delivered, she couldn't fault the firm's owners for taking issue with her dress. Clothes shopping had long ago failed to interest her as she always had far more pressing ways to spend money.

When she did purchase clothing, her first priority was price. The suits she wore to the office were those she'd purchased for her parents' respective funerals. Fashion hadn't been at the top of her mind at either time, not that it ever was. Aside from making sure there was enough room at the shoulders not to pull, she hadn't thought much about sleeve length. One pair of her dress pants was definitely too wide; she *had* lost weight since her father's death. And she'd moved toward more, not less, comfort over the years in her footwear. Hours of waitressing made it imperative. The shorter heels she'd adopted caused the hem to drag onto instead of graze the floor.

Jess had been tactful enough to take TJ into her office to discuss the clothing situation instead of mentioning it in front of other staffers. She also hadn't assumed TJ would shoulder the expense herself. TJ couldn't blame Jess for offering to help. It wasn't Jess's fault that she came from money and wouldn't know how sensitive TJ was to getting costly things for free.

Initially, part of TJ's vexation had been the lack of any substantive work to do. But Jess was now demonstrating a willingness to hold up her end of the bargain. That meant TJ would have to meet her partway. She could think of worse things than having luxuriously soft material lightly touch her skin.

CHAPTER SEVEN

Had this been last week, TJ's irritation with Jess's antics would have been chart-topping. Who actually practiced putting in their office? But there Jess stood, on her roll-out putting green, hair in a twisted updo, wearing golf shoes with her skirt, taking shot after shot toward the two holes at the far end of the green.

TJ knocked on Jess's door frame. She was wearing a Hugo Boss navy suit with a light-blue point-collar blouse. Although the Jimmy Choo pumps added polish to the outfit, she couldn't shake the feeling she was playing dress-up. She hoped she at least appeared assured on the outside.

Jess glanced up and smiled. "Are you still talking to me then?"

"You're my boss. Do I have a choice?" TJ smiled to soften her words.

"Colleague. But we can email or instant-message if you'd prefer."

"You don't want to have to look at me?" TJ gestured to her attire, keeping her tone light.

Jess pretended to block her eyes with her elbow. "Yes. You're hurting my eyes. I might survive one, two in-person meetings, tops. After that, it's IM or email only."

"Then I better make the most of this one. May I come in?"

"Please. How's Kara?"

"Still in pain, but improving. Her bruises are nearly as colorful as the under-the-breath cussing she thinks I can't hear."

Jess returned to putting. "Glad she's doing better. What's up?"

"I'm spinning my wheels a bit and was hoping for some pointers. Is this a good time?"

"Yep. Shoot." Her next putt circled the cup before rolling off the green. "Dang it."

Not the most open invitation, but TJ needed help. "You've already identified some of these folks as city treasurers. For them, I'm supposed to identify potential next steps to landing their business, right?"

"Mm-hmm."

"Within budget."

"Yep."

"On my own. Unless I want outside help."

"Could you roll that over here?"

TJ nudged the golf ball with her shoe and sent it back. "I'm not a marketer."

"No."

"I'm not sure where to start," TJ said.

"Start with what you know."

"Not much."

"Not true. How do they get their jobs?"

"I suppose most are elected."

"And how many of them—dang it," Jess said as she missed another shot. "How many of them are experienced in money management?"

"I've no idea."

"It's in the information I gave you."

"You told me only to look at the lists."

Jess finally raised her head. "So I did." Jess leaned her putter against her desk and sat at her conference table, indicating that TJ follow suit. "Okay. Here's the thing. These people aren't experts. They may or may not have a finance background. What they have in common is they can't take gifts, they have a boring job, they want to get reelected, and they want to travel on the city's dime. Get paid for a day off from the usual. How do you reach them?"

"Invite them to some sort of educational seminar, subsidize their travel costs so they can stay somewhere decent yet justifiable from a budget standpoint, and have someone interesting as a speaker?"

"Sounds expensive."

"I have a pretty big budget."

"This is only one target segment. You also have HNWs and other money managers. Plus, one celebrity speaker could wipe it out."

"I wouldn't know," TJ said, frustrated by her lack of knowledge.

"Hey." Jess touched TJ's forearm and waited until TJ met her eyes. "Don't get down. Don't focus on what you don't know. Focus on reaching these people. Your idea's a good one. So how do you get a speaker you can afford?"

"Find someone who isn't too high on the food chain but wants to be or used to be."

"That works. So what's your next step?"

"Check out recent headlines for someone who's been in the news for any kind of financial reform or related commentary?"

"Go on."

"A politician or an ex-CEO, maybe. Someone who'll still be relevant by the time of the seminar."

"What else?"

"We can offer a workshop on fixed-income securities and bond markets—things that sound safe and risk-free."

"I like it. There's an association of public treasurers we may be able to work with too. What's the end goal?"

"New clients. We'll have a captive audience. After the speaker, we can offer up our investment advisors to meet with them individually to go through their concerns and issues. In the literature we provide, add credibility by listing municipalities that are already clients."

"Leave-behinds. Yes." Jess stood and pretended she was wiping her hands clean. "My work here is done." She snatched her putter and set three golf balls at the edge of the green. The first shot sank cleanly. "Was there something else?"

TJ stared. Jess had succinctly addressed her questions and given her ideas to work with. "You made that so easy."

"I didn't do anything. You came up with the ideas." She sank another putt.

Why did she insist on taking no credit? Why was she engaging in this display of idleness?

"I've got a one o'clock tee time. Call my cell if you need anything," Jess said. Her final ball missed the cup and veered into TJ's foot.

TJ covered the ball with her toe and watched as Jess changed shoes, grabbed her purse, and glanced around her office as if ensuring she wouldn't forget anything. She flipped off the light and held the door. TJ didn't realize Jess was waiting for her to depart. Jess stood beside her and smiled.

Not just smiled. Dazzled.

It was as if TJ saw her for the first time. Everything in TJ's peripheral vision seemed to fade until all she saw was Jess's face opening to her as if a tulip to the sun. Although Jess's office was dark, there was enough light from the main room to illuminate her face. Assorted shades of blue sparkled in her eyes. Jess was no longer simply a pretty face. She was a compassionate woman with a keen mind. Her responses to TJ's questions were like flint on steel, sparking within TJ a sharp interest she barely recognized from years of dormancy.

Jess's smile dimmed. "Are you okay?"

TJ wanted to scream, "No!" Questions popped through her head in rapid fire. Why do you feign ignorance? Why act obtuse? Who put you up to this or, rather, tore you down to this? Can't you see how incredible you are? May I kiss you? The last question gave her pause.

TJ didn't think her eyes gave away much, but she didn't want to give Jess any reason to feel uncomfortable around her. Having her eyes virtually peel Jess's blouse from her shoulders would not be appropriate in any work setting. She shifted her focus to Jess's mouth. It was a mistake.

When Jess gulped, TJ raised her gaze from Jess's lips and realized she should speak. "I'd wish you luck, but I've a feeling you're very good at the game."

Jess pulled the door closed behind them, confusion evident in her eyes. "Far be it for me to disavow you of that notion. You should see me play."

"I have." To keep open the possibility they were talking about golf instead of Jess's veneer, TJ pointed through Jess's glass office walls to her putting green.

Jess laughed unsteadily. "That's right. You have. Okay then. See you tomorrow."

Before Jess took five steps, TJ called out, "Wait."

Jess turned and steepled her brows.

"I believe I'm still waiting for my welcome lunch. Al's Sandwich Shop tomorrow?" TJ asked.

Jess smiled. "That'd be perfect."

The two of them entered Al's, and Jess studied the large menus on display above the staffers behind the counter. TJ didn't look because she knew what she wanted.

"What are we having?" Jess asked.

"Do you eat meat?"

"Yes."

"Chicken pesto panini on ciabatta bread?"

"Perfect."

TJ placed their order. Jess removed a wallet from her handbag and, before extracting any bills, eyed TJ. TJ held out a five. Jess smiled, and they each handed five dollars to the cashier. They deposited their change in the tip jar.

"You just tipped something like forty percent," Jess said. "Doesn't that go against your miserly ways?"

"Servers work hard and they're always on their feet. They rely on tips."

TJ capped their water cups while Jess gathered the napkins and utensils for the coleslaw. When their lunch was ready, Jess tossed the items into the bag and followed TJ to the park.

The day was glorious. They walked under a tent of cypress trees that allowed only shafts of sunlight to touch ground. As they headed toward the benches at the coastline, TJ enjoyed the shift in the wind that kept away the diesel fumes of the highway behind them. The air now smelled of salt water and seaweed, and it was easy to forget the madness of the city. Seagulls floated aloft in the ocean breeze.

TJ spied an empty bench and inspected it for bird droppings. It was blessedly clean. She sat at one end and set their cups down. Jess sat and removed the outer paper from the sandwich before handing a wrapped half to TJ. TJ crossed her legs and took a small bite as she scanned her surroundings. Behind them on the other side of the highway sprawled multi-million-dollar homes.

"What do you see?" TJ asked.

Jess finished chewing and drank some water before responding. "Is that a trick question?"

"No. Look around and tell me what you see."

Jess turned her head slowly. She glanced back at the houses. Raising her chin to them, she said, "Prospects." Pointing to the harbor, she waited until TJ followed her line of sight to a sleek black-and-white yacht returning from its voyage. "Prospect." She nodded toward the beach. A barefoot man with rolled-up pant legs, wearing a wide-brimmed hat and large earphones passed his metal detector over the sand as if he were a priest absolving sinners beneath him. "Not a prospect."

TJ had difficulty understanding what she'd just heard. They were overlooking the majestic Pacific Ocean on a calm, cloudless day. The sun was bright but brought welcome warmth instead of overbearing heat. Few people were about due to the weekday, but those here were enjoying themselves. Two dog owners played fetch with their four-legged companions. One used a ball launcher to throw to her black Labrador, while the other took turns tossing a Frisbee to his border collie and a tennis ball to his Jack Russell.

Seabirds ran into the departing waves, fed, and retreated again once another wave ran aground. A group of brown pelicans bobbed a couple of hundred yards from shore as if on siesta. The contrails of a passing jet created cloud formations like ski tracks in blue snow. Indentations in the sand made by the occasional passing shoreline runner were slowly swallowed under the constant pummeling of the waves. A young girl squatted near the water, using a plastic shovel to sculpt a clump of damp sand into something that vaguely resembled a coffee can, which to her mind probably rivaled the tallest spire of Sleeping Beauty Castle. Interesting, magnificent things surrounded them.

Jessica Spaulding was in one of the most beautiful settings in the country, yet the only thing she could see within it was work.

Moreover, that prospects were her highest priority in life was completely at odds with everything TJ knew of her. How did this fact reconcile with the woman who came in late, left early, and embraced the role of coddled diva?

"You must really love your job to sit here in all this glory and think only of people you have to court. You're lucky to feel so connected to it." However, even as she said it, TJ didn't think Jess was lucky. There was something profoundly sad about someone who couldn't see the exquisiteness before them.

Jess took another bite of her sandwich and seemed to consider this remark as she chewed. "I wouldn't know how to disconnect from it. I'm a Spaulding."

"Like I said, you're lucky. Most people would take this opportunity to *not* think about work. They want to get away."

"I didn't say I don't want to get away. But getting away means different things to different people. Lots of people see this and feel they're away, which means they're appreciating something out of their ordinary. But if this," she extended her hand in an arc as if presenting the beach, "is your ordinary, what's your escape? Where do you get away?"

She has a point, TJ thought, and some part of her felt a small tug, a pinprick of desire to toss a lifeline to this woman. As if she were adrift, which made no sense. Jessica Spaulding had more resources available to help her through any possible issues that might arise in her life than

TJ would ever have. Still, Jess's melancholic tone caused TJ to respond to the rhetorical question.

"Maybe you don't need to. Maybe you have to find ways to look at the same things in new ways."

Jess stared at TJ skeptically. "What do *you* see?"

The question surprised TJ, who figured Jess would be more interested in hearing herself talk than learning about her. Another assumption upended. "Let's finish eating and I'll show you."

After lunch, TJ led the way down sand-covered steps to the beach. At the bottom, she pulled off her shoes, rolled up her slacks, and waited for Jess to do the same. She led them to a tide pool where they found tiny crabs, mollusks, sea urchins, hermit crabs, and anemones. They perched on the rocks closer to the water.

"Look, breathe, listen, and touch. Tell me what you see, smell, hear, and feel," TJ said.

The rock under Jess wasn't smooth, and TJ watched with amusement as she tried to lose herself in the moment. "Water. Sand." She turned to TJ. "I know. Duh." She faced the ocean and took a deep breath. "Crashing waves, like thunder. Seaweed or something salty, but not like a margarita. Is this what you mean?"

"Yep. Keep going."

"The air is slightly damp as we're misted, so gently it's like a breath instead of a spray…seagulls cawing…children laughing…the coolness of the wind interspersed with the warmth of the sun through the clouds. The sand hugging my toes. My butt falling asleep on this uncomfortably jagged rock."

TJ burst out laughing. "You were really good at this until then. Come on. Stand up and continue."

Jess stood and shook her bootie as if enjoying that sensation was returning to her nether parts. She looked around. "Blue. Endless blue. Clouds like spun cotton on an invisible wheel. Sailboats like tiny corks pierced by a white flag on a toothpick, floating, disappearing, returning. Birds bobbing. Whitecaps appearing and disappearing. Children running, stopping, assessing. Dogs chasing, bounding, begging."

"Amazing."

"That I'd forgotten all about that little detail called the ocean? The feeling you get when you're trying to find your sunglasses and they're on your head?"

"Not even. You're a natural."

"As natural as my stepmother's hair color. When you asked, 'What do you see,' I had the distinct impression you've asked that question many times before. Is Kara your usual audience?"

TJ nodded. "We never had much money growing up, so for amusement we used to tell stories about the things we'd see and touch around us. We were only limited by our imaginations, which is to say, we weren't."

"Give me an example."

"Well, here at the beach, for instance. When Kara was young, I might take her to a tide pool, point to a crab, and say in a silly voice, 'That's Henrietta the Hermit Crab. She doesn't like other crabs. Why is she so crabby?' Kara would giggle and then launch into some story about how Henrietta was bullied as a baby crab, which is why she built a shell around herself. And it took Studly the Starfish to bring Henrietta out of her shell or some such."

"Do you still play?"

"Not often. It's hard to compete with electronic gadgets no matter how much more flexible and extensive our imaginations are. But sometimes. In fact, we played the other day in her hospital room. Kara's always been a good storyteller."

"How much younger is she?"

"Eleven years. She's sixteen."

"You seem close."

TJ nodded, though closeness was a fickle companion. Some days, Kara talked to TJ as if they were best friends, sharing intimate details, admitting vulnerabilities, laughing. Other days, TJ was lucky to receive a grunt and an eye-roll. She didn't remember her own moods oscillating so much at Kara's age. But she suspected they probably did, and like the way the recollection of the pain of childbirth dulls conveniently the moment a mother contemplates having more children, the amnesia of what one really was like as a teenager was a requirement for the survival of the species. Otherwise no one would have kids.

TJ started heading back.

"Wait. We're leaving?" Jess asked.

"My boss is pretty strict."

Jess laughed. "Completely untrue."

"Maybe. Not sure yet. She's sort of an enigma."

"Oh, right. Complicated and confusing, that's me."

"I stand by my assessment. Thanks for the outing. I appreciate that the daughter of Derrick Spaulding deigned to take the intern to lunch."

"Haven't you learned by now? All the important jobs go to me."
TJ heard the sarcasm and wasn't offended. "Hey. I was kidding."
"I was too, but I really shouldn't. Your program bears my father's
name and you're in the first class to graduate. We have a vested interest
in you." Jess's attempt to smile was obviously halfhearted.

"I see." TJ didn't understand why the idea of having a stake in TJ's
future made Jess seem glum. Was it because it made their relationship
into a calculated thing that wasn't the basis of a real friendship? Was
it because TJ was one more work-related thing Jess had to deal with?
As much as she was beginning to like Jessica Spaulding, she was at
Magnate for an internship. This was professional, not personal. Best
not to lose sight of the fact that Jess was simply doing her job.

CHAPTER EIGHT

Gary knocked on Jess's office door frame. "Got a minute?" Without awaiting a reply, he entered and closed the door.

"What's up?"

"There's a girl up front who says she's TJ's sister, and I can't find TJ anywhere."

"She's at the printer."

"In what?"

"My car." At his doubtful expression, she said, "Don't ask."

"We can't leave this kid in the reception area. She's going to scare away our clients."

"She's in high school. How intimidating can she possibly be?"

"Black eye. Swollen cheek. Cast. Crutches. Great for a PSA against domestic violence, but not so good for people looking for a safe place to park their cash."

Damn it. "What's that got to do with me?"

"Your intern, your problem."

Jess had no experience with children. Youngsters, she corrected herself. Youths? Whatever. As far as she could tell, they were either self-absorbed thrill-seekers with too much free time, or dour fit-throwers who felt their every whim should be attended to once they could be bothered to look up from their smartphones. "Have the car service take her home."

"She insists on waiting for TJ."

Double damn it. "Fine." Jess marched past him. She was sending the kid home. As soon as she entered reception, however, she abandoned the thought. Kara's eyes held a mix of swagger and surrender, acting tough though her bruises spoke of frailty and pain. The idea of forcing this girl into a car, no matter how luxurious, to spend the afternoon alone, held no sway.

"Hi, Kara. Nice to see you again."

"Do I know you?"

"I'm Jessica Spaulding. They had you on some good drugs last time I saw you."

"Oh. The hot one."

"Sorry?" Jess hadn't heard that the temperature of a pharmaceutical was a thing.

"My sister mentioned you."

Wait. What? Was Jess the hot one in this context? Impossible. What a strange comment. "How about you come on back and wait for her in my office?"

"I won't bother anyone." Kara sounded like she thought she was always a bother. It pulled at Jess.

"You won't be bothering me, and I could use the company. Come on." With a flick of her head, Jess prodded Kara to follow.

Pushing to a precarious standing position, Kara coordinated feet and crutches and did so.

Jess had Kara settle at her small conference table, an ironic name for furniture at which no one ever conferred since coworkers had so few expectations of her. Today Jess's reputation worked in her favor. She could keep the youngster in her office all day if she wanted. Hell, they could play cards or board games. No one would question it.

Jess settled in her desk chair and watched the girl fish something out of her backpack. It was a magazine called *Hot Rod*, which she began to read. Why was she about to vie for this girl's attention? "So what brings you here today?"

Without looking up from her magazine, Kara said, "My sister."

Helpful kid. "You're supposed to meet her here?"

The response came in the form of a nod.

Not easily dismissed when she put her mind to something, Jess asked, "She's taking you to an appointment or something?"

Kara raised her eyes. Such fire there, crackling beneath the surface. Then, as if smothering a blazing comeback, she dropped her head and spoke into the magazine. "I have to come here after school from now on."

Ah, punishment. Still, couldn't she go to the library or a café or something? This wasn't the YMCA. Jess bit back the question. She didn't want to make the girl feel any less wanted. "You're in the doghouse?"

Another nod.

Teenagers! How did parents put up with this stuff? Jess corrected herself. How did TJ put up with it? Then again, what choice did she have? "What'd you do?" Jess asked.

Kara flicked her eyes in Jess's direction. "Borrowed a car."

Jess had trouble imagining why that was a bad thing. Then it struck her. "Without a license?"

"I have my license."

Then what was the issue? "Did you keep it longer than you were supposed to?"

Kara shrugged.

This pulling teeth was tiresome. "You stole it?"

Another shrug.

Finally. "I see. And you..." She pointed to Kara's cast and face. "Drove into a wall? Tripped on your way to return the keys?"

"Something like that."

The penny dropped. "Its owner hurt you?"

"He wasn't happy."

Jess wanted to yell obscenities. This ninety-pound girl was brutally beaten for *joyriding*? "Please tell me he was arrested."

Kara shrugged again. "I deserved it."

No one deserves to be beaten! Jess tamped down her enormous anger. She rested her chin in her hand and innocently asked, "What's his name and where does he live?"

Kara laughed. "She's going to be in so much trouble."

"A *woman* did this to you?"

"No. TJ. Never mind. I did it to myself."

Did she really believe she was responsible for her injuries? "You both committed crimes. But that's what our justice system is for. He had no right to assault you. As much as I'd like to find that creep and give him what's coming to him, this isn't the Wild West where people take the law into their own hands."

Kara shook her head and grabbed her crutches. "Look, Miss Spaulding, if you could just point me to my sister's desk, I'll be out of your way."

Jess raised a palm to stop her. "Okay. We won't talk about it. One more question, and you can get back to your magazine."

"What?"

"What was the car?"

Kara harrumphed. "Not a Rolls or Mercedes, that's for sure."

"Not very exciting then." Jess goaded her.

The pages grew louder with each flip of Kara's wrist. Jess had caught a live one. "1970 Plymouth Duster 340. Two-hundred seventy-five horsepower."

"Not bad." She'd never heard of it.

Kara snapped the magazine shut. "Not bad?"

"Probably the best you could do around that part of town." Jess had no idea where the incident had taken place.

"What would you know about it?"

Not much. But if she played her cards right, she could pretend otherwise. "So what's the draw?" Jess inclined her head toward the crutches and indicated her own face to mirror Kara's bruises. "To make it worth it. Is it the particular car or the ability to steal it?"

Kara flipped a couple pages of her periodical, making Jess wonder if she'd heard the question. "I like muscle cars. Fixing 'em. Restoring 'em. Driving 'em."

"You fix cars?"

Kara shrugged.

If she received one more shrug in reply, Jess was going to scream. If the girl had to have gotten hurt, couldn't it have been a shoulder? "Doesn't seem as though you care too much about getting caught."

"Maybe I want to."

The bravado was so B-movie, so over-the-top, it made Jess contemplate the statement more than she otherwise would have. She parsed the girl's comment and began thinking it through. Did Kara want to get caught? If so, why?

She got back on track. "So no interest in an already restored, cherried-out classic that starts faster than lightning?"

The magazine rolled into the shape of a telescope in the teen's lap.

"Yeah. No challenge in that." Jess glanced at her watch before focusing on her laptop screen. "She should be back any time now."

"What kind of classic?"

Jess feigned confusion. "What? Oh. Never mind. Not your thing. I get it." She waved Kara off. "Forget it. My friend's probably sold it by now anyway."

"Sold what?"

"'57 Corvette Fuelie." The only year, make, and model combination she'd ever committed to memory. She hoped this was her version of *Jeopardy*—whipping out some long-held, useless fact in the hope it became useful one day.

Kara tsked and resumed her reading.

Mutely replaying the last few seconds to ensure she hadn't misspoken, Jess opted not to cave in to her desire to ask why the self-proclaimed hotrod devotee wasn't interested in such a revered automobile. Game over. The room was quiet as seconds ticked by.

"The two fifty or the two eighty-three?" Kara asked.

Double Jeopardy. "Two eighty-three."

Kara laughed. "Right. You expect me to believe your friend owns a car they only produced about a thousand of?"

Jess fought to relax her facial muscles, which were rebelliously intent on forming a smug expression. "You expect to believe I'd have the slightest clue about any of it had I not been subjected to his incessant fawning over that car?"

"Ohmygod. He really has one?"

And because she simply had to, Jess shrugged.

Kara's eyes grew wider than a pug puppy's. "Can I see it?"

"Do you think your sister would be interested in joining us?"

The girl's exuberance immediately cooled, and she shook her head.

Jess wondered at the change but didn't hesitate. Smartphone in hand, she swiped to her favorites and clicked on the familiar name. After more than a dozen rings, she heard his greeting and replied, "Hey, handsome. Up for some company?"

❖

The service center never ceased to awe Jess. Mechanics, service managers, clerical staff, and customers moved about the place like a busy anthill. Her driver dropped them off at the main entrance. Certain her hobbled passenger would be able to keep up, she marched past the waiting area to a door marked PRIVATE, which she pulled open and held. Kara shuffled past, then stopped to allow Jess to retake the lead. At the end of the corridor was another door. Jess keyed a code into the security device, and the steel door unlatched. She pushed this one as well and again allowed Kara to pass.

But Kara stopped in the doorway, mouth open. Jess had expected as much. It was an impressive sight. The well-lit hangar-type facility was the owner's private showroom. Four pristine classic cars were backed into spaces along one wall. Opposite were two others. Beyond them was a man working beneath another car raised by a hydraulic platform. Though the area smelled vaguely of grease, the air conditioning and ceiling vents minimized its impact.

Jess recognized one of the vehicles as the Corvette. Two others she identified as an MG and a Porsche. She had no idea what the others were.

"Knock knock," Jess shouted over Bob Seger's "Old Time Rock & Roll." The man glanced over and waved. Dillon. He broke into the smile that still melted hearts, though hers was no longer one of them. He placed whatever tool he was holding onto a nearby tray and hit a button on a remote that reduced the music volume. He peeled off his gloves, removed and hung his shirt on the corner of the tool chest, leaving him in a white T-shirt. "Hey, beautiful," he said as he walked over to Jess, twirling her around and kissing her briefly on the lips.

Jess kept her arms around his waist, enjoying the intimacy they shared. "Hey, yourself. Thanks for seeing us." She turned to Kara. "Kara, this is Dillon Bradford. Dillon, this is…" But Kara wasn't paying attention. She was staring at the cars as if they were unicorns. "Kara." Jess stepped between Kara and the automobiles. "Kara." With the girl's focus finally on her, Jess extended her palm toward Dillon. "Kara, this is Dillon Bradford. Dillon, Kara Blake. This is Dillon's body shop and these are some of his toys. I thought you might like them."

Kara accepted Dillon's outstretched hand, but her eyes never left the autos as she said, "These are yours?"

"Yes, ma'am. Do they pass muster?"

Kara nodded like a bobblehead on steroids. "Is that…is that the Banshee? *The* Banshee?"

"It's not *the* Banshee. It's *a* Banshee. There were two that year," Dillon said.

Kara's mouth hung open and she turned to Jess. "You didn't mention that one."

"I didn't know." To Dillon, Jess said, "Is she new?"

Dillon smiled. "Picked her up at auction last month. Isn't she a beaut?"

"She's incredible. I can't believe you have all of these. '60 Camaro, '64 GTO, '68 Road Runner Hemi, '73 911 Carrera RS." Kara pointed to the MG. "Is that a seventy or seventy-one?"

"Seventy."

"Not much of an engine but not bad for its size."

"She's faster without the emissions equipment."

With four large pendulum steps, Kara surrounded herself amid the automobiles. "Can I sit in one?"

"You can sit in all of them if you'd like," Dillon said. While Kara took him up on the offer, he asked Jess, "What have you gotten yourself into?"

"The better question is, what have I gotten you into?"

"I don't think I like the sound of this. Who is she?"

"Your new intern?"

Dillon dropped his chin without taking his eyes off her.

"She knows a lot about cars," Jess said helpfully.

"She wants to work in an auto shop?"

"I don't know yet. But if she does, can she?"

"Is this Chad's little sister or something?"

"Of course not." Chad was a subject they usually shied away from because it wasn't healthy for their friendship. Jess didn't like Dillon's accusatory tone but recognized it stemmed from his concern for her. It wasn't that Dillon hated Chad. He just believed Chad was wrong for her. Though she agreed, dating Chad allowed her to sideline Lilith from her annoying matchmaking, and she didn't want to admit to Dillon she was using Chad. He disapproved whenever she acquiesced to Lilith, himself having once been the target of Lilith's intolerance.

Jess softened her tone. "Her sister's an intern at the firm. My guess is she wants to keep Kara away from people who don't discourage her from doing stupid things that get her hurt. But she hasn't figured out how to do that. I thought this might be a way."

"It's what it looks like then? She was beaten up?"

"Yeah."

"Damn."

"Yeah. The thing is, Dillon, she was caught joyriding." She needed to be up front with him.

Dillon seemed to weigh this information carefully. "You've brought a kid with a propensity for stealing cars *here*? And you want me to hire her."

"If she's interested, yes."

The tapping sound of crutches signaled Kara's approach. She wore a grin the size of Texas. "This is better than any museum! These are so beautiful and amazing." Her expression was one of pure joy as she stuck out her hand to Dillon. "Thank you so much, Mr. Bradford. I'll never forget this."

Dillon and Jess locked eyes briefly before he shook Kara's hand. "Any time."

Jess reached into her purse and retrieved her phone. "Would you like me to take a picture?"

Kara's eyes widened. "That would be awesome!" She turned to Dillon. "Would that be okay?"

"Sure. And you're welcome to pop the hood on any of these babies."

"Really? Even the Banshee?" At Dillon's nod, Kara seemed to forget about taking photos and made a beeline for the Pontiac.

"Enthusiastic kid," Dillon said.

"This could be so good for her. If I can convince her sister, say you'll think about it."

"What's in it for me?" He waggled his eyebrows suggestively.

"You wish," she said before hugging him. "Thank you."

"I like this side of you. I don't get to see it often enough."

She pulled back and gave him a questioning look.

"The side that veers off path."

Jess's path had been the main sticking point throughout their romantic relationship. Veering off it was what first brought them together during Jess's junior year in high school. Yet its pull, like gravity, was strong and unwavering. When her stepmother had forced her to choose between Dillon and the plans she'd set for her, Jess stayed the course, and their relationship ended. She'd hurt him deeply and he'd been slow to forgive. It had been difficult for them to transition into platonic friends, but it was the right choice for both of them. Jess loved Dillon the way she loved Derrick: wholly and unconditionally.

"I'll talk to her sister and let you know."

She snapped some photos of Kara before they left.

❖

The drive back to the office started off as quietly as the ride over. Kara pored over the photos Jess had texted to her, scrolling and zooming in on certain parts of the vehicles. Jess scanned the passing streets, not really seeing anything, trying to figure out her next steps with TJ.

"Is he your boyfriend?" Kara asked without raising her head from the prized pictures.

It was the first personal question Kara had asked. "No," Jess replied.

"Huh."

Clearly, Kara thought she was lying. "He used to be."

"So you are Polish."

"I'm sorry?"

"Private joke. Straight. You're straight."

Why would Kara be contemplating Jess's sexual preference? Did that mean she'd been discussing it with TJ? The thought gave her a little thrill in an unexpected way, as if someone had touched her with an ice cube on a warm day. Before she could respond, Kara continued.

"What happened? He's hunkalicious."

Jess enjoyed the contentment that always accompanied thoughts of Dillon. Like a mental sigh. "Noticed that, did you?"

"I have a pulse."

"Dillon was my first real relationship and my shot at…I don't know. Expression." Jess didn't know why she was opening her kimono, but she wanted to connect to this young woman, and the best way to do that was to be forthcoming.

Kara looked up questioningly.

"Ever been to Disneyland?" Jess asked.

"Once."

"You know how once you're strapped into a ride and it starts, you can't get out? Can't leave? Those rides aren't for everyone. People may tell you how great it is and how lucky you are to be on it, but for some, it's a jail sentence until it stops."

Kara seemed to mull this over. "Kind of like purgatory."

Jess nodded.

"He pulled you off the ride?" Kara spoke with an understanding beyond her years.

Jess nodded again.

"And now?"

Such a simple question. Yet so complicated. "Strapped in."

"I know what you mean."

Coming from any other teenager, it would have made Jess laugh. Out of Kara's mouth, it was unsettling. And believable. "Yeah?"

"Yeah. College."

"Purgatory?"

Kara lips settled in a tight line.

How should Jess respond? Part of her believed Kara was too young to know what she wanted. Part of her remembered being Kara's age and feeling the same way. Not about college, but about the expectations that came with being Jessica Spaulding. Some kids grew up faster than others, and it wasn't necessarily a good thing. Still, the conversation had gotten too serious.

Jess pulled out her phone and opened one of several photos of Kara with the automobiles. "Never heard of a—what'd you call it— Banshee before."

"That was so cool! It was a concept car that influenced lots of GM models."

"I still like the Fuelie."

"It's pretty sweet."

"Any interest in interning there?"

"In my dreams."

Right answer. "I can't promise you'd get assigned as a mechanic. You might have to start in the office or in parts or something, but if you're interested, I'm pretty sure I can get you in."

Kara visibly brightened. "Really?"

"Really."

"I could only do it for a few hours after school." She wilted like a thirsty vine. "And I'm kind of grounded right now. I probably won't be allowed to. TJ doesn't like me working on cars."

"Like I said, I don't know that you will. You might be relegated to the office."

"But I might not be?" Kara's enthusiasm rebounded and was five shades of delightful.

"You might not be."

"Cool. But maybe I won't lead with that."

The limo stopped in front of the firm's offices. The driver opened Jess's door and she stepped out. Kara struggled with her crutches but eventually got them settled. Jess waited for her and they walked side by side.

"Miss Spaulding?"

"Please. Call me Jess."

"Thanks for everything. Today totally rocked. Even if the work thing doesn't pan out, it was awesome."

Jess opened the front door and allowed Kara to pass. "You're very welcome." When they approached TJ's desk, she said, "She's just up ahead."

TJ stood and gave Kara a warm smile. "There you are. How's the leg?"

Kara peered at her cast. "Stiff."

"And the head?"

"Hard."

"I don't know." TJ mussed Kara's hair. "Might be a little soft up here. But I love you anyway. What have you been up to? I expected you earlier." Kara's last class had ended hours ago. TJ sized up her sister's countenance. "Clearly you haven't been hanging out in the reception area, reading money magazines. Why the grin?"

Kara pulled out her phone and showed TJ a picture of her with the Banshee.

"You had a field trip today?"

Jess's voice came from behind. "We did. Do you have a minute?" A perplexed TJ nodded. "Take my seat. I'll be right back." TJ followed Jess into her office. "You're here late."

Jess sat at her desk. "And we need to talk about why."

TJ took the seat across from Jess, growing concerned by the formality Jess was assuming. "What happened?"

"This is no place for Kara to stay while she waits for you." Jess raised her hand as if anticipating TJ's protest. "I know what you're trying to do. But you can't keep an eye on her here. I understand you want to minimize whatever's influencing her, but this is an investment firm, not a gym with complimentary child care."

TJ could only nod, the lump in her throat at the thought of Kara spending time contemplating trouble making it impossible to reply. She dropped her gaze.

"A friend of mine owns an auto body shop here in Montgomery Hills. It's extremely reputable. Given Kara's interest in cars, it might be good to let her work there for a few hours a day after school—hear me out." Jess raised her palm again when TJ opened her mouth. "If she sees the nonglamorous side of the business—answering phones, processing payments, ordering parts—maybe it'll curb her enthusiasm. And no matter what, she won't be surrounded by stolen cars or the men who take them."

"She needs an education. Not a job."

Jess put up her hands as if in surrender. "I'm not telling you what to do, TJ. I'm offering a solution. She can't loiter here, and my friend's willing to take her on as an intern. It's up to you whether to take him up on it." She stood and grabbed her purse. "Give it some thought."

TJ's hand was on the door when Jess added, "And TJ?" When she turned, Jess said, "Just a suggestion, but maybe ask Kara what *she* wants."

❖

Conversation was absent during the first part of dinner. TJ normally took advantage of this time together to get up to speed on whatever Kara cared to share about school and friends—typically a quiet conversation. Yet it was their only dedicated one-on-one time while TJ interned.

Tonight, TJ struggled with Jess's proposition to land Kara a job. She said, "What kind of car was in the photo you showed me, and where did you see it?"

Kara's face lit up. "'64 Pontiac Banshee. Concept car they never made because GM brass were afraid it would threaten Corvette sales. Only two prototypes were ever built. And I got to sit in one. So sick." It came as no surprise that the longest sentence Kara had uttered in weeks related to cars.

"Where was it?"

"This guy Miss Spaulding knows. He's got this private showroom in the back of his auto-repair shop. You should see his cars, Teej. They're beautiful. I have pictures of all of them."

"Show me after dinner. What were you doing at his fancy garage?"

"You weren't at the office when I arrived. When I told the receptionist I was waiting for you, she called some guy who came out and said I couldn't wait there. I'm like, nice *reception*, receptionist. Dude. Lame. A few minutes later Miss Spaulding asked me to her office. We got to talking about cars, and she mentioned her friend owned a '57 Corvette Fuelie. We went to see it, and he had six other cars too."

"Including the Banshee."

"I got to sit in it *and* check out its engine."

"Was it hard to come back down to earth?"

"It will be."

"That good, huh?"

"The best." Kara's grin lingered for several moments until her expression turned serious. She dropped her gaze and began pushing her food around on her plate with her fork.

"Kare? What is it?"

Kara stared at her plate. "No fire trucks though."

In one of the few frames hanging in the family room was a photo of an eight-year-old Kara sitting in their father's lap as they rode atop an antique fire truck in the annual Kids' Day Fire Truck Parade. One of

Jack's friends was the son of the fire chief several towns over, and Jack had called in a favor to get his youngest daughter on the truck. Kara had been so thrilled by the event she chattered to TJ endlessly about it on one of TJ's holiday breaks from college, even though it had happened many weeks prior. It was the last photo Kara would ever take with her father.

The current iteration of the frame had an acrylic face, which TJ had found to replace the glass after their mother had broken earlier versions during fits of rage and despair. Spiraling out of control, fueled by alcohol and grief, Evelyn had screamed at the memories that hung on the wall, reminding her of the husband she'd lost. Thankfully, Kara hadn't been home to experience them.

Initially, TJ had stored the family photos following Evelyn's death. While Evelyn was alive, TJ reached a point of wishing she wasn't. The wish materialized, leaving her struggling not only with its truth but also that she had desired her sister's mother dead. Yes, their mother was one and the same, but now that TJ was Kara's guardian, it took on additional meaning, knowing she had longed for Kara's mother's demise. What kind of person did that make TJ?

She didn't want to think about it. Or Evelyn.

But friends and neighbors had stopped talking about their parents, and it wasn't okay. As if by not mentioning them, life for Kara and TJ went back to "normal." TJ didn't want her father forgotten. And while she hadn't concluded whether that was true with respect to her mother, she refused to take away anything more from Kara than the universe had already stolen. So she rehung some pictures. Happy memories of her mother existed in a compartment of her brain, however walled off, and she wasn't going to grease the wheels of familial amnesia for Kara by refusing to display the photographs.

And now, as she watched Kara eye the fire-truck photo, TJ was swept in a wave of sentiment that buoyed her spirit. They didn't often talk about Jack, and TJ was moved that Kara's sudden sadness stemmed from missing him, missing out on something she might have shared with him. Yes, he was gone. But he wasn't forgotten. That meant everything. To an eight-year-old, a father is bigger than life. Now, to this teenager, he might have simply been a man who shared his daughter's enthusiasm over a fancy car.

TJ said, "If Papa were there, he'd have wrestled you for the driver's seat. Or swiped your crutches so you couldn't get to the Banshee first."

Kara smiled. "If it meant he was with us, that'd be okay. More than okay."

TJ squeezed Kara's hand. Maybe she should give in. If working at this auto shop was going to remind Kara of their father, TJ would be all for it. And if it kept Kara off the streets surrounding their building, it would be a positive outcome. "We have to set some ground rules."

Growing wide-eyed at the implication, Kara asked, "I can work there?"

"If you promise to maintain your GPA, among other things, yes."

"I totally promise."

"Stop bouncing in your seat before you hurt that leg," TJ said before she was enveloped in a tight hug.

CHAPTER NINE

A nother yawn meant another glance at the clock. 1:54 a.m. It was the second night in a row TJ had stayed up late to work on the marketing project. Technically she could have gone to bed far earlier had she limited her research to the project instead of the project's creator. The USB drive Jess had given her was a treasure trove of information regarding previous initiatives, targets, budgets, and results.

Jess employed multiple advertising agencies to assist with different aspects of the marketing efforts and seemed to rotate through them, rarely using the same agency for back-to-back years. Since that was atypical—usually you stayed with an agency that yielded great results—TJ dug around to ascertain why.

Aside from blog posts by industry leaders and aggregated reports that provided expected ranges for certain types of campaigns, TJ could find little additional data. But everything she did find, including the quarterly performance reports put together by the agencies, drove her to one conclusion: Jess blew away the competition. Or at the very least, the campaign goals. The return-on-investment of Magnate's marketing initiatives was astounding, not because the numbers were repeatedly off the charts—there would always be the occasional huge hit that couldn't be replicated, such as Nike's "Just Do It." Rather, the success came in the form of consistently beating the averages and goals.

Were the goals set falsely low? No. Too many agencies were involved for all of them to be treating Magnate differently than other clients, lowballing every effort. And based on the limited data TJ could pull from the Internet and the aggregated median data on the agency reports, the goals fell within an expected range for the types of campaigns Magnate was running.

Was Jess that much better at selecting agencies and approving ad creative than others in her industry? No. These agencies worked for clients willing to pay them. Their employees didn't alter their routines or veer widely from their training from client to client. Many of the agencies worked for Magnate's competitors at one time or another. Were they also seeing such success? No.

Jess didn't work crazy hours. From what TJ could see, she barely logged fifteen hours a week in the office. And she had no staff (other than domestic staff, TJ corrected herself). Magnate was a small firm, and prior to reviewing these files, TJ hadn't been surprised that its marketing department was a staff of one. Now she wasn't as sure Jess spent so little time doing actual marketing work. Perhaps Jess worked from home, and none of the Magnate personnel realized it.

But *why*? That was the burning question. If TJ's assessment was correct and Magnate's marketing performance record was that of an industry leader, why hide that fact? Why would Jess practically parade around the office as if her brain weighed that of a newt's? Why wouldn't she take pride in delivering such repeatedly positive results?

TJ wasn't particularly underhanded, but she was scrappy. When she put her mind to something, she didn't concede defeat until she had explored all avenues. If TJ was correct that Jess was far more deliberate and knowledgeable about the marketing aspects of the business than she purported to be, TJ was determined to get to the bottom of it.

As she drifted off to sleep, she contemplated how to go about getting Jess to come clean. TJ had the feeling that if Jess knew she was being observed for signs of intelligence, she'd play dumb.

❖

"What do you have for me?" Jess asked as TJ took a seat in her office. It was Friday, the day TJ was to report on her first marketing project.

TJ handed across the USB drive Jess had given her and set her laptop on the desk, turning the screen so both could see. Realizing this wasn't ideal positioning, TJ suggested they sit at Jess's conference table.

She pulled up the slide deck she'd prepared. "I went in a different direction than we discussed earlier, though that's a project I'd like to get back to. I've come up with two different initiatives that are doable within the respective budgets. They're both centered around the philanthropic aspect of Magnate. You didn't give me a timeline for landing new clients, only that I use the lists. This route should yield the most clients, albeit over a longer period. The budget dollars should stretch farther under the assumption that some of the media outlets and the creative agency would donate their services."

Slide after slide, TJ presented her ideas, careful to leave the minutia out of the deck and reserve it for any questions Jess had. Jess did ask several questions, to which TJ responded as best she could, acknowledging that given her limited marketing knowledge and the short time frame of the project, she'd left some aspects of her proposal too vague. Once the slide show ended, TJ awaited Jess's assessment. As seconds ticked by in silence, TJ focused on breathing evenly and projecting confidence, sitting back and holding her head high. Jess's opinion mattered to her in a way it wouldn't have at the outset of the week, before she'd come to realize Jess's competence.

When Jess finally spoke, she said, "It's obvious you're biased by your graduate program in that you went after the philanthropy angle. And you're making fairly large assumptions as to the pro-bono services you can expect to receive. I'm doubtful your budget will stretch as far as you've proposed."

TJ firmly believed she was on the right track with highlighting the things Magnate's founder was known for on the charitable-giving front. If a client could expect to achieve not only above-average returns but also get good press for choosing a firm that cared about social issues, it was a no-brainer.

TJ nodded, having expected to be admonished for the very things Jess called her out on, yet not expecting it to feel like she had failed to meet expectations. She'd delivered a proposal she believed would appeal to Magnate's clientele as well as celebrate the charitable goals of its founder. It was true her propositions relied heavily on procuring catchy ad creative that would garner media attention. Perhaps she'd been too hopeful or naive that the initiative would bring in Hollywood types willing to donate time.

"That said," Jess continued, "your instincts are sound. We've actually used similar initiatives, and one in particular is ongoing even today. Unfortunately, it doesn't come close to sticking to a two-million-dollar budget, but you get high marks for the concept. I'm impressed. What you've put together in four days would easily rival the best ideas I could expect from any of our agencies, and you're not even a marketer. Good job, TJ."

Warming as if descending into the Earth's core, TJ let out a breath.

"Thank you." Jess's words felt better than a hot bath after an especially trying shift at the restaurant. She wanted to ask Jess why she pretended to her colleagues that she was incapable of or uninterested in leading Magnate's marketing efforts when it was clearly not the case. Part of her also felt fortunate to get this one-on-one time with Jess. Marketing wasn't the focus of her class assignment, but at least she was learning something from a master in her field. TJ worried that if she called Jess out on her front, Jess would revert back to the same antics TJ had seen during her first week in some kind of defense mechanism. Defense against what, TJ wasn't sure. But something made Jess act differently in front of others, and for now, TJ was content to enjoy the glimpses of who she was discovering to be the real Jessica Spaulding.

As TJ studied the warmth in Jess's eyes, the obvious pleasure Jess took from TJ's work on the project, TJ realized she was enjoying more than glimpses. Today Jess was wearing a simple sleeveless black dress. A clip made her blond hair fall behind her back that, along with the V-neck of the dress, exposed the smooth planes of her neck and shoulders. Hit with a sudden memory of Jess's light perfume when Jess had hugged her after dropping her off after the hospital, TJ focused on the creamy skin at her collarbone. She imagined catching that delicate scent while she trailed her mouth along Jess's throat and under her chin, imagined hearing Jess moan softly beneath her touch.

TJ raised her eyes and saw from Jess's expression that she'd been caught daydreaming. The image of such an intimate interlude was so clear, it was as if she'd projected it onto every wall of Jess's office like a drive-in movie. TJ's lips curled under in an unsuccessful attempt to hide her smile as she felt a blush blossom in her cheeks.

Seemingly amused, Jess said, "I'm not sure where you went just now, but I'll gladly purchase a ticket. One-way, please, as I don't think I'll want to return."

The fact that her boss dated men wasn't sinking in the way it should. How could TJ get herself to settle down and focus? "What do you have in mind for my next project?"

"City treasurers," Jess said without skipping a beat.

That did it. The remark might as well have been a polar-bear-club plunge. "City treasurers," TJ repeated unenthusiastically.

"You said yourself it was a project you'd like to get back to. They're responsible for millions in assets and are on the lists I gave you."

TJ nodded.

"I know what you're doing," Jess said.

"What's that?"

"Stereotyping. Thinking they're boring people who carry slide rules, sniff paste, and tell tax jokes at parties."

"No. I'm thinking they don't party. Ever. The most excitement in their week is when they feed the fish in their aquariums."

"Don't underestimate the face-off over those flakes. Those fish can get a little *American Gladiator*."

"Wow. Who knew city treasurers liked to stir up so much trouble? And we're thinking of putting said financial officers together in one room?"

"Make sure to budget for security."

CHAPTER TEN

Jess took a sip of wine as her eyes settled on their quarry: Muriel Manchester, the frequent target of money managers seeking to put her substantial assets under their control.

Jess admired Muriel, a capable and ruthless businesswoman who suffered no fools. Muriel liked her women young and handsome and didn't try to hide that fact. The good-looking brunette holding court with her was no exception. Jess smiled. She appreciated Muriel's openness about her sexual orientation. That her parents continued to invite Muriel to social functions was less a testament to their acceptance of gays and more of their endless pursuit of new assets to manage. Less clear was why Muriel continued to come to these gatherings, though they did have a number of mutual friends.

Tapping the toe of her Manolo Blahniks, Jess realized the band's rendition of Sammy Davis Jr.'s "Love Me or Leave Me" was putting her in the mood to swing. Chad wasn't a good lead, which made her sit out more often than she wanted. Muriel and her date were on the dance floor, but it became quickly evident that even Muriel's considerable skill couldn't overcome her companion's inexperience. Instead of swinging, they broke apart and danced next to each other. Jess briefly toyed with the idea of cutting in to give Muriel the dance she wanted.

Brooke leaned forward and spoke to her sister. "Her dates seem to get younger and younger. She's like a lesbian cougar."

"She's got a lot going for her. Brains, wealth, power, looks. And let's face it: she can dance. What woman doesn't appreciate that in a date?"

"Well, I certainly didn't appreciate their behavior during that last slow dance. Must they paw each other in public? Get a room."

"They weren't acting differently than any of the other couples."

"No one wants to see that. Live and let live and all, but don't subject everyone else to it."

Jess glared at her sister.

Brooke's eyes narrowed. "Don't tell me the intern you couldn't even get to show up tonight is pushing that agenda on you?"

Jess took another sip. Brooke was a barracuda who wouldn't let anyone out of her grasp once she bit. In that respect, she was glad TJ had apparently decided not to come.

"I take it back. Tell me the intern's shown up, and that's her," Brooke said.

Quickly pivoting, Jess followed Brooke's line of vision to the only other same-sex couple in the room. Her mouth dried at the unsettling sight, and she turned away from the approaching TJ, heart hammering. Not only had TJ unexpectedly donned a dress for the event—a short-sleeve side-ruched black number that fell just above the knee—she wore it impeccably and assuredly. It was simple yet stunning, showing off her figure in a way Jess was surprised TJ was comfortable with, even down to the muscled calves it revealed. TJ was nothing short of gorgeous.

No less unsettling was TJ's date, the emergency-room physician who had treated Kara. Of course TJ would nab a doctor—an elegantly dressed, svelte one at that. Why should it rattle Jess? After all, she had her pick of them should she choose—Lilith practically stack-ranked them by specialty. She faced her sister and assumed an expression of indifference. "The very same."

Brooke lowered her voice. "Muriel's going to love her."

TJ stopped at their table and glanced between them. "I hope we're not interrupting?"

Brooke stood and offered her hand. "Not at all. Brooke Spaulding. You must be TJ. Very nice to meet you." She turned to TJ's date. "Hi. I'm Brooke."

"Rebecca Stanfield." The women shook hands.

Jess abandoned the idea of taking a large swig of wine before joining the pleasantries, making an effort not to dwell on how good TJ looked. She wished she wasn't wearing a dress because she needed something to do with her hands instead of reach out for TJ. She had a full-blown crush and thought it aptly named. It was overpowering, as if a strong force were pressing against her chest, making it difficult to breathe. "Dr. Stanfield, so glad you could join us. Jessica Spaulding." After their greetings, Jess nodded to TJ. "TJ. Welcome."

"Thank you." TJ turned to Rebecca. "Care to dance?"

"I'd love to."

And they were off.

"You did good, Jess. This has got to score us points with Muriel."

Jess wasn't in the mood to care about landing new business. She felt dirty, like they were the owners of some sideshow, only instead of exhibiting their freaks, they were showing off perfect examples of the female form. It sickened her to think she'd asked TJ to take part in such a spectacle. She finished her wine and wanted another glass. It was a feeling she'd carry through much of the evening.

The next hour dragged like a small predator trying to tame its larger, fallen prey. TJ and Rebecca made a captivating couple, Jess admitted. She hadn't picked up on any intimacy between them at the hospital, but they were getting along swimmingly this evening. TJ's hand often rested solicitously on Rebecca's lower back while they mingled with other guests. Jess wondered why she noticed and was irked with herself for being annoyed. She plastered on a practiced smile when she saw them approach.

"I'm afraid I'm needed at the hospital. I wanted to thank you for having me this evening. I've really enjoyed myself." Rebecca extended her hand. "It was great to meet you, Jessica. I hope to see you again soon. Please extend my thanks to your family."

"It's been our pleasure having you," Jess said. For all her disquiet about Rebecca, she seemed genuinely likeable, which irritated Jess like a sunburn.

Rebecca addressed TJ and held out her hand. "Walk me out?"

"Certainly," TJ said as she took the proffered hand and tucked it under her arm.

When TJ returned, Jess was speaking with another couple, who soon headed to the dance floor.

"Dr. Stanfield seems lovely. How long have you been seeing each other, if you don't mind my asking?" Jess asked.

"She's quite lovely, and I told you, I don't date."

Jess laughed. "Interesting way not to date someone."

"Her uncle was in the hospital the first time Kara got hurt. We were both worried about loved ones and kind of bonded. She's become a friend." TJ glanced at her watch. "That page was from her husband, planned ninety minutes into our arrival. Since she was all dolled up, they decided to make a date night out of it."

"Wow. You seemed so...close."

"I told her the situation and asked if she'd mind my hands on her. She said, 'Hell, no' and wished her husband was attending so I could do it in front of him—thought it might help her get lucky tonight."

"In that dress? She'd have him at hello."

TJ smiled. "Yeah."

"Thank you for, gosh, doing all that. That's certainly going above and beyond."

The band started playing Madonna's "Hanky Panky." TJ inclined her head and raised her voice to be heard over the music. "Dance?"

Jess loved the song but wasn't comfortable doing the random-moves thing TJ had done with Rebecca. "No, thank you."

"You don't like to dance?"

"I love dancing. But not your way. I like to swing."

TJ brightened. "Let's go." She escorted Jess to the dance floor. Suddenly TJ's right hand was on her shoulder blade and their hands touched lightly. TJ led her through basic moves with practiced ease. Although Jess had been tense when they began, it melted away with each step, and soon she was in a zone, enjoying the music. They transitioned seamlessly into the next tune, the Stray Cats' "Rock This Town." TJ didn't improvise much, but she was a good leader, providing sufficient direction and space.

Since Jess had been relishing the opportunity to let go and dance her concerns away, the music ended too soon for her taste, and the band shifted to a slow ballad. After thanking TJ, she made it only two steps before she felt a hand on hers.

At TJ's raised eyebrow, Jess understood she was being challenged. The safe route was to exit the floor, and Jess wasn't much of a risk taker.

"It's why I'm here," TJ said, tugging Jess closer.

Jess was out of her comfort zone. But at TJ's words, she reminded herself this wasn't a date. They were colleagues working toward the goal of changing Muriel Manchester's opinion of the firm, however slight the chance. Decision made, Jess stepped forward and embraced TJ, whose arms enfolded her waist.

It was uncomfortable, this lack of distance. And damn it—exhilarating. TJ's gray eyes searched hers as if questioning her ability to handle the situation, which was absurd. Because what was scary about a slow dance? Spinning it to herself that way helped relax her somewhat.

TJ was taller, but Jess's heels were higher, making them nearly the same height. Jess studied the face she'd only been this close to once, when TJ tried to dismiss her in Zelda's. At the time, TJ's eyes had been fierce and penetrating. Now they were kind and welcoming. Her lips glistened. The recent exertion added a little color to her cheeks, and light perspiration beaded her forehead. Inches separated them, and for a moment, the distance felt too wide. Jess tamped down the desire to be closer, dismayed to enjoy having her arms around TJ's shoulders.

"You've surprised me," Jess said.

"I could say the same thing. But I have a work question first."

The last thing on Jess's mind was work. It was a good reminder that TJ was here as an employee, someone with a duty to perform. Whatever Jess was feeling, it was inappropriate and unprofessional. Casually, she added a bit more space between them. "Of course. What is it?"

"Are we on the clock?"

It didn't sound from TJ's tone that she was concerned about getting paid. Interested in following the conversation where TJ wanted to take it, Jess replied, "No."

"I'm glad you have a boyfriend."

How nice of TJ to help with the calling-Chad-to-mind thing. Which she really should be trying to do. But rather than saying, "Me, too," she asked, "Why's that?"

"Because otherwise I'd be tempted to do something really stupid, like tell you how beautiful you look and how much I've enjoyed dancing with you. Instead, I hope you'll take it as a compliment that I think your boyfriend's a lucky guy, and that by saying so you won't be uncomfortable around me at the office."

Definitely not what Jess was expecting. "I don't think I could ever be uncomfortable around you." As soon as she said it, she realized it wasn't true. Her core had warmed a good twenty degrees at TJ's words, and an image flashed to mind of how it could be cooled. Eventually. She had no intention of sharing it. "And thank you for saying that. My sister's the one who usually gets the compliments."

TJ found that hard to believe. When she had entered the mansion's elegant ballroom, she'd immediately searched for Jess, certain no one else would give her the time of day. At Jess's table had been a beautiful blonde with features similar to Jess. Though more traditionally pretty than Jess, the woman exuded an ego the size of Alaska, which tainted her otherwise flawless appearance.

"No disrespect to your sister, but from where I stand, there's no comparison." As the song came to a close, TJ stepped back. With her palm, she gestured that Jess should take the lead off the dance floor. TJ needed the space. She hadn't expected sparks to fly between them and wanted time to process their interaction. Something in the way Jess had been looking at her had changed of late, as if she was mirroring the same thing building within TJ.

The rest of the evening passed slowly for TJ, during which Jess introduced her to Chad as well as other guests she couldn't recall. How Jess remembered every person's name was impressive. Less so was the deference she showed to the men. One such conversation between Chad, a man named Monroe, Monroe's wife, and Jess, was particularly egregious.

"I say, Astor, what do you think of our good Senator Grantham? He waffles more than any breakfast," Monroe asked.

TJ wasn't sure she was more galled or amused that Monroe directed the question solely to Chad, altogether sidelining the three women surrounding them. If she'd cared more, gall would have won out. But the corpulent man with the reddened face and his equally bulbous wife seemed so cartoonish as to minimize her vexation. Had Monroe been sporting a hat, TJ could imagine him saying, "I'll gladly pay you Tuesday for a hamburger today."

"His latest stance on gun control is intolerable," Chad replied.

"To think he was the NRA's choice two years ago," Monroe said.

"Hardly their fault, is it? Grantham's done a complete one-eighty on the issue."

"Indeed. Woeful independent streak. This voter prefers that his candidates stick to the platform."

"I agree. What kind of elected official does that make him?" Chad asked.

Though the silence was preferable to TJ than listening to them, it was jarring her into action. Was the question rhetorical? Why didn't Jess join the discussion? Mrs. Monroe's smile seemed stuck in place, as if she'd been shellacked in acrylic, so TJ surmised the woman wouldn't be participating. TJ wasn't sure of proper protocol at such a swanky event, but she wasn't the type to duck and cover. "The kind that weighs the evidence and makes an informed decision," she said.

"By listening to the liberal rhetoric of a Stanford law professor?" Chad asked.

"By being open-minded to a different conclusion reached by over thirty years of statistics." The story had lit up the Internet and made headlines in newspapers and cable news networks. TJ was well aware of Senator Grantham's left turn on the issue.

"Statistics are manipulated to tell the story the author wants to tell." Chad's tone slighted TJ in the way of young people in the grocery checkout queue impatiently waiting for an elderly patron to write a check.

"Right-to-carry laws are associated with substantially higher rates of aggravated assault, robbery, rape, and murder. 'More guns, less crime' is an outdated notion based on incomplete evidence," TJ said.

"I agree with Astor. There are no facts; simply an agenda and a set of figures. An individual's politics will surely alter any relevant information to reach the desired conclusion."

No facts? Clearly Mr. Monroe hadn't made his substantial sums in the field of science. TJ was interested in Jess's opinion. Turning to her, she asked, "What do you think of Grantham's about-face?"

The pitch of Jess's laugh was unlike anything TJ had heard from her. Was she auditioning for a *Legally Blonde* sequel?

"Jess isn't much for politics, Ms. Blake," Chad said.

"Ever the proper lady," added Mr. Monroe. "You won't find my Trudy having any part of it."

The insult wasn't lost on TJ. She wasn't a proper lady by any of this set's measuring sticks if it meant acquiescing to a man's stance on an issue by virtue of his being male.

Jess laid her palm against Chad's chest. "Let's avoid such unsavory talk while at my father's party."

"Does attendance preclude thoughtful conversation?" TJ asked.

Chad seemed to expand under Jess's touch the way a tampon might, as if to absorb a flood of potential barbs headed her way. He snaked an arm around Jess's waist. "With the Granthams of the world snubbing the voters who brought them into power, I can't say I fault the request."

Jess winked at TJ. "Words like robbery must be handled delicately in public venues. We wouldn't want anyone thinking we're speaking of their investments with us."

"Another time, perhaps." TJ raised her glass to Jess, took a sip, and set it down. "And on that note, I'll bid you all a good evening." She nodded to each guest in turn as she said her good-byes, fighting the urge to snap her fingers in front of Mrs. Monroe to see if she was a figure out of Madame Tussauds wax museum.

As TJ made her way toward the estate's main entrance, a commanding woman in her mid to late forties stopped her. "Pardon me," she said as she held out her hand to TJ. "Muriel Manchester. And you are?"

"TJ Blake."

Muriel took TJ's elbow and steered her away from the entryway. "What happened to that beautiful woman you were dancing with earlier?"

"Jessica Spaulding?"

Muriel furrowed a brow. "No. I'm well acquainted with the Spauldings. No, the woman with the chestnut hair."

"I'm afraid she was paged. Were you wishing to speak with her, or is there something I can do for you?"

"Oh, there are many things you can do for me, TJ Blake. But let me start with the basics. Are you and she exclusive?"

"Are you usually so forward?"

"Yes. And I'd like to get to know you better."

"I imagine your date wouldn't be thrilled to hear that."

"Ah, you noticed us. I take that as a good sign."

"Hard to miss the only other same-sex couple here."

Muriel laughed, a rich, melodic sound that TJ found welcoming. "Are you suggesting a lack of diversity in these ranks?"

"It's a private party. It's not for me to judge."

"Speaking of private parties, I'm having one next Saturday. You're invited."

"How private is this party?"

Muriel laughed again. "There will be dozens of us, I expect. You're welcome to bring a guest, of course."

"You don't even know me."

"Join me, and we'll change that. Shall I send the invitation to Magnate?"

"What makes you think I work there?"

"Darling, you must be new to the firm. You're certainly not part of Derrick and Lilith's social network. As they're hardly known for their inclusive practices, it wouldn't surprise me if the Spaulding clan is pulling out the stops to try to get my business by inviting you here."

"I don't know if I should be flattered that you'd think of me as some sort of weapon, insulted that's the only reason you think I'd be invited, or impressed that you could see through such a scheme, if that's what it is."

"Rule number one: never care what others think. As far as the rest, you're most definitely a great addition to anyone's arsenal, I don't flatter myself to think I'm the only reason you're here, and feel free to be impressed. It's been my pleasure to meet you, TJ, and I hope you'll consider accepting my invitation. Now if you'll excuse me, I must return to my table."

When the energetic wave that was Muriel left, TJ found herself awed. Muriel was straightforward, confident, and sharp. No wonder she was CEO of a major corporation. TJ was surprised to have garnered Muriel's attention. She'd noticed Muriel and her date during the course of the evening. The date was far younger than Muriel, perhaps TJ's age, and seemed to have a bit of an edge to her, not unlike TJ. As TJ retrieved her wrap and purse from the designated coat-check area, she wondered whether the invitation was real or whether Muriel had taken her aside to fuel her date's jealousy or keep afloat the rumor that she was a player.

She looked out across the expansive curved driveway, admiring the organized valets and the automobiles they tended. The driveway was lined with tea-light candles in small paper bags, as was a wooden bridge that rose above a side garden and pond. Small white lights illuminated the surrounding trees as well as the columns and terraces in front of the mansion. TJ couldn't imagine this being her view each day she left for work.

A couple waited for a valet to run and fetch their car. TJ's pumps had already pummeled her feet into white-flag-surrender territory, and the thought occurred to her to ask the couple for a ride to the nearest bus stop, wherever that was. She had arrived in Rebecca's car, and poor planning had left her standing here, contemplating her options.

"TJ!" She turned to see Jess descending the stairs toward her. "How are you getting home?" Jess asked as she stopped next to her.

The question surprised her. How did Jess know it was an issue? TJ had been disappointed earlier by Jess's unwillingness to participate in substantive conversation. Her acquiescence to the political views espoused by the men was unsettling. Did Jess prefer not to share her private views in a public setting, or did she hold no opinions? The latter idea clashed fiercely with TJ's independent nature. American women had fought too hard for too long to secure suffrage in order to toss it aside as casually as a used paper towel.

Complicating the matter was the vision of Jess's hand centered on Chad's chest. TJ had been so irritated by the discussion between Monroe and Chad that she hadn't focused on Jess and Chad's physicality. But now that Jess was beside her, holding her forearm, TJ chafed at the memory. She stared at Jess's hand and recalled the way it had pressed against Chad in a gently controlling fashion, the opposite gesture one would expect from a submissive girlfriend. Was Jess meek or commanding? Why did she seem to always be acting in diametrically opposed directions?

TJ wanted to get to know the Jessica Spaulding she'd danced with for several blissful minutes earlier in the evening, the one whose body moved flawlessly in step with hers with so little effort it was like dancing with her own shadow. Only this shadow was corporeal, with Jess filling out the curves of her dress more deliciously than the caramel center of a dark chocolate shell.

"I'll figure something out. Maybe I'll call a cab. Please don't concern yourself."

"Nonsense," Jess said and headed straight for the lead valet. TJ couldn't hear the conversation, but the valet took off down the driveway. "One of our drivers will be at your disposal in no time."

"That's not necessary. I'm perfectly capable of finding my way home."

Jess smiled. "You're perfectly capable of a great many things, one of which is allowing me to thank you for agreeing to come here tonight by procuring a ride for you. We have a service on call to ensure everyone gets home safely, and I say we use it."

TJ clenched and unclenched her jaw as she worked through a response. She could really use the lift home but wasn't comfortable being needy.

"Is it my help specifically or help in general you find so difficult to accept?" Jess asked.

TJ let out an exasperated breath. Truth be told, she didn't know the answer. "I don't have any way of repaying you for your kindness."

"If I expected repayment, it would no longer be kindness," Jess said reasonably.

It was a good point, but TJ couldn't control her discomfort at the idea of accepting. TJ inclined her head toward the entryway. "Isn't there some conversation you could be in there dodging right now?"

Jess shifted her focus to the entryway and appeared to scrutinize it. Then she gave TJ a beseeching look that quickly shifted into resignation, almost as if she'd rather be here with TJ but accepted she had other obligations. Obligations that somehow required her to don a feebleminded persona. With a sad smile, she slowly nodded. "Your ride's here. Good night, TJ."

Before Jess had taken ten steps, TJ said, "Wait."

Jess paused in the middle of ascending the stairs. But she didn't turn around and, after a small shake of her head, continued her trek upward. Impulsively, TJ ran after her and stopped her at the top of the stairs with a hand to her upper arm.

"That came out wrong," TJ said. It wasn't her place to judge Jess for putting on a front in company. TJ was one hundred percent convinced Jess was so much more than she let on, and in this moment, the only thing that mattered was to let her know. "What I meant to say is, you're kind, intelligent, and charming."

TJ reached for Jess's hand. She had no desire to offend Jess by saying something detrimental about Chad or the way Jess handled herself in group conversation. "Please don't let anyone who can't see you for all that you are have any say in all that you can be."

Emotion swirled in Jess's eyes at the comment. TJ squeezed Jess's hand briefly before letting go. "Good night, Jess." She walked backward for several steps to linger in Jess's gaze before turning and taking the stairs to the waiting car.

❖

"What are you still doing up?" TJ said as she locked the apartment door, greeted by the familiar sight of Kara manipulating a game console while focused on the television screen.

"Taking advantage," Kara said without glancing up.

"Appreciate the honesty. I'm glad you're up. You can help me get out of this thing. Pause it and unzip me." TJ sat on the couch next to Kara and presented her back.

As Kara unzipped the dress, she said, "How'd it go?"

"I survived." TJ strode to her bedroom and changed into a T-shirt and pajama bottoms. She grabbed a glass of water from the kitchen and parked next to her sister. Kara was playing a violent first-person-shooter game that had a number of weapons at the character's disposal.

It made her recall the earlier conversation about guns, and her thoughts returned to Jess. She'd spent the entire car ride home thinking about her. Why did Jess mill about the party as if she were as hollow as a cheap chocolate Easter bunny? By refusing to engage the men in any meaningful conversation, Jess's feebleminded persona rendered her the equivalent of a piece of jewelry on Chad's arm. TJ much preferred the company of the woman who challenged her to think things through. Not for the first time, TJ wondered if there were two Jessica Spauldings, identical twins who got their kicks by weaving in and out of each other's lives to see if anyone noticed.

TJ watched as the character on screen suddenly left the safety of his hiding place and ran into the middle of a zombie-infested room, firing in every direction and taking numerous hits. His life force quickly dwindled to zero and he died, whereupon he was summarily eaten by ravaging zombies. Bloodletting ensued.

Kara set the console on the coffee table.

TJ blinked and turned to Kara. "What's up? You rarely die."

"You've sat here for twenty minutes letting me play the only video game you never let me play. I put it in before you got home to see how long it would take before you noticed. I guessed ninety seconds, tops. You tell me what's up." She crossed her arms as if to say she could wait all night. "Or should I say, who?"

TJ brought her knees to her chest. "Doesn't matter."

"Dimwitted heiress?" Kara asked.

"She's not dimwitted!" TJ snapped, as if looking for a fight.

Kara grinned.

Bolting off the couch, TJ ran a hand through her hair and began to pace. "Kare, she's so smart. You should hear her in her element. But God, when others are around, she acts like an imbecile."

"Maybe she's shy."

"She's not shy!" TJ exclaimed. "Hello. You've met," she said sarcastically. TJ stilled and pinched the bridge of her nose. For as much as the topic fueled her fire, TJ didn't want to lash out at Kara. "Sorry. I wish there was a way I could call her out on her pretense, but she'd simply brush aside my attempts to get her to admit anything."

"Why the need for her to admit it?" Kara asked reasonably. "What if she's happy?"

"That's like assuming an Arctic tern would be satisfied living in someone's backyard."

"Never heard of it."

"Seabird that migrates something like fifty thousand miles a year."

"Maybe it's a nice backyard."

A sharp retort died on TJ's lips. Indeed, Jess did live in a nice backyard—a multi-million-dollar one, to be exact. Perhaps Kara was right. Maybe the luxury of the confinement trumped the fact that it was confining. From behind the couch, TJ leaned over and hugged her. "It's an amazing backyard, to be sure. Thanks for your wise counsel as ever, Dr. Blake. Good night. And turn off that terrible game, please."

CHAPTER ELEVEN

Jess was surprised by Kara's text inviting her to join TJ and her at the classic-car show. Kara instructed Jess to text once she parked so they could come out to meet her at the entrance. Having thought of nothing but TJ for the last twelve hours, Jess concluded that a lighthearted day outside, yucking it up with the Blake sisters, might be just the trick to pull her from her more serious musings.

She was experiencing all the telltale signs of infatuation: jealousy of Muriel and Dr. Stanfield, irritation with Chad and everything he represented, longing to spend time alone with TJ. The realization she could never act on her blossoming feelings, the knowledge TJ could never be interested in her once she discovered how truly shallow she was, had put Jess in a somber mood. A frivolous day walking among tricked-out automobiles might give her a reprieve from her self-flagellation.

The parking lot at the fairgrounds was enormous, reminding Jess of the football games she had attended during college. Impeccably maintained classic cars and trucks lined the rows closest to the ticket booth. People sat in folded chairs under umbrellas or stood talking to one another nearby. Their expressions emanated the same satisfaction and pride she'd seen on Dillon's face countless times as he worked on one of his "babies."

Children should be treated this well, she thought as she passed the polished metal bodies that sparkled as radiantly as the sets of silver in her father's mansion. If parents spent as much time with their children as these owners obviously spent on their vehicles, kids would never know loneliness.

The train of thought led to Kara. How much love and attention did she receive, given that her parents were dead? Jess shook her head when she immediately realized she could ask the same thing about TJ. Did the eleven years separating them mean the pain of such a devastating turn of events had impacted TJ any less than it did Kara? She doubted it. The difference was Kara had someone to care for her. TJ had stepped into the role of guardian, taking on the significant responsibility at a young age. What toll was it exacting?

TJ worked hard, somehow managing to attend a demanding graduate program and care for her sister at the same time. A pang of guilt made Jess's stomach clench. Why had Kara invited her? Shouldn't just the two of them spend this day together? Their one-on-one time together was limited. Jess was intruding. As she considered heading back to her car, she saw TJ and Kara waiting for her near the gate. Kara raised a crutch to draw her attention.

Once TJ caught sight of her, confusion registered on her face. TJ spoke into Kara's ear, but Kara's smile didn't change and her gaze didn't waver. TJ's elbow quickly jabbed into Kara's side, though she smiled politely.

Too late to turn around, Jess approached. TJ wore a black polo shirt and charcoal jeans that clung to her like honey on a spoon. The shirt was open at the collar, the sleeves stopping where her defined triceps began. Her large silver watch provided exactly enough jewelry to give her a slightly feminine air. It annoyed Jess the way stylish Hollywood power celebrities did—they were so damn perfect, you could never measure up. How could something as plain as a polo shirt and jeans make TJ look delectable? Cotton-mouthed, Jess was grateful she could still speak. "Hey, guys," she said. Maybe this wasn't such a good idea.

Reaching into her jeans pocket, Kara retrieved a ticket and offered it to Jess. "Thanks for introducing me to Dillon."

Jess reached for her purse and sought her wallet. "Don't be silly. There's no need to thank me for—" TJ's hand on her wrist stopped her. "Ah ah ah. Please," TJ said.

Jess glanced between the sisters. Kara seemed so pleased at the prospect of treating her to the show, she could hardly decline. She took the proffered stub. "Thank you. Your texts made it sound as though you and TJ wanted me to join you today." Turning to TJ, she said, "But I've a feeling you weren't expecting me."

"We both wanted you to come," Kara said.

TJ cocked her head and raised her eyebrow.

"Don't give me that. Just because you didn't say anything doesn't make it untrue," Kara said. "Let's get this party started." Kara led the way, excitedly chattering about some of the cars in the winner's circle, not slowed in the least by her crutches. TJ and Jess followed.

"I think my sister's been taking lessons from your stepmother," TJ said.

"God. Don't say things like that."

TJ leaned close and whispered conspiratorially. "I think she's trying to set us up."

Jess smiled. "So I wasn't imagining you weren't expecting me?"

"No, but I'm glad you're here."

"Are you?"

"I can think of worse things than being in your company."

"Flatterer."

TJ laughed. Jess loved the joyful sound and the way the skin around TJ's eyes crinkled. She wanted to make TJ laugh time and again. Seeing her carefree and happy felt as good as a hug from an old friend.

"You want to tell her the rules, Kare?" TJ asked.

Jess pretended to be more interested in the surrounding spectacle than her colleague. "Rules?"

"More like games, really," Kara clarified. "Pick your favorites. Like, pick your favorite date-mobile, outfit, artery-hardener, date, etcetera. You have to say your reasons and we all vote."

"Date-mobile?" Jess asked.

TJ chimed in. "You know, like Greased Lightning. Usually something with bench seats. Something good for, you know, necking."

Jess laughed. "Necking? That's still a word?"

"Lame," Kara said.

"Oh, and making out makes more sense? At least necking gives you the gist," TJ said.

"Favorite date?" Jess asked, not wanting to think about necking with TJ so close.

"Checking out the crowd and picking the person you'd want to take home if you could." Kara's expression turned thoughtful. "In your case, I guess that could be anybody."

Jess offered an amused smile. Seemed Kara was operating under the assumption that Jess was interested in men and women alike. Maybe she was. "I'd like to think I'm a little more selective than merely checking for a pulse."

Kara shrugged. "Sorry. Sometimes I think out loud. None of my business. You can be straight, gay, bi, pan, ace, label-less, whatever.

My school has all kinds. Personally I think it'd be cool to work a larger section of the spectrum, but it's not really up to us, is it?"

How did a sixteen-year-old know this stuff? "You're way more ahead of the game than I was at your age," Jess said.

Kara nodded at TJ. "That's what she's always saying."

TJ said to Jess, "You have no idea. Light-years."

Jess addressed Kara. "I take that back. You're way more ahead of the game than I am now."

Kara used a crutch to point to an extremely muscular, heavily tattooed, early twenty-something man wearing a baseball cap and a wife-beater. "My vote so far for favorite date, though I reserve the right to change my mind."

Jess nodded. "He's pretty hot."

TJ rolled her eyes, but the sparkle in her eyes gave away how much she was enjoying herself.

Kara smiled. "I think I'm going to like this year's judges." She ambled away on her crutches.

"So am I," TJ said before following her sister. And as TJ did so, the thought flitted across Jess's mind that she wouldn't mind spending more than an afternoon with these two.

CHAPTER TWELVE

The invitation arrived via courier, and the receptionist carried it back to TJ's desk. It was beautiful, wrapped with a satin bow and made of thick paper stock. A tiny red-and-white origami sailboat fell onto the desk as she opened it. With a gray-and-black raised border and a small red image of a cocktail glass, it was elegant yet whimsical. It was official: Muriel Manchester had invited her and a guest for a sunset cruise on Saturday.

The other thing that was official: TJ would be completely out of her element. If Derrick Spaulding's party had taught her anything, it was that she fit in with the rich set like almonds in a Mounds bar. The only thing she had in common with them was a love of good coffee, proven by her affair with Magnate's espresso machine. She'd already done her part to help Magnate win over Muriel. Why continue pretending Magnate's people were any more different than slices in a loaf of Wonder Bread?

But it gnawed at TJ to throw her hands up. She'd worked hard to arrive at the place she was in her life and didn't walk away from a challenge. Waitressing meant dealing with folks up and down the socioeconomic ladder. There wasn't much a person could throw at her that she hadn't already seen in some capacity. Her goal to one day head her own nonprofit meant she'd have to court the one percent—the small number of Americans who control nearly half its wealth. Perhaps she should consider the invitation a training ground.

She stared at her laptop screen. Inspiration on planning the city-treasurer event had been sporadic, though she'd made progress. It had become a little more fun once she imagined the guests as a roomful of people wearing Pee Wee Herman costumes, holding an abacus in one hand and a glass of prune juice in the other. Jess was right. TJ had been stereotyping. She knew as little about government financial officers as she did about the uber wealthy, and she wasn't proud of herself for her presumptions. She didn't appreciate when people put her in a box based on her address, clothes, or sexual orientation. She'd learned from waitressing that you couldn't tell what kind of tipper someone would be from what they wore, their accent, or how much they chatted you up. You could only start to tell once they showed attitude or couldn't have their persnickety requests met, and even those hints weren't foolproof.

Why had she reverted to compartmentalizing people she didn't know? The thought brought her back to her conversation with Jess the day they met, when Jess had asked if she'd nix dates because they earned too much. Most people would do the opposite and ax dates because of poor prospects. Leave it to Jess to call her out on it. She chuckled at the memory.

"What's got you in such a good mood?" TJ turned to see Jess leaning against TJ's cubicle wall. "Hmm?" Her playful expression changed once she spotted the invitation on TJ's desk.

"I was thinking about you, actually." TJ glanced at the computer clock and stood. "Eleven twenty. You're here early." TJ smiled. Jess had remained true to her word, ensuring TJ stayed busy with honest-to-goodness work that kept TJ on a steep learning curve, but she continued to maintain minimal office hours. Knowing Jess was putting in significant time elsewhere and was available via phone at any time, TJ no longer cared. Jess gave TJ complete access to her during the short time she came in each day, and it was plenty helpful.

"Had to check on you. If you have any questions, come on in." Jess headed to her office and TJ followed, invitation in hand.

"I do." TJ sat in the guest chair and slid the paper to Jess.

Jess scanned the card and returned it. "Not surprising. I saw her speaking with you at the party."

"What's your take on it?"

"Muriel has a reputation as something of a lothario. I imagine she's invited you because she's interested. Maybe you can be the first to tame her." TJ hadn't heard this caustic tone since her first, disastrous week at the firm.

"I never said I was interested."

"You didn't have to. Muriel Manchester's hard to resist. The media's tied her to some of the most beautiful women in the world. She's smart, attractive, rich, and influential. You could do worse."

This was unexpected. Jess had made no bones about the reason TJ had been invited to Derrick's party. But this went well beyond trying to show Muriel another side of Magnate. TJ worked there as openly lesbian and as such, knowing Jess had no issues with it and no one else seemed to, hadn't minded playing the part. But this was far more than taking one for the team. Magnate employees had no business interfering with TJ's personal life.

"I'm not asking your opinion on my love life. I want to know if *the firm* has any particular stance on my attendance at the *event* since the card arrived *here*. If the firm considers this a strictly social engagement, I don't need your input."

Jess took a deep breath and closed her eyes. When she opened them, her expression softened, as did her tone, which immediately settled TJ down. "This isn't a Magnate-sponsored event. It's a personal invitation to you from someone who happens to be of interest to the firm. You've already gone over and above what any employer could rightfully expect of you. I want you to do what's right for you."

It was the professional thing for Jess to say, but something felt off. Jess had been so cheerfully welcoming mere moments before. Now she was all business. "What is it about this that's bothering you?" TJ asked.

Jess offered one of her infuriatingly polite half-smiles TJ had come to know as a veneer. "Not a thing. From Magnate's standpoint, we wanted Muriel to notice we'd actually hired someone who wasn't a straight white male, and we succeeded. Your invitation's a testament to the effort you made with Dr. Stanfield."

More slick words that sounded hollow to TJ. Something was eating at Jess. "You don't like her," TJ said.

"TJ, stop fishing. Muriel and I aren't friends, but we certainly aren't enemies. I've known her for years through my parents' functions. I've nothing but respect for her. She's a straight shooter who doesn't suffer fools gladly. I think you'd enjoy her company." She raised a palm. "And please don't take offense at that. It's not an endorsement or recommendation. I'm not trying to steer you in a particular direction."

Perhaps it was the resignation in Jess's tone that signaled she was withholding some key piece of information. TJ tried a different angle. "It could be good for me, getting more comfortable with people of her caliber in terms of money and power."

"I agree."

"It could also be excruciating. She could have country music piped in through the sound system, and I'd be a prisoner with no escape except to jump ship."

Jess lips curled up at TJ's hyperbole. "Can you swim?"

"I can."

"Then you'll be fine."

"Somehow I get the sense you're not concerned for my safety. This could be death by Olivia Cruise."

Jess didn't appear troubled by the prospect. "The only risk you face on Muriel's boat is catching flies because your mouth will be agape at all the beautiful women surrounding you."

"A lesbian Hugh Hefner? Dear God, why invite me?" TJ rolled her eyes before taking note of the change in Jess's expression. "What? I know what agape means. You don't have to demonstrate."

"You're not serious," Jess said.

"Yes, I really do know what it means."

"About why she invited you."

"No clue."

"She invited you because she enjoys surrounding herself with extremely attractive women, especially—though not exclusively—those that play for her team. *That* is why she invited you."

Unsure of how to respond, TJ sat quietly. Did Jess really think she was attractive?

"If I knew all it took was a compliment to get you to pipe down, I'd make an audio file full and play them for you on an endless loop," Jess said.

Was it possible the change in Jess's demeanor at seeing the invitation was due to jealousy? Did Jess think Muriel was actually interested in her? TJ didn't have high hopes Jess was starting to feel more for her than she did toward any other colleague, but the idea intrigued her. And TJ wasn't the type to use one woman in order to gain another's attention. She preferred a more honest approach.

"Come on the cruise with me." TJ said. "Be my plus-one."

"If Muriel meant for a Spaulding to come, she'd have invited one."

"I'm inviting one."

"You'd be too polite to leave my side for any stretch because you'd want to make sure I was having a good time. If you want to get to know Muriel, perhaps attend by yourself."

I want to get to know *you*. "You give me too much credit. I might ditch you at the first sign of one of the luscious ladies you insist will be milling about, hopefully all bikini-clad and single." TJ waggled her eyebrows to communicate she was being purposely absurd.

"And in four-inch heels, no doubt."

"A spectacle you simply have to see. As Kara would say, it'll be epic."

"Wow. It sounds so...appall—appealing."

"You'll come?"

Jess's face crinkled into a wince as if she were preparing to offer her regrets.

Before Jess could decline, TJ said, "Think about Magnate. If I go by myself, it says nothing about the firm. If I go with you, she'll know there's at least one Spaulding who's not afraid to be the minority in a sea of lesbians. If you want to start chipping away at her misperceptions of Magnate's staffing practices, join me."

After some hesitation, Jess said, "All right. Now, shall we get to work?"

TJ nodded but made no attempt to leave. "What are you working on?"

Jess raised an eyebrow.

It was now or never. TJ hadn't been brave enough to broach the subject of Jess's Magnate endeavors while they were out enjoying the sunshine, fresh air, and overt sexism of yesterday's car show, but she hadn't gotten the subject out of her head either. Once home, she and Kara had discussed ways to get Jess to come clean, but because TJ preferred a far more direct approach than anything Kara suggested, they'd stopped batting ideas around.

Deciding to take the plunge and see where it led, TJ said, "I realize I've never asked. You've been giving me special projects and teaching me a lot, but I haven't worked on anything you're working on."

"I'm a Spaulding. I don't have to work on anything."

"Perhaps not. But you do. Can I help?"

Jess's jaw tightened. "Our deal was to teach you what I know. Am I not living up to my promise?"

"Very much so. But I—"

"If there's nothing else?"

TJ was being dismissed. She hadn't wanted to make Jess uncomfortable. She wasn't sharing Jess's secret but wanted her to know she had someone to confide in, if she so chose. "There is one more thing." TJ fortified herself with a deep breath. "Kara and I discussed ways in which we could get you to admit you're sharper than you let on. I'm sorry if that stings, but it's the truth. I realized if there's something I want to know about you, I should ask. I know you work hard for this firm. I don't know why you hide it, but there you go. I hope one day you'll let me in, and I hope you know I would never betray your confidence."

TJ exited quickly, upset by her dispassionate tone when she was anything but indifferent. Seeing Jess's trembling chin made TJ's heart clench. She wanted to go to Jess, wrap her arms around her and tell her she cared, tell her she didn't have to hide. But the next step was up to Jess. It was Jess's secret to maintain or share as she saw fit. All TJ could do was be honest and respect Jess's privacy.

Moments later, Jess left the building.

CHAPTER THIRTEEN

Tuesday came and went without word from Jess. TJ was grateful to be buried by the city-treasurer project. It helped take her mind off Jess. But whenever her thoughts strayed, they landed squarely on her colleague.

Had she been right to call Jess out on her facade? Unless Jess was straying from their agreement regarding the internship, it wasn't any of her business. But even that wasn't accurate. Jess was becoming her business because TJ cared.

Wednesday afternoon, Jess was back at Magnate and went straight to TJ's desk. "Are you at a stopping point?"

TJ turned to her and felt her face light up. "I can be. What's up?"

"Field trip."

"I don't know. My boss is pretty strict."

"She won't notice. Grab your things. You're not returning today, and you'll be home in plenty of time before Kara gets off work."

The drive was a silent one. TJ was excited yet anxious, unsure where they were heading but relieved Jess was still talking to her. She hoped Jess was taking her to wherever it was she did her Magnate work. TJ wanted to get a sense of the place that inspired Jess to accomplish so much on a daily basis. Part of her hoped seeing it would give her a better sense of what made Jess tick. Another part wanted Jess to acknowledge her role in Magnate's success.

They pulled into an underground parking structure next to the tallest building along the Montgomery Hills shoreline. Jess left the car with a valet, and TJ followed as she strode to the elevator. They rode two floors up, exited at street level, rounded the corner to another bank of elevators, and took one to the top floor. Upon exiting, Jess walked down the hallway to a door she opened with a key card. She pushed it open and inclined her head, allowing TJ to enter first.

What TJ saw took her breath away. "Oh, Jess." Two levels of floor-to-ceiling windows provided unobstructed views of the Pacific Ocean. A monitor sat atop a simple, modern desk that faced the windows. Off to the side was a seating area with a bar counter that shared the lower half of the same view. Above it was a bedroom she couldn't see much of. A contemporary kitchen with white cabinets and black granite countertops was on the same floor as the office, and in what TJ suspected was supposed to be the dining room lay a larger version of the putting green Jess had in her office at Magnate. "You really do golf," TJ said.

"Actually, I don't. I need to get up and stretch throughout the day, and putting is a great way to very quickly get my mind off work for a few minutes. Meditation of sorts. Something to drink?"

"Water, please." TJ stood in front of one of the many windows and took in the view. The sun's angle should have made it tough on her eyes, but some sort of UV tinting on the glass protected the unit from the light's intensity. A glass of water moved into her peripheral vision. Jess was at her side. "Thank you." TJ took a healthy drink. "I'm sorry if I pressured you."

Jess laughed. "No, you're not."

"I won't lie. I'm interested in finding out more about you, but honestly not at the expense of taking you out of your comfort zone. You work *somewhere*, that much is obvious."

"Obvious? I've been at Magnate since I graduated from college, and you're the first to make the connection."

"I'm the first who's been forced on you like a barnacle. My question is why."

"You know as well as I the circumstances of your internship."

"I know why I've been forced on you. My question is why do you hide how smart you are?"

Jess walked to an area of the loft where four bar stools were placed beneath a counter that overlooked the expanse of ocean below. She pulled out a stool and sat, then indicated that TJ follow suit.

"I was asked to," Jess said.

"I don't understand."

"When I was in ninth grade, a national math competition was held the same night as our homecoming dance. My teacher told me I had a solid chance of winning my age group because I tested far above my grade level. When I chose to attend the competition instead of the dance, the friends in my clique told me I was more interested in formulas than boys, and they abandoned me.

"I was a wreck. My newly minted stepmother told me their reactions were understandable and that my priorities were wrong. She said it was unbecoming for girls to compete against boys and that I was damaging my stepbrother Gary's ego because I was way ahead of him in math and science even though he's two years older.

"My stepmother told me to 'dumb it down' and enrolled me in innumerable classes that had nothing to do with smarts and everything to do with perception. I learned how to walk, talk, flirt, entertain, and still my tongue at every sexist, racist, classist, homophobic remark uttered by the people within my socioeconomic status.

"Aside from Dillon, you're the only person who knows any of this. At the office, no one expects anything from me. In truth, I work seven days a week. I singlehandedly run marketing for a multi-billion-dollar enterprise and am treated as though I sell lemonade curbside for five cents a glass."

TJ tried to process it all. She hadn't known what to expect, but this certainly wasn't it.

"You're shaking your head," Jess said.

TJ didn't understand. Jess and Derrick were close. Jess revered the man. Why would he acquiesce to a plan desiring Jess to be anything less than she was capable of? It was the opposite from what her own father had done, urging TJ to be every bit as much as she could be. Fearing any negative comments about Derrick would push Jess away, TJ asked, "Doesn't it bother you? Letting people think you're only on payroll because of nepotism?"

Jess shook her head. "It used to. But it was worth it to me not to make waves between me and my stepmother. Daddy was devastated when Mom died and threw himself into work. When Lilith came along, he got a spring back in his step. I'd almost forgotten what he was like when he was happy. So when she mandated how I was to behave, it was easiest to comply, though I always hoped he would stand up for me."

"But at what cost to you?" For the first time, TJ compared people's misperceptions and prejudices regarding gays to her own regarding the wealthy. It was common to hear stories about judgmental people condemning gays for their "sins" and "lifestyle" until they actually met a gay person. Then they understood that the world wouldn't end simply because not everyone was heterosexual and that people should be judged by their actions, not their labels. Now that she'd befriended an extremely wealthy woman, TJ realized she was as guilty of having preconceived, erroneous notions as anyone else. Rich people had their own troubles; having money was not a panacea.

"I made a choice rendering that question moot," Jess said.

"What choice?"

Jess walked to the wet bar, poured herself a cocktail, and took a sip as if fortifying herself. "When I was a senior in high school, Dillon wanted us to build a life together. When I told my dad and stepmother I wasn't going to college, that I was going to marry Dillon, Lilith flipped. Dillon didn't come from a family that met her stringent requirements of a suitable husband, and it was inconceivable that I not attend college. She didn't care that I *learned* anything there, mind you, but a child of Derrick Spaulding's having merely a high school diploma was unthinkable. So she made me choose. I could either go to college or I could marry Dillon, in which case she would ensure I was cut off from my family's fortune." She took another sip before facing TJ squarely, raising her chin as if preparing herself for a dressing down.

"I chose the money. I wasn't willing to give up the creature comforts I'd grown accustomed to for an uncertain future with someone who loved me for exactly who I was, not who I pretended to be. I wasn't willing to leave my father behind, and Lilith promised she'd do everything possible to ensure that's exactly what would happen. I couldn't believe he'd acquiesce and cut me off financially or emotionally, but it didn't matter. I didn't want a life like you've had, TJ, where you've toiled for everything you've gotten. I took the easy way out. I chose the money.

"So you see, the question of the cost to me is irrelevant. I made my choice. Her world. Her rules. Her money."

"It's unconscionable that she made you choose between your family and Dillon."

"It's unconscionable that I chose my bank balance. You never would have done that."

"Far more than money was at stake. You had your whole family to consider."

Jess shrugged as if she didn't believe it.

"You were seventeen. That's not a decision anyone should have to make at any age, but certainly not seventeen."

"If it were you, you would have—"

"Don't. I haven't walked in your shoes. We don't know what I would have done."

"I do." Jess swirled her drink and stared into it as if it held answers. She set it down without taking a sip and faced TJ squarely, self-reproach written across her face. "You wouldn't have let money influence your decision."

"I've never had enough for it to matter." TJ ran her hand through her hair. "Jess, money isn't everything, but it's something. You can't blame yourself for taking it into consideration. You were put in an impossible situation and did the best you could."

"How can you say that? You've seen how I am. I always choose me."

TJ took Jess's hand and smiled. "You had your father's happiness in mind. And by continuing this charade, you still do. You helped us keep our health care when I didn't deserve it. You helped Kara get a job she loves. The other night, you left a party to make sure I had a ride home. You're not a selfish woman, Jess. You're bright, beautiful, and benevolent." TJ pulled her hand away because of what she was about to say. "I'm sorry to say this, but your family should support you. You should be praised for your brilliance, not chided for it, not hidden away. You shouldn't have to pretend you're something you're not, because what you are is pretty special."

Jess gazed at TJ with an unreadable expression, and TJ grew increasingly anxious about the words she'd uttered. She didn't want Jess to mistake her earnest comments as a come-on. Her attraction to Jess was burgeoning, but Jess was her colleague. More than that, she was her boss.

Then TJ saw the misting in Jess's eyes. She needed to apologize, but she wasn't sure Jess was disturbed by hearing potentially sexually harassing words or hurt by her reproach of Jess's family. Before she could respond, Jess took her hand.

"You're kind to say so," Jess said, rubbing the back of TJ's hand with her thumb. She dropped her focus to their joined hands, then brought her other hand into the mix and continued to gently stroke TJ's. Her hand stilled, and she let TJ go before rising and heading for her keys. Whatever Jess was thinking, she was keeping it to herself. "I'll take you home," Jess said as she tucked her purse under her arm.

"Thank you for bringing me here and sharing this part of you."

Jess nodded sadly, as if she'd been offered condolences instead of thanks.

TJ sensed Jess's unease but didn't understand its source. TJ said, "Your secret's safe with me."

"I'm certain that's true," Jess said as she opened the door, waiting for TJ to exit.

As TJ passed, she stopped in the doorway next to Jess. Attempting to lighten the mood, TJ asked, "Because you're going to tape my mouth shut?"

This remark elicited a barely perceptible upturn of Jess's lips. "There are better ways."

Standing close, TJ noticed Jess's gaze drop briefly to her mouth. TJ's belly tightened. With a short lean forward, they could be kissing. She stood still, as if in the path of an endangered animal, not wanting to frighten it away. "Better ways?"

"To keep you quiet," Jess said in a low voice.

Mouth dry as a perfect martini, TJ quietly asked, "Such as?"

Jess visibly swallowed. Light danced in her eyes, and all traces of melancholy vanished. "Tape would hurt when removed. I'd use something...softer."

Wanting Jess's mouth on hers more than she ever wanted anything, TJ's synapses misfired and her brain stopped functioning. She couldn't respond. She caught a trace of Jess's perfume and had to force herself not to sway toward its source.

"Would you like to know what it is?" Jess said above a whisper.

TJ shook her head.

"No?" Jess asked, a deliciously sexy smile on her lips.

"My imagination's doing nicely, thank you," TJ said.

Jess pushed TJ out of the way so she could close the door. "So's mine."

CHAPTER FOURTEEN

The end of the week was quiet. Though Jess still came in for one to two hours daily and addressed any pressing questions TJ had on the marketing front, they kept to themselves. Gone was the easy camaraderie they'd achieved before Jess's confession.

As Saturday neared, Jess became more uncomfortable at having agreed to join TJ for Muriel's sunset cruise. Eating became a chore, and she picked at her food disinterestedly. The idea that she might have to watch Muriel's seduction of TJ was making her sick to her stomach.

Though TJ's forgiving reaction to her admission had surprised her, she held no illusion TJ could find her remotely appealing as anything more than a friend. It saddened her to know her revelation would ruin any chance, however small, they might have had to explore something beyond friendship, but Jess wouldn't lie. Her past choices rendered her undeserving of someone with TJ's integrity, but at least she was showing TJ all her cards. She should feel grateful TJ was still offering friendship.

By the time Saturday rolled around, Jess decided to send a car for TJ versus picking her up herself. Jess wasn't up for one-on-one time during the ride to the harbor. She needed to save the happy-go-lucky energy for the actual cruise.

Jess stood on the dock, gazing out at the water while waiting for TJ's arrival. As guest of an invitee, she hadn't wanted to board the vessel without the half named on the invitation. Try as she might, Jess couldn't stay focused on the fact that she was here as a Magnate envoy. Beautiful woman after beautiful woman boarded the yacht, and none held her attention. All she could think about was TJ, the only woman who'd ever stirred any kind of arousal within her.

"Fancy meeting you here," the familiar voice said from behind.

Jess turned to see TJ smiling at her. TJ had paired one of the vests Renee had selected for her with a white, long-sleeve shirt, cuffs rolled close to her elbows. The shirt fell untucked just over her jeans, and she looked fantastic. "Small world," Jess rejoined, wishing she could slide her hands beneath TJ's shirt.

"Where's your helmet and body armor?" TJ asked. "In that sundress, you're going to need something to keep the lesbians at bay."

Jess took TJ's arm and started walking them to the ship. "Isn't that what you're here for? To protect my virtue?"

TJ laughed and covered Jess's hand with hers. "As if I had a chance."

The rebuttal confused Jess. If she received so much as a smile or nod from another woman during the entire cruise, she'd be shocked. It wasn't as if TJ was going to have to intervene on her behalf. As they approached the gangplank, Jess asked, "A chance with what?"

Eyes twinkling, TJ said, "A chance with you."

The statement compounded Jess's confusion. Was TJ being serious? Or was she merely being playful?

With an exaggerated bow, TJ extended her hand in front of Jess in an invitation to step onto the gangplank. "After you, m'lady."

Once TJ was by her side, Jess again took her elbow. She considered her options. As hard as it would be to watch Muriel's overtures with TJ, at least Jess respected Muriel and understood her appeal. But if Jess were forced to observe multiple advances on TJ from the string of pretty women aboard this vessel, she might retch. Best all-around if she didn't subject herself to the experience. Jess said, "I know I'm your plus-one, but please don't feel you have to stay by my side. I'll be perfectly happy making small talk with the other guests." The lie came easily.

"The ship hasn't left port and you're already trying to ditch me?"

"I don't want you to cramp my style."

TJ laughed. "I see. Would it bother you if I stick close by? Understanding, of course, I'd merely be trying to pick up tips from a master?"

The suggestion infused Jess with a feeling of contentment she'd not encountered in months. She adored TJ's playful side. "Not at all."

Not unexpectedly, Muriel was in high demand, and it took half an hour chitchatting among her guests before she freed herself up enough to welcome them. Unfortunately from Jess's point of view, the greeting occurred while Jess was in line at one of the bars. While the bartender mixed their drinks, Jess watched as Muriel took TJ's hands, kissed her cheeks in greeting, and leaned in to whisper something in her ear. Jess's blood began to boil in a way she'd never experienced. She always thought the phrase spoke of a puerile instinct she'd never succumb to, but the cabin seemed to heat up, not at all gradual in its climb. While she flipped through murderous images involving Muriel's untimely demise, such as death by aggressive seagull, tidal wave, and giant squid, the large tentacles she imagined wrapping around Muriel and pulling her off the deck withdrew from her mind as a woman's voice said, "Excuse me."

Jess took a few seconds to focus on the gorgeous woman in front of her instead of visions of giant suction cups latching onto Muriel's body and tugging her overboard. "Hello."

The woman, who appeared to be of Italian descent with olive skin, long wavy black hair, and warm brown eyes, handed Jess two drinks. "I believe these are yours. They've been sitting here a little while, but the bartender wasn't able to get your attention. I'm Carmela, by the way." Her slight accent convinced Jess she'd guessed right about the Italian thing.

Jess took the drinks and smiled. "Jess." She held up a glass. "Thanks for these. My mind was elsewhere."

Carmela's gaze followed Jess's. "Is she with you?"

"Who, Muriel?"

"No. The young brunette."

God, how to answer this simple question? Jess's eyes wandered back to TJ and Muriel. Muriel said something that made TJ laugh, and Jess conjured another image of long tentacles reaching into the cabin to yank Muriel over the rails. Jess turned to Carmela. She could offer no reply but simply smiled.

"If you're looking for company, I'd be happy to make your acquaintance."

Was this woman flirting with her? How did women traverse this path? How could you tell if a woman was interested or merely being friendly? As flattered as Jess was to get Carmela's attention, she wasn't in the market. Not that it stopped her from slowly appraising Carmela's incredible body. Carmela's dress wasn't leaving a lot to the imagination, and Jess could definitely appreciate the sight, but it was more as if she were viewing a work of fine art. It made her ask herself what it would be like to feel TJ's skin against hers.

Realizing she was staring, Jess raised her eyes. Carmela offered a smile. "I'm all set, thank you," Jess said as she nodded and made her way over to TJ, who was watching her. Muriel was nowhere in sight.

Handing the beverage to TJ, Jess was about to ask where Muriel went off to when TJ asked, "Who's your friend?"

Jess followed TJ's gaze. "That's Carmela." She turned to TJ and asked cheerfully, "Would you like me to introduce you?" though she had no desire to initiate a meeting.

"Did she hit on you?" TJ took a sip of her drink and kept her eyes on Carmela.

"I'm not sure. I really don't know how you tell, short of something concise and obvious such as, 'Would you like to go out with me?'"

"Did she ask to spend time with you?"

Jess curled her lips with amusement. "Why? Are you jealous?"

TJ rolled her eyes. "Please."

"You are. You're jealous."

TJ slung her arm around Jess's shoulders playfully and sized up Carmela. "Pfft. Of what, her Marilyn Monroe figure and a smile that could have started the Trojan War?"

"Don't forget the sexy accent."

"Seriously?"

Jess held up two crossed fingers and bit her bottom lip in a failed attempt to keep a straight face. "Swear."

TJ removed her arm, much to Jess's disappointment. "Details," she said with a mock pout.

"That's okay, tiger. You can dance, and that's what matters."

Meeting Jess's eyes, TJ asked, "Yeah?" Gone was the kidding tone, as if TJ was really asking if she had something Jess liked.

Jess nodded. "Yeah."

Their eyes met as they sipped their drinks. Jess felt something stirring between them and wanted to explore it. But she didn't know how.

At first it appeared as though TJ would make a move, perhaps ask Jess to dance or take her on deck to enjoy the view. The moment passed.

"Where did you learn to dance, by the way?" Jess asked.

"Library."

Jess stared at her. "Your *library* offered dance lessons?"

TJ shook her head. "Video rentals. We couldn't afford live dance lessons, so I found some instructional videos. Kara and I taught ourselves. It was a cheap form of entertainment and something we could do together. Those were the days before video games and cars commanded her attention."

"Impressive."

"Not as impressive as Car-mel-a."

Jess smacked TJ playfully on the arm. "Stop. You know I only have eyes for you, tiger."

The band changed from R&B covers to the classic swing-dance tune "Mack the Knife."

"Speaking of dancing, Muriel made me promise her one. I think that's my cue." TJ set her drink down and leaned in to whisper, "Don't do anything I wouldn't do." Then she headed to the dance floor where Muriel waited with an outstretched hand.

As TJ led Muriel around the dance floor, the pang in Jess's stomach resurfaced. There was no doubt: *she* was jealous. She wanted TJ's hands on her, not on Muriel. Watching the two move together adeptly was doing nothing to mitigate the feeling. Instead of stewing, Jess decided to head to the top deck and enjoy the city lights.

The water was calm, the weather almost perfect. Now that the sun had set, there was a chill in the air, and Jess wished she'd brought a sweater. She turned slowly in a circle, taking in the views. Mindful of TJ's earliest reprimand, she tried to appreciate a panorama she'd seen a thousand times. A number of couples were sharing some quality time on deck, and Jess found herself eyeing a pretty couple who were adorable together, kissing, nipping, laughing, snuggling. She didn't usually stare, but something about these women made her gaze linger. What would TJ's lips taste like, feel like? Having had TJ's arms around her for part of the evening, she knew she enjoyed the closeness. She wished they were here as a real couple, not as colleagues trying to make an impression.

"We meet again." Jess turned to find Carmela approaching.

"Hi, Carmela. It's a lovely evening, isn't it?"

"Lovely's a perfect word for it," Carmela said without taking her eyes off Jess.

Okay. Jess was pretty sure Carmela wasn't simply being friendly. She was being hit on. She smiled, silently congratulating herself for reaching that conclusion. She found something incredibly flattering about being the object of this Italian beauty's attention and decided to let the situation run its course. TJ was otherwise occupied, and they'd come here in part to mingle.

Conversation with Carmela was easy. She was a charmer and an undeniable head-turner. The faint Italian accent didn't hurt matters. Muriel's laughter shot out in the night sky, interrupting them, and both Jess and Carmela followed the sound with their eyes. On the other side of the deck, Jess spotted Muriel with TJ. They were standing close together—too close, in Jess's opinion. Jess suddenly felt like a lobster in a heating pot. Then it was quiet, too quiet, and Jess realized Carmela had spoken. "I'm sorry. What did you say?"

"Those two." Carmela inclined her head in Muriel and TJ's direction. "You're not happy about it."

Jess watched them while she decided how to respond. She saw no reason to lie. "Not particularly, no. But it's none of my business."

"Isn't it?"

Jess slid her eyes to Carmela. "What do you mean?"

"You care about the younger brunette."

"Yes."

"But she doesn't know."

"No," Jess said.

"Tell her."

Jess laughed mirthlessly. "Carmela, if I had half your charm and looks, I might have the confidence to do just that. As it stands, I don't."

"You're as beautiful and charming as they come, but the way she looks at you, you don't need it."

"I don't understand."

"She has feelings for you. Explore it. Muriel will turn her attention elsewhere. And since I'm striking out tonight, who knows, maybe it will turn to me." Carmela leaned in and spoke softly in Jess's ear. "Bella, trust me. Go to her." She kissed Jess on the cheek. "You can thank me later. Go."

Jess fixed her gaze on TJ, who gave her a beseeching glance before refocusing on Muriel. Steeling herself with a deep breath, Jess marched over to them and extended a hand to TJ. "Excuse us, Muriel." She smiled to Muriel in part to soften the sting of the interruption and in part because it felt good to take charge.

Jess tugged on TJ's hand and led her to an empty section of the deck. Words poured out almost stream-of-consciousness. "I should say I'm sorry for interrupting. But I'm not. She's wrong for you, TJ. Sure, she might be attractive. And confident. And clever. Not to mention charismatic and interesting. Pretty wonderful sounding, actually." This was quickly spiraling off topic, and Jess felt heat in her cheeks. "Damn it. I'm not making sense. Shit. The thing is, I can't stand seeing you together."

Confusion etched across TJ's face like a cracked windshield. "You said you didn't dislike her. I thought you wanted me to mingle with her."

"I thought I did too."

"What's changed?"

Plan A wasn't working, so Jess improvised with Plan B. "This," she said as she slid her arms around TJ's waist, rose onto her toes, and kissed her.

Wide-eyed, TJ didn't move. Deer-in-headlights was not the response Jess was looking for.

Rapidly losing her nerve and thinking Plans A and B were falling into the Chevy Nova camp of bad ideas, Jess said, "Let's try this again. Put your arms around me." TJ complied. "Good." Jess moved her hands behind TJ's neck and pulled her close. "Now kiss me."

TJ's expression morphed into understanding, then into—anticipation? Initially hesitant, TJ drew closer, never taking her eyes off Jess's. The inches separating them dwindled slowly, slowly, and just before their lips touched, TJ closed her eyes.

The kiss started gently, and Jess sank into it as if edging into a hot bath, so good it was almost painful. Yet it was over all too quickly. And far too chastely for Jess's taste. Like Maria von Trapp, Jess was not cut out for the convent. She needed far more than TJ had offered. Her dismay at the prospect it had ended must have been conspicuous, quite possibly due to her vise grip around TJ's shoulders. Or perhaps it was the whimper. Because TJ, who remained inches away, quirked a brow, dropped her gaze to Jess's lips, and descended unhurriedly to capture them in a fiery kiss.

Although Jess had previously liked TJ's mouth for its expressiveness and shape, her appreciation of it was climbing precipitously. It was demanding, teasing, and marvelously skilled. She didn't care that a soft moan escaped. It wasn't as though TJ couldn't tell she was enjoying this. Their tongues explored and tantalized while their hands leisurely wandered. Had they not been in a semi-public place, Jess wouldn't have hesitated to slide a hand to one of TJ's breasts and see what it was like to touch another woman that way. As the thought took shape, she became gradually aware of the lack of privacy and pulled out of the embrace. She cupped TJ's cheek and offered another too-brief kiss.

TJ took that hand and curled it in both of hers against her chest. Their eyes searched each other as if simultaneously processing what had just happened as well as lingering as long as possible in the intimacy of the moment. Jess broke the silence. "Roshambo for who speaks first?"

The question made TJ smile, but after a quick brush of her lips to the back of Jess's hand, TJ shook her head as if to say, "Not it."

"Is that how it always feels to kiss another woman?" Jess asked.

Biting her lip as if uncertain how to respond, TJ shook her head again.

"So that was just us?"

TJ nodded.

"Well, good. I'd hate to think I was missing out on that my entire adult life when I could have grabbed any one of my friends and gone to town."

TJ laughed. "You're handling it well."

"Don't worry. I'll be up all night processing."

Stepping back as if to allow more space between them, TJ slid her hands into her pockets. "It doesn't have to be a big deal."

"True."

"At least now you can say you've kissed a woman." TJ shrugged. "Cross it off the bucket list."

"You think that's what I was doing? Ticking a box?" A prick of anger arose within Jess.

"I'm not offended." TJ appeared to take in the scenery, the twinkling city lights, and the couples dotting the perimeter, looking everywhere except at Jess. "If you ever wanted to try kissing a woman, you couldn't have picked a better atmosphere."

"You're going to go there? Completely downplay what just happened between us?" Jess was incredulous. TJ was usually the first to lose her cool whenever they argued, but Jess was doing nicely on her own, thank you very much.

"I don't want you to feel pressured into believing it was something special."

"I thought we established it was."

"It was," TJ spoke softly, her attention on the ground between them. "It is."

The quiet admission caused Jess's anger to dissipate like the air in a freshly untied balloon. She stepped toward TJ and took her hand. "Good. I want—no, I need your honesty. Is that something you can give me?"

TJ nodded.

Jess leaned close and whispered, "And something else."

"Name it."

"That mouth." Jess first pointed to TJ's lips and then her own. "Here. Now."

"Bossy," TJ murmured before doing what she was told.

As expected, Jess couldn't sleep. She felt good. She liked someone, and someone liked her. It was simple in a sixth-grade-crush kind of way, and she was okay with that. Simple lacked drama. All she could think of was reprising their roles from Hot Lesbian Kissing, Volume One.

This should be harder, moving into the realm of girl-on-girl action. Girl-on-girl action? Was she suddenly a member of a fraternity? Whatever it was called, lesbian or bisexual or gay, she was game. TJ made her feel things she'd only ever had an inkling of. Dillon had been her first love, and their relationship held a special place in Jess's heart. Attentive, fun, and faithful, he'd been her best friend first, lover second. Over time they'd learned how to please each other, Dillon an eager and giving partner, but something had eluded her.

Or was that true? It had been ten years ago. She'd been young and, she thought, in love. Why question it? Comparisons weren't helpful. They existed in romance novels with characters who *never felt that way before*. Yes, being with TJ felt wholly new and wonderful, but was part of her labeling TJ that way and telling herself she hadn't been in love in order to justify the depthless choice she'd made at seventeen?

Though she desperately wanted to be someone TJ could fall for, and all earlier signs tonight had been positive, it seemed a little too convenient to pretend TJ would overlook the kind of person Jess was. It had probably been an in-the-moment thing.

And still, the cookie jar was too close. She was susceptible to its lure. Her happiness served as an amnesiac that allowed her to ignore the differences between them, the type of people they were.

Tonight was about indulgence. It was about reaching for and drowning in the depths, breadths, and heights that poets wrote of. The heat between her and TJ had sizzled like oil in a hot pan, consuming her in the way of a wildfire through a drought-ravaged forest. She couldn't wait to once again be set aflame. And TJ's mouth. God, that mouth. She failed in her weak attempts not to let her mind wander to places that mouth could linger.

She was being ridiculous, she knew, ascribing so much to a few kisses. Yet here she was thinking of sonnets, sizzle, and sex.

Perhaps she'd have to rethink how little time she spent in the office.

CHAPTER FIFTEEN

Though thoughts of a certain blue-eyed blonde had completely dominated the rest of her weekend, TJ had awoken Monday with a clear objective: talk to Gary about being reassigned. She'd yet to get her hands on a single client record or any information related to the firm's investments, and weeks were ticking by. Jess had kept her busy with projects, and in truth she was learning a lot. Jess had turned out to be a proficient teacher, managing to provide the right level of explanation without undermining her requirement that TJ think through issues on her own.

Marketing, however, was merely a tangent of TJ's assignment, and though she'd probably learned more about the field under Jess's tutelage than during a semester in any classroom, TJ's grade depended on writing about the thing that set Magnate apart: its investment strategy.

Even if she took the tack that marketing *was* the thing that gave Magnate its edge, now that she was—what was the word? Involved with? No. Interested in?—Jess, someone could construe their relationship as giving TJ an unfair advantage over the other students, which was unacceptable. Regardless of whether TJ wrote the entire paper on her own, she was well aware of the power of perception. She would be solely responsible for what she turned in. But would this action build trust in and credibility to the MBA program? If things between Jess and her progressed, anyone could point to their relationship and turn a skeptical eye as to whether TJ had received help with the case study. Her ethics demanded she either spin down what was starting to develop between them—which she had no desire to do—or move on to the investment side of the house.

The latter was the only option. Her assignment was clear, and she was already woefully behind.

Part of her *did* want to write a marketing case study to show to the world—to show her professors, at any rate—the infrastructure and processes Jess had built. TJ was proud of Jess's work, which undeniably contributed to the success of Magnate. She wanted others to see how truly capable Jess was.

But Jess didn't want to let that secret out, and TJ wouldn't be the one to out her. It had to be Jess's decision.

Everything kept coming back to TJ needing access to the investment records.

The meeting with Gary hadn't gone well. Either he didn't understand the purpose of her internship or was refusing to grant her the access she needed to delve into the investments. In response to her request, he asked whether working with Jess was proving not to be valuable. TJ tried to explain that he misunderstood, but he didn't budge. His take on it was that either she was learning how Magnate's marketing machine ran, in which case there was no need to revise TJ's reporting structure, or she wasn't learning enough, in which case he would be discussing the matter with Jess.

As had been their routine, TJ allowed Jess, ever the late arrival, to settle in before seeking a meeting. Then TJ would knock on Jess's door frame and go over her questions or provide a status. Today, less than two minutes after Jess came in, TJ could hear her on speakerphone with Gary, who requested her in his office.

Jess disappeared for a short time before returning and shutting the door. The only time TJ had seen Jess's door closed was when the two of them met. Otherwise, Jess seemed to have an open-door policy because, in truth, no one else came to see her, so she rarely required privacy.

Minutes later, Jess's door flew open, and she strode down the hall and out of the building.

The abrupt departure left TJ to wonder what had transpired and whether it had anything to do with her earlier meeting with Gary.

At nearly four o'clock, Jess returned and stopped by TJ's desk. "Do you have a minute?"

TJ rose, followed Jess into her office, and closed the door.

Jess looked upset, as if she wanted to be anywhere but here, having this conversation.

On the edge of her chair, TJ asked, "What's wrong?"

In a tremulous voice, Jess said, "I'm sorry if I've made you uncomfortable at the office. I wish you'd have spoken with me about it first, but I understand it's probably difficult at this point."

"What are you talking about?" TJ's concern escalated.

"You wanting to change departments. If I came across too aggressively or you felt I was harassing you in any way, I'm so sorry. I really thought we were on the same page, but I'm obviously new at this and totally misread things."

"I don't understand."

"Gary told me you don't want to work with me anymore."

TJ was stunned. That wasn't even close to accurate. "I can tell Gary didn't play Telephone well as a child, because that isn't remotely what I said to him."

Jess waved her away. "I didn't mean to put you on the defensive. You feel how you feel. Rest assured, we'll have you report to Brooke or someone else as soon as possible." She stood to signal that the conversation was over.

TJ wouldn't be so easily dismissed. "Jess, I don't know what Gary told you. I approached him this morning and asked to be given access to the investment records and managers because my *assignment* is to write a business case study on what differentiates Magnate from its competitors. To me, that means using the single most important metric in the industry: investment returns."

Jess was unmoved.

"Please sit down. You're making me nervous." When Jess didn't sit, TJ tried again. "Please." Jess reluctantly sat, and TJ continued. "It's not to say there aren't other important aspects of the business, aspects it's also clearly succeeding at, such as all you're accomplishing on the marketing front. But the focus of my internship is clear. I'm here to write a case study on what differentiates Magnate from the rest of the players. I haven't seen a single analyst opinion or been allowed to view the investments underlying the client accounts. I didn't ask to be reassigned away from you so much as I asked to be assigned to whoever can help me achieve my goal."

It took Jess several moments to digest this information. "Your graduate program sets the focus of your internship, not the business you intern at?"

"That's right."

"Magnate has no discretion when it comes to what you'll learn here?"

"All the businesses that agreed to sponsor the inaugural class have to adhere to the same general curriculum so it's fair to all students. Not every student is interning at an investment firm, for example, but each business excels at something in particular. The interns are required to identify it and document that factor extensively."

"Then why did you tell Gary you needed to transfer out of marketing regardless of whether he agreed to give you access to the investment files?"

"Because I..." She stopped and took a deep breath. The office seemed an inappropriate venue in which to be admitting this. Though no one but Jess could hear, TJ lowered her voice. "I was hoping to see you again. In a non-professional capacity."

It was Jess's turn to be confused, given her creased brow and cocked head.

"Jess, if we continue to see each other, any paper I turn in related to Magnate's marketing could be seen as being unduly influenced or possibly exclusively written by you. Even if we don't, anyone on Muriel's yacht could decide to call into question whether the material I turn in is completely my own. The risk is negligible, but my actions need to engender confidence in your father's MBA program, not undermine it. So, yes, I asked Gary if I could report to someone else."

Jess blinked the way a seventies computer console might as it processed information. "You want to see me outside of work?"

If not for the change that overcame Jess's expression—like a child in time-out who'd just been offered a cookie—TJ might have been irritated to have to repeat herself. But Jess looked so completely adorable, TJ had to smile. "If you're amenable."

Jess nodded, her eyes shy and hopeful. "A date?"

"Yes." TJ felt her face fall. "No."

"No?" Jess asked, her expression mirroring TJ's.

"Oh, Jess. I don't know. It wouldn't—couldn't be anything like you're used to."

"That might be the point."

"The thing is, this is going to sound incredibly miserly, but can we set a budget? You have so much, and I...I can't afford the kinds of—"

"Say no more. I understand. Really, I do." Her eyes misted.

TJ grew worried. "I didn't mean to offend you. I know I shouldn't be concerned by our differences, but I am."

"I know, and I'm not offended. You caught me by surprise is all. In a good way. We're going to rock this town without so much as an ATM card in our pockets."

"Yeah?" TJ asked hopefully.

"Leave it to me."

TJ smiled. "You're the boss."

"Glad you recognize your place," Jess said with a wink. "Now that that's settled, here's the thing. Gary's not budging. You're to stick with marketing even if you were to report to someone else. He's concerned your report could compromise our market edge." She held up a palm to stop TJ's protest. "I don't agree with him. It runs contrary to our role as mentor, trying to help you succeed. And none of the businesses would underwrite the internships if their intellectual property were at risk. It would undermine the program."

Pulling out a sticky note, Jess wrote two lines and handed it to TJ, pointing as she spoke. "This is the network folder where the investment program and client database reside. And this is a password. Use Gary's email as the login. If you can't get in, swap a two for the one, then try a three, etcetera. When the system forces him to change his password, he appends it with a new number and then starts over once the system no longer remembers the earliest one."

"I don't want to run afoul of the end-user license," TJ said.

"Of course you don't. But Magnate owns the software outright. It's our proprietary system."

"Don't you have a login?"

"No. My job's to bring people to the firm, not manage their investments. That's for the associates and analysts. I only know Gary's because he uses the name of his first dog as his password for everything." Jess rolled her eyes.

TJ hesitantly took the paper. "Are you sure?"

"TJ, until today, I had no idea you had a specific assignment. I thought you'd decided to write your case study on marketing. Gary balked when I told him we should transfer you to the investment team like you wanted, so please don't share with anyone that I've given you file access. I have no idea how helpful our database will be to you without someone to train you on it, but hopefully you'll find something you can use."

❖

Once Jess turned onto Mountain Avenue, TJ asked, "We're going to GU?" Griffin University was where she was studying for her degree. Jess cast TJ a sideways glance. "We are."

"Are we here to study?"

"In a matter of speaking."

At the guard kiosk, Jess handed over her driver's license and a GU ID card.

"You're an alum?" TJ asked.

With a wink, Jess said, "No. Family discount."

"Ah." Given that one of the university's graduate programs was in Derrick Spaulding's name, TJ understood the perk. In all likelihood, as a member of a family that had donated millions to the university, Jess had access to every nook and cranny of its hallowed grounds and halls.

"Don't go thinking you know what you're in for, because I assure you, you don't." Jess stuffed her identification cards back into her purse and accelerated.

"I'm with you. Surprises are the norm."

Jess parked in one of the staff lots at the Performing Arts section of campus. She pulled an insulated carrier from the trunk and headed up the walking path. "Follow me."

Winded after climbing the many steps to the top of the hill, they stopped and caught their breath. "Hear that?" Jess asked as their breathing returned to normal.

"Piano?"

"*Eine kleine Nachtmusik.*" Jess paused to listen. "Not that piece specifically, but that's what we're here for: a little night music. Come on." Jess headed for a set of small cabin-size buildings that rested on the path's decline. She stopped at a picnic table several yards from the first cabin. "Have you been here?" At TJ's head shake, Jess said, "These are piano practice rooms. Anyone can come here to play." She waved TJ over to sit next to her. "The soundproofing's good but far from perfect. If you're in a room, you can't hear much on the outside. But if you're outside, you can get a flavor for the musician. Occasionally, one will invite me in to listen."

The person in the room closest was practicing scales. Jess started down the path and stopped outside the second cabin. No sound emanated from its walls, and the darkened skylight in the angled roof indicated it was empty.

As they made their way still lower, TJ began to hear another piano. It was subtle, as if a sea of pillows surrounded the instrument. The pianist was well into whatever song it was, as far as TJ could tell. Jess's eyes grew wide, and she covered her mouth before excitedly pointing to TJ to sit on the picnic-table bench outside the small building.

The music was magnificent. TJ couldn't imagine that a student's hands were bringing the piece to life. Surely this had to be some sort of maestro? TJ was familiar with the music but didn't know its title or composer.

When the piece concluded, silence again filled the night sky except for faint notes echoing from the other piano rooms. "That was sublime," TJ said, not sure why she whispered. With whatever insulation was built into the rooms, it seemed no one but Jess might hear her for miles.

"*Liebestraum* by Franz Liszt. Gorgeous."

"Do you know who's playing?" TJ asked.

Jess shook her head. "I rarely do. We got very lucky tonight. It's a crapshoot. But that's part of what makes it unique and satisfying. Listening to someone play such a beautiful piece so gloriously is wonderful, but I also enjoy hearing various skill levels. There's something about the process I find intriguing. Someone is always coming to it fresh, hoping to play like that one day. And I love the optimism inherent in that, the belief that someday, they will." Jess's eyes again widened and she pantomimed her request for silence. She whispered in TJ's ear. "Bach's *Prelude in C Major*." She put her hand over her chest and closed her eyes.

The wishful melody combined with the rise and fall of Jess's chest reminded TJ of the preciousness of life. This was a moment and a woman she wouldn't soon forget.

Once the song ended, Jess flipped her legs over the bench seat and rose from the table. "Come on," she said as she strapped the bulky bag over her shoulder and led TJ down a different footpath. "Time to work for your dinner."

Jess reached for TJ's hand and held it as they walked across campus.

"You seem surprisingly comfortable with the whole holding-hands-with-a-girl thing," TJ said.

Smiling, Jess said, "I'm comfortable with you."

With their arms swinging back and forth with each step, TJ reveled in the simplicity of Jess's statement. There was no drama, which was odd considering the class differential between them. Shouldn't there be drama? She shook her head in mystification and mirrored Jess's smile. Oddly, she was comfortable too.

"I've never walked through this part of campus," TJ said. "I didn't know any of this existed."

"Then I've a good chance of surprising you." Jess pulled open a heavy door. TJ could immediately hear the hustle and bustle of activity inside. A sharp crack to her left caught her attention, and she immediately recognized the sound. The nearby pool tables confirmed her suspicion. Several dartboards lined the walls and most were being used. They were in the corner of a warehouse-size room. Ping-Pong, foosball, and indoor shuffleboard tables rounded out the gaming activity TJ could see. She followed Jess to a counter serviced by a student.

Jess slid her GU ID card to the clerk and asked for darts. They were directed to one of two open dart lanes, where Jess promptly set down her carrier at a round bar table. "We'll start here, and if you can't stand the heat, we can move on to a different game. Once you beg for mercy, we'll grab dinner."

At the line, Jess threw her first set of darts. The first two landed just outside the outer bull's-eye, and the last landed inside the triple ring. She pulled them from the board and handed them to TJ with a wink. "Good luck, tiger."

Competitive energy surged through TJ as she took the proffered weapons, though she hadn't played in years. Her first two throws hit the flat-tire area next to the numbers. Her final throw struck just inside the double ring. As she handed the darts to Jess, she asked, "How do you know about this place?"

"As you know, my dad's a GU grad. He loves the campus. I can't tell you how many times he's given me the grand tour." Jess let fly three zingers. Two outer bull's-eyes and a small pie later, it was TJ's turn. While TJ took hers, Jess said, "I can be anonymous here. Students come to the game room to burn off steam and socialize. It's not really a pick-up joint, and since there's a large grad-student population here, no one questions my age. Or my bank-account balance."

Appalled at her showing, TJ quickly plucked the darts from the board and relinquished them to Jess. She took small consolation that she hadn't yet thrown wildly enough to hit the wall. She was outmatched. "Do they usually?"

"My most popular attribute is my wealth. Type Jessica Spaulding into any browser address bar, and you'll see the search-term suggestions append my name with the words wealth, assets, or rich, indicating what people typically search for." Jess hit the bull's-eye and grinned. "Here I'm just Jess." Another two small pies later and TJ again took the darts.

"Well, Just Jess, I only have one thing to say to that." To TJ's chagrin, her next dart hit the wall. "Let's not keep score."

❖

"Almost there," Jess said as they strolled hand in hand to the soccer field. Though the sky was bright, it wasn't until they passed the lower dormitories that the grounds opened up like an Ansel Adams photograph. The moon was nearly full, a one-eyed sentry that seemed twice its normal size as it hung above the Pacific Ocean and illuminated the grassy hill below.

TJ stopped, mesmerized. "No wonder you come here."

"Not too shabby, is it?" Jess tugged TJ's hand. "Come on. It's just as beautiful from over here." Jess led them to the field before setting down the insulated bag. She withdrew a blanket from an outside mesh pocket and fanned it out for them to sit on. Then she removed two covered containers and handed one to TJ along with utensils. A half bottle of champagne was next, and Jess set up a small stand designed to steadily hold two flutes on uneven ground. With a pop, the bottle opened and Jess poured.

"This is where most of my budget went," she said as she handed TJ a glass. "Life's too short for bad champagne. Or plasticware." Raising her glass, she said, "Thanks for joining me tonight."

"Thanks for inviting me. I'll never think of GU the same way." They clinked rims and sipped.

Jess removed the lid on her container and nodded to TJ's food. "Mixed greens with figs and a raspberry vinaigrette, sesame-crusted mahi-mahi with toasted coconut, garlic-ginger green beans. You'll notice it's a fairly light dinner because we're saving room for dessert, my favorite part of any meal." She wagged her eyebrows and took a bite of salad.

TJ surveyed the contents of her bowl and slid Jess a wary gaze. "This isn't exactly Swanson's."

"I don't know what that means, but don't give me that look. I'll have you know these are all leftovers. Nothing here was made specifically for our date, so I'm not counting it against my budget. And the flutes will return to my bar."

"These leftovers are nicer than anything you can get at Zelda's."

Jess set her hand on TJ's forearm. "TJ, at Donatello's, you rightfully chastised me for not appreciating the experience. Don't make my mistake. Look around us. Take in that view. Enjoy this wonderfully warm weather and the smell of the grass. Listen. Hear that? Birds. Crickets. Laughter. Savor each bite of this meal. And most importantly," she lightly brushed her lips against TJ's, "be in this moment with me."

TJ blinked. Jess was right. She was in a glorious field on a gorgeous night with a beautiful woman who had painstakingly adhered to her request that they not spend an outrageous sum. It was clear Jess had given their date much consideration. Did it matter that what constituted a typical or leftover meal differed between them? "I'm here now." She leaned forward and kissed Jess. "Thanks for the reminder." Taking Jess's hand, she kissed her palm and smiled. "And for all this."

They ate in companionable silence for several minutes.

"How often do you come here?" TJ asked.

"Not very. Sometimes when I need to reconnect with my father. It's indirect, but it works. He loves this school and what it represents."

"Represents?"

"A chance for students with a strong work ethic and a philanthropic sensibility to excel without regard to their socioeconomic status. Can you tell I've heard that line before? My father wasn't the strongest academically, so his scholarship opportunities were limited. He came from a working-class family and had trouble making ends meet during college because he was working full-time. At GU, he found educators who believed students learned in different ways and didn't fault him for not maintaining a 4.0 GPA."

"Tell me about him."

Jess smiled. "You'd like him. You're very similar. Hard-working, smart, stubborn. His college friend Philip—Professor Ridge to you— pitched the Derrick Spaulding MBA program to my dad a few years ago. The student-selection process, the service requirement, and the nonprofit focus intrigued Daddy, which of course is exactly why Philip crafted it in such a manner. My dad's always been acutely aware of how lucky he's been and is constantly looking for ways to return some of his wealth to people who need it. It was a match made in heaven."

"It's the perfect program for me for exactly those reasons. I was never a straight-A student, in part because I was usually working and in part because I was never super strong in math and science. Unlike you."

Jess laughed. "Don't let anyone hear you say that or they'll call the men in the white coats."

"They're already coming for me for dating a Spaulding."

Jess took another sip of her beverage, and her expression shuttered.

"That was a joke," TJ said, trying to stave off a withdrawal.

"Was it?" Jess set down her glass.

"Jess, it was a thoughtless quip. I don't want to fight with you."

"I won't apologize for being a Spaulding, TJ. My father's worked extremely hard to get where he is. Yes, my mother's wealth and Lilith's uber wealth improved his connections, but it's my father who founded Magnate and his efforts alone that have turned it into *the* go-to investment firm of our time. His efforts, mind you, that created the quote 'perfect' graduate program you're in and without which I'd never have met you. *You* have money issues, not me. I understand we have differences where it's concerned, and I intend to remain conscious of them to do what I can to put you at ease. But God damn it, you need to meet me halfway."

Jess shook her head and threw her fork into her food container, lidded it, and began repacking some of the picnic items. Jess was right. TJ did have money issues. And while she wasn't about to get over them in a heartbeat, the least she could do was take a step in Jess's direction. She owed her that much.

She reached over and stilled Jess's hand with her own. "Please don't end our evening prematurely because of a thoughtless comment."

"Well, then give me something to work with," Jess said, exuding frustration. "I feel I'm out on a limb by myself."

"You're not," TJ said as she gently tugged Jess's hand. "Hey." She tugged again and Jess finally met her gaze. "You're not." It meant something to hear Jess imply she was pleased their paths had crossed. "You're right. I do have money issues and I've been unfair to you because of them." TJ lay sideways on the blanket, facing Jess, propped on her elbow.

"My dad was a job-to-job kind of guy known more for joining in a game of jump ball than taking an extra shift. He didn't want Mom to work, and she preferred being a stay-at-home mom anyway, so we never had much money. During my first year at community college, he surprised me one day and told me to apply to any college I wanted to, regardless of cost. I thought he'd lost his mind, but he insisted, and I got into my top choice. Near the end of my first semester as a sophomore, he showed up unexpectedly at my dorm room. Pale as a ghost and thinner than I'd ever seen him, he told me this crazy story about how some bar customer had left a sealed package with him one night when he was closing. The man asked my father to keep it safe until he returned for it one day. A year or two later, Dad stumbled across the hiding place and it triggered his memory. Sure enough, the package was still there.

"It contained three thousand one-hundred-dollar bills. Since the man never returned, Dad started to spend it. Bought my mom a new car and me a year's tuition. Apparently the local—I don't know—mafia noted his new spending habits. Who knows, but these guys found their lost money and threatened my dad.

"With what he hadn't yet spent, what he was able to sell, my parents' meager savings, and mostly loans from friends of his I'm still repaying, he managed to pay back the entire sum. But these guys, I'm sure they wanted to send a message.

"That day in my dorm room, Dad said, 'Don't take something for nothing. Work for everything you get and it'll never lead you wrong.' He made me promise Kara got a proper education and not to let mine go to waste. He told me he loved me and was proud of me. It was the last time I saw him. They delivered his wedding ring to my mom in an envelope with no return address.

"And Mom..." TJ couldn't go there. Rage flared unbidden at the thought of Evelyn's alcoholism and what she'd put Kara and her through. She sat up and wiped angrily at a falling tear. "I lost everything because of money. Someone else's money." As another tear fell, she jumped up and told Jess she needed a minute. She strode farther down the field to put some distance between them.

She laughed bitterly. Money issues? She had more of those than Greece. No wonder Jess had called her on it.

A warm body pressed against her back and caring arms wrapped around her waist. She felt the gentle pressure of Jess's chin against her shoulder. Swiping at the last of her tears, TJ whispered, "Sorry."

"Don't be," Jess said. "There's nothing for you to be sorry for. I can't imagine how hard it's been for you."

TJ broke from the embrace and turned on Jess. "I don't want your pity."

"And you won't get it. What you have is my admiration."

"For losing a father to poor judgment, a mother to heartbreak and alcoholism, and a sister to street thugs?"

"For holding on to your values. For never wavering from your integrity. And you haven't lost Kara. She's doing great, thanks to you."

"You mean, thanks to you. Her health care, her job. You did that."

Once again, Jess put her arms around her. "Let's not keep score."

"You're in a far better position to be able to help me than vice versa," TJ said.

"I disagree."

"Why am I not surprised?"

Jess tapped TJ's nose with her index finger in a playful rebuke before twisting TJ's hips so that Jess was once again standing behind her. "Look around. Tell me what you see. Or feel. But this time, you only get one word to describe it. Take a few deep breaths before you do."

TJ obliged. She closed her eyes. Inhale. Exhale. Inhale. Exhale. She opened her eyes and took in the beautiful night sky. The stars winked as if on a sketchy power grid, whereas the moon shone as if it had just won an Academy Award. Its light kissed the surface of the ocean with a pale glow, like warm breath on a cool window. The horizon stretched open wide in the way of an embrace, offering endless possibilities.

The thought brought TJ's mind to the woman holding her. She folded her arms over Jess's and soaked up the sensation of being held by her. It felt good. Better than good. She felt cherished. Could she say it? It seemed too soon for such sentimentality, though the feeling was undeniable.

"Only one?" TJ asked.

"You've opened up a lot tonight. I don't want to wear you out. At least not by talking." Jess gave TJ a brief squeeze.

"You're kind of a hussy, you know that?"

"One word."

One word. What was she seeing, feeling? Words flitted in and out of her brain like moths to a porch light. Cherished. Scared. Possibility. Wonder. Gratitude. Hope. She was feeling *a lot*. What she wasn't feeling was brave. Jess was right—TJ had shared enough. Could she put herself in such a vulnerable position by admitting the truth?

"Vulnerable." It came out before TJ could censor herself.

Jess slid around TJ's body until they were in each other's arms. "That's a good thing," she said, her smile easily visible in the moonlight. "You're letting me in."

"Yay," TJ grumbled.

Jess laughed. "You could have picked a thousand other words."

"Like you said, I need to meet you halfway. Try, anyway."

"So honorable." Jess kissed TJ softly on the lips. "I like that about you." Jess put her arms around TJ's neck and whispered in her ear. "You know what else I like?"

TJ's stomach tightened. Was she ready for the answer? "Tell me."

"Dessert."

"Dessert?" It seemed far too soon for them to be entertaining the type TJ immediately called to mind.

"Mud pie." Jess gave TJ a quick kiss and threaded her arm through TJ's as they walked back to the blanket. "The student café here sells it, and it's to die for. Chocolate-cookie crust, your choice of mocha almond fudge or mint chocolate-chip ice cream, topped with a fudge swirl and whipped cream. This date's taken far too serious a turn, so after we indulge my sweet tooth, I'm marching you straight back to the game room for a round of pool, where you can attempt to redeem yourself after your poor showing in darts." Jess grabbed the carrier and stepped off the blanket, leaving TJ to shake it off and fold it.

"You're not some sort of pool shark too, are you?"

"When you're sent to college for reasons other than to study, you find ways to kill time. Just look sexy for me while you watch me run the table."

CHAPTER SIXTEEN

T ell me again why we live on the fifth floor?"
     TJ ducked her head around the wall separating the kitchen from the living room and grinned at her sister. "What are you doing home so early? I'm not done making your surprise." The chocolate-chocolate-chunk muffins were still cooling so she hadn't yet topped them with the cream-cheese frosting Kara favored.

Kara dropped her backpack on the couch, set the crutches down, and wiped her brow. Maneuvering up the stairs with the banister in one hand and crutches in the other usually took their toll on her energy when she first entered the apartment, but today was different. Making sure TJ was watching, she gingerly turned around while attempting a silly disco move of pointing up to her right and down to her left.

When TJ had received Kara's text that the doctor said the bone was healing well and had removed the cast, she asked Jess if she could duck out early. "Happy to have the cast off, I take it?"

"You've no idea," Kara said as she limped past TJ and headed straight for the utensil drawer. "She said to 'let my pain be my guide,' but I told her I didn't want you involved."

TJ laughed. "I left the spatula in the bowl for you."

Quickly returning a spoon to its compartment, Kara scooped as much of the chocolate batter remnants onto the spatula as she could before attacking it with her tongue.

"How's it feel?"

Kara made a face. "Eh. I can wean myself off the crutches depending on the pain. She gave me some exercises to do, and I'm supposed to start PT next week."

"That's great." TJ pulled out a package of small candles and set them on the counter. "I wanted to celebrate your freedom by greeting you with your favorite dessert, but I didn't expect you so soon."

Kara scraped up the last of the batter and grinned. "That's 'cuz I didn't take the bus." She waggled her eyebrows before licking off the rest of the chocolate.

"Someone give you a ride?"

"Nope." Kara's eyes twinkled.

TJ's thoughts turned dark. Kara was still recovering from her last joyride, which hadn't brought joy to anyone. Surely she wasn't returning to her old tricks? Allowing her to work at Dillon's was one way TJ thought she could curb Kara's desire for auto-related mischief because she'd be surrounded by car brouhaha in an above-board setting. How did she get home?

"Could you grab my backpack?" Kara asked as she set the bowl in the sink.

It was unlike Kara to ask for help of any kind, so TJ's concern immediately shifted from Kara's transportation to her injury. She lifted the bag and returned to the kitchen, watching Kara favor her leg as she made her way to the table. "Are you in pain?"

Kara opened her pack and rifled around for something. "Not really. My foot's a little tingly because I haven't put weight on it for so long." She removed an envelope and set it down. Then she fumbled in her pocket and set a key on top of the envelope. "I got paid today," she said with a smile.

TJ took a seat across from her and eyed the objects. "Is that your paycheck?"

Kara shook her head and slid the tiny pile to TJ.

TJ pulled the envelope from beneath the key and opened it. Confusion set in as she scanned the document. "This is a certificate of title. I'm the owner of a...1992 Ford Ranger?"

"Once you sign it and submit it to the DMV."

"I don't understand."

"I bought it."

"Kara, you're not making any sense. What's going on?"

Kara rolled her eyes. "Don't be dense. Some guy abandoned his Ranger at Dillon's thinking it wasn't worth the repair cost he was quoted. Anyway, there was an auction and nobody bid so it's been sitting there. Dillon said if I paid for the parts and fixed it myself, I could have it." She picked up the key and held it out to TJ. "Wanna check her out?"

TJ didn't know how to proceed. Part of her wanted to throw her arms around Kara for her generous gift, while another part wanted to know what the chances were Dillon happened to have an extra vehicle lying around that hadn't been worth selling. She didn't want him thinking they needed a special handout. Many times she'd considered purchasing an older car but chose to limit their expenses while she was still paying off her father's loans and her mother's medical bills. She figured she'd buy one if she was lucky enough to line up a job at graduation.

Still another part couldn't wrap her head around the fact her sixteen-year-old sister had bought her a truck. Teenagers bought music, clothes, and video games. Not major household purchases. Was life without their parents forcing Kara to grow up faster than other kids her age? Was TJ forcing her to do it? Was she giving Kara enough of a chance to simply be a kid?

"I thought we agreed you were going to buy a couple new games and put the rest into savings."

"That was before I knew about the Ranger."

"You know I don't expect you to contribute your paychecks to the household, don't you?"

"I know."

"Then what are you doing this for?"

"Because I can."

Was it really so simple? TJ watched Kara carefully for any kind of insight into what she was thinking. In these rare moments when Kara did utter more than two sentences, she was always forthright. Nothing in her expression said otherwise. If future paychecks followed the same path as this one, she'd intervene. But for now, the pride showing so brightly in Kara's eyes meant TJ might have to swallow her own. Yet she swelled with it as she considered the kind of person Kara was turning into. Maybe she wasn't doing everything wrong as a parent after all.

"Don't get mushy," Kara said.

"I'm not getting mushy," TJ lied as she snagged the key and got to her feet, needing a distraction.

"Uh-huh."

TJ tore a paper towel from its roll, folded it, and placed a warm muffin on top. "Here," she said as she set it in front of Kara. "No frosting but I'm sure you'll manage." She scooped up a crutch in case

Kara needed it to traverse the stairs. "Now get off your derriere and let's go for a drive."

❖

As Jess sat down to lunch, Brooke said, "Tell me the rumors aren't true."

If Jess was correct about where this conversation was headed, she wasn't sure she wanted to dine. "Rumors?"

"Don't play coy. Rumors of you locking lips with a woman."

Jess pretended to study her menu. The time she and TJ were spending together was too important to trivialize or deny. TJ wouldn't. "Then let's not deal in rumor. I've kissed a woman, yes. The crispy chicken-leg confit with couscous and olives sounds good."

Brooke pushed down the top of Jess's menu until it hit the table and spoke in a quiet yet anxious voice. "Are you kidding me with this?"

As patiently as she could, Jess said, "I've met someone who makes me happy. Is that a crime?"

"Jess, when I said we needed to embrace diversity, I wasn't talking about literally folding your arms around another woman."

"Why don't you tell me what's really on your mind? You don't take well to the idea that your sister's dating a woman, is at the very least bisexual, and possibly even gay." Jess perused the menu. "I think I'll go with the chicken with artichokes and angel hair."

Brooke ripped the menu out of Jess's hands. "I don't give a good God damn whether you're dating a woman or the Cat in the Hat, but our clients will. Why are you making light of this?"

"Because it's none of their business." Jess crossed her arms defiantly. "Or anyone else's."

"Did you hit your head?" Brooke gave Jess the three-finger salute. "How many fingers am I holding up?"

A waitress took their drink order and promptly moved away.

"What our clients can and can't handle on a personal front has no bearing on me. We're there to increase their assets appreciably. Who I sleep with is of no consequence."

Wide-eyed, Brooke whispered, "You've slept with her?"

Although Jess and TJ hadn't had sex, it didn't prevent Jess from imagining it. The smile she failed to quell likely revealed the train of her thoughts.

Brooke's voice increased at least half an octave. "Are you forgetting who your stepmother is? Our lives are as much our own as individuality gets expressed in paint-by-numbers."

"Are you honestly worried that my love life is going to impact Magnate's bottom line? Because if that's true, we've really got to work on our messaging. The whole industry-leading-returns angle's got to go."

"I'm worried Lilith is going to blow a gasket the way she did when you wanted to elope."

Jess took a moment to study her sister. Had they deferred to Lilith at the expense of their happiness? "Do you think Dad wants us to accede to Lilith's wishes if it means squelching a part of ourselves?"

"Dad wants us to keep his sugar mama happy. Short of letting her lop off our limbs, he's not going to interfere. So unless you're in love with your lady friend, I suggest you toe the line."

"And if I am?"

"If you're what?"

"Falling in love."

Brooke blinked several times before throwing her napkin down.

Jess sighed as she watched Brooke thread her way through the tables and out the front door. Brooke's way of processing sensitive information while in a public place was to walk. In private, Brooke had no qualms about raising her voice. When others were around, however, she channeled her discomfort into her stride. Minutes later, Jess received a text from Brooke demanding Jess meet her outside. Jess refolded her napkin and motioned the waitress over. She slipped the woman a fifty-dollar bill. "If we're not back in fifteen minutes, please seat the next patrons."

From the entrance, Jess glanced right and left. The area was full of boutiques and restaurants that catered to the well-to-do. Strands of tiny white lights reminiscent of Christmas-tree decorations adorned the trees along the walkway.

Suddenly Brooke was at her elbow, propelling her down the sidewalk. "Tell me you're not doing this to win Muriel's business."

"I'm not."

"Does Chad know?"

"Since you do, he might. But unless he sees the possibility of a threesome, he won't care. Still, I'll talk to him."

"Is it the intern?"

"It is."

"God damn it, Jess."

Jess pulled them to a stop. "If you're going to berate me, please just get it over with. I don't need you to draw it out."

"I don't understand this. You never do anything to rock the boat. That's my job."

"Consider it my gift to you."

"Lilith's going to flip."

"I imagine," Jess said.

Brooke stared at her. "She's called a family dinner for Friday. I assume you heard?"

"Yes." When something threatened the family, as determined solely by Lilith, she called them together to address the matter. This resulted in everyone capitulating to Lilith, with the possible exception of Brooke, the lone loose cannon.

"She'll insist you stop seeing her."

"That's my guess."

Brooke shook her head in disbelief. "And will you?"

"Not if I can help it. And I'd appreciate it if you'd stop staring at me. I'm the same person I've always been."

Brooke shook her head again, and this time a small smile tugged at the corners of her mouth. She turned them around and headed back toward the restaurant. "No, you're not. And if you're going to be the target of Lilith's ire, I'm getting a front-row seat."

Jess stopped again. "Wait a second. You're not going to tell me I'm crazy?"

"You're crazy all right. Taking on Lilith is a death wish. But if she kicks you out of the will, Gary and I split your share. I say bring it on."

"I appreciate the support," Jess said wryly. Jess could rarely tell how seriously to take Brooke, who often said things merely to get a rise out of someone. There was no doubt Brooke would be happy to have Jess's share of the Spaulding fortune, but Jess hoped it wouldn't be at the expense of her place in the family.

Once again seated at their table, Brooke said, "Tell me what it's like to kiss that hot woman of yours. Spare no detail."

At least Jess would enjoy the subject.

❖

TJ stared at the screen. She was fairly adept with databases and spreadsheets, but the numbers either didn't make sense or were dead ends.

The client database was mostly as expected, accessed via one of the two main paths provided by the software: Clients and Investments. From within the Clients section, a user could search by first or last name or company name. Once the client account was onscreen, there were various tabs she could click into for additional information: Portfolio, Profile, and Statements. The Portfolio tab showed the positions held by the client. The Profile tab showed detailed client information such as address and social-security or employer-identification number, and the referring client, if any. TJ wondered whether Jess had this referral data in a separate place since referrals was a marketing field, and Jess had mentioned she didn't access the client database.

In fact, Gary didn't seem to access it either, which was odd. After attempting to log in with the information Jess had provided and getting up to Shadow3, she was successful. The guilt she felt for using someone else's credentials turned to concern when she saw that the last time the records were accessed was over six months ago. What did Gary do all day? And wouldn't he notice the next time he *did* sign in that someone had done so as him more recently?

The Statements tab showed the statements, but unlike her online-banking and credit-card sites, they were haphazard, not covering a consistent time period such as a month. Nor did they provide a running balance or provide the investment-return percentage. And some clients didn't have any statements.

The Portfolio tab was straightforward: a row for cash and one for Magnate Fund. When she clicked into cash, she saw deposits and redemptions, all of which were transferred into and out of the Magnate Fund. When she clicked into the Magnate Fund, she saw the same cash transactions.

Where was the data on the Magnate Fund? And why didn't any of Magnate's clients have outside investments?

TJ had taken enough finance courses to understand the basics of investing. One such tenet was diversification. It seemed all the firm's clients were invested in the Magnate Fund, which wasn't publicly traded. Perhaps they were diversified elsewhere and had chosen the firm to specifically be invested in the fund? That made sense. Multiple financial advisors across the globe probably serviced Magnate's clientele. People like Muriel Manchester would surely not entrust all their cash reserves to one institution.

The Investments section was a compendium of resources that accessed all manner of stock-market data such as trading, research, and news, but TJ saw no clear path as to how it intersected with the Magnate Fund. Since she didn't have anyone at the firm to ask for help besides Jess, she needed to figure things out for herself. How well would it go over with Derrick Spaulding that his intern had decided to adhere to the original assignment rather than be taken off course to write about marketing? Then again, he likely had no idea anyone was even interning at his firm. Besides, if she could figure out in layman's terms how the firm did what it did, the case study might help yield additional clients who would hear about it through academic circles.

The thought of a new sales vertical to target brought Jess to mind, causing TJ to smile. Another avenue for Jess to market to and use that kick-ass brain of hers on. Her smile turned to a frown as she contemplated Derrick's accedence to his wife's wishes. She couldn't imagine telling Kara to tone down her intelligence for any reason, but especially for finding a spouse. Spouses were supposed to lift each other up and inspire each other to be better people. And parents? What kind of father found it acceptable to allow his daughter to be shaped into a role beneath her capabilities?

She might have promised not to divulge Jess's secret, but no way was she was going to remain silent when she was in Jess's presence.

CHAPTER SEVENTEEN

Jess slid into the booth across from TJ and eyed her surroundings skeptically. For this date, TJ had navigated them to a place called Joe's Tavern, a converted barn that included straw on the floor as part of the decor, and Jess wasn't thrilled with the idea of eating in a place that had once housed animals. And their loo.

A waitress promptly appeared and asked for their drink orders. When Jess ordered a glass of Chardonnay, the waitress laughed. "Darlin', we've got beer, beer, or beer." She flipped Jess's menu over. "One hundred kinds of bottles from all over the world. And this here's what we got on tap." She glanced at TJ. "Help her out, sugar. Back in a few."

"They serve beer but not wine?" Jess asked.

"Unless you like your wine from a box, be grateful they don't offer it," TJ said. "Besides, we're not here for the beverages."

"They're known for their food?" Jess couldn't fathom eating off this water-stained table.

At that moment, the array of TV screens hanging from the tavern ceiling flickered on. "Time for Trivia Tuesday!" popped onscreen.

TJ grabbed the electronic tablet attached to the table.

"What? We're playing?" Jess asked.

"You bet. We need a name for our team."

Jess rolled her eyes.

"Okay, the Eye-Rollers it is." TJ typed into the keypad.

"Wait. That's not a name."

"In and confirmed. Now, pick a beer and get ready to win."

"I'm terrible at trivia."

"Then just sit there and look sexy while I answer all the questions."

TJ winked as she delivered Jess's words back to her from their night at GU.

They ordered their drinks and listened as an announcer explained how Trivia Tuesdays worked, which was a version of the TV show *Jeopardy*. The top three teams received food and beverage coupons, and top prize was a fifty-dollar gift certificate.

Four-Letter Words, Sports, Food, Physics, Geography, and Authors made up the initial categories.

"Try to keep up," TJ said as the game got under way.

Jess quietly observed as TJ held her own through the first set of clues. As the game progressed, cheers, jeers, and laughter filled the tavern. Jess had to admit it was becoming harder to be the odd man out, especially when TJ would shake her head at a clue and say, "Hit me," trying to solicit input from Jess. It was so utterly ridiculous that Jess found herself starting to enjoy the evening despite her misgivings.

TJ correctly answered all five Geography questions, but was fairly uninspired when it came to Food. Jess found it ironic that TJ could know the highest point in Europe but not the answer to: *Carbonnade is a Belgian beef stew made with this alcoholic brew.* After all, the place only served beer.

Finally Jess could contain herself no longer when TJ balked at the clue: *These edible fungi thrive in chalky soil, and the best are the perigord variety.* "What are truffles?" Jess said, and TJ quickly wrote the answer into the tablet. It was correct, and when TJ beamed at her, all remaining excuses vanished.

"Now we're talking," TJ said.

Together they'd moved up to third place by the end of the game. Jess's competitive juices were in full swing, lubricated by beer. She was on her second by the time of the first break between games.

"How are you so good at this?" Jess asked, amazed by how much trivia TJ knew.

"Mom and I watched a lot of game shows and played Trivial Pursuit until the cards were dog-eared and faded. When it comes to knowing useless information, I excel."

"Did you bring me here to impress me with your skill set? Because it's working."

"I did. I thought if you were on the fence about me, all it would take to push you over the edge is to show you I know that the Pacific halibut can grow to more than eight feet long and the tallest mountain range in the Western hemisphere is Argentina's Cerro Aconcagua."

"Wow. I feel like I've won the lottery," Jess said.

"So, an ordinary day for you then?" TJ asked, offering a teasing smile.

Jess reached across the table and took TJ's hand in hers. "I'm beginning to think no day with you is ordinary."

"Jessica Spaulding, you say the sweetest things."

"You make me feel them." Jess realized the truth of that simple statement. Her feelings for TJ were turning her as maudlin as the Hallmark Channel's programming. My God, what was next? Nicholas Sparks novels? The idea caused her to burst with laughter.

"Care to share?" TJ asked.

Jess shook her head and squeezed TJ's hand. "Too embarrassing." But really, what was embarrassing about feeling happy and special? She shrugged shyly and tucked her hands into her lap. "I kind of like you a little is all."

TJ grinned. "Back atcha."

The announcer signaled the start of the next game. The categories were well within TJ's purview, and she again excelled. However, it was Jess who cruised them through Mathematics. She hit a Daily Double by answering "helix" to a clue, which prompted TJ to commandeer it as the name of her first cat. Then, feeling giddy from the alcohol, Jess told TJ to go all in once they learned the Final Jeopardy category was Scientists. With her response, "Who is Kepler?" to a clue about laws of planetary motion, the Eye-Rollers were in second place.

By the time they awaited the start of the final game, TJ and Jess were side by side in the booth, having shared their precious real estate with another couple, Jim and Karen, who took the bench opposite. Patrons stuffed the bar to the gills. Those that couldn't play due to a finite number of electronic tablets cheered for the nearest team and shouted unsolicited answers in a display of camaraderie.

Jess's third beer arrived before she'd placed the order. When the waitress nodded to the gentleman who'd paid for it, Jess held up the bottle, gave him a nod of thanks, and slung her arm across TJ's shoulders.

"Would you mind driving home tonight?" Jess asked.

"Not at all." TJ was still nursing her first beer, and now that it was probably warm, Jess didn't expect her to finish it.

"I'm having fun," Jess said before kissing TJ on the cheek.

TJ raised her chin toward Jess's bottle. "I noticed."

Suddenly Jess's chest constricted. "Is it okay? I don't want you to think, with your mom, that I…" She pushed the bottle away. "I don't need to—"

"Stop," TJ said with a squeeze to Jess's thigh. "It's fine." She slid the bottle back in front of Jess. "I'm glad you're letting loose and enjoying yourself."

"You're sure?"

"Positive. Just make sure it's me who takes you home and not your new friend." TJ tilted her head toward Jess's suitor.

"You're the only one I want to go home with," Jess said as she slid her hand over TJ's.

They stared at each other, grinning like fools, when someone snapped in their faces.

"Hey hey hey," Jim said. "You in? Or you gettin' a room?"

"We're in," TJ said before turning to Jess. "Unlike real *Jeopardy*, whoever's in first place after this round gets to select the final category."

"Then we'd better win," Jess said.

And win they did. Luckily Jim was a nurse, so he got them through Medicine. Karen knew her kings and queens as well as some famous quotes. TJ remained the anchor, dominating American Literature and Presidents, and together they limped through World Religion. The Eye-Rollers took first place.

The tablet at their table lit up, indicating they needed to select the category for the final three teams. TJ scrolled through the drop-down menu until she reached Mathematics. Before she hit the button to confirm her selection, Jess stopped her.

"What are you doing?" Jess asked.

"Choosing the category to win us tonight's tournament."

"But you said it's one of your weakest categories."

"It's your best."

"No, no, no. Don't put this on me. I'll lose everything."

TJ chuckled. "We're talking about a gift certificate. That's hardly losing everything."

"You know what I mean. You guys are killing it. Pick—I don't know—Literature or Authors, or…" Jess pointed to Jim and Karen. "Medicine. Royalty."

TJ appealed to them. "You guys okay with math?"

Jim held up the coupons the waitress dropped off at the table. "Yep. Your call. We're already way ahead of how we were doing on our own." Karen nodded her agreement.

"Math it is." TJ clicked the confirm button.

As soon as the category came onscreen, the crowd oohed. Math was apparently considered more challenging than most. TJ hid what she wagered on behalf of the team and squeezed Jess's thigh. "Jim, Karen, and I are here too. It's not all on you."

Clue: *He never revealed the proof of his last theorem but only hinted at it in a margin note.*

"No idea," TJ said.

Jim agreed. "I got nuthin'. Babe?"

Karen looked dumbstruck.

TJ turned to Jess. "They're not always this hard. Don't let it get to you."

Pulling the tablet closer, Jess keyed in her reply and quickly hit the confirmation button to thwart prying eyes.

TJ stared at the completely black screen for several seconds before meeting Jess's eyes. "You know this?"

Jess shrugged. She'd studied the mathematician in eighth grade when her fellow students were learning basic algebra and geometry. She focused her attention on the closest TV.

Erring with Pascal and Descartes, the third- and second-place teams managed to remain in positive dollar territory, meaning the entire game came down to Jess's answer.

TJ squeezed her hand in a show of solidarity.

The Eye-Rollers' bet flashed above—the entire $18,500 balance.

The announcer said, "Ladies and gentlemen. The Eye-Rollers' answer is..." *Who is Pierre de Fermat?* flashed onscreen. Seconds ticked by, ratcheting up the anticipation of the crowd and causing Jess to squirm in her seat. "Correct!"

A large green check mark lit up the screens throughout the bar. "With the fourth-largest grand total in the history of Joe's Tavern Trivia, with a score of $37,000, give it up for the Eye-Rollers!" Vegas-sounding electronic bells rang out and the crowd cheered.

Before Jess could process the announcement, TJ threw her arms around her. "I knew you could do it."

Jim and Karen joined in an awkward group hug, and soon after they headed for Jess's car.

"I should be angry with you for putting me on the spot like that," Jess said, swatting TJ's thigh once TJ slid into the driver's seat.

"Are you?" TJ asked.

"Not at all. I had fun," Jess said as she laced TJ's fingers with hers. "Do I want to know how many dates you've awed with your trivia savvy?"

"I've never brought a date to trivia night before."

"What made you think to bring me?"

TJ shrugged. "Why wouldn't I?"

"Uh-uh. I don't buy it. There's something you're not telling me."

"People play bar trivia because it's entertaining. Were you entertained?"

"Yes."

"There you go." TJ slid her hand out from under Jess's and put both hands on the steering wheel. "I could get used to this German engineering. This handles like a dream. Do you ever just go for a drive?"

Something gnawed at Jess, preventing her from accepting TJ's simple explanation. If TJ thought bar trivia was so enjoyable, wouldn't she have wanted previous dates to experience it? And why the sudden diversion about the car? "You wanted me to play. You wanted me to win. Why?"

"What's the fastest you've taken her?"

"TJ."

TJ sighed. "I didn't want to call attention to it."

"Well, you've got my attention now."

TJ reached for Jess's hand. "You told me you like the game room at GU because there you're just Jess. I wanted you to have a night of being just Jess, the one who's not only playful and fun, but smart." She paused. "No. Not just Jess. All Jess."

Jess's head was spinning. On one hand, she wanted TJ to stop the car so she could launch herself at her and smother her with kisses. It was a selfless, sincere act on TJ's part to want to give her a night of being judged for her knowledge rather than her clothing, assets, or connections. Nights Jess could be herself without having to inhabit the role long expected of her were blessings as rare as a US senator reaching across the aisle to strike a compromise. On the other hand, she would have preferred an evening without judgment of any sort, which she sensed TJ doing to Derrick for allowing Lilith to hold Jess to a lower standard.

Still, Jess couldn't fault TJ for being protective of her. If anything, it further endeared TJ to her. There was so much more to Derrick Spaulding than TJ could possibly know, and over time, Jess would share it with her. True, Derrick ceded too much control to Lilith when it came to rearing his own children, but Jess was equally submissive. She could have fought harder for Dillon, forcing Derrick to side with Jess or side with his wife. But she hadn't wanted to tear up the family, hadn't wanted to walk away from the life of comfort she enjoyed, and as she glanced at the woman she was falling for, she finally understood what she'd danced around but never before put her finger on. She hadn't chosen Dillon because she wasn't in love with him.

She'd wanted to punish herself for it—her lack of deeper feelings for him. How could she not want the most sought-after boy in Montgomery Hills, who loved her? He'd been her confidant, her champion, her friend, her lover. He was sweet and sexy and handsome, and without a doubt, she loved and adored him. Yet she wasn't in love with him. For as much as she despised Lilith for making her choose between Dillon and her family, or Dillon and her family's money, Jess could never have married him.

Until TJ walked into her life, Jess had felt unworthy of Dillon's love, felt something was wrong with her not to reciprocate it. Years of placating Lilith by stifling certain parts of herself and adopting her assigned role of airheaded princess seemed the proper price to pay for being the subhuman who couldn't love Dillon the way he deserved.

Was she worthy of TJ's love?

She didn't think so, but she knew unequivocally that she wanted to be. Leaning over as far as the seat belt would allow and pushing off the shoulder harness when it refused to give her the room she needed, she whispered in TJ's ear. "Thank you." She gently tugged on TJ's earlobe with her teeth and briefly sucked it before settling back into her seat.

"You're going to make it very hard to leave tonight, aren't you?" TJ asked.

"Who says you have to leave?"

In the dashboard light, Jess saw TJ white-knuckle the wheel. "I told Kara I'd be home by midnight. We're almost at your place, which means I'll have about twenty minutes before I have to head out."

"I'm sure she'll excuse a little tardiness," Jess said as she rested her hand on TJ's thigh.

"I try to lead by example. If I'm late, she'll push the envelope next time she's out."

"You're an excellent role model."

"You don't make it easy."

"Do you want me to?"

"No. Yes."

Jess chuckled and gave TJ's thigh a quick squeeze. "I'll behave." She clicked the gate remote in her purse. "Take the next right and follow the driveway around to the left. They'll have parked your truck next to my coupe." Since TJ had been running late for their date, Jess had saved time by meeting her at the front steps of the main house instead of the guesthouse.

As the path turned left, the immense grounds and gardens of the estate came into view, as much as it was possible this late in the evening. Much of it was lit in part by the moonlight and in part by lights that illuminated the walking paths, sculptures, trees, flowers, and benches. Jess knew TJ wouldn't have seen this section of the estate during the party.

"The guesthouse is on the right. Park next to your truck, and I'll give you the tour." After she complied, TJ handed the keys to Jess, looking somewhat shell-shocked. Jess might as well get it over with. There would never be a good time for TJ to see where she lived, and perhaps the enjoyable evening they'd shared would help soften her to the experience.

As Jess ascended the steps to her front door, TJ lingered behind, staring up at the massive structure. "This is the *guesthouse*?" TJ asked, her voice rising an octave.

"Yes. It's where I live." Jess noticed TJ's wide eyes and constant head-shaking, as if TJ couldn't believe what she was seeing. Maybe their fun evening wouldn't be enough to get TJ over the shock of Jess's not-so-humble abode.

Jess powered through the tour in record time, ten minutes from start to finish, and they hadn't even gone into the basement, which was far less a basement than an entirely self-contained five-bedroom unit. She ended at the kitchen. "My favorite room in the house," Jess said as she slid into the breakfast-nook bench, watching TJ tour the room.

"How can you choose just one? There are so many." TJ ran her fingers along the rail at the edge of the range. "This is the most beautiful range I've ever seen. Not that I've seen much beyond Kenmore."

"I don't know that one."

TJ turned and halfway smiled. "No. I wouldn't expect you would."

Jess chose to ignore the melancholic note TJ had struck, hoping she was misreading it. They'd had a fantastic evening, and she couldn't see why it should change. "You'd think with two ovens and all those burners at my disposal, I'd be a great cook."

"Not the case?"

"I make a mean microwave popcorn, I have to say."

Continuing her slow perusal of the appliances, counters, and cabinets, TJ asked, "Is it presumptuous of me to think you have your own cook?"

"My parents employ a private chef. She provides a three-course dinner nightly and either prepares breakfast the night before or is on-site to create a meal. Since I live on the lot, I reap the benefit of her service because it's only a hundred-yard walk to my front door. The bottom line is my freezer and refrigerator are always full of ready meals, and if I ate half of what was made, I'd be three times my size."

"Our lives are so similar."

And damn it, there was that wistful tone again.

Jess crossed the room and took TJ's hand in both of hers. "Let's not focus on our differences. I've enjoyed our evening."

TJ dropped her gaze to the floor and shook her head. "What are we playing at?" Jess heard the hopelessness in the sharp puff of air that escaped from TJ's nose.

An idea popped into Jess's head. They needed to find common ground, not play haves and have-nots. "Look around. Tell me what you see."

TJ scanned the room. "I see a kitchen that could fit half my apartment, a refrigerator the size of a garage, and a range that could double as a dance floor."

Stepping back to lean on the counter, Jess said, "Stop comparing it to what you don't see. Try again."

With a deep breath, TJ again began to survey her surroundings. "I see a hood above a range the size of a parking space."

"Stop it. You're comparing again." Jess pulled on a handle. "What's this?"

Clearly unamused, TJ crossed her arms. "A drawer."

Jess slid it back into place. "And these?"

"Hinges."

Opening a cabinet and indicating the space within, Jess asked, "And this?"

"Cupboard. Are you going to pull out some children's books and ask me to start naming the objects and animals? Because that's what this feels like."

"I might. Now once again, tell me what you see."

"Range. Hood. Pots hanging from hooks. Cutting board. Block of knives. Microwave. Sink. Shall I continue?"

"And do you have any of those things in your kitchen?" Jess asked.

"I get the point," TJ said gruffly.

"Do you?"

TJ's expression softened. "I'm trying."

"Try harder." Jess stepped to TJ and wrapped her arms around her waist. "The differences are superficial. What's important is what's here." Jess laid a finger at TJ's temple. "Here." She trailed it down TJ's face and neck, and spread her palm on TJ's chest. "And right now, here." She smoothed her thumb along TJ's bottom lip.

Jess leaned in, but TJ's gaze dropped to the ground and she shook her head. "I know you're right. It's just…" TJ scanned the room. "All this. It's a lot. I'm sorry."

Bringing TJ into her house had been a mistake they needed to get past. Jess scanned the kitchen for ideas and then remembered her purse. Scanning its contents, she found a tightly wound silk scarf. As she unraveled it, she patted the breakfast-nook table. "Sit here," she said. Jess folded the scarf and placed it gently across TJ's eyes, reaching behind TJ's head to tie it.

"What are you doing?" TJ asked, her voice dropping an octave.

"Helping you focus," Jess said as she stood between TJ's legs and held TJ's palms against the tabletop with her own. Jess explored TJ's face and neck with the gentlest of caresses from her nose, lips, and tongue. She nuzzled below her ears and chin. "You smell so good," Jess said as she let her warm breath skate across the tiny hairs on TJ's skin, causing TJ's breath to hitch and goose bumps to erupt where she traveled. Her mouth lingered on TJ's earlobe, and TJ writhed beneath her. "Taste so good," Jess whispered as she sucked it into her mouth and enjoyed the squirming she was causing.

Jess needed more contact but relished the sweet torture her body was experiencing. She pressed her chest into TJ's as she kissed TJ's throat, chin, and the corner of her mouth. "Feel so good," Jess said as she claimed TJ's mouth with her own.

Apparently no longer willing to submit to Jess's will, TJ reached around the small of Jess's back and pulled her close. They both moaned from the pleasure of the contact.

Suddenly TJ tugged off the blindfold and slid off the table, taking Jess's face in her hands. She stared into Jess's eyes, hunger etched on her face as well as something else Jess couldn't decipher. Jess half expected TJ to jump her, but instead she bent forward and kissed Jess unhurriedly, offering more eye contact than Jess was used to. It was a little unnerving, but TJ seemed to need another way to communicate. Something was growing between them, and apparently TJ felt similarly.

It didn't last. The heat between them ratcheted up several more notches, and eye contact became less important than physical contact. TJ's hands caressed her back and sides, whereas Jess's traveled up TJ's abdomen to her breasts. Soft and pliable at first, the nipples soon hardened against her fingers, and Jess felt a rush of power at being able to elicit such a response. TJ pushed into Jess's hands and offered a short whimper so unlike her that a pool of moisture flooded between Jess's thighs, knowing it was she who'd caused the sound. When she found herself backed against the table with TJ's thigh pressed to her center, she was already so close to exploding that she broke the kiss and tried to catch her breath. She didn't want her first orgasm with TJ to arrive so quickly and take place in her kitchen while fully clothed. Her body had other ideas, not minding whatsoever where they were or whether fabric lay between them.

TJ quickly kissed the corner of Jess's mouth before holding up her hands in surrender and taking several steps back. "I need to go or I'll be late."

"You did *not* just say that," Jess said, still breathing heavily. "Get back over here."

"You know I can't."

"You are the meanest woman I've ever met. And believe me, I've met my share," Jess said.

"And you," TJ said as she lifted Jess onto the table, letting Jess's legs surround her, "are heavenly." TJ kissed Jess so tenderly, Jess nearly cried. "Sweet dreams, princess," TJ said, giving Jess a fleeting kiss on the mouth before striding out of the room.

Seconds later, TJ was back, pulling Jess off. "But first, help me find the front door," she said as she pushed Jess in front of her. "I didn't drop any bread crumbs earlier."

CHAPTER EIGHTEEN

No, no, no," Jess had said to Brooke, who was ducking out of a press conference and forcing Jess to take her place. The conference was to announce their father's twenty-million-dollar gift to the Reilly Hospital for Children, and Brooke was supposed to briefly introduce Derrick after the hospital's president gave his opening remarks. Brooke claimed a scheduling conflict with a potential client and told Jess to fill in. Although Jess attended many Magnate events and was fine mingling, she didn't enjoy speaking publicly. Brooke hadn't left her much choice.

She'd been escorted through the hospital by an efficient staff woman who wouldn't stop raving about Derrick and the improvements in cancer treatments sure to be made as a result of his gift. He'd had an earlier meeting and told Jess he'd meet her at the hospital. Veering through hallway after hallway, Jess was led to a door with a sign indicating it was private. The woman held the door open for her and said, "He's in here. I'll see you all downstairs in a few minutes."

Abruptly stopping inside the doorway, Jess mumbled a quick apology—mostly to herself. She seemed to have stumbled into a costume party of sorts. People in Disney character costumes were chatting and laughing with one another, while some were attending to their makeup in front of various mirrors that didn't go with the decor, clearly brought in for whatever event this was. A tall Mickey Mouse, wearing his trademark long-tail black tuxedo jacket, white vest, red pants, yellow bow tie, and puffy white gloves, strode over to Jess in balloon-like black shoes and indicated the roomful of folks behind him. From somewhere within the plastic head, a muffled but familiar voice said, "Well? What do you think?"

Shocked beyond belief, Jess said, "Dad? Dad, what on earth?"

The mouse removed his head and revealed Derrick Spaulding, albeit without his typically perfectly coifed hair. "Suit up, honey. We've got kids to visit."

This wasn't what Brooke had led Jess to believe. "But what about the press conference?"

Derrick said, "Rumor has it you weren't happy about this event."

Jess frowned. "You know I'm not a huge fan of speaking in front of a crowd, but it's fine."

"That's not what I mean. You said I'd lost focus of the real importance of the gift."

Damn Brooke. Why couldn't she keep her mouth shut? Jess had told her she was thrilled with the donation but felt a press conference was overkill. Many marketers would think it a perfect avenue to tout the Spaulding name and values, but Jess preferred a softer approach. Such gifts should be about the causes, not the donors. She'd made the mistake of telling Blabbermouth Brooke how she felt, including saying she thought Derrick was starting to get dangerously close to narcissistic when it came to seeing his name associated with do-gooding. "Daddy, I was out of line. I didn't mean any—"

"You were right."

Wait. What? "I was?"

Derrick said, "If you were here fighting for your life, would you care that some muckety-muck at the other end of the hospital you'll probably never visit was giving some speech about resources, or would you rather meet some of your favorite characters?"

Jess processed the information more slowly than usual because she was so surprised. This was not a side of her father she'd seen in a long time. "So there's no press conference?"

"There is, but we've got better things to do with our time. I know big white polka dots and bright-yellow shoes aren't your usual style, but would you mind being Minnie for a few hours? I've got a great outfit for you." Derrick turned and asked something of someone who looked to be Cruella de Vil.

"We're visiting the kids?"

"We are. And every one of them is going to get their choice of a Mickey Ears hat, which we'll have shipped to them if they don't like any of the ones we've brought, plus a gift certificate to the Disney Store." Cruella handed Derrick a bulky outfit and a Minnie Mouse head. He, in turn, held them out to Jess. "What do you think?"

Ignoring that he had his hands full, Jess slid her arms around his waist. "I think you're wonderful. And not having to stand in front of an audience is merely icing on the cake." She pulled away and took the costume. "I'd be honored to be your Minnie Mouse today."

And that's how she found herself sitting across from her father in the back of his limousine as they headed to the office, wrapping up a conversation about how rewarding it had been to spend time with the kids. Considering most of the children were battling leukemia and other cancers, it was nice to be able to give them a distraction for a little while. They'd really enjoyed the characters, especially some of the newer ones like Buzz Lightyear and Sheriff Woody. Jess adored her father for giving her the opportunity to experience something she'd surely never forget.

"Are you sure you want to be wearing that outfit when you arrive?" Jess asked. "You're not your usually intimidating self in that garb."

"Am I usually intimidating?" Derrick asked.

Jess smiled. "You know better than to ask."

"As long as I don't intimidate my family."

"Only as it relates to work."

"I might be able to live with that. Speaking of work, how's everything on the marketing front? Brooke's never in the office, which means Magnate has you to thank."

"Because she's busy meeting new prospects or because she's out of your hair?"

"I plead the Fifth."

Jess laughed. "Things are good." An image of TJ popped into her head and she blushed. "Really good."

"Does this mean Chad's finally given up aiming for Playboy of the Year and wants to take things more seriously?"

Lost in her thoughts, Jess asked, "Who? Sorry. Chad. I've no idea. I hope that doesn't disappoint you."

Derrick made use of the bar within the vehicle's confines and poured them both a glass of bubbly. After handing one to Jess, he offered his for a toast. "You could never disappoint me. Especially if it means Chad's on the outs."

"I thought you liked him."

"I like a lot of people. Doesn't mean I want them marrying my daughter."

"Lilith thinks he's perfect."

"Uh-oh. Should I be worried?" Derrick asked with a glint in his eye.

"She's far too enamored of you to be considering replacements."

"Chad's a good-looking lad with a great name and a tremendous future. But he's only perfect if you think he is. And I've never gotten that sense from you."

"No." Caught between wanting to tell Derrick about TJ and not wanting to admit to herself she was so far gone already, Jess hedged. "I've met someone I really like, but I'm afraid to jinx it by making too much of it too soon. Would you be offended if I leave it at that?"

"Would you be offended if I gave you some advice?"

"Not at all. You're two for two on the important-relationships front, so you must know something."

"There's no such thing as making too much of a relationship with someone who's special. You each might be ready to take certain steps at different times, but there's no shame in admitting how you feel as you're feeling it."

"Even if it's scary as hell?"

"Especially. Loving someone means you'll have pain and joy, but it's the joy that endures."

"Love might be a little premature," Jess said as if trying to convince herself.

"Jessica, falling in love is like DNA. It's different for everyone. There's no universal timetable. I'm not trying to convince you you're in love, though the sparkle in your eyes tells a different story. I'm saying there's no such thing as too much or too quickly."

It was too big an opening not to take. "So if I tie the knot down at city hall tomorrow, I can tell Lilith you said it was okay?"

"I can safely say your elopement would be painful for me."

"Because you couldn't walk me down the aisle?"

"Because after Lilith got through with me, I wouldn't be physically able to. Have mercy, child."

❖

Technology was a blessing and a curse. The fact that parents could register for the high school's smartphone app that provided up-to-date test results of its students was a blessing. The fact that the records didn't lie was a curse. TJ had several hours from receipt of

Kara's latest test scores before they'd see each other at home, and TJ needed every second of that time to figure out a course of action. Kara had always been a straight-A student with the exception of physical-education courses, which she despised. Although TJ believed physical activity was important, she didn't consider Kara's poor PE scores to be compromising her education.

What was compromising her education, however, was the job at Dillon's. That much was clear from the B-minus in American Literature and C-plus in U.S. Government.

Since Kara had started working, she'd spoken more to TJ in the past few weeks than she had in months. She was excited about what she was learning, and it showed. Her enthusiasm was obvious even in the mornings, which Kara usually dreaded, no longer dragging her feet and pushing her luck when it came to getting to school on time. And in the evenings, instead of what was normally a teeth-pulling exercise to get her to say more than ten words during dinner, TJ now spent time listening to Kara chatter about the latest vehicle she'd worked on and how she'd helped fix some difficult mechanical problem.

TJ was loath to take any kind of step that would dim Kara's flame, but she'd promised her father she would ensure that Kara received a solid education. Her father's memory burned brightly in TJ's mind. Jack had often stated that his biggest regret was having never graduated high school. He believed his earning power had been less than a third of what it could have been had he gone to college. But in his younger days, he'd cared more about women than school, and by the time he figured out a college education would have been a more lucrative path, he had a wife, a young daughter, and a construction gig. Unfortunately he landed in an industry that was one of the first to feel the brunt of an economic downturn, and finding work took precedence over returning to school for a degree.

He'd pushed TJ throughout high school, and she was a good student, though the pluses became minuses when she'd started working at sixteen to help with expenses. Now his children's futures rested in her hands. She'd made it into a graduate program he'd be proud of, and she owed it to him to ensure Kara applied to good colleges with grades that would secure her acceptance.

TJ had to take the pragmatic approach. College would be far more beneficial to Kara over the long term than anything she could reap from Dillon's. She felt certain that if Jack were alive, he wouldn't allow

Kara to keep the job at the expense of her grades. Short term, TJ knew she'd be at the receiving end of a full-scale verbal thrashing. But soon thereafter, Kara would go back to being a typical teenager, sulking one day and joking the next. At least that was the hope.

When TJ heard Kara's key in the lock, she steeled herself to do what she felt was in Kara's best interest. As Kara's guardian, it wasn't her job to be Kara's best friend, even though she wanted to be. Rather, her role was to help guide Kara through this prickly world, be her moral compass, her champion, her supporter. And sometimes that meant making decisions Kara disliked, because it would lead to the greater good. This was one of those times.

"Hey, Teej. You wouldn't believe what happened today." Kara swung her backpack onto the couch and headed to the kitchen for a glass of milk. "This guy brought in a sixth-generation Suburban he'd taken to three other places. The guy's out, like, twelve hundred bucks by this point, and he's been told he needs to invest another twenty-two hundred to fix the problem. So Jimmy, one of our master techs, tells me to check it out with him. And we do, and it's so obvious what the…" Kara stopped her rambling after TJ slid her phone across the kitchen table. "What's this?"

"I think it's fairly self-explanatory," TJ said.

Kara slid the phone back to TJ and shrugged. "They're just test scores. Not midterms. It's not like it's my final grade."

"English is your best subject."

Kara shrugged again. TJ wished someone would make some sort of miniature version of a straitjacket for teenagers that you could put them in to immobilize their shoulders. But what would a teenager be without the ability to casually express indifference?

"How are your other classes going?" *Shrug again and I may claw my eyes out.*

Sure enough, the shoulders raised and dropped. Kara returned the milk to the fridge and set her glass in the sink. Ten steps later she was retrieving her backpack and heading for her bedroom.

"I'd like to discuss this with you," TJ said, raising her voice beyond what she'd prefer.

"What's to discuss?" Kara's phone was in her hand, and although she stopped short of the hallway, she was swiping at the screen.

TJ stood and squared off. "This is a drastic drop in performance over a short time frame. It's safe to say your job's having a detrimental effect on your studies. I'm not okay with that."

Kara met TJ's gaze. "What's the big deal? I've made Bs and Cs before."

"Not in the same semester and never in more than one class. And the one C you ever got was when you were out with the flu the week before. This isn't acceptable."

"I'll try harder," Kara said in a tone that conveyed she wouldn't.

"Yes, you will. Which will be easier once you quit your job. You promised to maintain your grades, and I can see what that means to you. You're going to give notice. Next Friday will be your last day."

Kara's eyes narrowed and her jaw jutted forward. Her breathing became more pronounced with each passing second, her nostrils twitched, and her eyes began to glisten. "I hate you!" she screamed before slamming her bedroom door.

The words were like a serrated knife pulled through a fresh scab, painful and jarring. And it was about to feel like aloe on sunburn compared to what TJ had to do next.

❖

"I thought you'd never get here," Jess said as she tugged TJ into her loft and closed the door. But before she threw her arms around her neck, she could immediately tell something was off. TJ stood as stiff as a wall. She looked like she wanted a kiss as much as she wanted a colonoscopy. "What's wrong?"

TJ pushed her hands into her pant pockets. "We need to talk."

Worst opening line ever. "Okay," Jess said, stretching out the word as if it were pizza dough. "Can I get you something to drink?"

TJ shook her head. "I need to put this on hold for a little while."

Jess's stomach clenched. She hoped she'd misunderstood TJ's vague statement. "This?"

"Us."

Jess took a sharp breath. They'd barely begun to be an "us." How could TJ be ending what had scarcely had a chance to begin? More importantly, why? She tamped down on her urge to beg TJ to reconsider.

She made her way to the wet bar and poured herself a drink, using the time to settle her thoughts. What was she supposed to say? "I see" would be a lie. "May I ask why" felt too standoffish. "Is it something I did" was unfair to herself. Arguing seemed selfish. Crying would be too dramatic. The burning sensation as the beverage went down felt apropos, like a devastating fire was ravaging her insides.

"I don't know what to say," she finally said. "An explanation would be nice." Jess felt as though someone else had spoken the words. They were too stiff, reflecting the distance her heart suddenly sought.

"Kara's grades have slipped. I think it's from a combination of her job at Dillon's and me spending less time at home," TJ said.

And more time with you. TJ hadn't said it, but the words stung as if she had.

"I need to rectify both situations," TJ said.

"I'm a situation?" Jess asked without emotion.

"I told you when we met that I don't date. This is why. Kara's always going to be my priority."

"I never expected otherwise," Jess said, her ire rising. Even though TJ wasn't technically a single parent, single parents dated. Of course their children were their priority. That didn't mean they couldn't meet someone and fall in love. Look at Mike and Carol Brady.

"It's not fair of me to put anyone in a position that's less than they deserve," TJ said.

"It's not fair of you to play God and make choices for that person. God damn it—me. Let's not pretend we're talking about some theoretical person. We're talking about me. There's no reason it has to be all or nothing. You aren't the first single parent trying to balance a new relationship and a child."

"This is hard enough. How much harder will it be when you mean even more to me than you already do? It would break me," TJ said.

God, what Jess wouldn't give to hear those words in another context. TJ was admitting some very strong feelings for her, and it was happening while she's breaking things off? "You're assuming I'm a liability. How much better a parent might you be if you're happy?"

"Like your father?" TJ said testily. "As long as I'm happy, let my wife steamroller my child while I don't lift a damn finger to stop her?"

Jess stared at TJ as if she'd owned to kicking a white cane from a blind man. Her breathing grew heavy and she barely suppressed her rage. "You have no right."

"I have every right. Parents hold their children up, not tear them down."

Jess snapped. "The way you're holding Kara up by forbidding her from doing what she loves?"

TJ blinked.

This was getting out of hand. Jess had no desire to wound TJ, no

desire to argue. In fact, she'd rather entreat her to change her mind.
"Please go before we both say more things we'll regret."

"I never meant to hurt you," TJ said.

"Then don't walk away from what's between us by unilaterally deciding what I do and don't deserve," Jess said.

The moisture reflecting in TJ's eyes didn't make Jess feel better. Backing away from Jess and heading out the way she came, TJ said, "I don't have a choice."

CHAPTER NINETEEN

The last time Lilith called a family dinner was during a social-media storm involving a photo of a naked Brooke lookalike being penetrated from behind by a man whose face was obscured. Lilith had upbraided Brooke for the scandal and demanded she issue a public apology. Brooke said she would do so if Lilith could prove it was her. Lilith turned crimson and issued multiple warnings about the effect of such behavior on the firm's reputation. Brooke turned to Jess to ask whether there were signs that the incident appeared to be harming Magnate. On the contrary, Jess reported a spike in web "contact me" forms and confirmed that several were bona fide prospects.

Brooke's partner in the affair was the son of a wealthy foreign diplomat, which by rule made him acceptable to Lilith. But in the event their relationship became serious, she didn't want to sour Lilith's impression of him by admitting the truth, which she did privately to Jess. She simply decided some PR was better than no PR and neither confirmed nor denied the affair to the tabloids. Indeed, over time not a single client seemed to have been lost, and several were gained.

Jess had been impressed by her sister's fortitude in facing down Lilith. She wished she could channel it.

Lilith, who liked to keep everyone waiting, finally joined her family and allowed everyone several bites before launching in with the subtlety of a missile. "Jessica, I heard a disturbing rumor about you."

Innocently, Jess asked, "Oh?"

"Did you go for a cruise aboard Muriel Manchester's yacht recently?"

"I did." Jess set down her utensils, knowing she wouldn't be eating any more of her meal. "Is there a problem?"

"Did you kiss a woman?"

"I did." Jess noted the absence of a specific reference to TJ and hoped Brooke was the only one who knew the woman was Magnate's intern.

"On purpose?" Lilith asked.

The question was so absurd, it was a feat to keep from laughing. How did one kiss someone accidentally, aside from possibly sharing a piece of spaghetti à la the dogs in Disney's *Lady and the Tramp*?

As if reading Jess's mind, Brooke jumped in with a sarcastic reply. "No, accidentally."

Lilith quieted Brooke with a cool stare before returning her attention to Jess. "It wasn't a joke or a dare?"

"Do you have an issue with it?" Jess asked.

"You know very well that's not the question, Jessica. It's whether it reflects poorly on the firm."

"My personal life has nothing to do with the firm."

"Those arguments are tiresome and untrue. You wouldn't say the same thing if your father were caught in a scandal."

"A, there's no scandal. B, he's the founder and CEO. Of course what he does in his personal life reflects upon the firm. C, he's married. I'm not."

"Gary, would you say our client base tends to be liberal or conservative on social issues?" Lilith asked her son, appearing to change tactics.

"Conservative," Gary replied. "Muriel's a rare exception."

"Brooke, when you entertain our clients, do you feel you're representing the firm?" Lilith asked.

Jess noted the very specific, leading question. It didn't allow Brooke much room for pushing back. "Of course I do, but Jess wasn't entertaining—"

Lilith's raised palm was enough to quiet Brooke. She turned to Jess. "Please see to it that such rumors cease. We can't have Magnate's reputation suffer because of poor personal choices."

That her father opted for silence and failed to call Lilith on her overreaching brought to mind TJ's issues with him. Jess had been so quick to defend Derrick and so angry with TJ for questioning his parenting, she hadn't recalled the many times she, too, had questioned his inaction. Was it fair to call TJ out for something she'd done countless times herself?

Nothing felt fair at the moment. Not TJ's decision to back away from their relationship, not Lilith's insulting demands on Jess's life, not Derrick's continued deference to his overbearing wife.

Taking a page from Brooke's playbook, Jess decided she wouldn't bow to Lilith so easily. "It wasn't a business-related event. I attended as a guest."

"Inconsequential. What's important is that it not happen again." Lilith cut a small piece of steak and chewed.

The easiest choice was to agree. After all, she and TJ were no longer dating. What would be the benefit of pushing back?

But tonight wasn't about easy. It was about standing up for what was right. All the years of remaining silent in the wake of Lilith's demands had exacted a toll Jess was no longer willing to endure. It didn't matter that she and TJ were no longer seeing each other. Family members were supposed to stick up for each other. TJ was right. Channeling TJ, she said, "The question shouldn't be whether my kissing a woman reflects poorly on the firm. The question should be, does she make me happy?"

It stung, saying the words aloud, and Jess fought back the tears threatening to spring forth. TJ did make her happy. Had made her happy. She wasn't used to thinking of TJ and her in the past tense. Didn't want to think of it.

Lilith remained implacable, as if she were the dealer in a high-stakes poker game. "The people at this table are the stakeholders of the firm. We are five, not one. We must act for the collective, not the individual."

"Your discomfort with my relationship reflects on you, not the firm. It's homophobia, plain and simple." Never mind that there is no relationship, Jess didn't add.

Lilith took a sip of wine and dabbed her mouth with her napkin before scanning the faces of her son and stepdaughters. "All three of you have firsthand experience with my—I must say, underappreciated—interference with certain of your *relationships*, so it may be a tad hyperbolic for such labels."

Jess hated the disdain in Lilith's tone, as if Jess's relationship somehow didn't qualify.

Lilith continued, sounding as righteous as ever. "I will not apologize for holding each of you to high standards and keeping the firm's reputation at the forefront of our collective minds." To Jess she said, "If you're in a *relationship*, as you call it, I suggest you *end* your relations."

Jess wanted to scream. Was there any point in continuing to argue? Lilith delivered the words they'd been called together to hear, and Jess didn't expect anyone to come to her defense. She couldn't blame Gary, who always did his mother's bidding, or Brooke, who generally had Jess's back but was put in a winless situation. Neither could step into the fray on Jess's behalf and expect to gain anything but excoriation from it. She couldn't even blame Lilith, who was acting exactly as she always had, though her homophobia was now in neon.

Yet she could blame her father for his muteness. Why didn't he stick up for her? Why did he allow Lilith to dictate family policy? Wasn't his acquiescence as much a sign of homophobia as Lilith's words?

TJ was a combination of so many wonderful things. To be ruled out simply because of who she loved was an offense of the worst kind.

Jess wanted to tell her family TJ was exactly the kind of person Derrick funded the graduate program for. Hard-working, dedicated, honest, family-oriented. Why did her lack of connections matter? Why did her bank-account balance matter? Why did her preference for loving women matter?

If she said anything about TJ, it was possible Derrick or Gary would contact the school to have TJ transferred to intern elsewhere. She hadn't considered that option before. Bringing up TJ's character at this point wouldn't solve anything, and a transfer this far into the internship would only hurt her.

Yet ultimately this wasn't simply an argument about TJ. This was about discrimination. If Jess had learned anything from TJ, it was that ethics mattered. If TJ were here, she wouldn't back down.

Neither would Jess.

"You believe Magnate's reputation so precarious as to be far more impacted by the private lives of the people who own it than by the investment returns it achieves for its clients?" Jess asked.

Lilith set her utensils down and laser-focused on Jess. "I believe it to be unforgivably selfish for any of you to knowingly behave in a manner that might negatively affect our livelihood."

Okay, that did it. Lilith invoking "livelihood" as if their next meal depended on their tilling the soil was intolerable. The woman had been worth hundreds of millions before she married Derrick. Now she was worth billions. Was "livelihood" the proper term here? TJ would balk.

"And I believe it unforgivably selfish of you to become involved with an industrious, considerate, intelligent person, yet forbid me from doing the same." Jess rose and pushed in her chair. "Thank you all for the insightful conversation," Jess turned to Lilith, "and the *suggestion.*" She followed her usual manners and kissed Derrick's cheek before leaving. "Good night, Daddy. Love you."

❖

TJ rubbed her eyes before turning them to the alarm clock. Two nineteen. Once again she'd worked late into the night, having logged into Magnate's servers remotely using a secure virtual private network. She couldn't make sense of how the investments worked, and at this late stage of her internship, she needed help.

The only person who could help was Jess. Jess could direct her to anyone within the firm she needed to talk to or, on TJ's behalf, could ask questions as if coming at something from a marketing angle. And Jess could probably figure out the solution to the matter in half the time it took TJ, maybe less.

She felt terribly lonely. Neither Kara nor Jess was speaking to her beyond the absolute minimum necessary to get through a day, though in truth, she wasn't seeking time with Jess. She had no one to blame but herself. It had been her call to force Kara to stop working as well as to put things with Jess on hold. Although who was she kidding? Why would Jess, or anyone for that matter, wait for TJ for the next nearly two years until Kara went off to college? No, their relationship wasn't on hold. It was over.

It had been mere days since they—she—ended things, but time moved as slowly as if the hourglass were filled with quicksand.

Dinners with Kara yielded as much conversation as pigs in mud, with TJ receiving the odd grunt in reply to a question or comment. Their only discussion not involving logistics was Tuesday morning, when Kara said, "You ended things, didn't you?" She was scraping a spoon against the bottom of a plastic yogurt cup, intent on getting every possible dollop.

TJ had been running late but was reluctant to stave off conversation, since they'd been as frequent as thunderstorms in Las Vegas. Still, she didn't relish the topic. As she continued to pack her lunch, she said, "I need to focus on my work if I'm going to finish researching this case study and find time to write it."

"You didn't seem to think that last week. Or the week before. Or the week before that."

The decibels on the cup scraping were ratcheting up, along with TJ's temper. She yanked the container from Kara's hands. "It's *empty*, Kare."

Kara glared. At least she was making eye contact, TJ thought, irritated with herself for her impatience.

"No. You are," Kara said before placing her spoon in the dishwasher and returning to her room.

Kara had been right. TJ felt as empty as a bag of Oreos left out during first-grade recess. Her own excuses felt hollow to her, though they'd seemed unimpeachable mere days ago. She didn't want Kara or Jess to get her leftovers—those parts of her that were too exhausted to fully engage in a way both deserved. If she couldn't give her best to Jess, she should care enough to let her go. And she did care.

The alternative—taking away from Kara the last family member she had left—wasn't a possibility. Kara wasn't negotiable. TJ wasn't foolish enough to believe she was the perfect substitute parent, but she was the only option, and she did her best. Her best didn't include spending time away from Kara to selfishly follow her heart.

Oh, how she wanted to follow it.

Jess's argument about TJ possibly being a better parent if she was happy had hit home. TJ couldn't deny that her mother had been a wonderful, doting parent when her father was alive. It was only after his death that she became a shadow of who she'd been, losing her mind to her grief.

Was it self-serving and wishful to buy into that way of thinking? Or did Jess have a valid point? TJ's own experience suggested the latter, but she also realized her feelings made her susceptible to believing any contention that being with Jess was better. She *wanted* to believe it.

How could she still be having this same argument with herself every moment her mind wasn't occupied with the Magnate Fund? At what point did the brain decide to take pity and simply decide something was right or wrong, and let it go? TJ had already chosen. Why did her mind wantonly rehash her conversation with Jess as if she hadn't?

She shut down her computer and slipped under the covers. In moments, she'd be with Jess the only way she was able. In her dreams.

CHAPTER TWENTY

By midweek, Jess was no longer thinking normally. Sleep had touched her fleetingly, and makeup wasn't sufficient to mask the circles under her eyes. TJ avoided their daily check-ins as if Jess's office had become quarantined. Indeed, the strain in their relationship had popped up as quickly and as welcome as an infectious disease. Jess missed TJ's warmth and vitality. Although she wasn't satisfied being relegated to the role of friend, she wasn't willing to lose a friendship that had come to mean so much. Surely they could work through this incredibly painful time and come out the other side as something more than temporary colleagues.

She approached TJ's desk and found her working in a spreadsheet. "TJ, I'd like to see you in my office when you have a minute."

After TJ took a seat in Jess's office, Jess realized the confidence she'd grown accustomed to TJ projecting was missing. TJ was reluctant to meet her gaze in the way an abused puppy was hesitant to approach its mercurial master.

Jess cut to the chase. "You're avoiding me. Why?"

Immediately shifting uncomfortably in her chair, TJ said, "You have better things to do than educate me on aspects of the business that are outside your purview."

"Let's agree you shouldn't make decisions for me as to how best to spend my time." Jess hadn't wanted to take such a sharp tone, but she couldn't easily disentangle the personal from the professional. She took a calming breath before proceeding more neutrally. "We've had daily briefings ever since you agreed to return to the internship. There's no reason they should cease. Are you getting what you need from the client records?"

TJ took her time in responding. "I'll figure it out."

"Already back to not being able to accept my help?" Again Jess failed to set the right tone. She swiped her hand through the air as if to strike the comment from the record. "I realize you're used to depending on yourself for most things, and it's an admirable quality in an employee. But good employees also need to ask for assistance when they're spinning their wheels. Now, what can I do?"

"I don't understand how the Magnate Fund works," TJ said, frustration evident in her voice. "As far as I can tell, all client funds are invested in it. We seem to offer great resources to our staff for trading, so there must be client assets invested in other vehicles, such as stocks, mutual funds, and bonds."

Jess considered this question for some time. "The Magnate Fund is a hedge fund. By nature, we'll invest in a wide variety of financial instruments not limited to those you mentioned. Investors enjoy the additional diversification that comes from what we can offer, unlike more traditional vehicles. I imagine the trading resources are available simply to have everything easily accessible to our staff."

"It would be great to see what instruments the fund holds. It would also be helpful to be able to log in to the records of an individual client or two, because I don't understand the ledger transactions. The only client records I could find showed cash deposits and redemptions, but nothing in between. I can't see what investments a client owns at any particular time."

"I'm sure it's easy enough to explain. It might just be a particular set of screens Gary doesn't readily access. I'll look into it. Anything else?"

"No." TJ said. "Well, there is one more thing. When I logged in, the system showed that Gary's last login was over six months ago. As COO, wouldn't he be constantly monitoring everything?"

Jess smiled. "There's your answer. He probably has both an admin and a user login, and I must have only given you the latter. I'll flesh it out with him." TJ returned her smile, which was bittersweet for Jess. It was tepid, as if TJ was purposely holding back the heat Jess knew she could unleash in a second. Jess wanted TJ's sexy smile to return, but any smile was better than nothing.

TJ stood. "Makes sense. Thanks for helping." Before slipping out the door, TJ added, "And get some sleep."

❖

Instead of taking the direct path to the guesthouse, Jess strolled along the pool toward the gardens. The pool was always so inviting on calm nights like this, the underwater lights casting the pale-blue walls in a glowing serenity. She often went swimming here in the evenings, enjoying the solitude as well as the tranquility that came with unplugging from the world for a short while.

Occasionally, her father would join her. Unlike Jess, Derrick no longer swam laps, but he enjoyed the outdoor hot tub. The sense of freedom that the expansive night sky offered proved far greater a temptation than tubbing indoors ever would.

She missed him. Long gone were the days he carved out family time with "my girls," reading them bedtime stories and, as they got older, insisting they read to *him* each night. Weekend mornings, Derrick had allowed the girls to burst into his bedroom and pile on top of him, and the three of them would tell stories in a round-robin, where one person would make up the beginning of a tale and then pass it to the next, who either went with it or took it in a completely different direction.

These days, it seemed Derrick was always working, just as he had after Jess's mom died. Back then, on the rare nights Jess and Brooke were still awake when he would come home, he'd kiss them on the cheek with as much emotion as one butters toast. The evening caregiver would take him dinner and his Gibson, and he'd ascend to the Moonlight Room, where he wasn't to be disturbed. There he'd sit in the same chair night after night, appearing to Jess as if he was looking out over the expanse of ocean without really seeing anything.

One night, as Jess watched from her hidden vantage point on the stairs, Derrick dropped his head into his hands, and his shoulders bobbed as he cried. Jess ran to him and hugged him, not caring about the punishment she was sure to receive from defying his commands. "I miss her too, Daddy," Jess said, intuiting his thoughts. He slid to his knees and held her as he sobbed. She'd never seen him so distraught and simply held him until he could cry no more.

"I can't do this alone, pumpkin," he said.

"You're not alone, Daddy. You have Brooke and me," Jess said. "Don't you love us anymore?"

"Of course I do, sweetie. Why do you say that?" he said as he wiped away her tears with the pads of his thumbs.

"Because you're always at work, you're mad all the time, and you never read us stories anymore."

"I haven't been a very good daddy lately, have I, pumpkin?"

"It's okay."

"No, it's not." Derrick lifted Jess into his arms and held her. "Would you like me to read you a story tonight?"

Jess nodded enthusiastically.

"How much does Daddy love you?" It was his usual question, but she hadn't heard it in months.

"To the moon and back," Jess exclaimed.

He shifted her onto his shoulders and held her ankles. "Let's go find us a good book."

From that night, though Derrick continued to put in long hours, he made it a point to check in on them at dinner, come home in time to read them a story at bedtime, and reserve weekend mornings so they could be together as a family.

As Jess wandered past the pool, she recalled it was Derrick who had taught her how to swim. She would gladly give up her *things* to spend more time with him. But she and Brooke had long been adults, and Derrick and Lilith had been married for many years. Perhaps it was simply the natural order of things that she'd see her father less and less.

The gradual descent into the garden occurred by long, wide stairs requiring at least three steps per level before reaching the next stair down. Parts of the path were covered by trees, most of which were dimly lit by the lights along the walkway. Jess headed for her favorite statue in the garden: a bronze cheetah sitting in a slanting tree. The magnificent cat was leaning forward on its front paws, its rear legs seated near the top of the tree, its tail appearing to swing off the back of the fallen trunk. It stared straight ahead with stunning intensity, ears back and alert. It was a gorgeous work of art, and as Jess studied it, she wondered how often Derrick stopped to enjoy the incredible beast or any of the other pieces in the surrounding grounds. He took morning walks through the gardens, but how much did he notice? When was the last time someone had asked him to describe what he saw?

Inevitably, as they did of late, her thoughts turned to TJ, the woman who'd reminded Jess to take more notice of the things around her. Jess missed their playfulness, their easy interaction, their flirtatiousness. She wasn't sure when it had happened, but TJ had gotten so far under her skin as to be muscle and bone. TJ had hurt her terribly, yet for some reason, Jess couldn't remain angry with her. TJ had lost both parents in tragic ways, and Kara was her only remaining close family.

Of course if TJ believed something was compromising Kara's future, she'd shoulder the blame. She was fortifying her defenses by turning into herself the way a turtle might.

But Jess wasn't the problem. Jess firmly believed they could be stronger and more helpful to Kara and to each other by being together. Yet she didn't know how to convince TJ.

Jess continued along the path, appreciating the windless, balmy evening. It was the perfect night for a stroll with a lover. The thought was like a kick in the gut, because the only person she thought of that way was TJ. They hadn't crossed that line, but Jess felt TJ was more her lover than any of her actual lovers had been. Tears stung her eyes. None of the grandeur surrounding her mattered if she couldn't share it with someone she loved.

And she couldn't.

She passed another of her favorite statues, a small boy carrying a lamb across his shoulders. But she could hardly see it for her tears. Escape was what she needed, escape from the art she couldn't share, the gardens she couldn't share, the feelings she couldn't share.

As she came around the corner and ran up the stairs to her front door, she nearly tripped over her father, who was seated outside waiting for her. Jess regained her balance and swiped at her cheeks with the back of her hand. "Sorry, Daddy. I wasn't expecting you."

Derrick held his arms out as if to steady her, but pulled back upon seeing she wasn't going to fall. "Are you okay? Honey, what's wrong?"

Jess shook her head. "I'm fine." Squaring her shoulders for an argument, she was about to ask what he wanted but realized she didn't have the energy. Instead she asked, "Can we please do this another time? I can't argue with you tonight. I'm tired, I'm…" Miserable. She swallowed hard.

"I'm not here to argue."

"You're not?"

"May I come in?"

Jess was powerless to deny his request. She pushed open the door and Derrick fell in step behind. She ducked into the bathroom off the hallway to grab some tissues before following him into the study, where Derrick headed straight for the wet bar and Jess for one of her favorite couches.

"Drink?" he offered.

"Sparkling water, please," with a Long Island Iced Tea chaser, she didn't add. Alcohol would definitely take the edge off, but she wanted all her faculties for this conversation.

When he finished making his Gibson, Derrick brought Jess her drink and took a seat next to her on the couch. "Cheers," he said, offering a toast. "Or should I say, cheer? It looks like you could use some."

She clinked glasses with him. "I could use a friend."

"How about a father? He went missing earlier but he's been returned. The microchip was a good call."

Jess wasn't in the mood for his humor, which was a first. "I'm not going to tell you what you want to hear."

"What do I want to hear?" Derrick asked.

"That I'm regretful. That I apologize. That I believe my actions have been detrimental to the firm."

"I know her methods aren't always agreeable, but Lilith's understandably protective when it comes to the firm. Magnate wouldn't be what it is today without her assets and connections."

Jess's jaw tightened. Derrick was putting his spin on things, as he always did. He was the consummate salesman, always trying to get you to buy. In this case, he was selling Lilith's actions as reasonable. But she believed Lilith's *suggestion* to be as acceptable as killing elephants for their ivory tusks. Was he trying to make Jess into an ingrate by reminding her of Lilith's contributions to their collective wealth? She stilled her tongue for fear she'd say something to pit her against Lilith, which she desperately wished to avoid. She feared whom he'd choose if it came to that, and she couldn't lose him, her bedrock.

Derrick set down his drink. "But I didn't come here to defend her. I was hoping Lilith would back down when you didn't. I didn't want to berate her in front of Gary and Brooke, but I should have said she was wrong. Because she was. Before I walked down here, I told her as much and that it wasn't open for debate."

"What are you saying?"

"I'm the one who's regretful. I'm the one who should apologize. I should have stuck up for you sooner. The only thing I want to hear is that you forgive me."

Rapid blinking wasn't preventing more tears from welling. Full of emotion, Jess couldn't speak, so she nodded.

Derrick moved closer to Jess on the couch and put his arms around her. Jess could no longer suppress her sobs, leaning into his chest and covering her face with her hands. He was finally being the father she so fiercely missed, so desperately needed, and she let go.

It was a bittersweet moment, feeling wrapped in the love of the most important man in her life yet melancholy over the state of things with TJ.

Finally ready to collect herself, Jess sat back on the couch and wiped her nose.

"Is it this woman?" Derrick asked.

Jess nodded and dabbed her eyes.

"I thought she made you happy."

Jess half-laughed, half-sobbed. "She did."

"What's the problem?"

"She's the guardian of her little sister, who's in high school. She feels guilty for spending time with me because that's time she could spend with her. Or something. I don't know. And if she's anything like me, she's also feeling scared as hell because I mean something to her, and she doesn't know what to do with it. So she put on the brakes."

With an expression laced with challenge, Derrick asked, "What do you plan to do about it?"

"What can I do?" Jess said, exasperation evidenced by raised decibels.

"Fight for her."

When no other words seemed forthcoming, Jess felt as lost as a small child dropped into the middle of Grand Central Station.

"You might get hurt, honey, but you're already hurting. You have to ask yourself if she's worth it. If the answer's yes, you've very little to lose and everything to gain by fighting for her."

Few of Derrick's words mirrored Lilith's. So few, Jess was compelled to confirm her understanding. "Even if it impairs Magnate's reputation?"

"It won't." Derrick stood as if needing a break from all the sentiment. "For every Jerry Falwell, we'll find a Muriel Manchester. And we'll be stronger for it." He took a final swig of his drink before setting it down and holding his arms out to her. "I haven't said this in far too long, but I'm proud of you."

The new tears threatening were those of joy. "Thank you, Daddy." Jess practically leapt into his embrace.

"Thank *you* for giving your old man another chance. I never want to disappoint you."

"You never will."

"Now figure out a way to get your girl."

"I'll try."

CHAPTER TWENTY-ONE

Jess's phone started playing "Fun, Fun, Fun (Till Her Daddy Takes the T-Bird Away)." Dillon. With a smile, she answered. "Hey, handsome."

"Have you seen Kara?" Dillon sounded frantic.

Jess gripped her chair's armrest. The ridiculousness of the question and its serious tone quashed a sarcastic reply. "No. Tell me what's wrong."

"She stole my GTO."

Wide-eyed and immediately thinking the worst, Jess stopped herself from asking whether he was certain. Dillon wouldn't make such an accusation otherwise. "How long ago? Have you called the police?"

"According to the security cameras, about an hour ago. And no, I haven't. Yet."

Jess wasn't sure whether to feel relieved. If the police were apprised, Kara would get into serious trouble. If they weren't, she could get seriously hurt. Or worse. "Why haven't you?"

"You tell me. Why am I in this mess to begin with?" Dillon asked accusingly.

The remark stung. Jess wasn't responsible for Kara or Kara's actions, and Dillon had no right to insinuate differently. But she *had* used her influence to encourage him to give Kara a chance. "I'm sor—"

"I'm sorry. I didn't mean that. It's not your fault." Jess heard him expel an exasperated breath. "I wanted to talk to you before I did anything."

Jess smiled sadly. Dillon's kind-hearted nature was shining through as always, and she wasn't sure she deserved his decency on the matter. Although she'd taken an immediate liking to Kara, she'd done so in part because she was intrigued by her sister. At the time Jess had hit up Dillon for the favor to employ Kara, how much did Jess really know about her? "Thanks, but I need you to do what's right for you. She's old enough to know right from wrong, and she has to face the consequences of her poor choices."

"I agree."

Jess heard the hesitation in his voice. "But?" she asked.

"She's a smart kid. She's seen the security cameras. She'd know I'd know it was her. So why do it?"

"You think she's trying to get caught?"

"I don't know."

"Have you told her sister?"

"Yes. She was surprised and extremely apologetic. She said she didn't think Kara would skip town, and when she checked her room, nothing seemed missing, as in, she hadn't packed anything. She was going to call some of Kara's friends and then head out to some of Kara's favorite hangouts to see if she could track her down."

TJ must be frantic with worry. Not only could Kara get into trouble with the law over this, but she could get hurt. If she really was trying to get caught, she might be in a frame of mind to do something stupid—not that she wasn't already killing it on that front. "That makes sense. What can I do?"

"There's not much that can be done except wait things out and call the police."

"Then call them."

"And if she's out for a joyride? I'd hate for her to get charged with grand theft auto. It's a felony, Jess."

"Jesus, Dillon. She stole your car. How can you be so understanding?"

The response was so slow in coming, Jess considered repeating the question in case they'd lost their connection briefly. But then she heard him say, "I think you know why." For her. He was doing it for her. She loved him for it. She and TJ might not be together, but that didn't prevent her from caring about TJ and, by extension, Kara.

"How about you give her until midnight, and if she or it hasn't turned up, call the police. If she's joyriding, she should be back by then," Jess said.

"That's what I was thinking."

"Great minds."

"That's you, Spaulding. I'm simply the meathead with the muscle cars."

"Ideally with the same number you started the day with. Call me if you hear anything, and I'll do the same."

"Will do. Love you," Dillon said.

"Love you too."

Jess considered calling TJ. But what words could she offer? She felt impotent, unsure of what she'd say or how she could aid the situation. Then again, she had unlimited resources at her disposal. Perhaps she could hire a private-investigations firm. No, they wouldn't have more eyes on the streets than the police, and if Kara was tucked away somewhere to hide the car, the extra eyes wouldn't help.

Maybe she could offer to split the task of scouting Kara's usual hangouts to cover more ground more quickly. This idea had merit, though TJ's pride would likely interfere. Still, wouldn't TJ rather find her sister and accept assistance, even if it came in the form of Jessica Spaulding? Jess thought so. Kara was probably the only thing in TJ's life that would cause her to swallow her pride. She placed the call, which went to voice mail. She left a message saying she'd spoken with Dillon and offered to help search for Kara.

Jess returned to the book she'd been reading, though it held no appeal. She wanted to be *doing* something. Was it a mistake not to call the police immediately? If Kara wished to be caught, involving the police would expedite her apprehension and get her off the road sooner, back to safety. Or would she be incarcerated, in which case her safety was not assured? The penal system had a terrible reputation for inmate safety. Kara didn't belong behind bars, and a felony record would seriously mar her otherwise strong prospects. What was the girl thinking?

Setting the book down after attempting to read the same page a dozen times, she went into her study to work. It was the best way she knew to get her mind off Kara's whereabouts.

As was often the case when she worked, Jess lost track of time. When the buzzer at the gate entrance signaled a visitor, it was after eleven. From her laptop she pulled up the security cameras' feed to see who was dropping by at such a late hour. She wasn't expecting anyone. Kara's image popped onscreen, the first angle capturing her head and shoulders, as well as a portion of the GTO's roof and driver's side mirror. The other cameras made it clear the GTO was intact. Nearly overwhelmed with relief, Jess felt some of the tension in her shoulders ease. Pushing the audio button, Jess said, "Kara? Are you all right?"

"I'm sorry to come by so late, but can I come through?"

"Of course. One sec." Jess hit the key to open the gate.

As Kara pulled into the estate grounds, Jess considered her predicament. This seemed like the kind of thing an aunt or grandmother should help with. In movies, the Kara character would have an older, wiser woman to turn to. Jess was not that person. How was she supposed to proceed? Should she berate Kara for her stupid behavior? Should she call the police and let the situation work itself through the juvenile justice system? Should she play dumb and pretend not to know what Kara had done and see if she came clean? Speaking of movies, should she cuff Kara to a pipe and call TJ to handle it?

The doorbell chimed, pulling Jess from her oscillating thoughts, except the lingering one that said she should have taken a shot of liquor. She rubbed her hands on her thighs in an attempt to wipe away her nervousness and calm herself. She'd follow Kara's lead but wouldn't let her off the hook.

Jess opened the door to a haggard Kara. "Come in." Deciding not to sidestep the issue, Jess asked, "Kara, did you take that car with Dillon's permission?" She needed to know off the bat whether Kara would be honest. Jess didn't doubt TJ's probity for a second, but she had very little experience with her sister.

Kara flicked her eyes to Jess before shoving her hands in the front pockets of her jeans and returning her eyes to the floor. She shook her head. "No."

Jess worked her mouth, contemplating how best to proceed. What would TJ do? Jess doubted TJ would shake Kara's shoulders and scream at her. Though it might feel cathartic in the moment, Jess knew it wasn't appropriate behavior. "I have to call him."

Kara's eyes shot up. "Can you wait? I was hoping to talk to you first."

"No, I can't wait. You can't take things that don't belong to you. He's already told me you took it, and he's extremely worried."

"I'd never hurt it."

"I mean about you. Of course he's upset you took his car, but what if you got into an accident? You could get hurt, or worse. And TJ—does she know you're here?"

Kara shook her head. "I turned my phone off."

"Kara..." Exasperated and overwhelmed, Jess fought to maintain her temper. Kara was acting like such a teenager. The fact that she *was* a teenager didn't make her actions any more palatable. Although she knew Dillon would wait until midnight per their pact, Jess said, "The police might be looking for you."

Tears welled in Kara's eyes, but she lifted her chin defiantly. "I'm ready for that."

"Well, I'm not. If there's a warrant out for your arrest, I could get in trouble for harboring a fugitive." It was complete BS, and Jess nearly laughed saying it, but the situation left little room for humor.

Slumping and speaking in a low voice, Kara turned for the door. "I don't want to get you in trouble."

Satisfied the girl still had something of a conscience, Jess grabbed her upper arm to stop her. "Stay. Give me two minutes to call Dillon and TJ to let them know you're okay. And hand me the keys."

"Please don't call her. Please."

Kids! Why were they so hard to say no to even when you were angry with them? No way could Jess sit on the news Kara was alive and well and with her. "Tell you what. I'll call Dillon and have him tell TJ you're okay but not divulge how he knows. Okay?"

Kara pressed the key into Jess's palm. "Thanks."

Jess lightly tugged Kara into the house. "Come on." She swept her phone from the entryway table and took Kara to one of the couches in the living room. She walked down the hallway to make a quick call to Dillon. Once she returned, she asked, "Can I get you anything to drink? Water? Soda?" At Kara's head shake, Jess sat on the edge of a nearby leather lounge chair. "Talk to me. What's going on? Why did you take Dillon's car?"

"Did he call the police?"

"No."

"Is he mad?"

"Yes. But mostly he's worried about you."

Kara's chin trembled before she set it, and her eyes gleamed rebelliously. "I don't need anyone worrying about me. I can take care of myself."

"Not until you're eighteen."

"I can petition to be an emancipated minor."

"I'm fairly certain you have to demonstrate your ability to be financially independent."

"I can be. I already know as much about cars as most of the mechanics in Dillon's shop."

"That may be true, but I'd be willing to bet you're not exactly looking at a glowing letter of recommendation at this point. You can't take what doesn't belong to you."

"I did it to get back at her."

"At TJ?"

"She said I can't work there anymore. Today was my last day, my last chance, and I...I don't know. I wanted to hurt her."

"By taking it out on Dillon?"

Kara jumped to her feet. "By taking it out on everyone! Why do *I* have to quit? Why do *I* have to give up what I want to do because *she* made a promise?"

"Sweetie, slow down. Start from the beginning."

"I don't know what to do." Kara wrapped her arms tightly around herself and began pacing a path behind the couch. "I got crummy marks on my last two tests. TJ said my job's impacting my grades and made me quit. But I don't want to! I've already learned so much. Dillon's showing me how to convert manual brakes to a power system on a sixty-nine Camaro. There's so much to think about and master. Leave them as drum or convert to disc? If disc, how much assist? Single diaphragm booster or dual? Eight-inch or eleven-inch or something in between? And what bore size do you need? It's all connected and so awesome.

"But all TJ cares about is me getting into college. I don't want to go to college! I don't *care* about college. Why can't she let me do what *I* want?" Kara swiped at her wet cheeks with her sleeve. "I can make a good living, just like Dillon. He knows so much. He would've kept teaching me if I hadn't..." She slumped onto the couch and hid her face in her hands.

Jess's lack of experience giving guidance to youngsters made her feel as though she were dropped into an air-traffic control tower and expected to safely guide incoming planes. Her appreciation for what TJ had to handle as Kara's guardian grew exponentially, and as much as Kara wanted to make TJ out to be the bad guy, Jess couldn't agree. She squatted in front of the girl and rested a hand on Kara's knee.

"Have you told her what you want?" Jess asked.

"Only a thousand times," Kara said disconsolately.

"Which is what?"

"Restore cars. I like fixing 'em too, but mostly I like making a rusty pile of metal into something beautiful and powerful. Dillon calls it extracting a butterfly's wings from cooled lava."

"And you thought taking his car would get your point across?" Jess suggested gently.

Kara shook her head. "At first I was angry. Like I wanted to get in trouble so she'd have to deal with it. But then..." She swallowed and wiped at fresh tears. "Then I wanted to get into enough trouble to go to jail for a long time."

"Why would you want to go to jail?"

"Because then she won't have to take care of me anymore." Her next words sounded haunted. "And I won't be in the way."

Though this quasi-parenting thing came with a host of uncharted territory, it involved certain precepts even Jess understood as sacrosanct. The bond TJ and Kara shared was as sure as tomorrow's sunrise. Jess sat next to her and placed a hand on her back. Without doubt or hesitation, she said, "Kara, sweetie, you're not in the way."

"She always puts me first," Kara said. "I hate it. Did you know she left college to take care of me?"

"Of all the people I know, TJ's the last who could be forced into doing something against her will. If she left college, it was her choice."

"Family means everything to her. If she has to choose between herself and me, she'll always choose me."

"Because she loves you. I don't fault her for that."

"I don't deserve it."

"Oh, sweetie. Yes, you do."

"No." Kara shook her head.

"Why do you think that?"

"If I'd been better, Mom wouldn't have..." Kara slid to the floor and pulled her knees to her, as if trying to shrink down so small she couldn't be seen. She repeatedly shook her head, and Jess wasn't sure Kara could continue, or if she wanted her to.

Finally, Kara drew in a ragged breath. Her voice was so soft and anguished, Jess struggled to hear. "I wasn't worth sticking around for."

Okay, that did it. No child should hold such an unfair and inaccurate view of themselves, and Jess didn't need to be Dr. Phil to know what to do next. She slipped to the floor, pulled Kara into her arms, and held fast.

The girl's sobs tore at Jess's heart. Jess repeated words of comfort while stroking Kara's hair and back, surprised at how petite she was beneath the boy clothes she wore. How had Kara arrived at such a terrible conclusion about herself? At sixteen, a girl is becoming independent and learning how the world works, facing pressures about her future, yet not sufficiently emotionally developed to maintain control over her feelings. Once she considered Kara in that light, Jess had an easier time understanding how she could move so quickly from angry to inadequate, from lashing out to breaking down.

Jess had only some idea of the circumstances that had caused TJ to become Kara's guardian. Losing a parent so young was hard, as Jess well knew. Losing the remaining parent to an unyielding self-destruction would have been devastating. TJ had experienced the same loss as her sister, yet instead of being of an age to continue attending school and striving to maintain a sense of normalcy by doing so, she was thrust into the demanding role of guardian and provider. No wonder TJ was so heavily self-reliant. With her parents gone, who else could she have turned to?

How much would it tear TJ apart to hear Kara's tormented words of doubt? How much might it mean to Kara's self-worth to work hard following her dreams, dreams that had nothing to do with attending college? Would TJ be able to let go of her wishes for Kara's education if it helped shore up Kara's self-regard?

"I can't speak for your mom, sweetie, but you're definitely worth sticking around for. She loved your father, yes?" Jess felt Kara nod against her chest. Recalling TJ's words about heartbreak and alcohol, Jess asked, "And she drank?" Again, Kara nodded. "After he died?" Another nod. "It sounds like she was battling severe depression over his death. Neither you nor TJ caused it, and it didn't make your mom love you any less. It's an illness, sweetie, and like any illness, if left untreated it can get worse over time. And adding alcohol is like trying to put out a fire with lighter fluid. She didn't stop loving you, but it was like she woke up alone in a room with no doors or windows, no light and no sound. You didn't change. She just couldn't reach you."

Kara mumbled a response Jess couldn't make out. Jess pulled back momentarily so she could hear.

"She didn't try," Kara whispered.

Jess didn't know how Kara's mother, a woman who produced two amazing daughters, could have lost sight of how precious and important they were. While the woman's loss had been profound, she'd tragically compounded it by focusing on her husband's death instead of the very alive and vibrant children who needed her. But depression was a complex, insidious beast that defied reason, and the woman apparently could no longer see the beauty and love surrounding her.

"I'm sure it felt that way to you, and it's a terrible feeling. But let me ask you this. Do you think TJ was worth sticking around for?"

This time it was Kara who pulled back. "Totally."

"You both were. Are." Jess tucked an unruly strand of hair behind Kara's ear, an oddly comforting yet fruitless gesture considering the girl's hairstyle was one of purposeful unruliness. "Your mom was sick, sweetie. You have to look at it that way and know she didn't leave you because of anything you did."

She watched Kara struggle to accept her words. Jess's comment about TJ being worth it had clearly registered, but it seemed too much for Kara to believe she was too. But at least Jess had gotten her to consider the possibility, given that she had likely struggled with her self-worth for years.

Kara scooted several inches away until she was out of reach. Jess sensed the girl was starting to feel embarrassed at her show of emotion. "Sorry to be such a minefield. Probably really makes you want to have kids, huh?"

Jess stared at Kara for a moment before bursting with laughter at the non sequitur. "I'm not sure anything would make me want to have kids, but I honestly haven't thought about it much. I think I need to find someone I can stand to date more than twice before I go down that path."

"You and TJ have gone out more than that."

Jess took a deep breath. TJ wasn't a subject she wished to broach. "Your sister and I are friends."

"You dated."

Not privy to whatever TJ had told Kara, Jess said, "Briefly."

"When did you break up?"

"I'm not sure breaking up is the right term. We never talked about being exclusive, and we were never girlfriends."

"It was last weekend, wasn't it?"

Jess didn't want to make it seem to Kara as though it was a big deal, as though it hadn't shaken her to her core. "Around then."

"She ended it, didn't she? She wouldn't answer when I asked."

Jess wanted to say it was none of Kara's business, but now wasn't the time to alienate her. She nodded.

"Because of me?" Kara asked.

"Of course not." Jess was adamant. In truth, Jess wasn't entirely clear as to TJ's reasoning, and TJ *had* implied her decision related to

Kara. But none of it was Kara's fault, and Jess wouldn't make Kara the scapegoat. No couple was insulated from the influence of people and pressures that could affect them. But if they cared enough, they could face and work through those challenges together. It didn't mean that they didn't need to perform certain juggling acts; it didn't mean other important people became somehow less so.

Kara's chin trembled. "You should be together." More tears threatened. "It's because of me you're not."

Kara was right. This was a minefield, and Jess was forced to traverse it without any detection tools. "We should be together. And I intend to fight for her. But I can tell you this unequivocally. You are *not* the reason we aren't together. TJ is. Actually she and I both are, because I gave up too easily."

"If I'm out of the picture, you—"

"Stop. Absolutely not. Kara, if you go to jail, you'll break your sister's heart. And mine." Frustrated at being unable to curtail the direction of the girl's thoughts, Jess took a different tack. "You are not in the way *at all*. I'm not going to bullshit you." Jess inwardly winced at her language, but hell, the kid was sixteen. It wasn't as if she hadn't heard it all before. "TJ's wrong about her and me, and I intend to tell her so. But if you're taken away from her, she'll be just as heartbroken over you as your mom was over your dad. Do you think I or anyone else would stand a chance if that happened?" Kara refused to meet Jess's gaze. "Look at me." Waiting until Kara raised her head, Jess repeated, "Do you?"

"No."

"Do you think she'd even be capable of a relationship if that happened?"

Kara shook her head and whispered, "I want her to be happy. You make her happy."

How was it possible for a heart to bleed yet expand in the same moment? Jess smiled and fought back her own tears as she brushed one from Kara's cheek. Then she cupped her chin and said firmly, "So do you." She cocked an eyebrow, waiting for Kara to agree. Then she tilted her head when a response wasn't forthcoming, letting Kara know she wasn't backing down. Finally, Kara nodded.

"Now, how 'bout we discuss this little matter of the car out front, hmm?"

Kara nodded again.

"What would you like to do?"

Kara twisted one of her hoodie strings. "I don't know. I've never kept one before. I know joyriding's, like, not okay either, but I've never wanted to actually steal anything, you know? But I did steal this one." She dropped the tie. "So I guess, maybe, you should call the police."

Jess prevented herself from rolling her eyes. Of course Kara would feel badly enough about herself and what she'd done to believe she ought to go to jail. "Hmm. Let's think about this. The car's out front and not damaged. So...not really missing. I'm not sure what I'd tell them. Plus I already told Dillon it's here."

"I can head back out, let you know which way I'm heading, and then you can tell them where you think I—"

"I don't believe you'd have come here if you really wanted to go to jail. And to be honest, orange wouldn't be a good color on you." That earned Jess a small smirk that inordinately pleased her.

Silent for several moments, Kara finally said, "I guess I should start by returning the car."

"A very mature step. I'm proud of you."

Kara snorted. "I stole a car and you're proud of me?"

"Not your finest hour, I agree. But we all make mistakes. The trick is owning up to them and understanding how we made them so we can learn not to repeat them."

"Can I have the keys?"

"Not on your life." Jess winked.

"But you just said you agree I should return the car."

"I said returning it would be a mature step, but I think we should let Dillon decide. We can let him know you're offering to return it, but it's his car. He'll probably want to drive it himself or bring his flatbed to pick it up."

"Do any bus routes go by here? TJ will come for me, but I don't want to ask."

"Tell you what. Why don't you sleep here tonight? I'll give Dillon another call, and we'll handle it in the morning. It's been a long day and the car's not going anywhere."

"Really?" Kara's face lit up.

"Yes, really. I have tons of room, and you're more than welcome."

Kara's smile dimmed as she took in her surroundings. "I've never stayed anywhere so nice. I don't want to ruin anything."

Jess laughed. "You're not cooking, so there's nothing to ruin, and clean sheets and towels are meant to be used. Give your sister a call while I call Dillon. Have you eaten?"

"Not hungry."

"Well, if you get hungry, feel free to eat anything you find. There's lots of stuff in the fridge. Make yourself at home after you call TJ. I'll be right back."

When Jess finished speaking with Dillon, she returned to find a frowning Kara scrolling through her phone. "What's wrong?"

"Five missed calls and a bunch of texts from TJ."

"Did you call?"

Kara nodded. "Went to voice mail."

The front gate buzzed again, and Jess opened the security app on her phone. A fretful TJ appeared onscreen. Jess showed Kara. "That would be why." She bypassed the intercom and opened the gate. "Why don't you shower and get your head together while I talk to her. Take any room down that way. Each one has a bathroom and fresh towels."

Kara shook her head. "No," she said joylessly. "I'll face the music."

"No doubt you will. But I'd like a word with her first, if that's okay."

"I don't want you in the middle. She likes you."

"A good thing considering she has to work with me."

Kara raised her gaze to Jess's and smiled sadly. "You know what I mean. If I wasn't in the way..."

"Stop. Saying. That." Jess caught Kara's forearm. "You're *not* in the way. She loves you."

Eyes downcast, Kara said, "I wish she didn't."

"Kara." Jess was frustrated that Kara didn't seem to be taking to heart their earlier conversation, but Kara had felt that way year after year until it was crusted over. "Someone who's in a great graduate program and interning at a top investment firm doesn't sound like someone putting her life on hold. But I'm not going to argue. Your choice, sweetie."

Kara made a face. "I'll save one of those clean towels for my mopping up once she's done with me." With that, Kara strode down the hall.

When the doorbell rang, Jess took a calming breath before opening the door. This would be the first time they'd seen each other outside of work since TJ ended things between them. Despite that, and despite the reason TJ was here, Jess was glad she'd come.

They stared at one another, neither comfortable starting a conversation sure to be even more awkward than this moment. Jess nearly whimpered at how good TJ looked, and it had nothing to do with attire. Concern over her sister's welfare made TJ at once vulnerable and commanding. An image popped into Jess's head of the formidable Cerberus, three-headed guard dog of the underworld. TJ's protection of Kara rivaled the beast's protection of Hades.

Jess broke the silence. "She's showering, and she's fine. Please come in." She stepped aside to let TJ by.

"I'm so sorry about this. Dillon wouldn't say anything other than he hadn't contacted the police and she was okay. I assumed she ended up here. It's probably hard for you to believe she knows better, but she does."

Jess shut the door. "I'm sorry you've been worried. She arrived a little while ago and told me what she'd done. I immediately called Dillon and asked him to call you."

"But not tell me where she was."

Needing time to gather her thoughts so this didn't deteriorate into an argument, Jess walked to the kitchen knowing TJ would follow. "Can I get you something to drink? Water, beer, wine, soda, cocktail?"

"Hemlock?" TJ suggested.

Jess laughed. "Sorry, no." TJ's attempt to lighten things up helped loosen Jess's tight shoulders.

"Water would be great, thanks." TJ leaned against the counter. "As soon as she's out of the shower, I'll take her home. I'll work out the car details with Dillon."

Jess took advantage of the time it took to gather the drink to figure out what to lead with. As she handed the glass to TJ, she said, "She was pretty upset when she arrived. Wasn't happy you made her quit."

TJ grimaced and gave a curt nod. "I apologize for involving you in our family squabbles. Our dirty laundry isn't exactly something I expected you to have to hear about." TJ's delivery was stilted, and Jess wondered whether TJ was uncomfortable at the prospect in general or whether she particularly disliked the idea that it was Jess specifically who got wind of it. Jess hoped it wasn't the latter, or they didn't stand a chance.

"Please don't apologize. She needed a friend tonight, and for whatever reason, she chose me. I'm glad she did." Jess meant it.

"Thanks for being there for her. I'm not always what she needs." The comment was strained and tugged at Jess deeply. The hurt in TJ's voice was unmistakable. It wasn't jealousy. No, Jess pegged it as fear—

fear of a rift beginning to tear the sisters apart the way a knitted sweater could unravel with the pull of one stray stitch.

"TJ, I really think it would be good for her to stay the night. She needs to process what she's done and how to make it right, and if you take her home, she's going to defer to you. It might be good for her to have the opportunity to devise her punishment with Dillon directly." And she won't be as likely to think she's in the way if you handle everything, she didn't add.

"He could have her arrested."

"He could. And if he does, she'll have to accept that. But he hasn't so far. Maybe sit back and see what they work out? He's a pretty reasonable guy."

"What's there to iron out? If she hadn't already quit, she'd be fired. She loses either way and yay, I win."

Jess heard the frustration in TJ's voice. "You don't sound too pleased by the prospect."

TJ seemed as though she wanted to say something and then changed her mind. "You know what?" She took a sip of water. "I'll let her know I'm waiting, and we can get out of your hair. Where can I find her?"

"I haven't convinced you."

"On the contrary, you're very convincing. You're probably right about everything." TJ spoke without irony, which made her renewal of her wish to depart even more confusing.

"But she can't stay?"

TJ shook her head. She shoved her hands in her pockets and refused to meet Jess's gaze.

Jess approached cautiously but intently. "What is it?"

Briefly biting her lip, TJ said, "The only...since before Mom died, the only nights I haven't been with Kara were when she was in the hospital."

It was apparent TJ felt selfish admitting it, but the unwavering protectiveness and love inherent in the declaration warmed Jess through and through. She tugged one of TJ's hands free and threaded her fingers with her own as she led her down the hall. She loved the feel of the firm grip, the warmth, the solidity of the connection. The third doorway on the right was closed to within an inch, which told Jess it was the room Kara had chosen. As she pushed it open, about to call out their entrance, she spotted Kara asleep on the bed, nestled under a large plush bath towel being used as a blanket. Jess turned to TJ with a raised brow, and at TJ's head shake, she backed them out and closed the door.

Without relinquishing TJ's hand, Jess pulled TJ back into the kitchen, where she stopped in front of her and met her eyes. Gently tracing her thumb along TJ's palm, Jess said, "Stay here tonight. You can take one of the rooms adjacent to hers so you won't have to be away from her. Say yes."

TJ looked down at their joined hands before raising her eyes to Jess's. Jess thought she saw the stirrings of desire there as their gazes held, TJ's eyes shifting between Jess's as if trying to communicate something vital, but then TJ broke the spell and squeezed Jess's hand gently before letting go. "You've already done so much. I'll come back in the morning."

You are the most infuriating woman! Why can't you accept anything from me? "Stay and talk for a minute at least."

"So you can tell me everything I'm doing wrong? I haven't been scrimping all these years so she can throw her future away on some unachievable dream."

Raising her palms in surrender, Jess said, "I didn't say anything."

"You're thinking it."

"I think she enjoyed her job." Jess casually walked to the refrigerator and grabbed a Diet Coke. She didn't want to have this conversation standing up, squaring off like boxers in a ring. Confrontational body language wouldn't help defuse the escalating tension.

"You know what she wants to do? Buy rusted-out classics and refurbish them. Do you know how few people actually make it in the car-flipping business? Those cars not only don't make money for their owners, they bleed money from them. It's the rare exception that a car is sold for millions at auction."

Jess slid onto one of the kitchen stools with her drink. "Dillon's done extremely well for himself. Kara seems just as tenacious and capable."

TJ snagged her water glass and leaned against the counter. "She needs to go to college. Once she has, she can choose to do whatever she wants."

"The reverse is also true. She can decide to go to college later. Plenty of people return as older students. I'm speaking with one."

"I made a promise."

"And that promise is worth more than her happiness?" Jess was pushing, but given the choices Kara had been making, something—or someone—needed to change.

The tight line of TJ's mouth suggested she was working to control her temper. "My parenting choices don't require your approval. Nor are they any of your business."

"It very much is my business when a kid shows up on my doorstep looking for guidance because her sister's too pigheaded to listen to reason," Jess snapped, jumping to her feet. "That girl came here as my friend, and I'm damn well going to look after her as such. She's staying here tonight with or without your approval, and if you don't like it, feel free to call the police. Please ask them not to park too close to the GTO." Jess's anger flared like steam from Old Faithful, and remaining polite wasn't doing enough to quell the pressure.

Jess whisked her phone from the counter and typed 911 before sliding it to TJ. "It's the green button." A stiff drink was in order, but mindful of the issues the Blake sisters had with their mother, Jess didn't want to go there. It took every ounce of energy to stand quietly and await a reply.

TJ stared at Jess as if she had no idea what to say. Seconds ticked by as she seemed to contemplate a response.

In a softer tone, Jess said, "She idolizes you on one hand and can't forgive you on the other. She's making ridiculously stupid choices because she so desperately wants to do right by you, when it's a hundred and eighty degrees from what *she* wants." The kernel of an earlier postulation suddenly blossomed into a full-blown proof. "Do you know why she returns the cars in the vicinity of the owners?"

"To see if she can get away with it."

"To see if she'll get caught. She wants to get hurt because she believes she deserves to be. Because she blames herself for your mother's death."

The veins in TJ's neck bulged and her jaw tightened, leading Jess to expect further argument. Jess reached out and took TJ's hand. TJ tried to pull away but Jess held tight.

"She shouldn't," TJ said.

Jess squeezed TJ's hand. "I know. And that's not all."   ·

"Isn't that enough?" TJ asked hoarsely.

"I think she wants to get into just enough of a mess to get pushed out of your life. She doesn't want to get so seriously in trouble that it's irreversible, because underneath her bad choices, she's a good kid, and

I think juvie or jail scares her. But she wants you to be free of her, free to live your life without having to look after her."

"I don't have to. I want to."

"I know, sweetie. But she thinks she's the reason you didn't give us a chance."

"That's completely untrue."

"Is it?" Jess squeezed TJ's hand again. "If Kara was in college, would you still have ended things between us?"

TJ blinked, her eyes misting as if she'd been slapped. "This isn't productive."

"Either she's right that you're putting your life on hold, or you're scared of what you feel for me and you're running away, or I don't mean to you what you mean to me."

TJ ran her free hand through her hair and closed her eyes for a moment before speaking again, quietly and plaintively. "Please don't do this."

"Talk to me. Which is it? I'm already hurting, TJ. I can deal with more pain. You're worth more pain. But I need you to be honest with me. It's one of the traits I love most about you, and if you're going to break my heart, I want it to be because you were true to yourself, not because you're doing what you think is best for me. So give me the truth."

TJ spoke barely above a whisper. "Kara's lost so much. I can't be the reason she loses any more. You're the first person I...you've become...It doesn't matter. Jess, I'm all she has left. If you and I keep seeing each other, I'm afraid she'll question how important she is to me. She needs to know she can count on me to be there for her."

"The best way to show her she's not in the way is not to put her there. How will she feel if she thinks she's the reason you're not giving us a shot? Scratch that. She already does, and—Jesus—she's trying to get herself incarcerated."

A spark of doubt flitted across TJ's face. Jess seized the opportunity to spread it like wildfire. "TJ, this isn't a zero-sum game. You don't have to lose a sister to gain a partner, and she doesn't have to lose a sister to gain a friend. You're forgetting two plus one equals three, not two or even one, like you seem to fear."

A disbelieving smile tugged at TJ's mouth. "You did not just make a math metaphor."

Jess drew her forward and slid her arms around TJ's waist. "I did, and I'll keep doing it if it means I'm finally getting through to you. Watch out or I'll start quoting Aristotle."

"'No great mind has ever existed without a touch of madness'?" TJ put her arms around Jess's shoulders.

"Is that a dig? I was thinking, 'The whole is greater than the sum of its parts,' but I can definitely work with yours."

TJ pulled Jess close and hugged her. "Touch of arrogance, maybe."

"Hey, I'm not the one who brought up great minds. But if the shoe fits." Jess melted into TJ's embrace as if she were chocolate in the sun. Warmth coursed through her, and she sighed with pleasure.

"I'm sorry," TJ said. "I've made a mess of everything."

"No. You're here. Kara's safe."

"Why are you giving me another chance?" TJ asked, leaning back within the circle of Jess's arms.

"We belong together, the three of us."

TJ chuckled. "You're volunteering to be involved in the life of a teenager?"

"Touch of madness," Jess replied, unable to wipe the grin from her face. "Now kiss me before I go completely insane."

TJ tugged Jess forward. "Pushy as ever," she said as she caressed Jess's cheek before kissing her.

Jess relished the feeling of TJ's soft, supple lips on hers and welcomed TJ's tongue inside her mouth. The exquisiteness of the sensation made their week apart seem like a frigid winter out of which she was coming indoors to dispel the cold. This, *this* was what she needed to chase the week-long chill away. "I've missed you," she said as she rested their foreheads together.

"Back atcha," TJ said.

"Did you just yawn?"

TJ nodded. "Sorry. I'm about as romantic as a Roomba, I know. But I'm emotionally drained and need to get some sleep," TJ said as she kissed the side of Jess's mouth. "Walk me out?"

Jess squealed in frustration. "That is so not happening." She tugged TJ's hand. "Come with me." Jess led TJ back toward the bedrooms and entered the one across the hall from the room Kara occupied. "You're staying here tonight. There's a robe in the bathroom, fresh sheets and towels, toiletries, and I'll bring you a T-shirt. The three of us are going to talk in the morning. And you're going to kiss me good night and not argue." She slid her arms around TJ's neck.

TJ smiled. "Demanding yet chivalrous. Enticing combination."

"If you weren't so tired, if *I* weren't so tired, I'd probably be as honorable as a whore in a brothel."

"You say the most romantic things," TJ said as she claimed Jess's mouth with her own.

❖

TJ tried to get comfortable in the massive bed she could easily share with five adults. It wasn't that it was uncomfortable—the mattress was a perfect mixture of firmness and softness—but the room was so large and the ceilings so high, she imagined trapeze artists swinging above. Unfortunately, they'd get tangled up in the chandelier in the center. Well, the center of the bed side of the room. A separate sitting area with two more chandeliers, chair, couch, and low, round table established the other half. A beautiful upholstered bench with intricately carved wooden legs nestled against the foot of the bed, across from which was the only anomaly in the otherwise old-fashioned suite: a large flat-screen television that occupied much of the wall.

She'd felt guilty moving the many decorative pillows from the bed in order to climb in, knowing full well she'd never remember how they were supposed to be resituated. Too late did she think to take a photo using her phone. Then again, Jess probably had household staff to attend to the sheets and position the decor.

She'd never learn to be completely at ease amid such opulent surroundings. But she was getting used to the idea of needing to accept them in the same way Jess would have to accept TJ would never have dwellings that could measure up. She was growing increasingly confident they could work through such differences. Jess hadn't criticized TJ for her lack of things but rather had been generous in her praise of TJ for jumping the many hurdles life had placed in her path.

TJ's heart filled at the thought of Jess, so earnest in her acceptance of Kara and fierce in her protectiveness. Jess had been open, forgiving, and, unlike TJ, willing to put herself out there. Jess was far braver than TJ imagined her to be, far more so than TJ herself had ever been.

It was 1:33 a.m. She wondered whether Jess was asleep, then decided she didn't care. There was a sweet, courageous, sexy woman down the hall, and she intended to risk waking her up in order to do the one thing she wanted in this moment more than anything.

Having remembered from her house tour where the master

bedroom was, TJ headed there. Its door was slightly ajar. Slowly pushing it, she took a step inside and waited for her eyes to adjust. Minimal light crept in from within the bathroom, enough to allow her to make out the bed. Jess lay on her side. TJ didn't want to wake her but didn't want to scare her either. At the bedside, she whispered, "Jess?"

"What's wrong?" Jess asked immediately.

"Nothing," TJ said as she slipped under the covers. She scooched until she pressed up against Jess's back, spooning her and resting an arm across Jess's torso. "I need to hold you." She pressed a kiss behind Jess's ear and snuggled close. "And I need to tell you that you scare me, and I need to tell you you're wonderful. And I need to say thank you. Now go to sleep."

TJ felt Jess's body shake with laughter. "What's so funny?" TJ asked.

"You say those things and expect me to fall back asleep?"

"Yes," TJ said before brushing aside some of Jess's hair and dropping a kiss on her neck.

"You're crazy."

"About you."

Jess caressed TJ's arm before covering it with her own. "I like you here."

TJ gave Jess a quick squeeze and settled in. "Good night, princess."

CHAPTER TWENTY-TWO

Warm. That was the first sensation Jess had upon waking. She was very warm, and it had everything to do with the firm yet soft body next to her. Jess lay on her back, and TJ had one leg slung over Jess's legs, one arm around her waist. Jess slept surprisingly well considering the furnace snuggled against her, and she was reluctant to move. Luxuriating in the feel of TJ, she stayed put as long as she could before her insistent bladder forced her hand. Slowly moving out from under her human blanket, she silently congratulated herself for not waking TJ.

It didn't take long to locate Kara, who was focused on the action playing out on the game room's large television screen and manipulating one of the many game consoles Jess kept for company. Jess appreciated Kara's consideration in keeping the volume low, though the room was designed to minimize sound travel. "I thought teenagers slept 'til noon," Jess said, tightening the robe's belt around her waist.

"Not when every video game I've ever wanted to play is at my fingertips." Kara stopped the game and the weaponry fell silent. "Is it okay?"

"This room is meant to be used. Can I get you something to eat? Drink?"

"TJ's keys are here. Did she stay with you?"

Damn, this wasn't exactly how Jess had envisioned the direction of this conversation. With everything they'd discussed the previous night, however, Jess wasn't going to lie. "Not the way you think."

Kara beamed and set down the controller. "Sweet!"

"Is it?" Jess hoped Kara wouldn't change her mind. The reality of her and TJ being together might be less exciting to Kara than the idea of it.

"Totally. She never stays the night anywhere."

"Maybe she's waiting for the right woman," Jess said carefully.

"Maybe she's found her."

The thought made Jess happier than a child playing with a litter of Labrador puppies. "Shall we come up with a game plan for the GTO?"

Kara frowned. "Reality sucks."

Jess laughed. "Come on. Let's figure out if we can unsuck it."

❖

An hour and a half later, Jess, Dillon, and Kara were seated at the kitchen table, talking and laughing when TJ entered. Jess was the first to notice. "Good morning," she said as the others turned. Kara reluctantly rose and, head down, walked over to TJ, who immediately opened her arms.

"I'm sorry," Kara mumbled into TJ's chest.

TJ held her tight. "You're in big trouble, young lady."

"I know."

"I love you, Kare."

"Love you too," Kara muttered before shuffling back to the table.

Dillon crossed the floor and offered his hand. "TJ, nice to see you again."

"Dillon, I don't know what to say. I'm so sorry about all this," TJ said, shaking his hand.

"We'll work something out. Grab some coffee and join us."

This was uncharted territory. Jess didn't know how she was supposed to greet TJ in front of Dillon and Kara. She knew how she wanted to but didn't want to pressure her. Taking the safe route, Jess headed for the espresso machine and pulled out a mug from the cabinet. "Espresso, cappuccino, Americano, or latte?"

TJ tilted her head back the way she came. "Do you have a sec?"

Jess set the mug down and followed TJ past the dining room into the living room. TJ hadn't reached for her, instead keeping her hands tucked in the front pockets of her jeans. Jess hoped she hadn't changed her mind from last night to this morning, but TJ's body language wasn't screaming "Hold me." Jess wasn't sure she could keep a handle on her emotions if TJ acted like nothing had changed between them.

"Does he know?" TJ asked.

"Yes."

"Thank God," TJ said, stepping forward to embrace Jess. "I didn't want to make anything awkward for you."

Jess relaxed, feeling as if whatever shield her body had raised in self-protection had instantly disintegrated. She stroked TJ's back, enjoying the combination of strength and softness she found. "He's my best friend. Of course he knows." She pulled back to meet TJ's eyes. "Thanks for not assuming, but know that I don't intend to hide how I feel about you. If people aren't comfortable with it, that's their problem."

TJ held Jess's head in her hands. "Still, I'd rather do this in private." What started as a gentle kiss of reconnection quickly escalated into one of passion and promise. When TJ finally broke the kiss, Jess was breathing heavily and wanting to take things in a more horizontal direction. "Now *that's* a good morning," TJ said, with one last nip at Jess's bottom lip.

"How are you so good at that?" Jess said hazily.

"It's not me. It's us." TJ gave Jess another peck. "Now that I know I can touch you, let's go see if we can loosen the noose around my sister's neck."

Jess took TJ's hand. En route back to the kitchen, she said, "We may have cooked up something in that regard."

"I figured you wouldn't have left them in a room with a block of knives if it wasn't safe."

"Keep an open mind."

"Yes, dear." They reentered the kitchen, where Dillon and Kara huddled over his phone, scrolling through photos of various automobiles. TJ sat down opposite. "Can we talk discipline?"

"Not until you've had your coffee," Kara said. "A latte for her please, if that's okay, Jess."

"Coming right up." Jess made the appropriate selection on the espresso machine. "We all proposed different aspects of Kara's punishment, which you have to agree to, of course," she quickly said to TJ before returning to the brew. "Kara, why don't you summarize?"

Kara spun her soda can in small circles as she spoke. "I can return to Dillon's conditionally and not until I get my grades back to where they were before I started."

"I'm listening," TJ said.

"And I have to maintain them, even if it means no more video games."

At TJ's shocked expression, Jess said, "Are you going to be able to handle this before coffee?" She placed the hot drink in front of TJ.

"Who are you and what have you done with my sister?" TJ asked Kara.

"Assuming I keep my grades up, for the next six months I have to split my paycheck three ways. I can keep fifty percent for myself and my expenses. Another ten percent goes to Dillon to repay him for the gas and insurance on the GTO."

"Dillon, why don't you tell TJ about the other forty percent, since it was your idea," Jess said.

"It goes to a charity of her choice," Dillon said. "I know the Blake sisters aren't quite at the Spaulding level of means, but she *has* opportunity, and I thought it important she recognize she shouldn't throw it away. I'm happy to continue mentoring her, but as she works toward what she wants, she might be able to help someone who doesn't have as good a shot."

TJ looked back and forth between Dillon and Jess, clearly becoming emotional. "That's more than fair." To Kara, she said, "You're on board with this plan?"

Kara nodded.

"And your expenses?" Jess prodded her.

"Oh, yeah. Jess thought I could maybe see a counselor to help me deal with mom stuff." She rolled her eyes. "But I don't have to continue if it's stupid. I only have to try a few sessions."

Jess reached for TJ's hand. "Like I said, it's up to you. We ran through a bunch of ideas and those were the ones that stuck. What do you think?"

Eyes glistening, TJ said, "You guys have been busy. I should sleep in more often."

Or over more often, Jess thought.

"What about the car?" TJ asked.

"I drove my flatbed rollback. I'll tow her back," Dillon said. He stood. "In fact, I'll do that now. Let me know how you want to play it." Turning to Kara, he said, "You get one more shot. Pull anything like this again, whether it's my car or anyone else's, I'll put out the word you can't be trusted, and you'll never work in another shop in this county."

Jess felt TJ go rigid beside her and apparently Dillon noticed. Dillon said, "You disagree?"

TJ pushed her chair back and stood in front of him. "I don't enjoy hearing anyone threaten my sister, but I don't fault your logic. If she pulls anything like this again, you have every right to warn your industry pals. In fact, you have every right to do that now." She stuck out her hand. "Thank you for your generosity and for giving her another chance. She won't disappoint you."

Dillon shook TJ's hand. "I don't doubt it for a minute." He pointed at Kara. "You behave yourself." Then he winked at her. Turning to TJ and Jess, he said, "Behave yourselves," and winked at Jess.

Jess followed him to the door and gave him a hug. "Thanks, Dill."

He gave her a quick kiss. "Don't mention it, beautiful. *I'll* mention it enough for both of us, because you owe me big-time."

She slapped his arm. "I know."

He grinned. "Big-time. Muah ha ha."

"Get out of here, you jerk," Jess said, laughing. Reentering the kitchen, she found TJ placing her mug in the dishwasher. "You couldn't have possibly finished your coffee."

"I didn't, but we need to head out." TJ nodded in Kara's direction. "This one and I have some things to discuss."

"So do we," Jess countered.

TJ took Jess's hands in hers. "Yes, we do." She gave Jess a gentle kiss. "Can I see you tonight?"

Jess shook her head. "Can't tonight." Damn. "Call me?"

"You got it." TJ gathered Jess in her arms and said, "Thanks for everything."

"You're welcome." Jess held an arm out to Kara. "Get over here, you."

Kara allowed herself to be wrapped in Jess's embrace and even gave a small squeeze in return. "What she said," Kara mumbled, obviously embarrassed by the affection.

"You're welcome here anytime." Jess hovered while the sisters gathered their belongings and walked them out. She hadn't even noticed when she'd said good-bye to Dillon that it was a glorious, cloudless day filled with plenty of sunshine. And as she waved to her departing guests, she realized she felt exactly like the day at hand: expansive and full of possibility.

❖

"Where are we going?" Kara asked on cue. TJ had expected the question as soon as she missed their usual turn and stayed in Montgomery Hills, heading toward state-park land. "A remote mountain area where you can dispose of my body?"

"Tempting. But now that you're going to be doing all my chores for the next two months, I think I'll postpone the more dramatic of your reparations."

"Two *months*?" Kara said with horror.

TJ gave her a quick glare before returning her focus to the road.

"How about one?" Kara asked.

"You want to work at Dillon's?" TJ asked.

"One and a half?"

TJ shook her head in amusement over Kara's constant attempts to renegotiate the terms of her atonements. "We'll see."

"Seriously, where are we going?" Kara asked again.

"Somewhere I should've taken you many times before now."

They drove in silence for another stretch of time until TJ turned into the Montgomery Sepulcher Cemetery.

"We haven't been here since Mom died," Kara said, sitting far more upright than she ever did.

"No. And I think it was my mistake."

TJ parked along the edge of a grassy field. There wasn't a designated parking area per se, so she pulled to the side of the narrow road to let other cars through. They walked to a statue of Mary. Under Mary's outstretched arms was a columbarium among whose sections housed their mother's remains. Their father's name was inscribed on the front of the niche along with their mother's, though his body had never been recovered.

Below the columbarium lay a valley closed to vehicles. Hawks circled high above. The faint murmur of road noise could be heard upon the wisps of the winds that occasionally wafted above the canyon.

TJ and Kara sat atop the granite-colored interment housing. TJ didn't know whether it was gauche to do so, but it seemed the designers of the grounds thought it appropriate since there were no other seating options. It was all very strange. She'd have to do an Internet search to see whether Emily Post or Miss Manners had anything to say about protocol. Her only real issue—perhaps superstition—was she never walked on the tombs. It seemed rude.

"So, you want to talk to a counselor about Mom?" TJ asked.

Kara shrugged. "Not really."

"Then why agree to it?"

"I'm being punished and it sounds like punishment."

TJ smiled. They sat quietly except for the occasional light thump of Kara's heel hitting the stone wall beneath where she sat. "Jess's idea?"

Kara nodded.

TJ remembered all too clearly what Jess had said: *She blames herself for your mother's death.* "I think it's a good one. Mom's a sore subject for me, but I should've encouraged you to talk about her." *Instead of letting you think you were to blame.*

"You still mad at her?"

"Probably."

"I would be." Kara lifted her heels and wrapped her arms around her knees.

The comment and its melancholic tone struck a chord with TJ. It was as if Kara was leaving off *if I were you.* "Why do you say that?"

"For having to drop everything to babysit me."

"I didn't *have* to do anything. I came home because I wanted to." Kara scoffed. "Right."

"Kara, I could go to community college anywhere and get a waitressing job anywhere. But I chose here."

"Because Mom went off the deep end."

"No. Because I love you."

"Whatever."

"I won't pretend it was Plan A, but I came home of my own volition. Think about it, Kare. If Mom and Dad had lived to be old and infirm, would you stay in the little bubble of whatever your life was at that point and say, 'Bummer for you'? Or would you figure out a way to help them because you love them? Just because we can't always continue along the first path we envision doesn't mean the new one's worse. In fact, it's often better. Should JK Rowling have stayed on welfare instead of writing her Harry Potter series? No. Do you know why?"

"Because it's a great story?"

"No. Because lesbians everywhere would never have had the opportunity to dream of Emma Watson, regardless of the fact she was underage in most of the films."

"Letch," Kara said with a slight upturn to her lips that pleased TJ enormously.

TJ laughed. "Seriously though. I've never once been mad at Mom for—how you seem to put it—dumping you on me. Don't ever, ever think that. I've been blessed to be so much a part of your life. I wouldn't change it for the world."

Kara picked at the molded foot bed of her Jack Purcell. "Then why are you angry with her?"

"Because she was unfair to you. You weren't even a teenager when she started killing herself. What she did to you...Kare, she had no right."

"Why bring me here if you feel that way?"

TJ took a deep breath. "I'm not sure I can forgive her. But I don't want to stand in the way of your doing so. Or maybe not stand in the way so much as give the impression I don't approve or make it seem like you can't talk about her with me. I had a lot more good years with her than you did. If you can forgive her, I think you should."

"I was never mad."

The despondency in the softly spoken words sliced through TJ like a cleaver. Anger at her mother stormed alive from the depths of dormancy. It was unforgivable that her mother still had the ability to hurt Kara this way. Kara had never been mad because she was constantly treading with such caution around Evelyn, it was like she walked a tightrope. TJ had seen it countless times. Kara had tried so hard to get Evelyn to care about something, to care about *her*, but Evelyn had stopped paying attention. Evelyn became one of the worst things a mother could ever be as far as TJ was concerned: indifferent. At least that's how it felt to TJ. Logic told her Evelyn was battling a dreadful illness, but her heart said Evelyn had stopped believing her children mattered.

Kara filled the silence. "Jess says Mom was sick and couldn't see us anymore. I don't think you should be angry with someone for getting sick."

"I don't disagree." TJ couldn't bring herself to go any farther than that, however; she didn't intend to lie to Kara by telling her she'd work on it when she wasn't at all sure she would—or could. "But back to you. I'll research folks who specialize in grief counseling, and you can choose whomever you feel most comfortable with."

"'Kay."

"You know what that means, though." TJ hopped off the wall and extended a hand to Kara, though she knew she wouldn't take it. "You actually have to talk in these sessions. You can't give the counselor your usual shrug and grunt."

"Then maybe you should find ones that specialize in teenagers."

"How about if I search for ones that only communicate via text message?"

Kara stopped.

"What's wrong?" TJ said, wondering if Kara had tweaked her leg.

"That's the most brilliant idea you've ever had," Kara said before she started walking again. "Second."

"What's the first?"

Kara smiled. "Jess."

TJ put her arm around Kara's shoulder and grinned. "You're not getting out of any punishments by buttering me up."

"I wonder what she sees in you."

"The wonder is that she sees it and still likes me."

"Maybe she's not as smart as we give her credit for."

"Good point, because she likes you too."

CHAPTER TWENTY-THREE

In order to get information to help TJ, Jess gave Gary a spiel about needing to access a client's view of his or her account due to certain marketing initiatives she planned that would show prospects the kinds of tools and information available to them once they invested with Magnate. As always, he complied without question, giving her access to everything she needed.

She started with the client statements, which showed dates of transactions, the names of the companies the client was invested in, the dividend-distribution amounts and the cash moving to and from the money-market sweep fund that held idle cash. They looked similar to those from the one brokerage account she held in her own name, the result of a bequest by her maternal grandmother.

The exercise wasn't exactly riveting, and Jess's thoughts shifted to TJ and their upcoming date. They hadn't yet figured out where to go, and Jess didn't care. It didn't matter whether a meal or entertainment was involved. She simply wanted to see TJ. Jess had to spend the first half of the week at a CMO conference. Rapidly evolving marketing technologies required her to routinely attend various events to make sure she understood the latest software tools available to her. The information she picked up was typically well worth her time.

From her hotel room during the evenings, she progressed on getting up to speed on the Magnate Fund so she could hand off to TJ what she knew. It was wise for her to become more of a technical expert anyway, so doing the work was good for both of them. But the days apart from TJ bordered on excruciating. Though they texted and video-chatted, it wasn't the same as seeing each other in person. She could hardly wait for Friday.

Returning her attention to the task at hand, she decided to take the extra step of matching a few of the dividend-distribution dates per the client statements to the companies' ex-dividend dates. She started with Merck & Co, PepsiCo, Walmart, HP, and United Parcel Service. Two of the first five dividend dates she checked occurred on weekends. She wondered why the statements wouldn't be correct. Weird. A minor computer glitch was likely the culprit. She'd have to touch base with Gary to find out which of the IT guys to follow up with.

Perhaps the most straightforward way of sifting through the array of information at her disposal was to take a look at a client's history from beginning to present. Randomly selecting several clients from the list, Jess set about getting a sense of how a client's funds were invested by Magnate by going through their accounts.

❖

"You're going to take all the wind out of my sails if you don't stop looking so dour," Brooke said as she took a seat. "What's got you in such a funk?"

Jess half-smiled as she settled into her chair. It was Thursday, and although she hadn't planned to leave the house until she'd figured out the puzzle that was the Magnate Fund, Brooke had insisted on lunch immediately upon her return from the conference. "Nothing that I'm sure whatever your surprise is won't fix." She was beginning to understand TJ's frustration with the fund, which in turn was fueling her frustration with herself. Now that she had all the firm's records at her disposal, there was no reason she couldn't form a comprehensive view of how it worked. For God's sake, if Gary understood the mechanics, she should be able to. The man practically needed instructions on how to open a book. "It couldn't be timed any better. So tell me. What couldn't wait?"

Brooke informed the waiter they were waiting for one more guest. "We're about to close Muriel Manchester."

The news should have made Jess happy. They'd been trying to win her business for years. But it only made her lose an already weak appetite. She couldn't shake the feeling that some aspect of the firm was operating clandestinely. Confidential matters were one thing, with certain ones requiring a need-to-know basis by staff. But she was a Spaulding. Shouldn't she be informed if any of Magnate's practices diverged from industry standards? "That's great to hear," she said with as much conviction as she could muster.

Brooke's expression soured. "That's great to hear? You sound like a mother telling her child how wonderful he sounds on his new trombone. Get your head in the game."

"I'll try."

"Try harder. She asked to meet with you specifically, and she'll be here any minute. What the hell, Jess?"

"Sorry. I'm just...You know the phrase 'healthy skepticism'?"

"Yes."

"It's not healthy."

"You don't think we'll close her?"

"No, it's not Muriel. It's..." Jess scanned the room to ensure no patrons were nearby and kept her voice down. "Have you ever wondered how our hedge fund was up more than five percent during the last bear market, when the S&P 500 was down nearly thirty-eight percent?"

Brooke stared at Jess. Then she broke out laughing. "That's what's bothering you?"

Jess winced in apology for even asking.

Brooke waved her hand as if Jess's question wasn't an issue. "You wouldn't believe how many meetings I take where I have to address these kinds of objections. In fact, Muriel had plenty herself. To answer your question, the fund is operating exactly as it should by diversifying outside the stock market to boost returns."

The explanation made sense. But there was more Jess needed to know. "What about its volatility? It's astoundingly low."

"I hear that one all the time too. The volatility's an illusion based on monthly and annual returns. On an intraday, intraweek, and intramonth basis, Dad says it's all over the place."

Jess nodded.

"Look, Jess, Dad's been in this business over thirty years. We've invested in the best technology for low-cost execution capabilities, we have incredible proprietary stock and options pricing models, and we have market intelligence derived from the massive amount of order flow we handle every day. Hell, you know this—it's from your own marketing material. Someone has to be the leader. That's us."

"Yeah, I know you're right." Brooke had a solid answer for everything. Something still felt slightly off, but Jess couldn't put her finger on it.

She took Jess's forearm. "It's not unreasonable to ask questions, but now isn't the time. We're on the precipice of getting half a billion from Muriel—for starters—so if you don't have faith in Dad and what we've built, leave now and ask questions later. Don't sabotage this deal."

"I won't." Jess did have faith in her dad. The simplest thing was to ask him how the fund worked. Just because things weren't adding up at first glance didn't mean anything improper was going on. It meant they were more complex than she imagined. On a regular basis, Brooke apparently had to address the kinds of questions Jess was asking. There would always be detractors and skeptics in the industry. Jess needn't be one.

Brooke cocked her head, apparently unconvinced.

"I won't," Jess repeated. She meant it.

Her sister's suddenly plastic expression signaled the end to their conversation.

"Muriel, hi. How lovely to see you," Jess said as she stood.

Muriel shook Jess's outstretched hand. "I'm sure your sister's informed you I'm interested in transferring some of my assets to your firm?"

As blunt as always, Jess thought. For some reason, Muriel's candor was more refreshing than vexing. "Yes. And we're delighted to have earned your confidence."

Muriel took a seat, though her eyes didn't stray from Jess. "How is that sinfully attractive girlfriend of yours?"

Nothing about TJ, including her looks, was relevant to the conversation. Jess ignored the question and merely smiled. "What made you finally decide to allow us the opportunity to become your investment advisor?"

"It wasn't a rhetorical question," Muriel said. "Sparkling water, please," she said to the waiter, shooing him away with her hand before he could interrupt.

"She's well, thank you for asking," Jess said stiffly.

Brooke chimed in. "As Jess mentioned, we're very honored—"

Remaining laser-focused on Jess, Muriel said, "And if I were to tell you my investment was contingent upon you ending your relationship and setting up a private meeting between her and me?"

"I wouldn't believe you," Jess said.

"She's worth losing a management fee on five hundred million?"

"You're either interested in investing with us or you're not. My relationships are irrelevant."

"On the contrary, I'm making them relevant. All I'm asking for is a meeting with a particular woman. Believe me," Muriel practically purred, "I can take it from there."

This game had gone on long enough. Whatever Muriel was playing at, Jess wanted no part of it. TJ had taught her that certain client behavior wasn't to be tolerated no matter the price. "I wouldn't disrespect her by ending our relationship in order to further my company's business prospects or by posing the question of whether she'd like to end our relationship for a guaranteed one-on-one with you. She's quite capable of deciding who she wants to spend time with, and apparently it's not you." Jess grabbed her purse and stood, ignoring Brooke's eye gestures that she retake her seat and pipe down. "Invest with us or don't. We earn people's business because we're the best advisor in the country. If you find a better one, by all means, move your money to them."

Before Jess could storm off, she felt a hand on hers, preventing her departure. "That's exactly what I wanted to hear," Muriel said. "I wanted to know the lengths to which you'd go to close my business. I'm glad to discover the firm truly has become more queer-friendly and what I witnessed on my yacht wasn't an act. The single most important attribute to winning my business is integrity. Magnate may be one of the top advisors, but until now I wasn't interested in working with you because our values weren't aligned." Muriel pulled a card from her clutch bag and handed it to Jess. "This is my accountant. Please give him the details for the wire transfer. And give my best to that ridiculously good-looking woman of yours." Muriel stood, nodded to Brooke, and left.

Brooke's mouth fell open.

Jess dropped the card into her purse. "Cha-ching."

CHAPTER TWENTY-FOUR

Panic, which had been entering Jess's bloodstream on an IV drip all week, was now coursing through her in a torrent. Having sequestered herself in her home office for two days straight except for yesterday's lunch, Jess had finally solved the puzzle of how Magnate achieved its unrivaled success, and it left a hole in her gut the size of Montana.

She wanted to scream and shout and fight against the irrefutable conclusion she'd reached, wanted to attack and beat it back into shadow, into unconsciousness. If only it were a tangible thing, she could carry it to the edge of a cliff and cast it into oblivion.

But it wasn't to be. The truth was no less real for its being inconceivable.

Public companies declare an ex-dividend date such that dividends are paid to holders of shares two days later. Days ago she had taken the additional step of verifying that the corresponding companies had declared the dividends listed on the client statements, all of which was a matter of public record.

The payable dates per the statements didn't match those of the investor relations website pages or SEC filings. Initially blaming a software bug, Jess upped her review from a handful to hundreds. Not only were many of the dates wrong, but a review of the client statements showed numerous other inconsistencies. Companies that paid quarterly dividends didn't often change their dividend schedule. But according to Magnate statements, a specific company's dividend would be listed one quarter, be missing the following quarter, and show up again the next. Investments in companies like PepsiCo were typically a buy-and-hold proposition, so turnover didn't explain the gaps and inconsistencies.

That wasn't all. On numerous days, trades were recorded using fake values, as the prices reported for the purported trades were outside the market-reported price range on a given day. Convertible securities were reported as being traded on days after the actual date of conversion reported by the issuing corporation. Transfers in and out of the cash-sweep account per the Magnate client statements went into a name and ticker symbol Jess couldn't identify because it didn't exist.

Topping off these already uncomfortable deductions was the work TJ had done, which showed the returns per the client statements—when compared to the broader market returns—to be easily assailable. TJ's spreadsheet listed one-, three-, five-, and ten-year investment returns as reported on certain client statements and compared them to various indexes and other funds. On an absolute return basis, the Magnate Fund wasn't a standout. However, it handily came in first over the five- and ten-year periods if measured by risk-adjusted return.

Jess's math skills came in handy here. Although its annual returns were fairly high for the investment strategies utilized, they were far more conceivable than Magnate's ability to sustain smooth, non-volatile returns over such a long period. Jess had taken a sample of the instruments reportedly invested in by Magnate and couldn't come close to replicating the returns claimed. Jess calculated the probability of their achievement to be so statistically insignificant as to be impossible without hindsight. Others who used the same strategies achieved nowhere near the same degree of success as Magnate, and now she knew why.

Oh, God, what had her father done? What had *she* done?

Was it possible her father hadn't created a massive Ponzi scheme?

Everything about Jess's world seemed suddenly built on sand, and the ground was shifting.

Her life was built on lies.

All her possessions had been illicitly obtained under the guise of enhancing investor wealth. What's more, her efforts provided the silk that allowed her father to weave a wider web.

A cold sweat broke out across her upper body, her abdomen clenched, and her throat constricted from sudden nausea. She ran to the bathroom and barely made it to the porcelain basin before unloading her stomach's contents into the bowl.

On her knees and holding herself up by the toilet rim, Jess couldn't hold back the tears that started streaming forth. Her mind and body were in turmoil, pulling her in opposite directions—her staggered breathing making it difficult to take in enough oxygen, her mind wishing her lungs would stop trying. Could she go on living, knowing what her father had done? Knowing her part in it? She sagged to the floor with her head in her hands and wept as never before.

As Jess lay in a heap, the warmth against her legs seeped into her consciousness like a black stain, providing an unwelcome reminder of the things she enjoyed on a daily basis that were paid for on the backs of Magnate's clients. Heated tile bathroom floors were one of the luxuries Jess noticed and appreciated daily. She once admitted to her dentist that her lack of cavities was due to lingering as she brushed her teeth, allowing her feet to soak up the warmth as if she were walking barefoot on a sunny day at the beach.

Now the warmth felt sweltering. She took stock of her surroundings. The previously wonderful spaciousness of her home felt instantly mausolean, as if she were entombed. Everything about the room made Jess's stomach churn. Everything about the house reminded her of what she hadn't earned, what none of the Spauldings had rightfully built.

Her makeup felt thick and cumbersome, as if someone had decorated her face with spackle. Her clothes, like her makeup, felt heavy, as if she'd run a marathon during a summer day in New Orleans. Were they even hers at this point? Did her underwear belong to someone else? The thought was repelling, as if maggots lined her hems. Out, out, out—she needed to get out of her garments. She stripped as if they were aflame. Even when she was naked, the air around her felt heavy, as if it were wet and hot and she had to take each breath through a sodden blanket covering her face.

She turned on the shower and stood beneath the flow of water. As it sluiced across her skin, Jess waited for the heaviness to ebb. This shower never failed to rebalance and renew her, as multiple showerheads sprayed her from head to toe. Today was different. Without opening her eyes, she turned off the valve. What right did she have to luxuriate in a spa-like setting as if the water could cleanse her sins the way it washed away the grime? Could she ever again be clean?

No. She was dirtier than the filth beneath the fingernails of a homeless man. Her jaw trembled and fresh tears anointed her cheeks. It was as if a freight train of greed had struck her innocence on its inexorable path of destruction. Had she been a willing passenger?

Jess wiped at her cheeks and appraised herself in the mirror. Her eyes were red-rimmed and bloodshot, her face blotchy and wet. Was this the face of a woman who could ignore the truth? She'd succeeded at putting on one kind of act of ignorance for so long, would this be any different?

Would she ever be able to look at her father the same way?

Oh, how she wanted to believe she'd misread and misunderstood all the evidence against him! For the first time in her life, Jess *wanted* to be the dimwit she'd portrayed for years. She didn't want to know what her father had done, didn't want to believe him capable of such nefariousness.

All she had was questions. She needed answers. She dried her face and rinsed her mouth before entering the closet. It had been one of her favorite rooms. Spacious, well-lit, and well-organized, it contained floor-to-ceiling racks of shoes, shelves for sweaters and tops, high and low garment racks for suit jackets, pants, skirts, shirts, and shorts, and a separate taller rack for dresses. Drawers hid her undergarments while additional shelves held her purses and hats. Now she looked at the colorful clothes and footwear as if through the eyes of a stranger. These things weren't hers. The clients whose assets had been pilfered to purchase them owned them.

Did anything in this room truly belong to her?

She opened the drawer to her gym wear and pulled on sweatpants and a sweatshirt, the drabbest clothing she possessed, even though they were still brand name. Anything more stylish would make her feel even more of an imposter.

She walked through the pool area to the rear of the great house. As was her standard practice, she entered without asking because she had permission to come and go as she pleased throughout the first floor. Rarely did she make use of the open-door policy without first texting or phoning her intention to drop by. The estate was secured on all sides so the family never locked their doors, as only friends or relatives were allowed on the grounds. The only stipulation—set by her stepmother—was that no one access the second floor without prior consent. Tonight she ignored the mandate and headed straight for her father's study. The door was always closed so she didn't know whether her father was inside. Knocking first but not awaiting a response, she pushed open the heavy door.

Derrick was seated at his desk. He glanced up from his work and removed his reading glasses. "What a lovely surprise, sweetheart," he said warmly. After a quick appraisal of her, he asked, "What's wrong?" He started to rise but heeded her open palm gesturing him to stop.

Jess closed the door and rested her back against it. This was the man who had comforted her time and again, no matter what, from scraped knee to broken heart. In order to remain strong and not seek solace in his arms, she needed physical distance. She studied him. He was his usual good-looking self, his slightly wavy hair graying at the temples and always trimmed to within a quarter-inch of the same length. Two parallel wrinkle lines across his forehead showed his concern at her unannounced arrival. He didn't appear to be a liar and a cheat, but then again, one didn't necessarily look at Ted Bundy and think serial murderer.

"How long?" Jess asked. She didn't know where to start or how to confront him. When Derrick cocked his head, she clarified her question. "How long have you been stealing from our clients?"

He sat back in his chair, appearing to consider how to respond.

"And don't say you don't know what I'm talking about. The growth you've been claiming isn't possible with your purported investment strategy. The dividends don't exist. You've only been able to pay them by getting new blood, which I've been doing my damnedest to win for you. How. Long." The acid in her stomach was threatening to make itself known again.

He rose and sauntered to the bar. "Drink?" he asked. Jess declined. After a few minutes perfecting his Gibson, he returned to his seat. He took a sip before setting his glass down. "Since Lilith."

Seventeen years. Seventeen *years*. Jess took a calming breath. Under such a time frame, the scale of the fraud must be astounding. "Does she know?" Jess asked.

"No."

"Does Gary?"

"No one knows."

Her father was the man who'd taught her right from wrong. How could he be behind this catastrophic abuse of trust? "Why? With Lilith's resources, why would you do this?"

He swirled his drink. "Early on, I made some poor investments with her money. I couldn't dig myself out of the hole without coming clean to her about the extent of the losses. This way, I didn't have to."

"She loves you. You could have worked through it."

Derrick smiled sadly. "Lilith isn't as forgiving as you give her credit for."

"You decided to steal from your clients because you couldn't face *your wife?*" No explanation could ever suffice, yet for some reason this was even more egregious than she was prepared for.

"Initially."

He didn't need to expand. His very public multi-million-dollar donations sprang to mind. She'd been concerned with his amplifying desire to be in the do-gooder spotlight, and it turned out she had ample cause.

Then something else hit her. "You let Lilith walk all over me for being too smart for my own good because you didn't want me figuring out your scam." She couldn't believe any of this, let alone that he'd allowed Lilith to treat her so poorly.

"I had no choice if I wanted you and Brooke by my side."

Such a twisted sentiment, wanting her to be part of the family business, yet, out of fear she'd get too close to the truth, complacently letting Lilith stifle a crucial part of who she was. He must have known all along how much business she brought to Magnate yet never said anything. He took advantage of her desire to keep him happy after her mother died to the point she felt she had to hide her contributions. How often had she longed to hear him acknowledge her work? Oh, her work. When Jess thought of her role in the deception, her stomach lurched. She barely managed to swallow the bile that threatened to spew.

Casually, Derrick moved from behind his desk to rest against it, assuming a conversational air as if they were fondly reminiscing. "We've done a lot of good, sweetheart. Don't lose sight of that."

"What?"

"We've given hundreds of millions to important causes, contributions that wouldn't have been made without our efforts."

Jess had expected an argument. Not this. Her father was off the deep end if he believed his words. "You're not Robin Hood! You can't take other people's money and spend it according to your wishes. You have no right."

"Think of the donations we help engender because of our status in the financial community."

Dumbfounded, Jess couldn't immediately reply. Was he trying to convince himself or her? "Charitable foundations that invested with us are going to fold because of you and your—whatever you call this— redistribution of wealth. You're literally robbing Peter to pay Paul."

As if she hadn't spoken, Derrick said, "Think of the incredible educational opportunities we're giving deserving students too. Students like your friend TJ."

TJ. So he knew, not that it mattered. TJ would never have entered the Derrick Spaulding MBA Program had she been privy to its funding sources. Jess's already unsettled stomach could barely take anymore, but she pushed down the nausea. "Don't you dare use her or anyone else to try to justify your actions. I don't believe for one second you can't recognize right from wrong. Otherwise you wouldn't have hidden this from everyone."

Derrick took a long pull from his drink. "I'm not saying it's right. But things aren't always black and white. We're doing a lot of good, whether you want to believe it or not. I've made a concerted effort to give back."

"It's not yours to give!" Jess shouted.

"You haven't minded."

Sucker punched, Jess's stomach roiled.

"Privilege comes at a price," he said. "Think of everything you have. You're willing to give it all up?"

An image of Kara popped into Jess's head. How would she answer the question if Kara were in the room? What kind of lesson would Kara need to learn from a case study on Derrick Spaulding?

"Absolutely," Jess said.

"You're willing to give her up too?"

Tears sprang into Jess's eyes and she swallowed hard, knowing exactly whom Derrick meant. Jess was on the brink of losing everything she cared about, everyone who mattered: her father, TJ, Brooke. No, she wasn't willing. But it wasn't her choice.

"No one ever needs to know about this conversation."

The way he let the suggestion sit between them reminded her of all the times she'd slid money toward someone with the expectation they'd do her bidding. Her own actions repulsed her. Did he actually believe her capable of ignoring her discovery? She hadn't exactly been the poster child of rectitude, but it hurt to think her own father could believe she was so shallow, even if he was its epitome.

She held her head high. Her path was clear and she would follow it unerringly, even in the face of debilitating loneliness and heartbreak. "If you were afraid of me finding out, then you must know what would happen once I did."

"Yes, although you can't blame me for trying to talk you out of it." Derrick emptied his glass.

Jess took no consolation from his confirmation. All these years she'd had trouble forgiving herself for choosing this life over Dillon, for being so shallow. It had taken precious time—and TJ—for her to realize she wasn't that person. How was it that restoring her faith in herself had to come at the price of having her faith in her father destroyed?

Jess ignored the tears sliding freely down her cheeks. She looked around the opulent study she knew she'd never again set foot in and then met her father's gaze. "None of this..." Her mouth trembled violently and she could scarcely speak. "I'd have taken you over any of this."

Derrick smiled sadly and his eyes misted. "I'm sorry."

She wasn't sure that was true or whether he was sorry for the fraud or for having been caught. Yet she refused to ask for fear of losing all hope of ever being able to forgive him.

She could only reply with a sob.

CHAPTER TWENTY-FIVE

Jess longed to be only one place: in TJ's arms. Before she went public, before she forced Gary to perform the inevitable, before anyone could arm TJ with more than a billion reasons to avoid her, Jess had to see her. This was likely Jess's last night of relative normalcy, where she could pretend she was simply a woman falling in love, supported by her friends and family, and working for a living. She wasn't yet a pariah with the reputation of having stolen the future from generations of children. Photos of her caught in unflattering moments would soon be splashed across trashy news-rag covers casting her as a monster. She'd probably be Photoshopped stabbing baby otters in their sleep while they floated on their backs, holding hands with each other. The new face of evil.

Though she longed for a lifetime of nights together with TJ, one was all she dared hope to be granted.

TJ was in the final stretches of the curriculum. What would happen to all her work when Jess went to the authorities? Once Jess lit the wick, the program would be blown to smithereens, all funding halted. And with its namesake behind bars, it would become so ridiculed that even in the unlikely scenario the inaugural class was allowed to graduate, who would hire them? The students wouldn't derive any benefit from listing it on a résumé. And graduating with an MBA from a "university—name withheld" would likewise be worthless.

What if Jess delayed her whistleblowing until after TJ's graduation and subsequent employment? Would a few months make a difference in the grand scheme of things?

A number of new individuals and organizations would become investors by then, expanding the reach of destruction. If TJ ever found out Jess had delayed going to the authorities because Jess was trying to protect her, TJ would never forgive her.

Not that TJ would forgive her for having spent most of her life using other people's money to fund her lavish lifestyle.

TJ's self-determination, resolve to bootstrap her and Kara's futures without financial assistance, and selection of the Derrick Spaulding MBA program for its post-graduation service requirement as a way to repay her education provided ample evidence she wasn't interested in taking the easy way. Her conviction that one's character and not one's means should inform one's success ran completely counter to all that would become associated with the program.

Even if TJ could forgive—Jess knew she had the capacity and heart to—she'd never be able to look at Jess the same way, never want to be with someone whose family would go down as among the greediest and most self-serving in history.

Worse, TJ would know the true role Jess played in securing more and more clients. Jess was damn good at her job, and TJ knew it. How could TJ ever consider Jess desirable once the truth came to light?

Good taste and fine breeding dictated it was far too late for Jess to stop by. Yet from this day forth the Spauldings would never be remembered for either, so what did she have to lose? She texted TJ another apology for spoiling their earlier plans and said she'd make it up to her. It was rude and presumptuous, but Jess needed to see her.

Though the day's revelation hadn't affected Jess's skin, it was as sensitive as if burned. All the material that touched it was filched and therefore filthy. Jess had a closet full of finery yet nothing to wear, nothing she could call her own. Covering herself with anything but a body bag seemed overly stylish, while normal clothing that touched skin felt too intimate to wear when it didn't belong to her. Even the sweats she'd had on earlier felt too rich, the material too soft, for what she deserved. Burlap would be more suitable, but she didn't own any.

Getting arrested at this stage was the least of Jess's worries, so she donned her oldest trench coat. She'd never gone commando before today, yet here she was ready to head to the worst part of town in nothing but flasher gear. It didn't matter. The coat felt as intimate as an arena, which made it easier to put on than her usual garb.

The only transportation options at her disposal were stark reminders of her father's treachery, flashy finery paid with misappropriated funds. Yet while there was probably a bus route in the vicinity, she hadn't the time or inclination to play planes, trains, and automobiles to get to TJ's. She slid into the Mercedes and took off.

❖

The roller-coaster ride Jess had taken her on lately confused TJ, but she knew Jess better than to think she was playing games. When Jess had said she had to bow out of their date night, TJ had been disappointed but understanding. Though she'd have preferred to learn the reason behind her canceling, she believed Jess wouldn't have done so lightly.

The faint knock at the door came as a surprise. It was after midnight. TJ had already settled in for the night, enjoying a mystery she'd picked up at the library. It provided a much-needed break from the puzzle that was the Magnate Fund. On Monday she'd have to get Jess to escalate the matter, be it through Gary or one of the analysts, as the presumption she could dive in headfirst and figure out the keys to Magnate's success without so much as a tutorial was proving false. But it was Friday night. She was tired of work and glad to let someone else—in this case the hapless PI from the novel—handle the investigating. At least TJ's troubles didn't involve a dead body and an unlicensed handgun.

In case she misheard, TJ waited before answering it. She didn't hear it again. Instead, her phone vibrated. It was a text from Jess asking if she was awake. When she replied in the affirmative, the next message asked her to open the door.

Without heeding her outfit—a worn T-shirt that didn't cover her underwear—she rushed to the door and found Jess standing in the hallway wearing a dark-gray trench coat and low-heeled boots. As she tried to put her jumbled thoughts in order, she watched Jess's eyes slowly travel down her body as if she were wearing the sexiest negligée ever designed. Jess's eyes seemed a shade darker and a hundred times hungrier than TJ had ever seen them, so much so that her sex clenched and her thighs tightened together in response.

"Where's Kara?" Jess asked in a low voice as she focused on TJ's bare legs.

TJ inclined her head toward Kara's bedroom. "Bed." She took a step back as Jess took two steps toward her and closed the door.

Jess briefly glanced behind her to flip the lock before resting her palms on TJ's chest. With a hair's breadth between their lips, Jess said, "One of my favorite words." She trailed the fingers of one hand down the channel between TJ's breasts before taking her hand and leading her to the edge of her bed.

"Jess, what are you—" TJ was gently pushed onto her back. Jess had an intensity—perhaps a desperation—she'd never seen before. As she considered turning on the overhead light in order to shift the mood that her reading light and Jess's assertiveness were quickly turning into a seduction, TJ faltered. Because in record time, Jess was out of her boots, simultaneously unfastening coat buttons as she untied its belt. An instant later, Jess was straddling her, palms next to TJ's shoulders, her gorgeous breasts dangling above her like tree-ripe fruit, fresh for the taking.

TJ swallowed hard. She wanted to know what was going through Jess's mind, but it was very hard to think with the expanse of lovely skin at her fingertips.

"Hi," Jess said in a shy voice that belied her extremely forward entrance.

"Hi," TJ managed. She was finding it difficult not to reach for Jess and wished she were stronger. In about two seconds, she'd be willing to push aside the conversation they clearly needed to have. Two. One. And just like that, those seconds passed and her hands started wandering over the luxurious planes of Jess's body. "What's on your mind?" She smiled wryly, knowing full well the answer.

"Oh, you know." Jess pushed the reading light to face the wall before leaning down and tracing her nose along the delicate skin beneath TJ's ear. "The price of tea in China." She placed feather-light kisses along TJ's neck. "Whether the Fed will raise interest rates." She trailed her tongue across TJ's chin. "Fracking's impact on clean drinking water." She lifted TJ's T-shirt to expose her breasts before lowering herself until their bodies touched. "Whether we're done talking." Jess kissed TJ in a way that removed any guesswork.

Conversation was out of the question now that TJ was rendered speechless. Jess had arrived on a mission, complete with mission control, and TJ could only take direction. She wasn't used to relinquishing control, but if this was the outcome of doing so, she might never try to retake it.

As Jess's mouth moved down TJ's torso, TJ felt a tug at the waistband of her briefs, which were swiftly pulled below her ass before being worked down and off her legs. Without Jess's weight on her upper body, TJ took the opportunity to quickly remove her own shirt. Knowing they were both naked, she couldn't help but tug Jess back up until they were face-to-face. She wanted to feel Jess against her fully, with nothing between them but love and trust. As Jess sank into TJ and their bodies connected from head to toe, skin on skin, they both released something between a sigh and a moan. To feel this woman above her, to know her heart and mind, was an experience TJ would never forget.

TJ's hands were in Jess's hair, and she kissed her as if starved, as if Jess were a rare food found only in the farthest reaches of the globe. Two hands were two—maybe four—too few to quench her thirst for Jess.

Jess, for her part, seemed extraordinarily competent, as if she'd been making love to women since puberty. Her lips, tongue, hands, thighs, and breasts moved together like a conflagration designed to make every molecule in TJ's body scream her name. She was also a tad impatient. Her mouth was between TJ's thighs before TJ could process she'd moved, since Jess seemed everywhere at once. Her talented tongue brought TJ to a climax TJ realized too late was taking place within the apartment she shared with Kara. Thankfully, like most teenagers, Kara was a notoriously heavy sleeper. Still, the sheer number of "Oh, Gods" she'd uttered made her pray Kara wouldn't ply her with questions about her new religion.

Before TJ's breathing returned to normal, Jess was caressing one of TJ's nipples with her tongue until it was erect and wanting. Jess took pity on the mute flesh by taking it more fully into her mouth. Indecently wet, TJ spoke for her overwhelmed body parts. "Jess, please." This time, Jess would not be rushed. She ran her tongue along TJ's throat, jaw, and neck, and took TJ's earlobe into her mouth while her fingers teased her center. With Jess's hot breath in her ear and Jess's hands tormenting her overly sensitive nerve endings, TJ again begged, "Please." TJ's wish was finally granted as she was instantly filled with fingers entirely too skillful to be neophytes in this arena. Not that she was complaining.

Sated and sweating, TJ finally caught her breath. She was riding mixed emotions, filled with wonder and delight on one hand, concern and caution on the other. Jess had taken her to physical heights, yes, but it was the emotional ones that had her reeling. She was on the brink of being inexorably tied to Jess by feelings she dared not name. Not wanting to dwell on her heart's response to Jess's lovemaking, TJ swung her attention to the woman instilling these new feelings within her.

TJ flipped Jess onto her back and kissed her soundly. "Can we mix up the agenda a little?"

Jess stroked TJ's back and ass. "No one else is invited, if that's the question."

"The question is," TJ said as she traced Jess's bottom lip with her tongue, "can I play too?"

Jess smiled and surged up to kiss her. "I thought you'd never ask."

TJ toured Jess's body as if she were a sleek sports car and Jess a mountain highway. Her mouth hugged Jess's curves the way the tires would cling to the road, creating a beautiful heat along the journey. She started with Jess's face, lingered along her throat and clavicle, spent a summer at her breasts, and finally moved south. At the first taste of her, TJ understood bliss. She'd known it earlier as she'd surrendered to Jess's mouth, but now, allowed to experience Jess in the most personal, vulnerable way possible, it was somehow expanded. Jess's moans of pleasure, the increased pressure she placed at the back of TJ's head, her attempts to widen her legs against the instinct to collapse them under the assault of TJ's tongue, all served to heighten TJ's already sky-high emotions.

Having relentlessly driven Jess to her peak, TJ tarried between Jess's legs a little longer, using them as protective walls to shield her from the onslaught of her emotions. After tonight, there was no doubt her soul belonged to Jess.

So why not tell Jess how she was feeling? Did keeping it to herself make it any less real?

Delivering kisses as she moved back up Jess's enticing body, she propped her head on her elbow and ran her fingers through Jess's hair. Jess caressed TJ's side, her face full of adoration. TJ decided she liked it. "You really know how to make an entrance," TJ said.

"You really know how to make a girl feel welcome," Jess said before leaning in for another kiss.

TJ traced Jess's lips with her finger. They were rosier and slightly fuller than usual, gently bruised from their lovemaking. It was incredibly sexy watching Jess's tongue snake out to take TJ's fingers into her mouth and feeling the warm wetness envelop them. "Mmm. I could get used to this mouth."

Once Jess had relinquished TJ's digits, she said, "I wish you could too," a little too melancholic for TJ's taste.

TJ took Jess's hand and kissed her palm. "I intend to."

Jess shifted her hand to cup TJ's face. She smiled in a way that appeared more sad than happy, as if she were trying to be strong in the face of receiving bad news from the internist. She appeared to be on the edge of saying something important when her eyes misted, and she held back.

Uncertain of what to make of Jess's reaction, TJ shifted until Jess was on her back, with TJ covering her. "Hey," TJ said. "Talk to me." A tear slid out of the corner of Jess's eye and TJ wiped it with her thumb. "Baby, please."

But Jess only shook her head slightly. "You make me happy."

TJ snorted and wiped away another tear. "I can tell," she said incredulously.

"You do. But you can make me happier," Jess said, planting a brief kiss on TJ's lips.

"Anything," TJ said and meant it.

"Make love to me," Jess whispered.

The entreaty melted away the last vestige of TJ's resolve to get Jess to open up. They could address whatever was plaguing her tomorrow. Right now Jess needed TJ to help her forget, and TJ couldn't deny her any more than she could cease breathing.

Jess awoke just after four in the morning. She was spooning TJ, one arm draped over her like a rabbit ear. Her nose was pressed close to the back of TJ's neck, and Jess could detect the faint smell of her shampoo. The scents of sex and sweat had faded, though the pleasant soreness of certain under-utilized muscles provided ample reminder of how she'd spent the night. Nuzzling TJ as delicately as a cotton ball so as not to wake her, Jess took time to enjoy the sheer pleasure of waking up to the woman she loved. How bittersweet it would be the last time she'd have the opportunity.

Extricating herself slowly from TJ, Jess crept to the closet and closed the door behind her before feeling for the light switch. She scanned the room's contents and grabbed a gray sweatshirt and sweat pants. Perhaps it was a little stalkerish, but she wanted to have something of TJ's against her skin, not clothing that had been purchased with stolen funds. She told herself she'd return them one day. Borrowing a bra or panties wasn't in the offing as she was curvier than TJ. Newly outfitted, she exited the closet and picked up her coat and boots. The floor creaked when she bent over, and TJ stirred. Jess froze. She didn't want to leave this way but had no choice. Saying good-bye forever after everything they'd shared was heartbreaking, but being together after what Jess was about to do was impossible.

After several minutes passed with no movement from TJ, Jess took her leave and left her heart behind.

CHAPTER TWENTY-SIX

Jess's phone buzzed and she picked it up. Dillon was out front. She swiped the application to open the gate.

She surveyed the entryway. Her two suitcases and boxes were packed. Her used cosmetics weren't worth anything to anyone else and were easily justified. The shoes and clothing were in impeccable condition. She rationalized taking them because she'd be facing tremendous public scrutiny, and she wanted Magnate's fleeced investors to see she understood the magnitude of the scam. That meant looking and acting the part of a credible witness. After her father was imprisoned, Jess would donate what little she was taking of her wardrobe. She'd borrow money from Dillon for replacements and figure out how to repay him. The two boxes contained personal items: gifts from friends and relatives, photographs, mementos from various trips she'd taken, books, and journals. Their monetary value was insignificant, but they meant something to Jess—even pictures of her father. Having debated whether to leave them behind—some of her favorites over the years were of the two of them together, snapshots capturing real smiles—she decided to pack them. She wasn't in the proper state of mind to make decisions as to whether irreplaceable keepsakes had any part in her future.

Once her father had admitted to the scheme, Jess had stopped seeing her house as hers. It was as much hers as a seat on a train, and she didn't have money for the fare. The extravagant surroundings became harsh to behold, as if she'd removed dark sunglasses from high atop a snowy mountain on a sunny day. The painstaking details created by the laborers, artists, and other craftsmen who'd built the guest home were like a mouthful of decayed teeth whose exposed nerves brought constant agony. Those details reminded Jess of the intricacies of her father's crime and made her feel filthy.

The doorbell rang and Jess opened the door. Dillon held out his arms and Jess sank into his embrace. During her earlier phone call, she'd been so upset he'd had difficulty making out her ragged sentences, but she'd managed to convey enough information to get him to drop everything and come for her. When she pulled back enough to look at him, she swiped at another tear, her constant companions of late. "I'm so sick of crying," Jess said with a pathetic laugh.

He smiled and brushed away a tear with a knuckle. "What can I do?"

"Being here for me is all I need." She picked up one of the boxes. "Could you grab one of the suitcases?"

Dillon took both suitcases and followed Jess out to his car. As he stowed the items, Jess returned for the last box. She peered around the grand entrance one last time and heard Dillon on the stairs. He pulled the box from her hands. "Is that everything?" She snatched her purse and phone from the side table, along with her laptop bag. Once she had time to save her files and erase the drive, she'd ship it back to the house for the U.S. Marshals or whoever to deal with. Dillon would have one she could borrow. And she intended to get a prepaid phone with the money Dillon would lend her.

Jess scrolled through the phone settings and selected the factory-reset option. The relief that she was taking steps to have TJ be rid of her once and for all replaced the guilt she'd first felt from not returning TJ's calls or texts. All Jess could ever be to TJ now was a disheartening reminder of everything her family had taken from TJ—and from scores of others. She turned it off and laid it next to her keys, as she wouldn't be needing the cars or house any longer. The heavy gold medallion with the Magnate logo that anchored her key ring might as well have been a lump of coal, so lost was its luster in her eyes. Once so proud to carry it, she left it behind with disdain. It wasn't real gold—wasn't meant to be—and the ersatz metal would only remind her that everything about Magnate was counterfeit.

Once in Dillon's truck, he said, "Bank, then my shop, then my shack?"

She nodded. During their earlier call, she'd blathered on about needing to leave everything behind. Dillon had immediately offered her his fishing shack and one of his repos. "Fishing" and "shack" were both misnomers. The only fish Dillon caught were red Swedish candies, and the structure was a spacious cabin filled with Dillon-type toys. It was his man cave. It had a wet bar, flat-screen TV with surround sound, Wi-Fi, gaming consoles, recliners, a poker table, electric guitars, an amplifier, and a dartboard. It also had a bedroom and full kitchen. Out back was a shed in which he kept two dirt bikes and two kayaks.

The cabin was on three acres an hour from town and would provide a good respite from the media circus Jess was about to enter.

❖

TJ was dragging this morning. Two days ago she'd awoken to an empty bed with no note of explanation after the most intimate evening she'd ever shared. Her texts and voice mails had gone unanswered, and she was worried. Jess had been distracted leading up to their night together and showed signs of carrying a heavy burden. Even the clothing—or lack thereof—she'd worn was very un-Jess-like. Always well put together, Jess had arrived without makeup, clothing, or having styled her hair. Almost disheveled. And her arrival itself seemed way off, almost desperate.

Having spent the weekend berating herself for caving in to her physical desire for Jess instead of urging her to discuss what was bothering her, and unable to get in touch, TJ was emotionally exhausted. It was akin to going door-to-door with lost-pet flyers in hand, searching for your beloved companion, only to return home empty-handed. Her heart felt heavy.

In an unprecedented move, Gary had swung by her desk and asked to speak with her. Though he usually seemed fairly clueless and rarely spent time on TJ's side of the office, TJ couldn't help wondering whether he'd noticed her flagging energy and was about to call her out on it. He was right to do so. She needed to get her head back into the game and find some answers for her case study.

Once they were seated in Gary's office, he didn't dawdle. "There's no easy way for me to say this, TJ, so I'm going to come right out with it. You're fired. If you sign the separation agreement, you'll be entitled to up to six months of COBRA reimbursement."

TJ's ears began to ring, drowning out most of his additional words regarding the termination paperwork and the return of the building security card and laptop. Although California was an at-will state in which employers weren't required to justify their actions with good cause or provide advance notice, it was a baffling turn of events. The only person within Magnate with whom she'd interacted regularly was Jess, and TJ could see no reason for Jess to let her go. Surely something else was at play here?

Deciding an argument wasn't in her best interest, TJ did her utmost to pretend she was listening to his words and understanding the documents she was signing. But when he asked if she had any questions, she took the opportunity. "May I ask whose decision this was?"

He didn't hesitate. "Your immediate supervisor, of course. Jess."

Blindsided.

That was the only word for TJ's reaction. It was like being hit by an Amtrak train while sitting in the stands of a football stadium—she never saw it coming. Jess had her fired?

TJ vaguely followed Gary's well-wishes that were incongruent with the rest of his message, took her personal belongings, and left the Magnate offices. As she drove home, she contemplated dropping by Jess's loft unannounced. She needed answers.

Was TJ's imminent firing the issue plaguing Jess these past few days? If so, why hadn't Jess discussed it with her? Jess had proved a good mentor, imparting knowledge and providing direction when TJ was stuck. Why then would she cease doing so? Did TJ's difficulties in understanding how the Magnate Fund operated change Jess's mind about her ability to succeed in the internship? Were TJ's questions about the fund coming across as her not being grateful for the immense opportunity of working for the man responsible for her graduate program? If so, why hadn't Jess come straight out and told her? Why pretend she'd look into TJ's questions if she had no intention of doing so?

No longer safe behind the wheel because of the tears welling in her eyes, TJ pulled over to get control over her emotions. On top of Jess's silence, she was like a boxer who'd been hit with a one-two punch that left her dazed and struggling to stay upright.

She'd gladly leave the internship if she and Jess could be together. Hell, she'd gladly leave the program if that were the case. But Jess seemed to be sending a message, and TJ didn't need a graduate degree to understand it.

TJ hadn't paid much attention to where she'd stopped the truck, but now she took in her surroundings. She was on a stretch of two-lane road that ran along a small river. On one side of the road lay commercial buildings. On the other side, beyond the water, old houses dotted a wide stretch of grassland. As she retrieved a tissue to blow her nose, TJ saw a house cat jump from its hiding place beneath the tall grass in an attempt to capture a white butterfly. The obviously well-fed animal wasn't attacking the insect for food. It was doing so for entertainment, for the thrill of the chase.

TJ watched the hunt for several minutes, silently rooting for the butterfly. Its haphazard flight pattern was beautiful in its randomness, darting and dropping as if purposely snubbing the laws of order. But this movement seemed only to fuel the cat's appetite for the capture and kill. Its front legs whipped about in a frenzy, trying to snare the tiny flitting wings. In an incredibly acrobatic move, the cat jumped high, stretched its paw, and snagged a wing with a claw. TJ lost sight of the butterfly once the cat brought it to the ground. The feline briefly monitored the insect's remnants before its preoccupation ebbed and it headed toward the river.

Her scathing inner self-critic asked whether she'd just witnessed a parody of her relationship with Jess, where as soon as the pampered princess captured the thing she was after, she lost interest.

Defeated, keeping control of her emotions with only the strength of a butterfly's wings, TJ headed home.

CHAPTER TWENTY-SEVEN

Something bopped TJ on the shoulder. Startled, she noticed an object rolling on the floor and watched it come to a stop. A grape. She'd been attempting to read a book on effective leadership, but her brain was retaining information like a sieve. The only thing she could effectively lead right now was the line for unemployment benefits.

"Sorry, I don't have any bread crumbs," Kara said from inside the doorway, setting down her backpack and holding a plastic baggie half full of grapes. "You're so lost in thought you can use these to find your way back," she said as she dropped the bag into TJ's lap en route to the kitchen, scooping up the grape as she passed. "You've got it baaaaad."

TJ heard the fridge door open and close before Kara plopped next to her on the couch with a glass of milk in hand. "You're home late," TJ said, setting the book in her lap.

Kara took a drink and nodded. "I texted you. Four times." She reached for TJ's phone and opened her messaging app. "All unread." She showed TJ the screen before setting it down. "Office hours with Mrs. Janikowski and then study group. Remember? Or are you so whipped you can't—what's wrong?"

TJ rubbed her face. "What isn't?"

"You didn't break up again, did you?" Kara asked with alarm.

"I was fired today."

"Are you serious?"

"As a heart attack."

"Fuck," Kara said before immediately covering her mouth. "Sorry."

This was as good a time as any to let it slide. TJ nodded. "Yeah, that pretty much sums it up."

"Why?"

"Wish I knew."

"What does Jess say about it?"

"I haven't seen or talked to her, but the decision was apparently hers."

"She must have had a reason."

"Thanks," TJ said dryly.

Kara set down her glass and crossed her arms. "That's not what I mean. You're the most capable person I know. Something's up."

TJ tossed her book onto the coffee table. "Something like she's a coward who refuses to return my calls and doesn't have the guts to fire me herself?"

"You don't know that."

"Maybe if we'd had a fight or something…I don't know." TJ shook her head.

"She wouldn't fire you over something personal."

"You have no idea what she'd fire me over," TJ said sharply.

"What if Mom and Dad worked together and Dad fired Mom? You think she'd go, 'What a Class A'? No. She'd be like, he must've had crappy choices and chose the least bad."

"I don't look to Mom for lessons in how to think or act."

Kara scooped up her backpack and glared. "Good thing you don't, because you know what? Jess deserves better." The bedroom door thudded closed.

I'm the one to lose my job without explanation, and Jess is the one Kara defends? Could this day get any better? On the bright side, Kara hadn't shrugged once during their brief conversation. That was a plus, wasn't it?

❖

Flying bugs buzzed past Jess as she sat on the small dock down the path from the shack. The lake was as quiet and still as bathwater. Birds occasionally darted by, but as it wasn't the time of the evening for their choir practice, they were silent among the trees. Traffic noise was blissfully absent.

Jess took a sip of hot cocoa, trying to enjoy the placid surroundings that were so different from the hustle and bustle of the FBI office she'd spent the morning in. She'd sat in an uncomfortable worn, gray chair for hours, under old fluorescent lights that seemed designed to sap energy. The agents were professional and courteous. After two hours, one had been kind enough to fetch her real coffee from a nearby café, apologizing for the sludge they'd initially offered and apparently routinely drank themselves. Its color and consistency had seemed more apt to be pulled from a car hose at Dillon's shop than suited for drinking, and Jess was grateful for the kindness.

Although she hadn't brought any records with her, she'd gone into great detail about what she'd found. To her, the most important fact was Derrick's confession, but given she'd sifted through a vast array of files herself, she informed them of everything she'd come across and the conclusions she'd reached. She'd wished she knew unequivocally whether Brooke, Gary, and even Lilith were innocent, but she'd only been able to relay what Derrick had told her.

Able to remain impassive throughout the questioning, she had let her emotions get away from her only once. The agent had asked Jess to confirm the date she first became aware of the fraud. That it had been so recent—mere days ago—was a guilt she'd have to live with for the rest of her life. Had she been less pliable to Lilith's demands regarding "her place," more curious to understand the complexities of the business instead of meekly accepting things at face value, more dubious about the long-running consistency of Magnate's returns, less acquiescent of her father's choice of Gary over Brooke or her or virtually anyone else as COO—God, if she'd been *anything* other than a spoiled rich kid who never really demanded to leave the nest and make her own way in this world—she might have been able to stop it before it ravaged so many people's lives.

When she'd exhausted herself of the tale and complied with requests to repeat certain statements, she was thanked for her cooperation and allowed to leave. She hadn't expected otherwise, though part of her believed she could be arrested for complicity because of her own role in bringing so many lambs to the slaughter. She wondered idly if there would ever come a time when she could forgive herself for working so hard to assure Magnate's success. But she knew the answer.

She watched several water striders dart across the lake's surface, and her thoughts shifted to her father. Throughout much of her life, Jess had believed he could practically walk on water. It had never occurred to her not to trust him. Normally people had to earn her trust. People like Dillon and TJ had done so over time through their actions. And yet, aside from his accedence to Lilith's ultimatum regarding Jess and Dillon, Derrick *had* earned her trust. He'd been there for her day in, day out. He was as good a parent as she could've hoped for. Until now. God, she'd been so wrong. How could she ever trust anyone again when her instincts were so far off the mark?

And yet, were they? Dillon had proved dependable and honorable time and again. And TJ was so principled she was sure to never want to speak to Jess again after tomorrow. The idea sent a shooting pain through her abdomen. She was greatly conflicted about their night together. If Jess had been truthful as to why she'd been distant and mercurial, TJ would've never allowed Jess to touch her. Part of her felt disgusted with herself, as if by leaving out the truth she'd done the equivalent of slipping TJ a roofie. Another part justified it as consensual lovemaking as crucial to Jess that night as oxygen. Perhaps most damning to her psyche was the fact she knew without a doubt she'd do it over again in the same circumstances. She'd had to know TJ's touch, had to touch her.

By tomorrow, assuming she'd read the news, TJ would understand why she'd had such difficulty making sense of the fund and why Derrick hadn't wanted her getting too deep in its files. She'd know of Jess's contributions to perpetuating the scam, and it wouldn't matter whether Jess was in on the deceit because she'd helped fleece folks of billions of dollars. Moreover, Jess had been the first to spend some of it.

Jess finished her tepid beverage and looked out across the water, considering it as a type of weapon. One could drown in it. For the first time, she truly understood Kara's desire to get beaten up, to be punished for what she believed were her own shortcomings. Jess didn't agree that Kara should ever be hurt in such a manner or that Kara was at fault in any way. But she thought she finally understood the inclination, finally grasped why someone like Virginia Woolf would don her overcoat, fill its pockets with stones, and walk into the water to end her days.

CHAPTER TWENTY-EIGHT

Wednesday afternoon, TJ arrived at the business school's offices for her meeting with Philip Ridge. As she waited, she noticed an uncharacteristic hustle and bustle among the staff. They were constantly on the phone, and as soon as someone would hang up, it wouldn't take long for it to ring again.

When Ridge finally opened his door and welcomed TJ into his office, he seemed even happier to see her than usual. Likely he'd already heard about her termination and was trying not to make it seem like a big deal. He was probably already working his back channels to see if he could set her up for a shortened internship. TJ was grateful for his belief in her and dreaded having to disavow him of it. After they exchanged greetings and Ridge asked what was on the mind of the "resident celebrity," TJ concluded she was the only one of her fellow students who'd been released from their jobs and this was his way of making light of it. She decided to get directly to the point of her visit.

"I'm here with bad news, Professor. I was fired from my internship because I got involved with someone I shouldn't have. I convinced myself it was above board but realize now it was wishful thinking, since the person's family runs the company. I can't finish the case study, and frankly, I wasn't making headway figuring out the formula for the firm's success anyway. I've let you down, I've let the program down, I've let myself down. There's really no way to sugarcoat it. I'm sorry."

During TJ's spiel, Ridge steepled his fingers and listened intently. "That's not how I heard it."

TJ's heart sank. She was too late. Of course someone at Magnate, probably Gary, would have already informed Ridge of her premature exit and must have provided a far lengthier explanation—hell, a sentence would have been more than she got—as to what had led to her termination. TJ was well aware of Ridge's history with Derrick Spaulding. They'd been college roommates, and their continued association had ultimately led to the Derrick Spaulding MBA Program at Griffin University. "I'm sorry you didn't hear it from me first. This was your earliest appointment, and I wanted to tell you in person."

"TJ, Derrick Spaulding was arrested this morning after confessing to running the largest Ponzi scheme in history. It's all over the news."

This was far too much for TJ to process. She spoke the only words she could manage. "I don't understand."

"Whatever questions you were asking were obviously the right ones. Jessica Spaulding went to the authorities yesterday and named you as the whistle-blower."

Jess did *what*?

None of this made sense. "Professor, all I did was get stumped. I didn't reach any conclusions about Magnate except that I wasn't savvy enough to grasp how it worked."

Ridge responded by pushing TJ on statements he'd read. Had she made inquiries as to how the Magnate Fund operated? (Yes.) Had she found some oddities in the information she was given? (Yes.) Had there been occasions she felt she was being purposefully sidetracked from her goal? (Yes.) Had she been fired without reason? (Yes.) Had Jessica already been investigating the matter before TJ started asking questions? (No.)

Jess had spun her version of the truth, TJ realized, for TJ's benefit. The details as Jess had apparently confided to the authorities were so close to being accurate that TJ had ended up seeming to corroborate Jess's story, which in turn only bolstered Ridge's contention that TJ was some kind of hero. The final nail: when TJ mentioned she hadn't known a scheme was afoot, Ridge said that according to Jessica Spaulding, TJ wouldn't want praise for her role in taking Derrick down. It was simply the right thing to do, and she would insist she hadn't done anything special. At every turn, Jess had preempted TJ's attempts to set the record straight.

Apparently attuned to TJ's frustration, Ridge told her that the truth didn't sell as much copy as sensationalism. If the public wanted a hero, the only guarantee was it wouldn't be a Spaulding. It would be a far flashier story to have a working-class David bring down a high-class Goliath. Instead of being credited for taking the incredibly difficult step of turning her father in, Jess would be vilified. Ridge said Jess was already being excoriated in the media. The pundits were saying it was improbable Jessica Spaulding hadn't been in on the deceit; she only turned her father in as a kind of plea bargain to minimize personal liability and maximize the assets they'd let her keep.

That's when TJ realized she had no such doubts about Jess. With every atom of her being, TJ knew Jess hadn't been involved in her father's scheme.

"Professor, there's no way Jess knew."

"Doesn't matter. She's being assailed for living a lavish lifestyle on the backs of unsuspecting investors and castigated for not being suspicious earlier."

"It's not fair."

"No. None of it is. The program will have to be cut immediately. There's no way the university could survive the PR damage of trying to keep the remaining funds, since they weren't Spaulding's to begin with. Due to your actions, thankfully no one should question the kinds of ethics we're teaching here, though we'll have to jettison any association with Derrick Spaulding ASAP. From a personal standpoint, I'm having trouble with it. Derrick's an old friend. A good friend. But what he's done…" Ridge shook his head. "TJ, was it Jessica you were involved with?"

TJ nodded.

"I don't want to insinuate myself where I don't belong, but if you're still…friends…I'm sure she could use one. I've known her since she was a child. She and Derrick have always been close. I can't imagine what she's going through."

TJ didn't know what she and Jess were, but Ridge's words resonated. Whatever was or had been between them didn't matter as much as letting Jess know she wasn't alone.

❖

The next two days flew by. At Ridge's suggestion, TJ helped out in the college of business's office while they put out various fires relating to the scandal and worked with other schools to see how, when, and where they could best transfer TJ and her classmates. Sprinkled throughout were interviews TJ granted as to how she discovered a fraud that had long gone unnoticed. Sticking with the corruption angle, reporters were quick to dismiss TJ's commendation of Jess and unwilling to allow that Jess had been as much a victim as anyone. At every turn, Jess was a pariah second only to her father.

Somehow by appearing shell-shocked on camera, Brooke, Gary, and Lilith all faced less public wrath than Jess who, by turning Derrick in, was seen as someone in the know and therefore culpable. TJ made the mistake of tuning into an exposé on Derrick's downfall that cast Lilith, her son, and the two Spaulding girls as spoiled spendthrifts. Brooke hadn't helped counter that reputation when it was reported she left the country to be with the wealthy son of a French diplomat, leaving her family behind.

At one point, Ridge's assistant transferred a call to TJ.

"TJ Blake."

A voice TJ didn't recognize said, "Ms. Blake, please hold a minute while I transfer you." TJ had little patience for these kinds of telemarketing ploys, though she couldn't understand why Ridge's assistant would put through such a call. A protest died on her lips when she heard, "Darling, it's Muriel Manchester."

The commanding voice left no doubt it was Muriel. She had a way of being slightly irritating yet very intriguing, like a sports celebrity. "Ms. Manchester. What a pleasant surprise. What can I do for you?"

"Several things, and you know better than to call me Ms. Manchester. First, what's your number so I can reach you more easily? The pit bull who answered refused to divulge your private information to my assistant."

TJ gave Muriel her mobile number.

"What's your employment status?"

"I'm helping out in the business-college office."

"Surely not for the long term?"

TJ didn't know what had prompted the call or the question, and it was none of Muriel's business. Yet while she didn't appreciate her derogatory tone, she thought it best not to strike an adversarial one. Knowing Muriel's deep pockets, she might be a donor of some significance, and TJ was representing the university. "You're a well-informed woman, Muriel. You must know my classmates and I are on a bit of a hiatus, so I'm assisting with the higher volume of inquiries at the moment."

"Perfect. I want you to be my compliance director, reporting to my chief compliance officer. Your name's associated with a standard of ethics every public company should aspire to and which my board takes very seriously. We'd be privileged to have you."

This offer was more unexpected than Muriel's call. The position was a solid jumping-off point to a career in nonprofit management and especially useful for establishing a reputation as someone mindful of asset stewardship. Days ago she'd been fired and all her prospects had dimmed. Now the CEO of a Fortune 500 company was seeking her. But TJ wanted to finish her degree. It was the best assurance she had of landing a management role in time and ultimately running the show.

"Muriel, I'm honored. But I can't accept. I need to earn the last of my course credits before I can graduate, and that has to be my focus at this stage."

"How close are you from graduating?"

"Very. But the program's been, well, it's in an unprecedented state given the overnight collapse of its funding. The credits earned are transferable, but it will take time to apply to a new program. Also the faculty has to determine how much credit, if any, can be earned for the internships and whether to keep the service requirement." TJ felt she was rambling and stopped. "Sorry. Probably more than you wanted to know."

"Not at all. I'll speak with your dean. I'm sure we can work something out, and I'm willing to accommodate your school schedule."

"I don't understand. Why would you want to help me?"

"TJ, darling—once you're my employee I'm going to miss being able to call you that—there's one thing I've managed to learn in all my years in business. Women, especially lesbians, need to look after each other. We need to hold each other up. Enough people out there strive to tear us down, and I've no intention of allowing that."

"That's...wow, that's very generous of you. Thank you. I'll certainly think about your offer."

"Please do. I want you on my team—my other team." Muriel laughed. "Besides, it's the least I can do after what your girlfriend did for me."

Jess. TJ had left countless voice mails and sent numerous texts. Every day she tried Jess's number multiple times in the hope it wouldn't go straight to voice mail. She'd driven by the mansion and the loft several times, but she never got any answer.

"I didn't realize she had business with you," TJ said. And girlfriend might be overstating things.

"I recently invested half a billion dollars in Magnate."

TJ cringed. She wondered how much of that money Derrick Spaulding had already used to pay dividends and returns of capital to earlier investors. Even if the independent investigator ultimately found that Muriel should be entitled to recoup some of it, it would likely be years before it was returned. "I'm sorry, Muriel."

"Don't be. Unlike the hundreds of unfortunates that seem to come forward daily, I won't have to admit to being one of them. My money was wired to me in full."

TJ wondered whether Muriel was more concerned about her reputation—i.e., of not having been duped—than the money. But it didn't make sense it had already been returned. "It wasn't used to pay off other Magnate investors?"

"It never made it to Magnate. Seems your girlfriend provided my accountant with the bank account details of the family attorney's escrow account to hold until otherwise instructed. And she later instructed the attorney to return the money. That's all he'd tell me."

TJ's heart soared. Performing one good deed after another was becoming Jess's MO. "I'm glad to hear it, though I can't say I'm surprised. But how about thanking her directly by offering her a job instead of me?"

"You're the famous whistle-blower, TJ. No offense to Jessica, but it's your name that carries weight. A much different kind than hers carries."

"Then how about a package deal?"

"I'm listening," Muriel replied.

"Your marketing department is about to get ten times better."

CHAPTER TWENTY-NINE

When Dillon entered the customer lounge area, he reminded TJ of Marlon Brando in *A Streetcar Named Desire*. How the man managed to look so dreamy when his clothes were streaked with grease was kind of hard on one's self-esteem. He held out his hand, which was absurdly clean given his outfit. "TJ, good to see you again."

"Thanks for making the time," she said as she shook his hand.

"Come on back."

Dillon led her through a door next to the payment window to the back offices. His was no different than the others they passed except it had less clutter. "Have a seat," he directed her, and she sat opposite his metal desk. "How's the mechanical prodigy?"

"Restless and studying like mad. She said to tell you she'll be back here faster than a Shelby Cobra."

Dillon laughed. "Glad to hear you haven't changed your mind."

"Not at the risk of a year and a half of silent treatment, occasional grunt notwithstanding."

"If our plan's still on, why the visit?"

"I need to get in touch with Jess."

He picked up a little black muscle-car toy and started squeezing it with one hand.

"Stress toy?" TJ asked.

He tossed it to her. "Yep. Sixty-nine Camaro ZL1. Only sixty-nine were made, and unfortunately, that's the only one I own."

"You don't keep it in the showroom along with the other collectors' items?"

"I see where Kara gets her sense of humor."

TJ set it on the desk and made it do a wheelie before getting down to business, barely suppressing the desire to make a screeching-tire sound along with it. There really was something fun and carefree about playing with toy cars, but this wasn't the time for it. "She doesn't answer at her house or loft. All my calls go directly to voice mail, and none of the texts I've sent show they've been delivered. Magnate's been shut down. I don't know how to reach her."

"What makes you think I do?"

"You're her best friend."

"Best friends look out for each other."

Having just confirmed he knew how to contact Jess bolstered TJ's resolve not to leave empty-handed. "Please tell me where she is."

"She knows how to reach you."

"Yes, but what if she thinks I don't want to talk to her?"

Dillon started giving the stress toy another workout.

"She's getting lambasted out there," TJ said. "Her supposed 'friends' are getting their fifteen minutes of fame by telling stories of how they spent money like it flowed from a tap and how they've no doubt she knew. Brooke took off with her rich boyfriend. That idiot Chad's the only one defending her, and his defense is that she's too dumb to have been able to figure anything out on her own. I'm not surprised she's gone off the grid and wonders who her real friends are."

"I can't help you, TJ."

"Can't? Or won't?"

"I'm sorry."

TJ had expected Dillon to be cautious, but she hadn't expected for him to stonewall her. She didn't know how to convince him of her good intentions without telling him how she felt about Jess, which she wouldn't do without first telling Jess herself. "I'm not asking you to be a go-between. That wouldn't be fair to you, and it wouldn't say much about our relationship if we can't figure things out ourselves. I don't know why she won't talk to me. All I can tell you is I care about her. What she did…" TJ's throat constricted as her emotions started to show, but she took a deep breath. "Dillon, what she did was one of the most courageous things I've ever heard." She closed her eyes momentarily, trying to hold back the tears that were threatening. "Please just let her know I'm so very proud of her." TJ rose, preparing to leave. "And while I'm disappointed to leave empty-handed, thank you for being there for her. You're a true friend, and I'm so glad she has you."

As she pushed open the door, Dillon's voice stopped her.

"TJ."

TJ turned.

"She doesn't have that number anymore and probably has no idea you've been trying to reach her. Here." He jotted something down on a notepad, tore off the page, and held it out to her. "This is where she's staying. I have your word you won't share it?"

Experiencing a relief so profound she fought to stay upright, TJ used her now-wobbly legs to advance upon Dillon and give him a fierce hug. "Thank you. You're the best, and you have my word."

"Be good to her," Dillon said as he squeezed back.

She gave him a kiss on the cheek and took the notepaper. "I will."

❖

When TJ entered the apartment that evening, Kara was seated at the kitchen table doing homework. She appreciated Kara's diligence in working to turn her grades around. More than that, she was grateful for the type of mentor Dillon undoubtedly was for her. TJ was nearly as excited about the prospect of Kara's return to work as Kara was, something she wouldn't have imagined a couple of weeks ago.

It had been a quiet week at home since TJ's dismissal from Magnate, with Kara emanating dissatisfaction with TJ from every pore. Their only substantive conversation was when TJ had informed her about Derrick Spaulding's treachery and Jess's role in his arrest. Thankfully Kara hadn't said "I told you so." Even her usual grunts were in short supply. TJ couldn't blame her. Days of soul-searching had led TJ to the same conclusion Kara had already reached. Jess did deserve better. And, TJ belatedly realized, so did their mom.

TJ sat across from Kara. "I met with a grief counselor from the GU student health center."

No response.

"For me, not you."

Kara raised her eyes.

"I'm seeing him again next week."

TJ had come to understand that Kara was right to have called her out on her peevish attitude toward Evelyn. The loving relationship their parents had was something to be emulated, not discounted, and for the vast majority of TJ's life, so was Evelyn's parenting skill. In TJ's shoes, Evelyn would have assumed that something Jess couldn't disclose had compelled her to fire TJ, which had turned out to be true. Had TJ followed Evelyn's example, Jess would already know she had more than Dillon on her side because Evelyn would have stopped at nothing to send that message. Since failing Jess wasn't an option, and TJ didn't possess the emotional tools to move forward, it was beyond time for her to consult a professional.

It was already bearing fruit. TJ was coming to understand that Evelyn had stopped caring because she was unable to care. Grief, not alcohol, had left her feeling hopeless and empty. By viewing Evelyn's alcoholism as a manifestation of her depression instead of the sole agent responsible for her decline, TJ was starting to forgive.

But it came down to something even simpler.

"I have a lot to learn from Mom and a lot to thank her for. One thing in particular. And when I remember that, I can't stay angry."

Kara repeatedly twirled her pen around her thumb. "What?"

"You." Just saying it infused TJ with a gladness she'd never tire of, and she let it show. As Kara wasn't much for sentiment, TJ expected her to scoff or dismiss what she said. Instead, Kara stilled the pen and held her gaze, which was a good sign.

"And I know where Jess is."

TJ hated the self-doubts Jess's disappearance had been stirring. It made her question Jess's motivations the night they made love, and she didn't want any negativity invading those precious memories. Uncertainty had been niggling at her like a virus, causing her to wonder whether Jess had come to her out of guilt for preparing to fire her.

TJ hadn't known Jess was in the throes of her world collapsing around her, but she clearly hadn't been herself of late. Jess had seemed nearly desperate when she'd arrived unannounced, as if she'd received a life sentence and TJ was her last meal. Her words, her touch, her mouth, her sighs—they weren't the signs of a woman offering a sympathy fuck or looking for a "wham, bam, thank you, ma'am." Her tenderness had been achingly sweet. Loving.

Could she really blame Jess for disappearing, when her life was imploding? Could she blame her for not telling her of Derrick's scheme, when TJ's reaction to so much less was to doubt everything that had transpired between them?

At least Jess hadn't been privy to TJ's insecurities. When Jess had needed her, she'd been there.

And more than anything, TJ wanted to be there for her again.

Even if Jess couldn't handle a relationship right now, or ever, nothing could keep TJ away. She owed Jess that much.

"I'm going to let her know we're there for her."

Setting the pen down, Kara sat back and folded her arms.

"I might be home in a few hours, or I might not come home at all. Whatever it takes and whatever she needs, I'm going to give her." Since TJ always made a point to come home, no matter the hour, this was the simplest way to convey the importance of her trip.

"About time."

"You're right. I'm new at this. I've got a lot to learn."

Kara's expression softened. "You're getting there."

"I hope so."

"Lucky you have me to help."

TJ beamed.

For the first time all week, Kara returned TJ's smile. It didn't come with any shades of doubt. It carried the confidence of someone who believed she was loved and lovable. TJ's heart soared. "Maybe you should get outta here and try to get lucky in other ways." Kara arched an eyebrow.

TJ felt heat in her cheeks. "She needs a friend."

Kara grinned. "With benefits?"

Knowing the conversation would only further devolve, TJ rose and walked over to say good-bye. Usually when she was leaving, she hugged Kara from behind. Now, Kara stood and wrapped her arms around her first. "Tell her we love her and we're proud of her."

TJ hugged Kara tightly. "I will."

❖

"It's open!" Jess said as she set down her laptop at the knock. Unless Dillon was delivering something, he parked in front of the gate at the top of the drive, so she wasn't surprised she hadn't heard his truck. "Why didn't you tell me you were coming? I would've…" The sentence died on her lips as she opened the door and saw TJ. Her throat closed as if she had a terrible head cold and swallowing was painful. "Please go."

"No," TJ said, stopping Jess's attempt to shut the door with her palm. "When did you find out about the scam?"

"I'm not going to have this conversation with you." Jess had had her fill of people assuming she was a liar. She wasn't naive enough to think TJ would believe her, but she was loath to have her confirm it. There was something strangely appealing about holding tight to a falsehood if that falsehood made you feel better. Just because a child came to learn the Tooth Fairy wasn't real didn't mean she wouldn't peek under her pillow at her next lost tooth.

"It was just before you came over, wasn't it?" TJ asked.

"I've known all along, or haven't you read the news?" Jess couldn't keep the bitterness out of her reply.

"I don't believe that."

"Let it go, TJ. You've done your duty. As you can see, I'm fine. Now please go. I don't need your pity."

TJ moved into the doorway and forced Jess back a few steps. "I'm not here out of pity. I'm here because I care about you."

Jess didn't doubt TJ's desire to do right by someone she considered—or formerly considered—a friend. If TJ spent even two minutes online or watching the news, she'd hear what people were saying about Jess and her protective instincts would kick in. But Jess didn't want to be TJ's moral obligation. She wanted to be TJ's lover and partner, which after this past week was as likely as Somalia medaling at the Winter Olympics. "Duly noted. You're officially released from further obligation. Now please go."

"So I couldn't possibly mean it?"

"If it makes a difference, I believe you believe you mean it."

"Do you discount your own feelings as much as you discount mine? Or are yours at least real?"

"I don't want to argue. Think what you will, but leave me in peace."

"I will if you answer one question. But I want the woman who had the guts to turn in her father to answer, not the one the media sees."

As if anyone besides Dillon would believe anything Jess said. She crossed her arms and cocked her head.

"Why did you stay with me that night? The truth."

What does it matter? Why rehash it? Let it be a happy memory away from the taint of Derrick's web of lies. "And you'll leave?"

"If you ask me to."

The fact TJ had come here asking about the fraud meant she knew very well Jess was responsible for firing her, getting her graduate program shut down, and ruining her reputation. They'd both lost everything. There was no candy-coating it. The only difference between them was that TJ had been a victim and Jess had been partly responsible for tearing her down. She might not be able to provide restitution, but she would own up to it.

"Because I wanted one night to forget I'm a Spaulding, okay? One night to try to forget I'd taken everything from you. One night to pretend I could be a woman you could fall in love with."

TJ peeled Jess's hand from her crossed arms. "The bravest person I've ever known is a Spaulding." She kissed Jess's palm. "The only person I've ever been in love with is a Spaulding." She placed it over her heart and covered it with hers. "And the only thing she's ever taken from me, I don't want returned."

Jess could scarcely understand what she was hearing. The past week had felt to her like she'd been living in a haunted house in which the ghosts of its previous owners rendered the place uninhabitable. As the new occupant, she was going out of her mind, tortured by images of heartbreak she'd had a hand in creating. But now it was as if the apparitions had received the justice they were seeking and could finally rest. They receded into the shadows along with their images of horror and destitution. She wasn't sure how they'd been placated, but she suspected it had something to do with forgiveness. Having her hand over the heart of the woman she loved settled her in a way she imagined those spirits experienced. She splayed her fingers and enjoyed the strength of the heartbeat under her touch. "Your gray sweats?" she asked, eyes gleaming.

TJ laughed. "That's where they went?"

Jess let her hand travel up until she cupped TJ's cheek. "Tell me I'm not dreaming. You really forgive me?"

TJ held her palm over Jess's hand. "Baby. Tell me what you see."

The sure and steady gaze TJ leveled at her made Jess's heart expand as if it were a blossom greeting the sun. "But your internship. And the program. And your credits. And your prospects. I've ruined all of it."

Once again, TJ kissed her palm. "What do you see?"

Compassion. Kindness. Devotion. Love. So many things Jess didn't deserve yet wouldn't question. TJ's assuredness wouldn't allow it. The answer was as clear as hindsight.

"My future," Jess said before wrapping TJ in her arms and kissing her.

EPILOGUE

No wonder TJ had been hurt when she'd been fired, Jess thought as she wound her way through the parking lot toward her borrowed car. It felt terrible. At least the emotional roller coaster she'd ridden for the past six months had helped in one small way—she was too drained to cry. Barbara Nichols, Muriel Manchester's chief marketing officer, had been against her hire from the start and, based on the case she'd just made against her, had gone out of her way to document issues with Jess's performance toward the goal of terminating her.

Not that Jess could blame her. Barbara was no different than nearly every other person she'd met since her father's arrest made headlines. People were as uncomfortable around her as if an Uzi were strapped over her shoulder. At least Barbara had honored the full probationary period.

A sound more pathetic than her internal monologue caught Jess's attention. Some poor soul's car wasn't starting. Jess followed the noise until she reached its source just as the vehicle's driver raised the hood and stared into the frame. "Need a hand?" Jess asked, though she no longer had access to a car service or an automobile club and knew as much about mechanics as heart surgery.

The female driver wore what Jess recognized as an Armani skirt suit in midnight blue, a look that contrasted sharply with the older-model sedan that refused to start. The woman shook her head and folded her arms. "Rookie move. I left the lights on."

Jess set down her small box of personal effects and pulled out her phone. "Let me see if I can help." She dialed Kara, who would be at the shop at this hour.

"Pineapple and Canadian bacon," Kara said by way of answering. "If you're calling to find out what pizza toppings I want for dinner."

"You're only saying that because it's my turn to cook."

"Yes, and I love you for it. I've never gotten to eat so much takeout in my life. What's up?"

"What's the likelihood you can walk me through how to jump someone's car battery?"

"Zero."

"Oh, come on. How hard can it be?"

Kara laughed. "You'll get dirty."

Jess pursed her lips and eyed the engine compartment. It seemed as if it had won grand prize at a soot-producing challenge, with black dust and grime covering every conceivable area. Hardly her cup of tea. She glanced at her clothing. The no-name skirt and blouse was nothing special, and now that she suddenly had free time, she could soak and scrub to her heart's content.

Armani woman fished through her purse on the front seat and held up her phone. "I'll just call roadside assistance. Thank you, though."

Jess held up a finger. "One sec," she told the woman as she scooped up her box. With her chin she indicated her destination. "I'm just over here. I'll block you." To Kara, she said, "I'll risk it. Tell me what to do and promise me you won't let me electrocute myself."

Kara laughed again, a sound Jess had come to enjoy as much as a warm blanket on a cool evening. "As hot as my sister thinks you are, not even you could get fried by twelve volts. For three slices of pizza, I'll walk you through it."

"Deal."

Miraculously the hands-on training went off with neither hitch nor call to 911. Dirt accumulation was minimal. Once her car started, the woman canceled her request for roadside assistance. Per Kara's instructions, Jess advised the woman to drive her car for at least ten minutes. The woman extended her hand.

"Susan O'Reilly. Thanks for the rescue."

Jess appraised her own palm and held it up for inspection. "Sorry."

Susan rummaged through the glove box and pulled out a napkin. "Here. This is my sister's car, and I'm not used to having to manually turn off the lights."

Jess wiped her hands, enjoying feeling useful. It had been elusive since she took this job. "Glad I could help. Good luck."

"What's half of our celebrity couple doing in the parking lot at midafternoon, rescuing damsels in distress?"

Of course Susan would know who Jess was. She wasn't famous

as much as infamous. Jess smiled. "Heading home. Today's my last day. Employees can rest easier knowing they don't have to clutch their wallets so tightly anymore."

"You quit?"

Jess shook her head but didn't need to get into the details with this stranger.

Susan frowned and consulted her phone. "On whose authority? I haven't green-lighted this. Has Muriel been informed?"

Jess didn't know Susan's role at the company and decided she didn't need to. "I wouldn't know. Nice to meet you, Susan." She stowed the cables and slid into the driver's seat.

"Wait," Susan said, blocking Jess from closing her car door. She had a phone to her ear and, with her other hand, held up her index finger. "Great. Trust me, she'll see us…Yes, go ahead and do that. We'll be right there." Susan swiped her phone and gave Jess her attention. "Would you mind speaking with Muriel?"

"Yes. I don't know who you are, but—"

"Senior Vice President of Global Human Resources. And you're Jessica Spaulding. Please. I'm quite certain there's been a mistake."

"And I'm just as certain there hasn't. Let's not drag this out. Especially let's not involve Muriel. California's an at-will state, and the list of my infractions is long."

"I'm not interested in whatever people say about you on social media."

"Thank you for saying that, but I mean my infractions here. In marketing."

"Let's let Muriel address them."

"Let's not."

"Jessica, come back inside with me. Worst-case scenario, we change your final day to be one week from today. Today can still be your last day on site, but I'll tack on a week's pay." Susan reached into her car and turned off the engine.

Jess was aghast. Her first-ever car repair had gone down in defeat. "After I just jumped you?"

Susan laughed. "Happily, you didn't. I'd hate to have to have that conversation with Cordelia."

Jess was confused by Susan's reply. "Cordelia?"

Now Susan appeared confused. "Cordelia Blake. Your partner, right? According to all the forms I have."

It was Jess's turn to laugh. "Ha! Seems I owe you one, so let me park and I'll come with you. She goes by TJ and has never owned up to her real name. Cordelia. Priceless." She laughed again. At least the day hadn't been a complete failure.

❖

"Have a seat," Muriel said.

Unlike in Jess's old office, Muriel had no chairs in front of her desk. Four chairs were situated at a round conference table, so Jess sat in one. The modern, minimalist furniture suited Muriel perfectly. The palette was white and dark brown, she had little in the way of art, and the lack of file cabinets or drawers beneath the desk gave the room a more open feel than the thick wooden behemoths most executives preferred.

"Barbara Nichols says things didn't work out with you. What do you say to that?"

Good old Muriel, always straight for the jugular. "I'd agree," Jess said, wondering why they were bothering with this conversation.

Muriel sat behind her desk, donned reading glasses, and appeared to read something on her monitor. "She says you're contumacious, overly experimental, and opposed to advertising."

Given the serious nature of the meeting, Jess shouldn't have smiled. She really, really shouldn't have. But she did. Contumacious was something you might call a particularly obstinate child or something TJ would consider Kara on her worst days; it wasn't something one colleague would typically say about another.

"You find that amusing?" Muriel asked.

"Not at all. She's entitled to her opinion." However hyperbolic, Jess didn't add.

Again Muriel referred to her screen. "She says when she's asked you to stay late to complete a project, you refused. On two separate occasions."

All traces of amusement fled Jess's system.

Viewing Jess over the rims of her glasses, Muriel must have noticed. She set them down. "No rebuttal?"

Jess shook her head.

"I'm not on a witch hunt, Jessica. I want facts. Were you unable or unwilling to assist with those projects?"

Part of Jess wanted to argue. Another part understood the futility. She'd fought the good fight. While she'd do it again in order to be sharing her life with TJ and Kara, and because it had been the right thing to do, the price was steep. An anathema could hardly expect a fair shake. The court of public opinion had sentenced Jess long before she'd even reached the grand jury. "Apparently."

Jess jumped at the sound of Muriel's open palm slapping the desk in a completely uncharacteristic move compared to her normally controlled demeanor. "Contumacious is sounding more accurate with each passing second," Muriel said angrily. She repeated her words in a staccato manner. "Were you unable or unwilling to assist with those projects?"

Pushed for a more comprehensive response, Jess said, "In my six months here, I've been unavailable on three work nights. Two in DC when I was invited to testify before the Senate committee on financial-advisor transparency—which I took unpaid leave for—and one when TJ and I had a parent-teacher conference. I wasn't going to miss either event. I put them on my calendar and notified Barbara weeks in advance. Three guesses as to the only nights I've ever been asked to work." Unsurprisingly, Barbara had failed to document that Jess routinely stayed late.

Muriel sat back in her chair and studied her.

Jess hadn't meant to add the snide remark and owed her lack of professionalism to being driven to the wall. But it didn't mean she couldn't own up to it. "I apologize. It's possible she and I got our wires crossed."

"But you don't believe so."

"I…" Jess stopped herself. She saw no point in arguing. Barbara was CMO; Jess was merely a director who'd been granted short tenure in a one-off deal.

They sat in silence for several uncomfortable moments—at least they were to Jess.

Muriel broke it. "Have you come across any practices we could utilize or overhaul to improve our marketing efforts?"

Jess examined her nail polish. She'd made a number of recommendations to Barbara she believed would improve sales but was powerless to implement them. The tear ducts she was so sure had dried up were threatening to reopen. Swallowing hard, she gave Muriel her attention and a brief nod.

"Have you shared them with Barbara?"

Jess nodded once.

"If you were head of marketing, tell me how you'd change things. There's no right or wrong answer."

"Between us?" Jess didn't want her ideas to taint whatever reputation Barbara had built for herself. Jess was untried. She knew marketing in the financial-advisor sphere. She had no experience in the world of global conglomerate.

"If you wish."

It's not as though Jess had been thinking of anything else work-wise for the past half year. Plus, she'd already been terminated. Why not speak her mind? "You need to become a content machine—creating content better than anyone else. Then connect with key influencers and have better relationships than everyone else. I see all these basic activity metrics floating around—clicks, followers, downloads. Those are fine indicators, but you need effectiveness metrics and revenue-focused calculations. There are marketing-performance tracking tools that you could and should be using. Without them, you're flying blind."

After months of having her ideas discounted, it felt good to let go in front of someone who'd never been inclined to belittle her. She only hoped Muriel wasn't the one behind Barbara, calling the shots like the Wizard of Oz.

"I don't place my faith in guesswork. I place it in people I trust." Muriel joined Jess at the conference table. "I've experienced more than my share of public criticism, and none of it comes close to the censure you've encountered. It's knocked you to the canvas, and only you can decide whether you can still stand and fight."

Muriel's words not only hit close to home; they were dead center. She continued.

"I care about this company. Not what people think of me. Not what people think of you. If you're going to be my CMO, I need you to want it and fight for it, knowing you deserve it. When my executive team takes issue with you because of the cardboard cutout they see in the media, I expect you to address their concerns with respect, and I expect you to demand nothing less than respect in return.

"You have a choice to make, Jessica. You can believe your defining moment is behind you. Or you can believe it's ahead of you."

Jess blinked hard, tamping down the emotion threatening to breach. Time and again, Muriel Manchester was proving to be every bit the leader she was reputed to be—demanding excellence and earning unparalleled loyalty among her staff, some of whom had been with her for over a decade. The opportunity she'd laid before Jess was astounding.

Muriel rose and returned to her desk. "I happen to believe the latter." She picked up her landline. "Send her in."

Seconds later, the door opened. Muriel's assistant gave Muriel a piece of paper and left; behind her, TJ strode in and appeared surprised to see Jess. "What are you doing here?"

"Take a seat," Muriel said, indicating the chair next to Jess.

"You okay?" TJ mouthed to Jess.

Jess nodded, still trying to wrap her head around Muriel's offer and counsel.

"You've had your degree for weeks now. Why haven't you been to see me?" Muriel asked TJ, who'd recently completed the credits she needed for her MBA. "You want to help bereaved children and their caregivers. How do you expect to do that here?"

TJ sounded unusually hesitant. "Yes, but I thought I'd stay—"

"Even if you worked for my foundation, it serves an entirely different mission than where your interest lies. This is about that service obligation you don't owe me, correct?"

TJ looked to Jess for help, but Jess didn't have any knowledge about this conversation or how Muriel knew where TJ's interests lay.

Muriel gave Jess a smug smile. "I back-channel all sorts of information," she said, as if she could read her mind. To TJ, she asked, "Are you familiar with Charles Fleming?"

"Of course," TJ said, sitting taller in her chair as if bolstered to finally be able to answer one of Muriel's questions. "He wrote the bestseller *Sharing the Dark* and founded the charity of the same name, which serves children who've lost both parents." Jess knew of it only because TJ considered it the standard by which she wanted to judge her future nonprofit efforts.

Muriel held out the paper to TJ. "He's a friend. His programs director is retiring. He's expecting to hear from you."

TJ took the proffered document and stared at it as if it were in hieroglyphics. Jess understood her confusion. She could hardly process it all herself. She had many unanswered questions of her own and almost didn't dare speak for fear it was all a dream. Taking a place by TJ's side, she whispered into her ear. "Say thank you."

The look TJ bestowed on her was full of such gratitude, Jess wanted to hold her face and kiss her softly, letting her know it was okay to accept gifts when they came into your life, much like how Jess felt that TJ had come into hers. Instead, she took her elbow and gave her a little nudge in Muriel's direction. "Sweetheart." It wasn't about taking something for nothing. It was about understanding that an act of kindness, however large or small, is never wasted.

TJ extended her hand to Muriel, who shook it. "Thank you."

"You're welcome. Jessica, I expect to hear from you shortly. Now if you'll both excuse me, I have some HR matters to address."

Once again TJ searched Jess for some insight into Muriel's comments, but Jess would save her updates for later. As they took their leave, Muriel's voice stopped them. "Your mother was a *King Lear* fan?"

TJ turned, and her entire face lit up in a radiant grin. "No, but she valued honesty. And other things I'm finally giving her credit for."

Her smile brought one to Jess's as well. Jess took her hand and tugged her through the office door. "Come on, princess." Jess hijacked the moniker TJ often used for her, hinting at TJ's given name. "Let's forge what's ahead of us."

About the Author

Heather Blackmore oversees finance for SF Bay Area technology startups. In a seemingly counterintuitive move, she got her MSA and CPA with the goal of one day being able to work part-time so she could write. The right and left sides of her brain have been at war ever since.

Heather was a finalist for the debut author Goldie award and runner-up for the Rainbow Award in the Contemporary Lesbian Romance and Debut Author categories for her first novel, *Like Jazz*.

Visit www.heatherblackmore.com and/or drop her a line at heather@heatherblackmore.com. She sincerely appreciates hearing from her readers.

Books Available From Bold Strokes Books

Basic Training of the Heart by Jaycie Morrison. In 1944, socialite Elizabeth Carlton joins the Women's Army Corps to escape family expectations and love's disappointments. Can Sergeant Gale Rains get her through Basic Training with their hearts intact? (978-1-62639-818-4)

Believing in Blue by Maggie Morton. Growing up gay in a small town has been hard, but it can't compare to the next challenge Wren—with her new, sky-blue wings—faces: saving two entire worlds. (978-1-62639-691-3)

Coils by Barbara Ann Wright. A modern young woman follows her aunt into the Greek Underworld and makes a pact with Medusa to win her freedom by killing a hero of legend. (978-1-62639-598-5)

Courting the Countess by Jenny Frame. When relationship-phobic Lady Henrietta Knight starts to care about housekeeper Annie Brannigan and her daughter, can she overcome her fears and promise Annie the forever that she demands? (978-1-62639-785-9)

Dapper by Jenny Frame. Amelia Honey meets the mysterious Byron De Brek and is faced with her darkest fantasies, but will her strict moral upbringing stop her from exploring what she truly wants? (978-1-62639-898-6)

Delayed Gratification: The Honeymoon by Meghan O'Brien. A dream European honeymoon turns into a winter storm nightmare involving a delayed flight, a ditched rental car, and eventually, a surprisingly happy ending. (978-1-62639-766-8)

For Money or Love by Heather Blackmore. Jessica Spaulding must choose between ignoring the truth to keep everything she has, and doing the right thing only to lose it all—including the woman she loves. (978-1-62639-756-9)

Hooked by Jaime Maddox. With the help of sexy Detective Mac Calabrese, Dr. Jessica Benson is working hard to overcome her past, but they may not be enough to stop a murderer. (978-1-62639-689-0)

Lands End by Jackie D. Public relations superstar Amy Kline is dealing with a media nightmare, and the last thing she expects is for restaurateur Lena Michaels to change everything, but she will. (978-1-62639-739-2)

Twisted Screams by Sheri Lewis Wohl. Reluctant psychic Lorna Dutton doesn't want to forgive, but if she doesn't do just that, an innocent woman will die. (978-1-62639-647-0)

A Class Act by Tammy Hayes. Buttoned-up college professor Dr. Margaret Parks doesn't know what she's getting herself into when she agrees to one date with her student Rory Morgan, who is fifteen years her junior. (978-1-62639-701-9)

Bitter Root by Laydin Michaels. Small town chef Adi Bergeron is hiding something, and Griffith McNaulty is going to find out what it is even if it gets her killed. (978-1-62639-656-2)

Capturing Forever by Erin Dutton. When family pulls Jacqueline and Casey back together, will the lessons learned in eight years apart be enough to mend the mistakes of the past? (978-1-62639-631-9)

Deception by VK Powell. DEA Agent Colby Vincent and Attorney Adena Weber are embroiled in a drug investigation involving homeless veterans and an attraction that could destroy them both. (978-1-62639-596-1)

Dyre: A Knight of Spirit and Shadows by Rachel E. Bailey. With the abduction of her queen, werewolf-bodyguard Des must follow the kidnappers' trail to Europe, where her queen—and a battle unlike any Des has ever waged—awaits her. (978-1-62639-664-7)

First Position by Melissa Brayden. Love and rivalry take center stage for Anastasia Mikhelson and Natalie Frederico in one of the most prestigious ballet companies in the nation. (978-1-62639-602-9)

Best Laid Plans by Jan Gayle. Nicky and Lauren are meant for each other, but Nicky's haunting past and Lauren's societal fears threaten to derail all possibilities of a relationship. (978-1-62639-658-6)

Exchange by CF Frizzell. When Shay Maguire rode into rural Montana, she never expected to meet the woman of her dreams—or to learn Mel Baker was held hostage by legal agreement to her right-wing father. (978-1-62639-679-1)

Just Enough Light by AJ Quinn. Will a serial killer's return to Colorado destroy Kellen Ryan and Dana Kingston's chance at love, or can the search-and-rescue team save themselves? (978-1-62639-685-2)

Rise of the Rain Queen by Fiona Zedde. Nyandoro is nobody's princess. She fights, curses, fornicates, and gets into as much trouble as her brothers. But the path to a throne is not always the one we expect. (978-1-62639-592-3)

Tales from Sea Glass Inn by Karis Walsh. Over the course of a year at Cannon Beach, tourists and locals alike find solace and passion at the Sea Glass Inn. (978-1-62639-643-2)

The Color of Love by Radclyffe. Black sheep Derian Winfield needs to convince literary agent Emily May to marry her to save the Winfield Agency and solve Emily's green card problem, but Derian didn't count on falling in love. (978-1-62639-716-3)

A Reluctant Enterprise by Gun Brooke. When two women grow up learning nothing but distrust, unworthiness, and abandonment, it's no wonder they are apprehensive and fearful when an overwhelming love just won't be denied. (978-1-62639-500-8)

Above the Law by Carsen Taite. Love is the last thing on Agent Dale Nelson's mind, but reporter Lindsey Ryan's investigation could change the way she sees everything—her career, her past, and her future. (978-1-62639-558-9)

Actual Stop by Kara A. McLeod. When Special Agent Ryan O'Connor's present collides abruptly with her past, shots are fired, and the course of her life is irrevocably altered. (978-1-62639-675-3)

Embracing the Dawn by Jeannie Levig. When ex-con Jinx Tanner and business executive E. J. Bastien awaken after a one-night stand to find their lives inextricably entangled, love has its work cut out for it. (978-1-62639-576-3)

Love's Redemption by Donna K. Ford. For ex-convict Rhea Daniels and ex-priest Morgan Scott, redemption lies in the thin line between right and wrong. (978-1-62639-673-9)

The Shewstone by Jane Fletcher. The prophetic Shewstone is in Eawynn's care, but unfortunately for her, Matt is coming to steal it. (978-1-62639-554-1)

Jane's World by Paige Braddock. Jane's PayBuddy account gets hacked and she inadvertently purchases a mail order bride from the Eastern Bloc. (978-1-62639-494-0)

A Touch of Temptation by Julie Blair. Recent law school graduate Kate Dawson's ordained path to the perfect life gets thrown off course when handsome butch top Chris Brent initiates her to sexual pleasure. (978-1-62639-488-9)

Beneath the Waves by Ali Vali. Kai Merlin and Vivien Palmer love the water and the secrets trapped in the depths, but if Kai gives in to her feelings, it might come at a cost to her entire realm. (978-1-62639-609-8)

Girls on Campus, edited by Sandy Lowe and Stacia Seaman. College: four years when rules are made to be broken. This collection is required reading for anyone looking to earn an A in sex ed. (978-1-62639-733-0)

Miss Match by Fiona Riley. Matchmaker Samantha Monteiro makes the impossible possible for everyone but herself. Is mysterious dancer Lucinda Moss her perfect match? (978-1-62639-574-9)

Paladins of the Storm Lord by Barbara Ann Wright. Lieutenant Cordelia Ross must choose between duty and honor when a man with godlike powers forces her soldiers to provoke an alien threat. (978-1-62639-604-3)